P9-DOE-527

# CRACHE

## MARK BUDZ

BANTAM BOOKS

CRACHE
A Bantam Spectra Book / December 2004

Published by Bantam Dell
A Division of Random House, Inc.
New York, New York

Bantam Books, the rooster colophon, and the portrayal of a
boxed "s" are registered trademarks of Random House, Inc.

ISBN 0-553-58659-9

Printed in the United States of America
Published simultaneously in Canada

www.bantamdell.com

OPM 10 9 8 7 6 5 4 3 2 1

*For Tom Rogers,*
*who's been there from the beginning.*

## SPECIAL THANKS

To Marina, as always, my star of the County Down. Juliet Ulman, for her precise editorial compass. Jim Gettins, Bryn Kanar, and Ed Weingold, who helped make the lies more true.

# CRACHE

# 1

## BURDEN OF FAITH

The cross weighs on Fola. Even in the micro-g of the asteroid it seems to exert a downward pull. The sensation is more mental than physical. She knows that. The slave-pherions that bound her to the Jesuettes have been cut out with chemical scalpels. But her mind still registers the weight of the cross the way it would the phantom pain of a severed limb.

Scar tissue.

A good thing. That's why she wears the cross, to remember. What she was back on earth. Who she is now.

The cross is a mystery in other ways. Lately, the stone it was cut from has grown heavier, the need to remember more insistent. She finds herself fingering the glass—smooth surface and cracked fragments of embedded bone, absently polishing them in response to some vague, nameless anxiety.

Ephraim. It has to be. Her tuplet buddy's dour moods

are seeping into her, a slow capillary trickle through the biodigital wires that connect them. It isn't just concern for his sister. That worry was there from the beginning. This is different. Something else is going on. Another wound has opened up, spilling fresh blood.

Fola never feels comfortable visiting Ephraim, even though they're biochemical siblings and she should be able to empathize with him. His hexcell makes her uneasy. Her mouth goes dry, her palms clammy. A kind of reverse Pavlovian response, according to Pheidoh. Her IA is always offering unwanted and unhelpful psychoanalysis, datamined from the mediasphere.

What bothers her is the decor. Ephraim has graffixed the hexcell's wall panels with Moorish architectural designs and motifs. It reminds her too much of the house she grew up in, before her father sold her to the Church. Circular arches. Tessellated tile patterns that hint at some highly complex but underlying order to the structure of day-to-day life. She was twelve at the time and never saw it coming. That innocence still haunts her. It steals over her like a catchy tune. She finds herself singing along without conscious thought. When that happens she has to take a step back, force the song from her head and replace it with another before she gets too carried away.

Fola's not sure why Ephraim chose the motif—what he finds comforting or appealing about it. She's afraid to ask. Part of her doesn't want to know, doesn't want to get any closer than she has to. Because of that, and his sullen temperament, she really doesn't know all that much about him. Where he came from, what his background is. All Fola knows is that he has a little sister, Lisi, who is indentured to do some kind of uterine piece-work and is at risk for becoming mutilated. The details are fuzzy. But Fola gathers that she's gestating nanimatronic seed stock inside her and then giving birth to the full-grown product. If she isn't already sterile, she will be soon. And that's just the start of her medical problems.

Not all that much different from her friend Xophia, who had been saved from permanent physical injury by the Ignatarians. Fola counted herself lucky. Her father had indentured her directly to the Church. Four years as a Jesuette, shaking her booty for God, until Xophia arranged to cut her free.

Now, three years later, with the help of Ephraim and a promise to the ICLU to act as a point of contact for other refugees in the future, Fola was returning the favor.

"You seem nervous," Pheidoh says over her cochlear implants.

"Yes." No sense denying it. The IA knows when she's lying, can unerringly read her neural tea leaves.

"You'll do fine. The Mymercia KBO is not that much different from Tiresias and other large Kuiper belt objects."

She realizes that the IA is referring to her and Ephraim's upcoming work assignment on the surface of the asteroid, not her anxiety about Xophia or Fola's aversion to Ephraim's choice of interior decor. This is her first trip to the Mymercia. Until now, she hasn't actually had to go to the asteroid. All of her work on the latest Kuiper belt colony has been done from the orbiting construction station.

"I hope so," she says.

The timing couldn't be worse. The shuttle carrying Xophia is due any day, and she wants to be on-station when it arrives.

* * *

Ephraim is still getting dressed when she enters his hexcell.

"You're early," he says, his voice muffled by the acoustic lichen he's got growing on the walls.

Their shuttle pod to the arcology doesn't depart for another thirty minutes. But, as much as she hates his living quarters, they need to talk. In private, out of earshot of any bitcams or acoustic spores that could pick up their conversation.

She hovers just inside the arched doorway. He's partitioned the cell with tapestree screens, so much of her view of the interior living quarters is blocked. She can't actually see the cuenca tiles with their quiltlike patterns of interlocking mosaics. But she can feel them subliminally, like the screech of high-frequency sound, and there's this mental itch building that she can't scratch.

Instead her fingers go to the cross. The stone polished and smooth, comforting.

Ephraim appears from behind one screen. His biosuit hasn't finished taking shape and still looks a little foamy in places. He must have just slathered it on.

"Any word on the shuttle?" she asks.

Ephraim's gaze brushes the cross and her fingers. He shakes his head. "Not yet."

She lowers her hand. "When?"

He waves off the question. It drives her nuts when he puts her off like this, gets sullen and dismissive.

"Shouldn't you have heard something by now?"

Ephraim runs one palm over the bald top of his head. "Not unless there's a change of plan or an emergency. Usually, I get notified twelve to twenty-four hours before they arrive."

She notices that the graffitic on the inside of his right

forearm is still blank. The small bronze disk, approximately a centimeter in diameter, could pass for a birthmark or a mole. Otto, the ICLU sympathizer who had given her sanctuary when she first arrived, had a similar mark. The graffitic is the equivalent of a digital watermark. It contains embedded steganographics that, when decrypted by a secure datasquirt, reveals a hidden image. This image contains a second stream of ciphertext that gets run through a onetime key to provide the comcode for an incoming shuttle of refugees or immigrants.

"What if something went wrong?" she says. "You'd know, right? Someone would tell you."

He frowns. "I haven't heard anything."

"So everything's okay." She forces a smile, hoping to lift his spirits by raising her own. No doubt her anxiety is contributing to his bad mood, amping up his usually morose disposition.

"Right." A nod. "No news is good news."

Hardly the reassurance she was looking for. It's impossible not to fret when she knows what it's like to make the trip. Alone. In the dark.

She's been there.

Cold. Three days in a cramped storage locker, waiting to apply for asylum. Nothing to eat but old ryce cakes washed down with recycled water. The warm-blooded plants all around, dead to her without a softwire connection.

To pass the time and take her mind off her empty stomach, Otto gave her a pair of cellophane wraparounds, direct eyescreen access to the infosphere that streamed outward from earth. She soaked up the light, lived off it nonstop. Afraid to go to sleep . . . afraid of succumbing to the hard vacuum outside her cubby that hungered for each breath she took almost as much as she did.

Without the eyescreens, she would never have made it. The lenses focused not just her eyes but her mind. They helped her to be born anew, restoring depth and breadth to the world. She had done it alone. But it would have been better, easier, if someone had been there for her. With her.

"Promise me that you'll let me know as soon as you hear anything," Fola says.

She can't help it, this insecurity that verges on desperation. She hates it, hates that she can't seem to unlearn this part of the indoctrination that ghosts her myelin.

"Does it work?" Ephraim says.

"What?"

"Prayer." He nods at her hand, which has risen to the cross like a fish surfacing to feed. "Does it do any good?"

"It makes me feel better."

"But does it actually change anything? Make a difference?"

"It can."

"How do you know? If something good happens, how do you know it was due to a prayer and not coincidence or luck?"

"Cause and effect, you mean."

"Yes."

"Prayer isn't about getting what you want," she says. "Or affecting the outcome of an event. It's about finding strength in yourself, or God, or whatever, and giving that strength to others."

"Don't you have to believe in God? I mean, you said you don't anymore. Right? So how come you still have the cross?"

"I don't know," she admits. Some things can't be explained.

"I wouldn't worry," Ephraim says, leading her from the hexcell into the magtube that ascends like an elevator shaft to the docking bay at the top. "I'm sure the shuttle's fine."

Faith, she thinks. Like different varieties of flowers, it bloomed in many different shapes and colors.

# 2

## WHITE RAIN

White Rain. Adipose Rexx can feel the need for a quick dose rising like brackish water in the back of his throat.

A modified black-market biodigital, the drug is designed for direct softwire delivery to the neocortex. It's cleaner that way—no messy pills, liquids, or combustible materials—the equivalent of chemical acupuncture. The delivery system is a type of wireless RNA activated by a molectronic switch. Under normal conditions the riboswitch is inactive. Under the influence of the right narrow-band signal, the protein changes shape for the duration of the squirt. This new shape tells ribosomes to start producing the drug, which is synapse-specific and gengineered to nuke certain neurotransmitters. The resulting fallout induces a pleasant state of zazen. His mind fills with a mushroom cloud of well-being that obliterates all guilt, self-loathing, and the desire to give the antiquated Winchester twelve-gauge semiautomatic mounted on the wall a blow job.

The best way to do White Rain is in front of the window that looks out over Tiresias. From his second-level arcology room, he has a view of the comet's icy horizon and the stars beyond. What he likes about the window is that he doesn't have to close his eyes to imagine what pre-ecocaust Texas used to look like following a snowstorm. The sky crystal clear, the ground as white and pure as a freshly washed bed-sheet.

Rexx preps the dose online, via his wraparounds. The virtual interface he's set up resembles the artfully restored Philco Predicta he saw in a tech history museum. The twenty-one-inch screen is large and chubby faced, the pedestal-mounted dials sleek. Switching channels in a predefined combination, 2–7–4, accesses the digital sequence for the drug and transmits it. Turning up the volume increases the dose. Some days the volume needs to be louder than others, to drown out the voices prowling the perimeter of his consciousness. Otherwise the clamor is unbearable.

Jelena is there, and Mathieu, as well as his father and his mother. All of the people who have followed him, dead or alive, to the edge of the solar system. Sometimes, if he's not fast enough, faces appear on the screen, flickering rodeo images of Jelena sitting on a horse and Mathieu perched on a fence rail, waving.

To be sure that doesn't happen, Rexx cranks the volume, ropes himself to a magnetic flux line in front of the window, and waits for the molectronic circuits wired in his brain to convert the digitally stored data into neural spooge.

Gradually his thoughts dull to a cathode ray flicker. The White Rain descends, big flakes that turn into water as soon as they hit the memories, washing them away.

# 3

## GUEST WORK

The old Boeing 9x9 shudders as it descends, buffeted by turbulence over the Rocky Mountains. Joints groan, rivets creak. L. Mariachi can feel the palsied vibration deep in his bones, the metal fatigue that mirrors his own weariness. The plane, a pre-ecocaust relic that's been resurrected for nonessential cargo duty, is fast approaching the end of its usefulness. Like him, the years have worn it down. If it crashes and burns, no big loss. The three hundred migrant workers onboard can be easily replaced. There are plenty of other *braceros* in the world, ready to take their place.

He presses his face to the scratched, pitted window. One thousand meters below, Front Range City sprawls next to a barren hogback of shale-toothed foothills. FRC stretches for several hundred kilometers to the north and south, a thin ribbon of buildings shaded by UV-reflective umbrella palms and powered by circuitrees or rooftop arrays of solar panels where the concrete buildings poke above the leaves.

To the west, canyons dotted with drought-resistant aquaferns pipe condensation into underground storage tanks. To the east, a dust storm roils along the far edge of Colorado's eastern plains, kicked up by a low-pressure system over the Kansas dust flats.

The plane trembles as it banks into its final approach to the airport, still known as DIA, Denver International. At the southern tip of the terminal a single monorail track gleams in the harsh morning sunlight. The silver thread cuts through barren scab land to the vat pharm sixty kilometers away. The pharm's rash of bubble domes remind him of heat blisters, raise goose bumps on his arms.

Looking at his reflection, he can't tell where the scratches in the thick plastic end and the crease lines on his face begin.

The plane drops suddenly. His ears pop and the abrupt increase in pressure gives him a headache. His crippled left hand throbs. Around him, the rest of the guest workers on the flight stir, roused from naps or whatever in-flight media they're streaming on their wraparounds.

The man next to him grins. "Time to rock and roll."

L. Mariachi blinks. He hasn't heard the phrase in years. He searches the *chavo*'s face. But the man doesn't seem to mean anything by it. He's just a nostalgia phreak, lost in the past.

Cultural fundamentalism. It's happening more and more these days. Most people without a viable future find it easier to look back instead of ahead. The past is readily accessible, ripe for the picking. Except, of course, for those who have nothing to go back to.

* * *

Two hours later, after deplaning and clearing a Bureau
of Ecotectural Assimilation and Naturalization reclade
clinic, L. Mariachi and the other *braceros* crowd into a
ten-pod train on the monorail. Standing room only. A
few of the younger *braceros* joke with one another, talk
animatedly about women or music. But most are sullen,
withdrawn.

Compared to the flight from Atlanta, this trip is mer-
cifully quick; less than half an hour. Through the bubble
window closest to him, he watches the vat pharm
emerge from the brown, desultory haze.

After twenty years as a migrant, every job is the same:
scratch away the change in scenery, and they're interchangeable. For years he found that comforting. He
knew exactly what to expect. He didn't have to think . . .
didn't have to worry. He just had to go through the
motions.

From this angle, the domes are pus white.

*Ni madres!* He stares at the hard calluses on his
hands. He can't do this anymore.

Flimsy prefab trailers and old injection-molded cargo
containers have been brought in to house the workers.
They hunker down around the meager oasis of umbrella palms and circuitrees that marks the center of the
temporary town. He's assigned to a cubicle in a cargo
container that's divided into six rooms by folding parti-
tions. A shower stall and portable latrine have been
shoved up against the rear end. His room comes with a
gel mattress cot, fresh biolum strips on the walls, and
no windows. No problem, there's nothing to look at
anyway.

He tosses his duffel bag on the cot and sits down.
This is it, home for the next six weeks. Then, he promises himself, it's over. This is his last job. It's time to call
it quits. For real, this time. He's done enough penance
for two lifetimes.

# 4

## A SERPENT IN THE GRASS

Fola watches the butterfly turn into a ghost. One moment it's indigo, the next pale white. The wings quiver to a stop and the butterfly—translucent now as melting snow—hangs motionless a few centimeters from the saffron petals of a chalice-shaped flower.

A sketchy face appears on the underside of one wing. The image, an old hand-animated cartoon character, grins at her. She can't remember the name of the duck. Taffy. Duffy. Something like that.

Fola reaches out a hand. But before she can touch the face, the data packet the butterfly represents disintegrates into virtual air. Ditto the flower and a nearby bumblebee, fat with recombinant instruction sets.

Fola blinks, frowns, then queries Ephraim. No answer. She tries her information agent. "Pheidoh?"

Nothing. Her IA has dropped offline. A first; the information agent is nothing if not dutiful.

Unnerved, she signs out of the ribozone. The virtuality collapses and the datawindow image of the garden on the inside of her eyescreens is replaced by an in-vivo view of airless rock and ice.

Her stomach lurches at the foreshortened horizon of the asteroid and steep-walled canyon outside the window of the cliff-face arcology. She's never been good with heights. Plus, the image of the duck is still tattooed to her retinas. Where had that come from?

"Ephraim? Pheidoh?"

Still no response. Great. Now what?

Fola cranes her head back, searching for the team of molectricians she's assisting. She spots the three-person tuplet next to the carbyne-frame vault that supports the lush topiary of circuitree branches, parasol palms, and clumped bananopy leaves that are part of the budding warm-blooded ecotecture.

She opens a comlink to the team. "Is everything okay?"

Liam is the first to respond. All puffed up, full of goofy sarcasm and the snide, jug-eared attitude he tries to pass off as humor. "Why wouldn't it be?"

From the moment she arrived on Mymercia, he's given her a bad time. First, about being a Performance Evaluation, Enhancement, and Validation specialist— what he calls his pet PEEV. Second, about the time she spent as a Jesuette. Never mind that it was against her will. He can't resist teasing her. Nun for me. Nun right now, thanks. Nun too soon. Nun of your business. Silly jokes like that. Playful. He's like a schoolboy with a crush. Pretty soon he'll pull her hair. Still, it's good to hear his voice. She's not totally cut off.

"What seems to be the problem?" Ingrid demands, terse. Unlike Liam, the team's leader is all business.

Fola squirms under Ingrid's annoyance. "There seems to be some kind of glitch in the infostream."

"What kind of glitch?"

"I'm not sure. Data loss maybe, or a transmission error. I've never seen anything like it."

"Everything looks fine to me," Ingrid says, impatient to finish with the array of biolum panels they're wiring to the arcology's main power grid. The job is taking longer than expected. There's a circuit relay problem she's been unable to isolate.

Fola pinches the tip of her tongue between pursed lips. "I just thought I'd check. That's all."

Ingrid doesn't say anything. No surprise. What's weird is that Liam is quiet. Normally he jumps right in. She always has to cut him off to keep him from pestering her. Not only that, they've stopped all work. She can see them pointing and gesticulating at each other in confusion.

"What's going on?" she says.

Silence.

"Hello?" Louder this time.

Nothing. Her cochlear implant is dead. She's de facto deaf. Not only that, she's not receiving any input over the softwire link to the warm-blooded plants. She's totally disconnected. Isolated.

Her stomach constricts. Something's wrong. She can feel it . . . a presence slipping into her via the softwire.

The sensation starts in her fingers and slithers up her arm, wrapping itself around her nerves like a snake coiling around the branch of a tree.

Probing. Tasting. Hunting for a core part of her being. She tries to make herself small, to crouch hidden in a safe corner of herself. But the feeling tightens its grip.

Her throat squeezes. She reaches for the cross hanging
around her neck under the biosuit. . . .

> One, two, three, four,
> Christ's the one who we adore.

After three years, deprogrammed by the ICLU,
stripped of the slave pherions the Ignatarians had dosed
her with to turn her into a model Catholic, the chant
rises up out of nowhere. It's still part of her, indelibly
engraved.

> Five, six, seven, eight,
> Meet you at the Pearly Gate.

She fights a sudden wave of nausea, clamps her hands
over her ears in an effort to shut out the remembered
rhythm. Instead, the frantic movement shifts her center
of gravity, catapults her into an off-kilter wobble, away
from the aluminum trellis she's been using to steady herself in the low-g arcology.

> Nine, ten, eleven, twelve,
> Goin' with the saints to dwell.

It's no use. The cheerful ditty—recited on street corners, in refugee camps, and during pep services complete with a lot of enthusiastic clapping, pompom
waving, and jumping up and down for joy—has been
resurrected against her will, a safety mechanism that's
as disconcerting as it is autonomic.

The presence pauses long enough for Fola to shudder. Her skull throbs, filled with a dry abscess of longing. She feels horribly alone. *Abandoned*. Without the

physical and emotional support of Ephraim or the
warm-blooded plants, she's helpless against the past. It
lies in wait, a serpent in the grass that she can't seem to
step over or around. She can hear its breathy sibilance,
sense its shadow in the weed-choked thicket of her
darkest thoughts.

*Our Father who art in heaven . . .*

She knows that the conviction, the fervent belief in
God that the Ignatarians doped her with, wasn't genuine because it didn't come from her. She didn't choose
to believe. Faith was forced on her. But part of her still
worries that she had her chance to be saved and blew it.
What if the Ignatarians were right? What if she's going
to burn in hell forever because she closed her heart to
the one true savior, turned her back on indentured servi-
tude and, at the same time, life everlasting?

Fear rushes in, anaphylactic, and her throat clenches
in a painful reminder of the afternoon she was ripped
from the body and blood of the Church. . . .

Fifteen years old. Spreading the word with Xophia and
Joi on an arid street corner in Singapore, hurling slo-
gans at the Sin-O-Matic sexplex in front of them.

> *Hey, hey, whaddaya say?*
> *Let's all pray for Judgment Day!*

Fola added a few brazen shakes of her pompoms for
good measure, just to let the club know she was serious.
Not that anyone was paying attention to the Jesuettes
or what they had to say. Especially the four old guys
smoking cigarettes on a spit-stained bench by the curb.
They were probably deaf, anyway.

The sex-parlor-cum-VRcade was located in an old

three-level aplex that had been retrofitted after the eco-caust. The building was a hodgepodge of solar panels, wind generators, condensation collectors, photovoltaic windows, and thermoelectric mesh. It was totally independent of the public-domain ecotecture that provided the city with electricity, filtered water, clean air, UV protection, sewage treatment, and waste disposal. The ancient stucco building squatted in an oasis of almond-scented umbrella palms and circuitrees. Succulent aquaferns, rooted to the aplex's backup water supply system via a pair of massive stone urns on either side of the main entrance, formed an inviting leafy arch over the recessed doorway. Above this, a peeling biolum marquee advertising *Debbie Does Bang-cock* gave off a desultory glow that reflected wanly off the canopy of fronds.

Fola rubbed her sweaty arms through the rough cotton of her sprayon robe. Dry-swallowed the scent of cigarettes and espresso from the café across the street. Breathed in the fragrance of violinette flowers from the florist a couple of shops down. It was early afternoon and hot, even in the shade of the umbrella palms. A feeling of lethargic ennui had settled over the street. The sugary aroma of vat-grown melons at a fruit kiosk gnawed at her stomach. Her feet hurt. But that was all right. She felt peaceful, at one with the world and her fellow Jesuettes. The three of them were like a single person. Part of a larger unified whole that formed the body of Christ.

Plus she was outfitted in the latest Popeware, which always made her feel good. Carnation pink robe with gold embroidery. Teeny diamond-encrusted seraph brooches that took flight to form a halo of angels. The Divinely Incensed collection of deodorants, which scented her sweat with myrrh, spread a feeling of goodwill to anyone who came within one meter of her, and temporarily protected her from heathen pherions in the Singapore ecotecture. If she stayed too long the broad-spectrum antipher in the deodorant would wear off and she would become susceptible to any number of embarrassing and potentially fatal physical discomforts, ranging from incontinence, hives, and nausea to tongue-biting convulsions.

Joi and Xophia were similarly costumed. Except that Xophia had on this Joan of Arc face appliqué to keep from being identified by any surveillance bitcams or flitcams operated by the sex parlor. Xophia used to be a sex worker at a franchise Sin-O-Matic in Seoul, before her contract was purchased by the Church. The stories she told were awful. She knew firsthand just how degrading the place was. It was terrible what she'd had to endure. A mastectomy, a hysterectomy, and a clitorectomy. Synthapse nanosockets for prosthetic breasts and genitals. The mods enabled her to emulate the sexual attributes of a lot of different women and men. Even animals. With the plug 'n' play attachments, anything was possible. According to Xophia, most customers opted for the standard glam celebrities. Sphinxter or Lucy Fur, as well as golden oldies like Marilyn Monroe, Elvis, and Hitler. Those were the most popular requests. A few of the clients she'd serviced had more exotic tastes. These brought custom plug-ins to satisfy their particular fetishes.

"But how do they know what they're getting is . . . accurate?" Fola asked Xophia one morning as they were dressing for matins, the first prayer session of the day.

Xophia adjusted the straps of her bra. "How do they know what's accurate?"

"The . . . you know." Fola lowered her eyes, too embarrassed to say what she was thinking. Ashamed of her inability to suppress her curiosity.

Xophia grinned. She grew up among the street kids in Rio. Had seen things that Fola couldn't even begin to imagine. Didn't know the meaning of the word "shame." "The inserts?" She touched her panties in the area of her hairless crotch.

Fola nodded, looked away. A blush scorched her face. "I mean, how do people know the historical stuff is . . . anatomically accurate? The right size and shape?"

"The manufacturers can tell from the old movies. A lot of them had nude scenes they can extrapolate from."

"What about the people who were never on film?" she said. "Like Cleopatra, or Napoleon?"

Xophia withdrew her hand from her underwear, returned her attention to the bra. "Forensics."

"What's that?"

"It's where they reconstruct the physical characteristics of somebody who's dead. How tall they were. How much they weighed. What they looked like. The color of their skin and hair."

"How?"

Xophia scratched the rash around the nanosocket jack that had replaced her left breast. "From bones and DNA."

Fola shook her head, not wanting to get into specifics, the gory details about how, exactly, the reconstruction process worked. "I don't get it," she finally said.

Xophia waved a hand. "The technical details aren't important. It's the end result that matters. As long as people believe what they're paying for is accurate, they're happy."

"No," Fola said. "What I don't understand is the allure. The attraction."

Xophia pursed her lips. "You're not supposed to. That's the whole point of being an Ignatarian."

True. But it was different with Xophia. She knew— had known—what it felt like to be physically attracted to someone. Fola had never known, she'd been dosed too early. That part of her personality had been aborted. The only love she'd ever know was filial. She didn't even blame her father for selling her. She had forgiven him, sent him an e-mail thanking him, telling him how happy she was as an indentured servant.

"Do you ever miss it?" Fola said.

Xophia didn't answer.

> *Hey, hey, whaddaya say?*
> *Let's all pray for Judgment Day!*

Of course, it wasn't the sex workers she was condemning. At least, not the ones who were being held against their will. They couldn't leave, not without killing or seriously injuring themselves. Like Xophia, they were innocent victims, shackled to the club by slave pherions in the fake Turkish rugs, imitation Moroccan candles, and pornographic Chinese wallscrolls. No . . . it was the club's owners and clientele Fola was denouncing—consigning to eternal damnation.

It seemed to be working. No one had approached the Sin-O-Matic in the three hours since they'd taken up residence out front. That could just be the heat. But Fola liked to think they were *having an effect*. People seemed to be *getting the message*. Except for a couple of Euro caucs drinking coffee at the café, dudes in khaki pants and nylon mesh shirts, who kept staring at them.

Like the Jesuettes were proselytizing *for* the sexplex instead of against it. Which was unnerving. But not as bad as when one of them lifted his cup in an appreciative salute and whistled.

"Just ignore them," Joi advised. "They'll leave."

"I don't want them to leave," Fola said, brandishing her pompoms. "I want them to understand what we're doing."

So she flounced over to the café, all indignant, to confront the two slumhounds.

"Yum," the guy who had saluted her said, licking his lips as he appraised her pink robe. "Cotton candy." He was bald and had these tattunes on his head that kept changing, randomly going from one image to the next and playing different music. Like multistreaming a lot of different netcasts. It made her dizzy.

The man grinned. "You like my adwear?"

"No." Pompoms on her hips, emphatic. "I think it's disgusting." The outline of a tongue formed in the middle of his forehead. It looked poised to lick her.

"Then how come you're staring?" the second guy said with a wink.

"I'm *not* staring." The tongue began to morph into a phallus. Fola looked away, back toward Xophia. And felt a sting on the side of her neck.

Tried to open her eyes.

Couldn't.

She woke sometime later. Alone, disoriented, sticky with fear. She lay on a soft gel mattress in a shuttered room. Light from the window fell across her in narrow, diffraction-grating slats. Photon-thin. Too sharp to look at. Chills wracked her, a cold fever. She felt clammy inside. Syrupy.

Where was she? *Who* was she? Panic caught her in

unhinged jaws and swallowed, pulling her down into suffocating darkness.

When she woke again, it was night and cooler. With the passing of the day's heat her fear had evaporated, and with it her belief in God.

Mostly. The deindoctrination didn't get everything. A few stubborn neural pathways survived. Mainly the fear of missing out on eternal life, a Madonna-ish urge to remain chaste, and her friendship with Xophia.

Xophia, who had waved good-bye when Fola glanced back. A quick farewell before the agents took her.

Xophia had known. She was working undercover for the ICLU and had arranged for the agents to take her, set her free.

Because Fola was still legally contracted to the Church, and because the ICLU couldn't guarantee that she wouldn't be located by the Ignatarians and reindoctrinated, the two ICLU deprogrammers put her in contact with an unregistered IA. The IA made her an offer.

Would she be interested in reclading to a completely new environment? A gengineered ecology, radically different from any of the politicorp-designed ecotectural systems that had been built after the Armageddon of overheating, overpopulation, and overeverything, including the loss of 98 percent of the world's pre-ecocaust species?

Would she be willing to emigrate offworld?

Would she be willing to give up everything and everyone she'd known in order to become part of the new gestalt?

*Hey, hey, whaddaya say? . . .*

"Fola?"

She blinks and finds herself back in the cliff-face

arcology. Upside down, staring through a lightdome at the phosphor-limned petals of a solcatcher. Parabolic membranes stretched sail-taut over structural cartilage. The petals billow and spin in the faint breeze given off by the distant sun, providing thermal and electric energy for the arcology. Less than a kilometer away, the Kuiper belt is a pearl necklace.

Hard to spec if the other solcatchers in the array have opened or not. Without the softwire link, or a bitcam image, she has no way of knowing.

Air blowing somewhere, noiseless. As furtive and tentative as the breaths of the half dozen refugees she knows are hiding somewhere in the arcology. Waiting. Caught in a collective cessation of all activity.

"Fola?" Urgency frames the question, an anxious, peremptory concern. "Can you hear me?"

Pheidoh. The information agent's voice sends a wave of comfort through her, as clear and sustained as a struck note. Hard to believe how much she's come to rely on it—not just for information but companionship.

"I hear you." She flips. "What's going on?"

"Good question."

"Where are the others?" She reorients herself, looks in the direction where Ingrid and Liam were last working. "Are they okay?"

No answer. The IA is offline again. Not only that, her biosuit is flickering, strobing between solid fabric and something more diaphanous and fuzzy. She can spec her hand through the suit, make out the tracery of bones beneath translucent flesh.

"Fola?" Liam's face blooms on the inside of her wraparound shades. Eyes wide, brimming with fear. "Help . . ." His lips form an O as he struggles to speak and a bubble of saliva balloons from his mouth.

"Why?" she says. "What's—?"

He stiffens. For an instant his face resembles a papier-mâché mask with black-painted eyes, nose, and the grinning, cadaverous outline of teeth. A second later he's gone, little more than an afterimage.

The pain in her head spikes. She screams, vaguely aware of the cold, poisonous chill traveling up her arm.

# 5

## SURFACE TENSION

With one fingertip, A. Rexx traces a molecular sentence in the page of the genome he's editing.

The gene sequence is as soft as bordello velvet, smells of honeyed raspberries and belongs to a new strain of warm-blooded orchid he's gengineering. Subsequent pages and lines of geneprint in the architext describe the complete genome of the flower.

"Line edit," Rexx says, instructing his IA to remove a line of code from the page and thread it onto the molecular loom in the center slate of the architext.

"What magnification/location?" Ida Claire says with the deadpan formality the IA never fails to use when addressing him. As if the IA is parodying him, tailoring its speech to match the uppity manners associated with old-world caucs.

"Six hundred nanometer resolution. Interval 128–134 cM. Transcription node D1S412. Site1365."

The thread expands into a series of brightly colored capsule-shaped genes, strung end to end, that remind him of jelly beans.

"Nucleotide sequence name?" the IA says.

"P14587."

The sequence regulates the electroconductivity of the orchid. It's been requisitioned by colonists on Petraea, where it's needed to extract toxins from the raw meltage supplied by wells that have been drilled in the thick mantle of ice covering the asteroid.

"File retrieve," Rexx says. "Petraea work library."

A list of encrypted data set names populates the left-hand page of the architext.

"File name?"

"TG14590."

A second series of base-pairs, shorter than the first, fills the middle panel of the architext.

"Insert . . . here." Rexx touches a specific base-pair near one end of the P14587 sequence. In less than an eye blink, the TG14590 base-pair sequence insinuates itself seamlessly into the gene, which lengthens infinitesimally, like a snake adding vertebrae. The petals of the orchid flicker, then steady.

"The recombination appears to be viable/error free," the IA says after the staccato waver subsides.

"Okay. Compile and reprint."

Rexx shifts his attention from the architext—a trifold assemblage with pewter-hinged slates, a cherrywood frame, and tooled leather clasp—to gaze out the virtual office window beside him. The flower clings to a wrought-iron trellis. Pale white flecked with gold. Later, when the digital DNA has been downloaded and molectronically converted into its organic analog, he'll visit the in-vivo greenhouse to check on the test specimen, verify that the softwire link is intact and that nothing is out of joint. It doesn't happen very often but he likes to physically touch a plant. Until then it's not real. Not really.

As he's admiring his handiwork, a gate opens in the fence on the far side of the garden. Lavender and white wisteria garland the wrought-iron arch. A bent figure appears in the opening, dappled with shadows, motes of pollen, and clusters of butterflies.

Pilar Atienza. She's gussied up in a purple sari. A yellow headband ties back her long steel gray hair, which has the thickness and texture of worsted wool. Identical to the way she wore it the one time he'd met her in person. Which tells him that the image is probably real-time, a bitcam telepresence image projected on the fabric of the ribozone rather than an in-virtu avatar.

She crosses the garden to his window. "I hope I'm not interrupting."

He shakes his head—"Naw"—and forces a smile, acutely aware of the blubbery weight of his lips.

She tips her head to the orchid. A little bow of acknowledgment or appreciation. "Very nice."

"You think so?"

"Yes. It's beautiful."

"Appearances can be deceiving."

"Really." She cocks a brow. Quizzical? Bemused? Coquettish? "Mind if I come in?"

Rexx shrugs. He taps out a series of quick finger-strokes that reconfigure the walls around him to accept her clade-profile and iDNA security signature. The office window widens and lengthens, creating a doorway. As soon as her image steps inside, the door reverts to a window.

"What can I do you for?" he says.

As a segue, she smoothes her sari. "I need your help."

"With what?"

She signs open a wallscreen. The translucent rectangular screen, superimposed on the virtuality, fills one side of the room. "There's a problem with the new Mymercia ecotecture."

He frowns. "What kind of problem?"

A deft hand movement calls up an image of the arcology. The picture is low-rez and grainy. It displays what looks like a cathedral gourd. The warm-blooded plant covers an immense lightwell a hundred or so meters from the edge of a deep fissure. The plant appears to be dead. The outer membrane is shriveled. Ditto the array of light-gathering and focusing lenses that blister the surface. Some of the lenses have ruptured, leaving open pustules. Destroyed are the tiny pores that absorb carbon dioxide and the microminiature air locks that prevent oxygen and water loss.

"As you can see," Pilar says, "there's been a failure."

No shit. "What happened?"

She looks from the wallscreen to the side of his face. "That's what we want you to find out."

Surface tension. Rexx can suddenly feel it tugging at him, threatening to pull him under the smooth, unwrinkled existence of his day-to-day routine. Slow down too much, pause or change his trajectory, and he will sink. Death by coefficient of drag.

"Why me?" he says. "I don't know squat about the design or construction specs. I wasn't even involved in the project."

"That's exactly why the council would like you to head the investigation. You're an outside observer."

"You don't think an internal investigation can be trusted?"

"It's always better to have an independent opinion. Someone who doesn't have a vested interest in the outcome. Who doesn't have to worry about shouldering blame or pointing fingers."

Rexx shakes his head, unconvinced, then glances back to the grisly image on the screen. "Was anyone hurt?"

"Three workers were killed."

"How did they die?"

"We're not sure." She grimaces. "There's not enough . . . there's not much physical evidence to go on. The only remains we have is an arm. I'm afraid that's all there is for you to autopsy."

"I might be a lot of things, but one thing I'm not is a doctor."

"There's also a survivor," Pilar says, ignoring his protest. "She's in intensive care. Since the medical facilities on the asteroid aren't operational yet, she was shuttled up to the station immediately, before we knew the full extent of the problem." Pilar hesitates. "She's still unconscious. When she wakes up we're hoping that she can tell us something."

If she wakes up, Rexx thinks. He can read between the lines. The prognosis isn't good.

"Here's her file." Pilar squirts him the woman's biomed readouts.

He leaves the file unopened. "I assume construction's been put on hold."

Pilar nods. "For now. The problem is, there are almost a thousand workers trapped on the surface. They've got enough air and water to last for a few days. But beyond that . . ." She lets him fill in the blank.

"Can't you shuttle them up to the station, too?"

Pilar shakes her head, grim. "Not until we know what's going on. We can't take the chance that whatever happened on the surface will spread. Right now, we only have to isolate one person. That's manageable. Nine hundred isn't. Not with another fifteen hundred on the station who are potentially at risk."

"You got any idea what went haywire? Preliminary clues? Theories?" Anything at all to point him in the right direction.

"No. The project manager is still analyzing the sensor data. Putting together a regression model and sequence of events."

Rexx jerks his head in the direction of the partially collapsed lightdome. "Is that the only failure?"

"No. There are others throughout. Dead or dying plants."

"So the entire ecotecture was affected. Not just one component."

"Right."

Which means that something has gone wrong at the core code level. Rexx lets out a breath. "All right," he says. "I'll see what I can do."

"Thank you."

She gives his arm a gentle squeeze, the gratitude transmitted from her nervous system to his via the interconnective tissue of the eoctecture they share. Rexx flinches at the touch, embarrassed by the Gothic immensity of his flesh. He kicks his self-consciousness into submission. Like any self-respecting cauc who comes from a long line of holier-than-thou Baptists, he's well versed in the art of abstinence, denial, and the parsimonious communication of his true inner feelings.

His attention drifts back to the virtual flower. Even though it's just a construct, a symbolic representation of the ecotecture he's working in, he likes to watch the garden change and grow in response to the edits he makes.

Maybe because Jelena had liked to garden, and this is
one way to prop up the fantasy that on some level she
really had been happy as his wife. That it wasn't the
pherions she'd been doped with as part of the arranged
marriage. That it wasn't just his father's billions, or his
mother's upper-clade status. He likes to think that without any of those things she would have cared for
him . . . despite the fact that he was the son of a first-
rate bitch and had been gengineered to be as ostenta-
tious as his Texas bloatware father. At least he hadn't
succumbed to autoerotic asphyxiation in a Juárez
brothel. The fat and Jelena are gone now. All that's left
is a shell draped in elephantine folds of skin, a ponder-
ous, wrinkled overcoat that he can't bring himself to
throw out.

Adipose. Jelena had coined the nickname—a term of
endearment. "You're my Fats Domino and my Phat
Chantz," she told him once, "all rolled into one."

Without the artificial pair-bond created by pherions,
he was all hat and no cattle. So plug-ugly no one in their
right mind would be physically attracted to him. On her
own Jelena would never have found him cute or cuddly,
an overstuffed teddy bear worthy of a pet name. Without the pherions, she would never have endured the
blubbery groping that led to Mathieu, the only good
thing to ever come out of him. And in the end even that
had been taken away.

The coffins were made of injection-molded diamond.
They had flower petals embedded just beneath the surface. Lilies of the valley for his wife, and violets for his
son, whose favorite color had been purple.

The flowers—thought to be extinct until a couple of
years ago when a few dried specimens had been found

pressed between the pages of a scrapbook in Hong Kong—had cost more than the coffins and been paid for by his mother. Except for a picture-frame oval at face level, the petals completely covered the corpses. Other than Rexx, no one at the funeral wanted to remember the way his loved ones had died—only the way they'd lived. For Rexx, there was no way to separate their life from their death. That was the way he thought of them, as a single life undifferentiated from his own. His mother, a venerable sesquicentenarian who'd been born before the ecocaust and survived the die-off, seemed indifferent to their passing. As far as Rexx could spec, she felt nothing, not even fatalistic resignation. She was hardened against death—not just in herself but in others. She refused to discuss the accident, arguing that nothing could be gained by fixating on the details.

"An exercise in futility, my dear boy," she said. "Pointless."

It was the same attitude she'd adopted after his father's less than noble passing south of the border.

"A horse rears for no reason," she argued. "Tragic, yes. Worth killing yourself over, no."

*No. Not for no reason. The horse reared because . . .*

"If there's one thing I've learned," his mother said, giving his arm a firm squeeze, "it's that life goes on."

Her hand lingered. Intimate. Possessive. They stood outside the small chapel, in the granite-walled foyer of the mausoleum where the caskets would be interred. The chapel, modeled after one of the great pyramids, was a platinum-and-glass affair with sharp angles, tinted windows, and fountains that cascaded into reflective ponds.

"You never liked Jelena," he said. She had opposed the marriage from day one—which had been arranged by his father—and done everything she could to sabotage it.

"That's not true." His mother removed her ruby-gloved hand, leaving behind the extinct odor of geraniums. "She was very . . . industrious."

He didn't have the energy, or desire, to translate the euphemism. He was beyond caring. Beyond *her*.

"Mathieu was a fine boy," she allowed, the gold brooch in the front of her collar offering a sympathetic flash. "What will you do now?"

"I haven't decided," he said, the lie as dry as a bleached bone in his mouth. He met her gaze, the jaundiced apathy limning her eyes. All life had evaporated from her, leaving behind a dry residue. A bathtub ring of indifference.

"It's important to do *some*thing," she said, "*any*thing. It doesn't matter what. I assume you're working on a project."

He nodded. A saline-resistant grass for Alaska's emergent wetlands. The senior management team at Sygnostics—the gengineering corp he worked for—was hoping to develop a clade-compatible version for Siberia.

"Good. You'll find that work obligations and commitments can be a blessing at a time like this."

"Don't worry," he said. Unable to add, "I'll be fine," but allowing the implication to hang in the air.

It seemed to be enough. Satisfied, his mother withdrew into her hard outer shell of platinum lamé and bacteria-complected skin.

Two weeks later he was gone, reclated, riding a shuttle that would take him to the Kuiper belt along with twelve other emigrants looking for someone or something else.

\* \* \*

Rexx blinks, shifts his attention from the orchid to the architext. "File close," he tells his IA.

"Do you want to save your changes?" Ida Claire says.

"That'd be dandy."

Maybe the IA's unfriendliness is a heuristic fluke, something it has no control over, like bad gas or a weak bladder. Then there's the IA's name. Another barb? There's no way to know. There aren't enough caucs on Tiresias to establish a statistical basis for the IA's behavior toward him.

"When would you like to implement an in-vivo update?" the IA says.

"Later," Rexx says. The orchid can wait. He squirts a little White Rain, then opens the biomed file and begins to read.

# 6

## THE EZ LIFE

L. Mariachi hates merengue—can't stand the slick rhythms and seductive vocals that promise nothing but happiness—and that is what the band at the Club Pair-A-Dice is playing at the moment.

The franchise is new, sugarcoated to lure him into a sense of false security. The decor is imitation glass and chrome with cheap faux-wood accents over structural foam and lichenboard. The atmosphere is upbeat but low key—sensuous. The air is raging with pherions that have everybody swaying together on the dance floor and waxing optimistic about the future.

No discontented *braceros* tonight. All of the guest workers are laughing, satisfied. Giddy with change. It's always this way just after the migrant workforce has been reclad and relocated. A new assignment always brings with it renewed hope; the work will be easier, the *patrón* nicer, the wages better.

It's bullshit, of course. Wishful th.
will be better, it never is. Soon, it will
*tambo,* the prisonlike trailers, for a few hour.
fore they start work at dawn. Harvesting pha.
berries this time. That means he'll be wading in .cs
filled knee-deep with nutrient solution, breathing in the
fumes of whatever hazmat they're using for fertilizer.
The vats are sealed with plastic bubble domes. Which
means it will be not only hot but humid.

The beat quickens. The syncopated pulsing of biolum panels suspended over the bar and the dance floor
amps up, engulfing him in a staccato swirl of pastels. A
contingent of *cholos* in retro-gangsta regalia—oversized
T-shirts, loose sprayon khakis, and backward baseball
caps—take to the dance floor and launch into a wild
*quebradita.*

L. Mariachi shakes his head at the fuck-me dance.
He's too old for this shit anymore. The lights and music
are giving him a headache. Even his eyes hurt. It didn't
used to be like this. When he was only a few years
younger, back in his late forties, he could party with the
best of them. It was the only way to burn off all the
pent-up frustration and rage that came with being
trapped in a dead-end existence. The only way to keep
going was to vomit up one job and move on to the next.
Now he can't even do that.

"Had enough?"

The *cantinera* serving beer is a pretty *chinito,* Asian-
eyed with olive skin, long black hair, and a look of distaste that tells him she's new to the Entertainment Zone.

"*Ni madres!*" he says. Hell no!

She rests both elbows on the thin veneer of sprayed
mahogany that covers the cheap lichenboard bar. Behind
her, a wallscreen flickers between random channels. At

ıe moment it's streaming a indoor soccer match between the European Union and SEA, Southeast Asia.
"You should quit while you're ahead, *viejo*."

"Who are you calling old?"

"I know a *desmadroso* when I see one."

"I'm not drunk," he protests, voicing the obligatory
protest.

She consults a tiny display that materializes in front
of one eye, hovers long enough for her to read a datasquirt, then dissipates into gnat-size particles. "That's
not what your biomed feed says."

"Point one-five-six, to be exact," a nasal voice whispers over his cochlear imp.

His fucking IA. Num Nut. "What do you expect
from politicorp-owned software?" he says.

"*You're* politicorp-owned," the *cantinera* says.

"You make your living off the corpocracy, too," he
counters. "If it wasn't for the pharms, you wouldn't
be here."

"The Pair-A-Dice is an independent contractor. It's
not the same."

"Bullshit." He jabs himself in the chest with one
finger. "If it wasn't for us *braceros* there wouldn't be
any Entertainment Zone. You wouldn't be living the
EZ life."

She juts her chin at a man passed out on the floor in
a pool of frothy yellow vomit. "You call this easy?"

"Try working the vats for a few months."

"No thanks. This is as close as I want to get."

L. Mariachi raises his empty beer pouch. "*Que viven
los mojados!*" he shouts at the top of his lungs. Long
live the wetbacks! But his voice is swallowed by the din,
lost almost before it leaves his lips.

Her mouth twists in what might be pity or contempt.

"I didn't realize that being a migrant was something to be proud of."

It was at one time, he thinks, back when borders were arbitrary, abstract lines that could be crossed. It was a form of rebellion, of not accepting the status quo. It wasn't the physical barrier they were violating so much as the idea of boundaries. Only a couple of generations ago it was possible to blur the divisions between people, break down rigid ideologies and challenge differing philosophies of life. The ecocaust, and the clade-based ecotectural systems that grew out of it, put an end to unregulated integration. No more illegal mixing of genes and memes or the erosion of cultural, social, and economic identities. From now on, things would be controlled. It could even be argued that the biochemical segregation enforced by the various clades was a way of preserving diversity.

"Why do you do it?" the *cantinera* asks.

"The same reason you do."

She shakes her head, in puzzlement or denial, and then replaces his empty pouch of beer with a new one and charges it against tomorrow's wages. For some reason she's decided to let him keep drinking. Maybe she's bored. Maybe she's a politicorp informer, sent to draw him out, trip him up. No doubt the place is crawling with bitcams, acoustic spores, and sniffers looking for unregistered or illegal pherions manufactured on the black market.

Fuck it. What's a Sin City binge without a little gambling? Besides, it's not like he has anything to lose. The politicorp has already taken everything it can.

L. Mariachi picks up the pouch, peels the tab off the top. "All migrants have *patas de perro*," he declares.

She frowns. "Dog's feet?"

He sips the beer, squeezing the pouch, then nods. "We're restless. We can't stay in one place."

"Like gypsies."

"Migrants have always done the shit work," he says. "The jobs no one else wants to do. We're opportunists."

"Sounds like a lack of self-respect to me."

He grips the pouch tighter. Beer bubbles out the top. "What we have is freedom. We're not trapped in one place, or one job, like you."

"At least I have a home."

"We get free housing and medical care. Plus, we're independent. Not tied down to any specific ecotecture."

She wipes the bar with her sleeve. "That doesn't mean you're free. You're just as isolated or marginalized as the rest of us. The only difference is, you take your cage with you."

In the beginning that hadn't been the case. Institutionalized migration had been a way of remaining free, of not being absorbed into one single clade. Collectivism and solidarity were the migrants' creed. Their saving grace. A few *braceros* still believed in that. They hadn't lost faith in themselves or the future.

"Have you always been a migrant?" the *cantinera* asks.

L. Mariachi looks up, surprised to find her still there, chewing a stick of nicaffeine gum. "No."

"What did you do before?"

He puffs out his chest. "I was a *taxista* and a musician."

"Where?"

"Zamora."

"That's in Mexico?"

"Michoacán, a couple hundred miles from Mexico City. I drove a taxi by day and played clubs at night."

"You were in a band?"

He nods, the alcohol filling him with false bravado at

his *rockero* past. "Daily Bred," he says. "We had an on-line single that topped the charts with a billion hits. 'SoulR Byrne.'" It stayed in the number-one spot for a full hundred and twenty seconds before losing its place.

The *cantinera*'s gum pops. "I never heard of you."

"We were marketed as Mexitallic," he says. "A blend of ethnic *pirekua* rap with a speed metal beat."

"What's *pirekua*?"

"A traditional Indian ballad, from the Purépecha highlands. I played mandolin and electric guitar."

"Have you thought about playing in the EZ?"

He laughs, a short bark, and holds up his deformed left hand with its gnarled joints and crooked fingers.

"What happened?"

"Things didn't work out. So I signed up as a mi-grant." He raises his beer, squeezes out the last of it in one shot to wash down the bitterness.

"And now you're stuck."

He shakes his head, doesn't need to hear this.

"You can't go back," she goes on. "Can't get ahead."

"Fuck this noise!" He slams down the pouch, crum-pling it on the thin veneer, and stands. The wallscreen behind the bar has cycled to a newstream. Digital video of a contaminated aqua pharm on one of the Gulf Coast offshore settlements. The ancient oil-drilling platform looks familiar. He's harvested kelp there, on a previous job. Seventeen people dead in the last five hours, killed by some unknown toxin.

Tottering under the influence of a syrupy Pedro In-fante ballad and the chatter of the *cantinera*, he stum-bles for the exit. Weaves his way past the dance floor and the craps tables, where the gangstas are whooping it up, as if they're *estafadores,* big-time con artists who are going to beat the house. Thing is, the house never gets beat. They haven't learned that yet.

"Hey," one of the *cholos* complains, his heavy gold chains rattling. He's working on a mustache, a wispy collection of meticulously groomed strands that look like a bad comb-over plastered in place. His eyes are flushed, bulging with machismo. He's got swagger up the sphincter, deserves respect.

L. Mariachi waves him off—"Fuck your mother"— and shoulders his way out the front entrance.

In the street—surrounded by bars, restaurants, VR-cades, and solar-panel–shaded stalls selling everything from jewelry to fortunes—the air is bright and hot, feverish with activity and the insect hum of flitcams. A half moon is up, barely visible above the canopy of tall circuitrees that generate power for the EZ, aquaferns that supply water, and umbrella palms that block UV. There's no breeze, and a pall of dust hangs in the air. Maybe the air filters aren't working yet, or maybe they've decided not to turn them on to conserve power. Most of the buildings are new, assembled a day ago in preparation for the arrival of the migrant pharm workers. But a few are older and show signs of successive renovation to make them more energy efficient and eco-logically sound: sonic floor tiles, thermal wall hangings, piezoelectric siding, and photovoltaic windows, all soaking up the raucous energy given off by the crowd.

The party atmosphere reminds him of the old fiestas. The feast of St. Francis, still celebrated around the time of the original pre-ecocaust autumn harvest, signaled the end of hard work, frustration, and disappointment. A few months later, Easter heralded a fresh beginning, filled with renewed promises, hopes, and resolve. All that's missing are the bullfights and the *nazarenos*, the ragged procession of teenage boys who dressed in white robes and carried home-built crosses on their shoulders, reenacting the pilgrimage to Golgotha.

Instead the EZ's got carnival rides and imitation gangstas who are weighted down with boredom rather than guilt or reverence. Nothing is authentic anymore. Everyone, including himself, is living the idea of *norteño* migrant culture. The real culture is dead. It disappeared during the ecocaust, along with the plants and animals. They're not even Chicano anymore. They've lost their identity.

He passes an Xstream 2na sushi outlet, then a Nito Kino tattune parlor. Resists the sudden pang of hunger and vanity brought on by the airborne virals circulated by the businesses. Good thing he's not wearing his wraparounds. He doesn't have to look at all the shit they're selling. The viral ads are bad enough.

"It's getting late," Num Nut tells him.

He checks the time. Ten-ten. "Not that late."

Behind him, two of the gangstas from the bar have followed him into the night. The one he bumped, plus another.

"I think you should go home," Num Nut says. "Get some rest."

"What do you know?"

"You have a long day ahead of you."

He shakes his head. "I don't have shit." Not even a future. And the past is hardly worth keeping. Hell.

"Stop feeling sorry for yourself," his IA counsels.

"Is that what I'm doing? I thought I was getting fucked up."

"You are. *Muy borracho*. And you're going to regret it big-time in the morning."

"Along with everything else."

"Don't do this."

"What?"

"Berate yourself. It will only make things worse."

He glances over his shoulder. The gangstas are still following him. "How can things get any worse?"

"Let's see. . . ."

"Never mind." He really doesn't want to know, doesn't want to think about it. He's got other problems right now. Like how to pull a disappearing act before he ends up with a cut throat.

He stumbles across a large, open-air amphitheater where a group of badmash performance actors are staging a show. Some melodrama in which the actors wear different colored barbed wire to represent different clades. Crass social commentary. But the smart mob that has spontaneously gathered to watch it is really into the shared mood they're streaming, eating it up like cotton candy. Part of the reason for the smob is the free samples the troupe is handing out: deodorants and perfumes that represent the pherions used by the clades to limit access and control behavior.

L. Mariachi ducks into the smob, hoping to lose himself. It should be easy. He's as faceless as the next *bracero,* just as interchangeable.

*Quería hacer algo.* He wanted to make something of himself, the same as anyone else. But his ruined hand put an end to that. Now he can't even put up a decent fight. If he wants to save himself, he has to run.

He veers down a footpath that goes to a mission-style church, empty except for a few old women sequestered in prayer and frayed shawls. A rock skitters behind him. He cuts a quick glance back.

The gangstas have trailed him from the amphitheater. L. Mariachi darts left, into a palm-shaded garden with injection-molded statues of St. Francis and the Virgin of Guadalupe. Past the statues, the potted umbrella palms end and he suddenly finds himself at the westernmost edge of the EZ.

The barrier is invisible—no fence or signs announce the line—but he registers the demarcation as a faint tingle in his skin. With every step the warning amplifies. No way they'll follow him this far. He's not worth it.

"What are you doing?" Num Nut says.

Ahead of him loom the Rocky Mountains and the lights of Front Range City, just over the curve of the horizon. A green and yellow haze tinged with pink that stretches from Fort Collins in the north to Colorado Springs in the south. He hasn't been to a city in years. Not since he left Mexico City.

"Don't be stupid." Somehow the IA manages to sound patronizing and worried at the same time.

"I didn't know you cared."

"You're an idiot."

"Tell me about it." He's itching like a motherfucker and his stomach is upset, but there's no pain. Not yet.

"I don't know what you hope to accomplish. You won't get very far. You'll end up in the clinic, unable to work for days."

He keeps walking, stubbornly heading toward the light until a slow burn settles deep in his bones.

He turns. The gangstas are closing in, less than fifty meters away. Motherfuckers are persistent. Refuse to be deterred.

Another step. The heat increases. His nerves feel incandescent, as if they're throwing off electrons. It's getting harder to move and his lips grow numb, deadened by scorched myelin. It feels like he's being cremated from the inside out. Tears bleed from the corners of his eyes, trail down his cheeks to the oil slick of drool and mucus glazing the stubble on his chin.

He sinks to his knees and tilts his head to the sky. "*Dulce dolor*," he thinks.

"I'm calling for medical assistance." The IA's voice sounds far away and unreal, something out of a dream.

L. Mariachi collapses onto his side, his lips moving wordlessly, and sees the two gangstas walking toward him. Something sharp flashes in the lead gangsta's hands, a bright sliver of metal or glass. L. Mariachi's heart stutters. But there's nothing he can do. He's helpless as a lamb.

"Hurry," the gangsta with the lame mustache says, "or we're fucked."

They grab him by the arms and drag him across the hardpan, back to the garden, where they lean him against the base of the Virgin Mary.

The gangsta with the mustache uncaps the plastic ampoule he's carrying, jams it up L. Mariachi's nose, and squeezes.

"Now what?" the other gangsta asks, glancing around nervously. They can't be older than fourteen or fifteen and look like brothers. They have the same features, identical almond eyes.

"We wait," the older one says. "Antipher will take effect in a couple of minutes." He has the voice of authority, like he's speaking from experience.

The gangstas squat on their haunches. What are they waiting for? They seem content to take their time, make him suffer.

From where he's propped, L. Mariachi has a clear view of the Virgin. It looks like she's gazing down at him instead of the Christ Child in her arms. Her expression is beatific but he's not ready to give himself over to her loving embrace. In a few minutes, feeling starts to return to his lips and his limbs.

"Wah . . . ah?" he says.

The gangstas lean forward, elbows on their knees, and peer at him with a mixture of anxiety and expectation.

He tries again. "Wah you won?"

"We want you to play," the older one says.

"Pway?"

The young gangsta makes a strumming motion with his right hand. "At a *limpia* for our sick aunt."

*Limpia*. Healing ceremony, spiritual cleansing.

"Wen?"

"Tonight."

L. Mariachi shakes his head. "Don' haf inshamen."

"No problem," the older gangsta says, making it clear that L. Mariachi doesn't have a choice. "The *bruja* has a guitar."

A *bruja*. Where did they find a witch? He didn't know there were any traditional healers left.

L. Mariachi raises his left hand. Evidence that he can't help, that they should find someone else.

The older gangsta grabs his hand and, misinterpreting his excuse as a gesture for help, hauls him to his feet. Together, draping his arms over their scrawny shoulders, they lead him away.

# 7

## BAD SINNERGY

The music is as sad as it is angry. A fickle current, it carries her forward in fits and starts. First a torrent of harsh, badmash lyrics, followed by slow, amniotic chords that make her chest ache.

> *Don't let my heart go*
> *Up in smoke, burned by the sun*
> *For eternity.*

Instinctively, her right hand scrabbles for the cross. Cool, peroxide air caresses her fingertips. They close around nothing and continue to curl inward. Fingernails bite into her palms.

The cross is missing, its reassuring weight gone.

So is Ephraim. They're no longer softwired. His absence is palpable, both a relief and a distress. It's as if a damaged tooth has been pulled from her. The cavity left behind induces another kind of discomfort. An echo tosses fitfully in the space he once occupied.

No different from the Church after it was cut out of her.

She has nothing to anchor her. No *thing* to hang on to. Her only ballast is a vague heaviness in her lungs, brought on by the song. It seems to be the only thing holding her in place. Without it, she would float away. Her head would inflate and up she would go. Forever.

Which might not be a bad thing. Consciousness lies up there somewhere, beyond this rippling surface tension of light she can't seem to break through.

"Fola?"

The voice yanks her out of the song. She jerks and struggles to open her eyes, afraid of slipping back into murky depths. "Pheidoh?" Her eyelids crack. Light seeps in, thick and moist between the dark lines of her lashes. Blurred diffraction-grating images clot her vision.

"How do you feel?" the IA says.

She blinks. Finds herself staring up at the cornea-thick lens of a small lightdome set in a hexagonal ceiling grid. Through the pressurized membrane she can see other hexapods, clustered together like atoms to form a large central nucleus. "Where am I?" Her voice is a scratchy whisper. The words rub against one another, dry as rain-starved grass.

"A hospicell on the construction station. You were brought here immediately after the accident."

The accident. Liam's face surfaces out of watery gloom, buoyed by a sudden rush of panic. Gone is the brashness. Everything has been stripped from him, except the knowledge that he's going to die. Fola's breath

catches. She flinches at the memory of mummified skin
and jaundiced eye sockets.

"It's all right," Pheidoh says. "You're safe. Everything's going to be fine."

She tries to move and finds she's immobilized by a
sleepsac, held in place by gossamer tubes fastened to an
Intensive Care Module. She glances at the grid of biolum panels, the medical equipment mounted on black-
anodized racks, and a plain folding privacy screen that
has been moved to the side and secured to one wall. The
decor is pure Art Treko. All of the ceiling panels are featureless, depressing. There's nothing, no one, to keep
her company.

"Where's Ephraim?" she asks. He's dead. He has to
be. That's the emptiness she feels.

"He's fine," Pheidoh says.

Then why can't she feel him? "Where?"

"Here on the station. He wasn't involved in the accident."

Fola draws a relieved breath, remembers that he was
working in another section of the arcology.

She twists her head to the side. One of the hexcell's
walls is a window that looks out into an atrium. The
atrium is the node for a hexapod. Five other cells identical to hers grouped around it. Bananopy fronds and
tapestree limbs, woven together in an intricate macramé
of Celtic knot designs, etch shadows onto the glass. A
tight flock of scuttleaves dislodge from a limb to school
like tropical fish in an aquarium.

"What about the others?" she asks. "What about
Ingrid?"

"They didn't make it," another voice says over her
cochlear implant. "You were the only survivor."

The news is accompanied by a grainy bitcam image

of a man projected onto the wallscreen in front of her. The man is older, an octogenarian at least, and wears a benevolent smile as pink as his crepe hospital sprayons.

She wills her hands to unfold, her jaw to unclench. "Who are you?"

"My name is Gilles Villaz. I'm the doctor in charge of your case." His bushy bottlebrush eyebrows remind her of a species of hairy caterpillar, believed to be extinct, that has suddenly resurfaced in some backwater ecological niche. He has toffee-colored cough lozenges for eyes, a bulbous nose, and a hairless scalp populated with a menagerie of turtle, fish, and spider-shaped liver spots.

"How long since—" Bile froths up in her throat. She can hear Liam joking with her. *Nun of that, now.* She swallows. "How long have I been here?"

"A little over four hours."

Hours. Fola was certain it had been longer. Days, maybe, or weeks. Some of the tension in her loosens, calves off like ice from a glacier. If she were seriously injured, it would have taken her longer to regain consciousness. They would have kept her sedated for any viral surgery, kept her under for as long as it took to heal. So she can't have been hurt too badly. "How soon can I leave?" Except for the atrium, the sterile atmosphere in the hexcell gives her the chills. She wants to reconnect with Ephraim and the rest of her tuplet—Alphonse, Yulong, Lalya—as well as the warm-blooded plants. Especially the plants. She misses the calming effect they have, their slow circadian thrum.

"I'm not sure." Dr. Villaz itches his nose. "Soon, I hope." His smile is reserved but optimistic. "You've been placed in isolation until you receive a clean bill of health."

No wonder she can't feel the softwire connection to the warm-blooded plants, the autonomic stream of bio-chemicals. "I feel fine."

"A period of observation is standard. Nothing more than a precaution."

"How come I'm not allowed to get up or move around?" It occurs to her that this might be for her own good. That she might have a few broken bones that she's not aware of.

"When you first arrived you suffered a number of grand mal seizures. We thought it best to immobilize you, for your own protection."

That doesn't explain why she's been disconnected from the plants and her tuplet.

"We should know more soon," the doctor says, "when your latest biomed scan is complete."

"What happened down there?"

But the doctor is gone.

"There was a temporary instability in the ecotec-ture," Pheidoh says. "A transient mutation."

"What kind of mutation?" She was under the impres-sion that mutations were permanent. But maybe not.

The IA hesitates. "It appears that a small portion of the architext is corrupt."

The architext is the equivalent of the Bible for an ecotectural system. It contains the lines of molecular code that define all of the pherions, genes, and clade-profiles that make up the asteroid's artificial ecology. "How was it corrupted?" she says.

"A mistake."

"By who?" Ingrid? she wonders. Liam? Or one of the ICLU refugees Ephraim smuggled onto the asteroid. Could one of them have accidentally done something to trigger—

"It was an IA," Pheidoh says.

Fola blinks. "You're kidding?" IAs almost never make a mistake. "Has it been fixed?"

"I think so."

Pheidoh doesn't seem too sure. More hopeful than certain. Like the jury might still be out.

"Which IA was it?" she says.

There's a pause. "I can't say. It's confidential."

The information agent sounds embarrassed—upset the way some people get when they find out that someone close to them, a family member or friend, has done something terrible—as if it were personally responsible.

"What did it feel like?" Pheidoh says.

The question catches her by surprise. "What?"

"The accident."

Fola grimaces. Tilts her head forward to inspect her arm. It looks okay. Normal. She rubs her fingers together. They don't feel out of the ordinary—nothing like clay or papier-mâché. "It hurt," she finally says.

When Pheidoh doesn't answer immediately the doctor says, "You should try to get some rest."

Fatigue weights her lids. "No," she protests. "Wait . . ."

The next time she wakes, the sleepsac is gone. So is the tangle of tubes connecting her to the ICM. She's free to move around. The interior decor has changed, too. The wallscreens are dotted with Art Frisco flowers, a cheerful assortment of hot pink, lemon yellow, and lime green daisies. The ceiling panels are stained glass. But instead of saints there are delicate flower stems and long-waisted women.

"I hope you don't mind," Pheidoh says over her cochlear implant. "I thought a change of scenery might make you feel a little more comfortable."

It does. She feels calmer. "Who's the artist?"

"Mucha."

"You have visitors," Dr. Villaz informs her. He sounds pleased, about this or something else, she's not sure. Either way, it's encouraging.

The pink daisies on one of the wall panels fade to reveal the hexapod outside her cell. Her tuplet has gathered in front of the honeycomb window, anxious but smiling, trying to put on a good face. Without the softwire link between them, that's all she has to go on. Fola doesn't know firsthand what they're feeling. She can guess. But it's impossible to know for certain.

Fola shifts the position of her arms and legs, then pushes away from the ICM. She gyrates clumsily as she reorients herself, snares a magnetic flux line and drifts over to the window. Executes an unsteady pirouette so she doesn't splat against the glass like a bug on a windshield.

"How are you?" Alphonse asks, concerned. "They refuse to tell us anything about your condition."

"I feel fine," she says. "Except that I miss you all." She rubs her arms, chafing at the absence.

"We were worried sick," Lalya says.

The rest of them nod in unison.

"What about you?" Fola says. "Is everyone okay?"

"We're fine," Ephraim says. He looks less confident than he sounds. His lips are crimped tight.

All of them are nervous, apprehensive. The tension is contagious. She can feel it even without a shared nervous system. "What's going on?" she says. "Do you have any idea what happened yet?"

"Are you kidding?" Yulong snorts, gruff as usual. "They haven't told us shit." A former vat rat who worked for a major engineering politicorp, she has the least respect of any of them for authority.

"We're cut off from the asteroid," Lalya says, matter-of-fact. "That's what. They shut down the softwire link to the ecotecture so it can't contaminate us."

"From the mutation?"

"If that's what it is," Ephraim says.

Which explains why she's in isolation, under observation. If Mymercia was affected, then the orbiting station is vulnerable. The ecotecture is identical. Since she was brought to the station after the accident, that makes her a risk, a potential carrier.

Fola adjusts the orientation of her arms and legs, stabilizing herself. "Is the station in any danger?"

"Not if we're disconnected," Ephraim says. She knows him well enough to know that he's trying to convince himself as much as her and the others.

"That doesn't mean we haven't already been compromised," Yulong snips. "It just might not have shown up yet, that's all."

"If the softwire link is down," Lalya says, "then whatever infected the ecotecture down there can't be transmitted to us."

"We hope," Yulong says. "If it has, we'll be the last to know."

"Construction's been put on hold," Alphonse says. "Right now, that's all we know."

They seem to be in the middle of an ongoing argument, one that doesn't include her.

"So what have you been doing in the meantime?" Fola says, anxious to change the subject. Not only does she feel left out but she finds the discord irritating. She doesn't have the energy or the patience right now to deal with their bickering. It seems pointless. How did she ever put up with it?

Ephraim grinds his teeth in frustration. "Not much we *can* do." He's worse than the rest of them put together when it comes to sitting around.

"We've been analyzing sensor data," Alphonse says. "The last datasquirt from the solcatchers. With luck the sensor readings will be able to tell us something about the system failure."

"Unless the sensors are wacked," Yulong says. "They could've been looping bad data."

"True," Alphonse allows.

Looping, Fola thinks. She remembers standing in a circle. Pudgy Imanol Ealo on one side of her. Snooty Tatjana Soffel on the other. Her fifth-grade teacher, Ms. Udman, leaning over to whisper in her ear. A phrase.

"Your turn," Ms. Udman told her. "Remember to speak clearly."

Fola turned to Imanol, whose breath smelled of peppered soytein, and whispered the phrase into his ear. She formed each word carefully, the way she did her letters. Imanol giggled and whispered the phrase to the next person, who whispered it to the next person, and so forth. The phrase was "cystic fibrosis," and by the time it got all the way around the circle it came out as "sixty-five roses."

Bad data. Even if the input was good, all it took was a tiny misinterpretation here, a slight mistranslation there. She had spoken clearly, yet the phrase had come out wrong.

Garbage out didn't always mean garbage in.

"Are you all right?" Pheidoh asks when everyone has left.

She nods. "Just tired." Instead of energizing her, the visit had the opposite effect. She's exhausted.

"According to your biomed readings your blood pressure is elevated. So is your heart rate."

"It's just that . . ." She shakes her head. Bad sinnergy. That's what the Jesuettes called it whenever people weren't in group-hug mode.

"Maybe you should rest—"

"No." She's too amped to sleep.

"—or eat."

No way she can eat. Her stomach is cramped, ulcerous.

"You have a message," Pheidoh says after a moment.

"Who is it?" Other than Ephraim, she can't imagine who would want to talk to her.

"Xophia."

Fola blinks. Stares.

"The transmission is encrypted and was squirted over an unauthorized channel," the IA warns.

Fola moistens her lips, chapped with sudden nervousness. "Put her through."


Xophia has changed. Six months on the shuttle have thinned her. She looks tired. Travel weary. Fatigue occludes her eyes, shadows every movement down to the smallest eye blink. Dressed in a pink sprayon jumpsuit, she's floating close to a recessed, wall-mounted hospital bed covered with gauzy, antiseptic blue sheets. The gauze is wrinkled, twisted around a motionless figure that could be a gerontocrat or half-starved refugee. It's hard to know. Her view is partially blocked by a fold-down rack of linen-filled trays. Both the jumpsuit and sheets are speckled yellow-brown.

"We're supposed to maintain radio silence during the

trip," Xophia begins. "But under the circumstances, I think it's important for you to know what's going on."

A muscle in Fola's eyelid twitches. Her throat pulses.

Xophia shifts to one side. The flitcams streaming her image shift with her, bringing the patient into view. A frail-looking geront with wax-paper skin. The guy's bald scalp looks diseased—a hodgepodge of wrinkled tattunes that, on closer inspection, appear to be shriveled lips. Puckered, subcutaneous, cancerous. In addition to the sheets, the patient is restrained by g-mesh that limits the movement of his limbs, keeps him from bouncing around the icosahedron-shaped clinic. His face is sunken, caved in on itself. His cadaverous mouth forms a knot of determination around the siptube lodged between his teeth. The thick tube is clogged with brownish sludge. Fola can't tell if the stuff is going in or coming out. It occurs to her that this is the source of the crusty polka dots on Xophia's jumpsuit.

"There's been an outbreak of some kind," Xophia says. "Within the last twenty-four hours. A lot of people on the shuttle are starting to get sick." She frowns in irritation as the siptube slides free or is spat out and gobs of the paste erupt from the caldera formed by the geront's mouth, spewing in all directions.

Fola grimaces. But Xophia doesn't seem to mind. "Since I'm the only one on board with any emergency medical training, I've been pretty busy." She snags the loose end of the siptube, holds it absently. "The problem is, I have no idea what it is. According to the datastream from Earth we're monitoring, the same thing is happening back there . . . which is weird. The bruises that are showing up—the growths that people are getting—look a lot like historical stuff you'd find in the mediasphere. Old ad images and tattunes. Pre-ecocaust, mostly. I'm wondering if maybe it's an ad virus that mutated and went berserk. Whatever it is, it's being transmitted electronically through the infosphere. Otherwise, there's no way we could be infected since we haven't been in direct physical contact with anyone else for months."

She reinserts the siptube into the geront's incontinent lips, swabs his mouth with a damp cloth, and replaces his bib. She completes the maneuver deftly, with practiced ease and patience.

"Anyway"—she glances up—"I just thought you should know what's happening. A lot of the refugees on the shuttle are worried about family members and friends they left behind. But with the radio silence, there's no way to contact them to find out what's going on."

That's it. The datasquirt ends, a freeze frame with Xophia looking straight at Fola, her hand still holding the siptube in place. There's something on her palm. A malignant black-and-white face that Fola doesn't recognize. Then the transmission washes away in a downpour of static.

*Hey, hey, whaddaya say,*
*Let's all pray for Judgment Day.*

"Do you want to reply?" Pheidoh asks.

Fola nods, takes a second to clear her throat and rub her nose with the back of her hand. "What was on her palm?"

"An image of Sydney Greenstreet playing the character of Ferrari in *Casablanca*."

"Is that a digital video?"

"No. It's an old black-and-white flat-screen movie."

Fola hollows her cheeks as several flitcams, disguised as insects, emerge from the stained-glass foliage to transmit her image.

*Five, six, seven, eight,*
*Meet you at the Pearly Gate.*

# 8

## HACK JOB

The only flesh Rexx has ever cut into with a knife, besides a steak, is the scrotum of a deformed calf at the Hello Dolly Animal Pharm.

"If you wanna be a gengineer," his father had said, "you're gonna learn firsthand what genes are."

Rexx was ten at the time and had already decided that the last thing he wanted to do was follow in his father's footsteps. Part of it was that he'd always hated his name, which was an acronym for an ancient programming language—REstructured eXtended eXecutor—that his father waxed nostalgic about whenever he got drunk. Rexx might be saddled with the name, but he could hitch himself to another wagon. A different stereotype.

"Genetics is a messy business," his father said as he led the defective clone from the holding pen to a cutting table in the corral outside. "The sooner you learn that, the better."

In the searing afternoon light, the scarred tabletop was stained with dried blood and had an empty tin bucket set on the ground next to it. The air was clotted with flies, the stench of burnt cow hair, pig slop, and manure.

"Gonna fix this little feller right up," the pharm hand helping them said. "Don't want him shootin' his wad in the gene pool." He winked at Rexx, then wrestled the calf onto the table, pinning it.

His father pointed to the scrotum. "Them balls have got a load o' bad shot. They got to go."

"Go where?" Rexx said.

The pharm hand grinned, revealing thirty-two pearl-finished teeth. Each one a miniature replica of a Colt .45 grip, designed to pistol-whip his food into submission each time he took a bite.

His father grabbed Rexx by the hand, swallowing it whole in his blubbery whale-size palm, and forced Rexx's fingers to the squishy testicles. The calf flinched. Rexx jerked.

"Feel 'em, goddamnit! Ain't no different than yours. 'Cept maybe a tad bigger."

The balls quivered, then steadied as the pharm hand leaned his weight onto the calf. When the calf was calm, he took out a knife and handed it to Rexx. "Here ya go."

"Take it," his father said.

Rexx took the knife. The handle was hot, the blade bright.

"Don't worry," his father said. "I'll help ya." With his free hand he stretched the scrotum tight around one ball. "Okay, now cut here." He made an arc with the fingertip of his other hand.

Except for the trembling tip of the blade, Rexx remained motionless.

"Do it," his father hissed. "If you don't, I guarantee you won't get within spittin' distance of Darwin."

Rexx inched the knife closer. His head spun. Sweat steamed off the calf, sharp and dank.

"Do it!"

Rexx closed his eyes, then, holding his breath, plunged the knife blade into the membrane. . . .

Cutting into the remains of Liam Vitt's left forearm leaves Rexx with the same rancid burn in his throat.

Instead of a cutting table the severed limb lies in a sealed chamber, held in place under a carbon nanotube biosensor. On his eyescreens, the arm appears pale and bloated. In addition to a realtime bitcam image, he's set up a virtual datawindow on the wallscreen behind his desk. The left pane of the window displays architext, the line-by-line molecular code that describes the composition and the structure of individual molecules and longer nucleotide sequences, including DNA. The right pane of the window displays a ribozone construct, the visual—and in Rexx's opinion, overtly poetic—representation of this code. Information packets are rendered as butterflies. Flowers signify pherions, the viral pheromones that make up clade patterns and profiles. Trees, bushes, and other vegetation represent the physical elements in an ecotecutural system that interacts with the warm-blooded plants—everything from water reclamation and distribution systems to heat storage and power generation.

In the ribozone, Rexx is represented as a collection of vines and flowers growing on a wicker-frame figure. One nice aspect of the ribozone is that he doesn't have to worry about coming into direct physical contact with the severed limb. It's several thousand kilometers away on Mymercia. But to prevent anything unpleasant from contaminating him via the softwire ribozone link—a mutant strand of biodigital code, for example, that the molectronic circuits in his body could convert into live proteins—he's set up a firewall and saturated himself with antiphers.

Rexx starts the autopsy with a close visual examination of the limb. In addition to being torn off at the elbow, the tissue shows damage from prolonged exposure to a vacuum and absolute zero. The ribozone image isn't much prettier—a twisted branch of dead graying wood with a few shriveled flowers clinging to the bark with the tenacity of a tick.

"Ready to slice and dice?" he asks Claire.

A pause. "Yes."

Nausea wells up from a pinprick in the base of his skull. As the queasiness spreads, his hand twitches, a prosthesis connected to some vast disquiet, intimate and yet distant. Invasive. Abruptly the nausea subsides, the tremor ends, and with it the feeling of dislocation.

Rexx works the tension from his fingers. "Let's get started, then."

The CNT biosensor consists of a monomol cutting wire and a sensor pad attached to the end of what is essentially a remote-operated cattle prod. The prod is controlled with a virtual glove that responds to finger kinesthetics and directs the movement of the prod a nanometer at a time in any direction. The monomol wire, strung between the horseshoe arms of a U, performs the same function as a cheese cutter. It carves off carpaccio-thin slices of skin and bone for analysis. The sensor pad is little more than a glorified brush. It bristles with billions of hairlike carbon nanotubes that have been functionalized at the tip with probe molecules. By running the pad over a slice of tissue, Rexx can determine its exact structure and composition. If anything out of the ordinary is present—a corrupted molecule, mutated nucleotide sequence, or foreign protein—it should show up.

Rexx moves the sensor tip into place over the sample, and slowly brushes it over the surface. Immediately, molecular code populates the architext window and a butterfly lands on a knuckle on the hand, updating the ribozone construct with data gathered by the probe.

The work is tedious. He doesn't have time to cross-section the entire arm, start at one end and work his way down. At a few molecules per slice, that would take centuries. Instead he relies on Claire for input on where to gather random samples.

He's not sure what he's looking for. Mymercia isn't like any of the other Kuiper belt arcologies. It's been modeled after a nineteenth-century tropical island. The interior design temperature is a balmy fifteen degrees centigrade. Ten degrees warmer than Tiresias and Petraea. In keeping with the jungle theme, the plants are based on species that were once indigenous to old-growth equatorial forests. Parasol palms. Bananopy leaves. Hanging tapestree vines that decorate the arcology's warren of arboretums. Eighty percent of the biome is located on the face of the kilometer-deep chasm. The asteroid has been rotated so the canyon wall faces the sun at all times. A large solcatcher array gathers additional light and power.

What makes the warm, wet biome possible is the large quantity of ice on the asteroid. Not just on the surface but below, locked up in hydrous minerals. The geology of Mymercia is atypical. Mixed in with the usual nickel and iron are basalt and granite as well as carbonate deposits. This composition is similar to Tiresias and, along with the six-billion-year age, hints at an extrasolar origin. It's believed that the two Kuiper belt objects may have formed a single chunk at one time. Seismic analysis indicates the presence of numerous gas-filled pockets in the rock core of the asteroid, some fairly large, filled with hydrogen, oxygen, and possibly methane.

Less than an hour in, his hands start to cramp, and he has to take a break. Give his fingers a rest.

"I feel like I'm pissin' down a gopher hole," he says. So far there are no anomalous readings. "What's the status of the latest datasquirt from Mymercia?"

"Still pending."

He's waiting for the arcology's construction manager to transmit sensor readouts from just prior to the accident. This includes not only biological readings but physical measurements of material properties such as thermal load, expansion, contraction, shear, and torsional stress.

"What seems to be the problem?" he says.

"I have no idea."

Rexx curls and uncurls his fingers, cracks his knuckles, then gets back to work.

Five minutes later, as he slices off a wafer of bone, a flower petal flares to life on the dead limb in the ribozone, then evaporates.

He shifts his attention to a jumbled line of text associated with the burst. "What the heck was that?"

"Unknown," Claire says. "The atomic structure is not on file."

Rexx frowns, his loose jowls sagging precariously.

"You're telling me the molecule, nucleotide sequence, or whatever, isn't cataloged in *any* library?"

"Correct."

So the gobbledygook isn't from another ecotecture. It hasn't been accidentally copied or inserted during construction. Seed plants cultivated in greenhouse vats on established arcologies are often used to kick-start the growth of a warm-blooded biosystem. Occasionally, these seedlings are defective, or suffer damage before being transplanted. But in this particular instance, that doesn't appear to be the case.

"A random mutation, then," he ventures. "Or sabotage." There aren't many other possibilities.

"There's nothing to suggest sabotage."

Rexx repositions the biosensor pad, ratchets up the bitcam magnification until the atoms on the surface of the tissue sample are a collection of acnelike bumps, and goes in for a closer look. In the location where the flower bloomed, there's nothing but a crater. A quantum hole.

He noses around for a few minutes, sniffing each of the nearby atoms with the tip of the probe. "Where'd it go?"

"I'm not sure. I'm not registering anything."

Rexx massages the wrinkles of skin on his forehead. "It can't have just up and disappeared."

He spends the next two hours dissecting the arm, shaving off nanometer segments, before pausing to take stock. "Any bright ideas?"

"No."

He returns to the line of gibberish in the architext. "Is there any way to model the damn thing with the information we have—figure out what the hell it is, and what it does, that way?"

"Not without nucleotide/instruction sequences."

"So what I'm hearin' is that we need a physical sample. Or we can't do squat. Is that about the size of it?"

"Yes."

"What about . . . what's her name—?" Rexx knocks his forehead with the heel of his hand. "The survivor."

"Fola Hanani."

"Right." He repeats the name to himself. He's seen her face three or four times on the biomed scans, but can't raise a clear image of her. It's as if he's already buried her. Given her up for dead. "How's she doin'?"

"I don't have her updated/current condition. Her latest biomed readout hasn't arrived."

"It's overdue? By how long?"

"Two hours and six minutes."

"No sensor readings yet either, I s'pose. What the hell's going on over there?"

Rexx doesn't wait for an answer. He signs out of the ribozone and drops offline.

Finds himself floating under the lightdome of his hexcell. It's night. His side of the Tiresias arcology has rotated away from the sun. Stars, as hard and bright as rhinestones, gleam on the ivory white ribs of the geodesic dome and the blue anodized grid of thermal mesh that insulates the faux marble walls of the room. The veil-thin curtains ripple with an unspoiled image of west Texas scrub, circling buzzards, and a sky smeared with mucus yellow clouds.

Rexx gazes at the desertscape for a spell, then reorients himself relative to the room's magnetic flux lines. The sheet-diamond floor, inlaid with tiles of pressed lichen, flips to become the ceiling. The lightdome becomes a pond of black water littered with sequins.

"Arrange for a shuttle pod," he says.

"Where are you going?"

"Where do you think?" He lassos a flux line and rides the current to the door.

"You can't. You don't know what you're getting into." The IA sounds alarmed at the prospect.

"You're probably right," Rexx admits. "But I've chewed about as much cud here as I can."

# 9

## BRUJA-HA

By the time the gangstas finish hauling L. Mariachi to their temporary barracks, his head is throbbing to a killer downbeat and he has to pee. The real pisser is that his bladder is about to explode and he's no longer drunk. Fucking EZ beer isn't worth shit. In the interest of worker health and productivity, it's been brewed to wear off quickly.

The *tambo* is a cluster of recycled trailers that have been hauled out of storage in the past twenty-four hours to house the incoming *braceros*. Fabricated out of stucco-textured structural foam sprayed over a wire frame, the trailers are stacked like cargo containers in precise anal-retentive rows. The dirt around them is bare. The politicorp didn't bother to spray the ground with grass to hold down the grit. A ragtag collection of umbrella palms and circuitrees furnish some UV protection and power. Not much, considering the number of migrant workers that have been sardined into the units. A bad sign. The *patrón* is a tightwad.

There are more *malavisos*, bad omens. For one, the place is dead quiet; no traditional *banda* or up-tempo *norteño* beat blasting from any of the trailers. No thrashup synthonica to keep the blood flowing. He can't stop thinking about the absence. It's as if the lack of music is a wound that needs to be licked, no different from a dog cleaning a raw sore. Not because it feels good but because it hurts more not to. The lack hints at some deeper, unseen illness. Maybe that's what's wrong with the sick woman—what the witch is trying to cure.

These *braceros* are more like *pollos*, he thinks. The frightened chickens who used to migrate between clades illegally, covertly, by dosing themselves with black-market antiphers. This was long before the *bracero* work exchange program was formally institutionalized and placed under the administrative control of the Bureau of Ecotectural Assimilation and Naturalization. Now the migrants are officially BEANers. A term that is no longer derogatory, according to the politicorps, because it applies equally to everyone who signs up for the employment program, regardless of race, religion, or economic and cultural background.

"*Pinche güey*," L. Mariachi mutters under his breath. Goddamn.

"What?" Balta, the oldest gangsta asks, steering him toward a trailer at the end of one row. The unit looks like a last-minute addition. It's whiter than those around it, as bright and shiny as a filling in a mouthful of rotting teeth.

"I have to take a leak," L. Mariachi says.

"Me, too," the younger gangsta, Oscar, says. Grinning. As if this creates some special bond between them that transcends their background and any other differences they might have.

"This is it," Balta announces, pressing a thumb to an iDNA sensor on the door to let them in.

L. Mariachi isn't sure if the kid's referring to the trailer or what's about to happen. When the door opens he's assaulted with the aroma of incense, rose-scented candles, tortillas, and hydroponic chili peppers.

Inside the trailer is a big rectangle divided into smaller rectangular rooms by thin lichenboard panels clipped to modular fasteners. The fasteners make it possible to change the floor plan, or redecorate, but the holes they leave in the exterior walls look like shit. For the most part, these have been papered over with old *videocentro* movie posters, hologram printouts of pop singers downloaded from online netzines, and black silkscreen images of Jesus, the Virgin Mary, and innumerable saints. The furniture is standard *bracero* mix-and-match, a menagerie of secondhand gel cushions and pillows on folding plastic frames. Interior light is provided by peeling biolum strips stuck to the walls and the ceiling. The windows, paned with photovoltaic cellulose, are black as the night and reflect the sad-ass squalor of the place, including himself.

A few steps into the room, Oscar locks the door behind him. Dead bolts click into place.

He's greeted by a man in his late forties—João, the uncle-in-law of Lejandra, the sick woman. He sports a big mustache, has watermelon seeds for eyes, and is wearing a loose sprayon tank top over the tattunes on his pectorals and biceps. One is a topless woman whose breasts rattle *ka-chooka chooka* when she shakes them. Another depicts a heart that drips blood. The blood trickles down his side before getting reabsorbed into his

skin. He's got scars, too. Thick keloid welts that look
like permanent leeches. He's been roughed up, and not
by another *bracero*. The welts are the scarlet letter of a
BEAN interrogation.

Great. Not only has he been hulled by the gangstas,
he's going to turn up on a BEAN list of suspicious persons. Assuming he doesn't get hulled permanently at the
end of the evening.

"Thanks for coming." João offers a gruff, callused
hand, each finger tattuned so it resembles a snake. "I'm
glad you could make it."

"Sure. No problem." L. Mariachi does his best to ignore the writhing Medusa hiss of serpents and return
the squeeze. Then he quickly excuses himself and heads
into the bathroom.

The closet-size stall is windowless. There's no way
out. Not even a fan vent he can use to call for help.

"You were lucky," Num Nut tells him as he's relieving himself. "It's a good thing they showed up when
they did."

"Yeah, right. No telling what horrible shit would
have happened if they'd left me alone."

"For one, you could be hungover. Wallowing in
self-pity."

L. Mariachi offlines the IA. He doesn't want to listen
to it berate him, especially if he actually has to try to
play. He tucks himself in, then shambles back out to the
front room.

João's wife, the sick woman's aunt, is waiting there
for him. She doesn't look happy to see him, introduces
herself as Isabelle. She's in her midforties; has raven
black hair tied back in a ropy braid, is rocking fresh
sprayon jeans, a pretty but modest floral-print blo

and cheap company-store wraparounds made out of pink-tinted cellophane.

"I hope you know what you're doing." She stands with her arms folded across her chest.

L. Mariachi glances around, notices the faint, chalky outline of an equilateral triangle scratched on the floor. At each corner he can just make out the shiny residue of low-grade glycerin wax. His gaze travels to the windows and hallway. Sure enough, the windowsills and doorframe have each been marked with an equi-armed cross.

"The *bruja* was here already?" he says, trying not to sound too optimistic. Maybe he's off the hook—won't have to play for the witch after all.

"That's from last night," Oscar says. "The spell didn't work."

His sense of reprieve falters. So she's coming back again tonight—moving on to the next stage of treatment.

"She's on her way now," Isabelle tells them. "I just got a message from her. She'll be here soon."

"You want to meet Lejandra?" João says.

"We already told her you were coming to play," Oscar says, working hard to play up L. Mariachi's celebrity status as a musician, stroke his ego. "The *bruja* asked for you specifically."

"She did?" A washed-up *rockero* like him?

"Come on." Balta tugs at L. Mariachi's sleeve.

"Maybe we should wait for *la bruja*," L. Mariachi says, hedging. There's still a chance she won't show.

"We need to wake Lejandra up anyway," Isabelle says. "For the *limpia*. It would make it easier if you're there."

No way he's getting out of this even if the *bruja* doesn't show. They aren't taking no for an answer. So he lets himself be led down the hallway to a bedroom in back. The room's only window is curtained with threadbare sprayon gauze that hides the yellowed photovoltaics. Under it, the family has set up an altar table. A vase on the table sprouts a bouquet of yellow marigoldlike flowers he can't identify. Some knockoff hybrid. There's a cross made out of two green chili peppers tied together by a red ribbon, even a festive sugar skull. The biolum panels on the walls have been muted. The only light in the room is given off by a votive candle made out of myrrh-scented glycerin, the chipped plastic holder etched with a colorful image of the Virgin Mary cradling the Baby Jesus.

L. Mariachi turns to the bed where Lejandra is asleep, resting uncomfortably under sweat-stained sheets. The woman, thirty-something, has a haunted look. Troubled. Her face is gaunt, her skin jaundiced but glossy. Just under the translucent flesh the bruised outline of her skeleton is visible, as if her bones have been scorched black. In contrast to her sunken cheeks and pursed lips, her tightly closed eyes are huge, bulging with fever or some other internal pressure. The pulse in her neck is rapid, as if fueled by a high-octane nightmare.

A flesh-and-bone Day of the Dead skeleton puppet, he thinks. That is what she looks like. Under the illness, something else about her is familiar. The association vague, unpleasant.

"Did the *bruja* say what's wrong with her?" L. Mariachi asks.

"She did a reading," João says. "The cards indicated she was suffering from ghost fright."

Ah. The tarot deck.

"Lejandra was shivering real bad," Balta explains. "She couldn't get warm no matter what."

That explains the triangle on the floor, the crosses ove

the windows and doorway. According to the old tales, people who have been badly frightened by an encounter with a spirit are susceptible to evil air—sometimes known as *aire de noche,* night air—which gives them chills. Usually the ghosts that cause evil air sickness are of people who have died violently.

"Did she sprinkle holy water?" L. Mariachi asks.

Isabelle nods. "Wherever she found a cold spot."

"But the exorcism didn't work."

João shakes his head, the corners of his eyes drooping almost as much as the ends of his mustache. "That's why we've decided to do a cleansing."

"What about a doctor?" L. Mariachi says. "Did you take her to the clinic for an examination?"

"Two days ago. All of the tests came up negative. They said there was nothing the matter with her."

Which is why they contacted the *bruja.*

"The politicorp doesn't want us to know what's wrong!" Balta blurts out. "The fucking *patrón* is trying to hide it from us."

"Why would he do that?" L. Mariachi says. It doesn't make sense. If there's a virus or some other kind of transmittable disease going around, it's in the best interest of the politicorp to keep it from spreading.

"We think they accidentally exposed us to something, and now they're trying to cover it up," Isabelle says.

She goes to the side of the bed and rouses Lejandra by brushing aside a tangled strand of matted hair and kissing her on the forehead. Then she blinks, straightens her head, and stares at the eyescreens on her shades. "She's here."

João and the two brothers hurry to the front room. Isabelle stays with Lejandra, one hand caressing the side of her face. L. Mariachi drifts uncertainly into the hallway, following the others. He hears a knock on the door, then two more, before the boys let her in.

"Doña Celia," João says, all respectful. "Welcome back."

The *bruja* is old and stooped, a thick stump of a woman in her white cottonlike dress, freshly sprayed. Her hair is a smoky white bun, coiled on her head. She's dosed herself with cleansing/deodorizing bacteria that reek of copal-scented cologne or soap. She's carrying a black mesh duffel bag in one gnarled hand and a battered instrument case in the other.

"You've been burning the candle." Her voice is a scratchy rasp, as soft as frayed canvas around the edges.

João bows his head in polite submission. "Just like you said."

"Good."

She glances from João and the two brothers to L. Mariachi. Skewers him with a bird-quick eye. "You're the musician."

"Yes." The word curdles on his tongue like a lie.

Her gaze settles on his left hand. "Your heart is crippled, too," she says. "Heal one, and you will heal the other. If you don't, the disease will spread and you will die."

Before he can respond she brushes past him, down the hallway. The four of them trail after her, pulled along like dead leaves in the wake of her movement.

When L. Mariachi gets to the room, she opens the instrument case, takes out a battered acoustic guitar and hands it to him. "It's made from the wood of the Angel Tree," she says.

Whatever the hell that is. He's never heard of it. Rather than reveal the depth of his ignorance, he nods once. "What do you want me to play?"

"Music that's close to your heart, that makes the soul burn."

"SoulR Byrne," he thinks, knee-jerk. It takes him a second to realize that what she actually means are the traditional and largely forgotten *pirekuas*.

"When do you want me to start playing?" he says.

"You'll know." She turns away from him and busies herself with Lejandra and the duffel bag.

L. Mariachi watches her pull out the contents—a green plastic egg, a clear plastic glass, which she has one of the boys fill with water, a spray of dried herbs, a crumpled pack of Siete Machos cigarettes, and a fire-blackened palm-size ring of stone. The stone is embedded with fossils. Odd-shaped bones from some mythical beast that send a chill down his spine. Lastly, a miniature parrot emerges from a side pocket on the duffel. Based on images he's seen online, the bird is maybe a quarter the size of a regular parrot. It's a child's toy. The bird moves with cheap nanimatronic clumsiness. Its purpose in the ceremony is unclear. Perched on the *bruja*'s shoulder it seems more of an annoyance than anything else, nibbling at her ear and clawing her hair into tangles.

While the *bruja* sets up, L. Mariachi focuses on the guitar. Amazingly, it's in tune, and the action of the strings is good. The sound isn't bad, either. Mellower than he would prefer but seductively resonant. The tone doesn't seem to have been adversely affected by the fragments of polished rock and worn bone inlaid in the soundboard. Fossils, similar to the *bruja*'s charred rock, arranged in a cryptic design.

He's more concerned with the frets. The action is higher than he's used to. He's not sure he can get the fingers of his left hand to cooperate. He attempts a song, letting the fingers of his right hand whisper over the strings. His left hand staggers through the chords, stumbling from one note to the next.

It sounds like shit. Worse than shit.

Not that anyone is going to be listening. He guesses that his role in the ceremony is mostly *ambiente,* atmosphere. He's here to add to the overall effect, to make the woman feel good. Palliative, like a circus clown. Still, he doesn't want to screw up. He onlines Num Nut.

"I need some painkiller," he tells the IA. "For my hand."

He hates to dip into his current allotment. There's no telling when he'll need it later on, after he starts working in the vats.

"How much?" the IA says.

"Two hundred milligrams." He can always take the second half of the dose if the first doesn't do the job.

"You should take it easy," Num Nut counsels.

"Just download it."

He waits for the drug dispenser jacked into his spine to start pumping out the analgesic, then concentrates on getting his left hand to obey. It's stubborn, as stiff as an old hinge. The area of his brain responsible for the control of his creaky fingers squeals in protest. Rust flakes off his joints and sweat beads on his forehead.

He tries a second tune, then another. It's no use. His fine motor control is shot and his hand refuses to cooperate.

*Me cagué!* He curses under his breath. It's been too long since he played. He's out of practice, even without the burden of his hand.

He's fucked. He looks up from the instrument to tell them he can't go on, that he's too handicapped, but it's too late. The ceremony has started.

Doña Celia smoothes the sheets over the woman's bony shoulders, rib cage, and sunken chest. She grips the egg in one hand and runs it up and down the woman, passing it over her to draw out some of the sickness. The woman quivers at the touch. Muscles spasm in her arms and legs. Tendons stand out on her neck.

A soft keening starts up. It begins as a feeble wail that gradually swells in volume to fill the room. L. Mariachi looks at Lejandra, then realizes the sound is coming from the guitar.

He looks down. His fingers are possessed, moving on their own to coax forth notes and rhythms. Some of what he's playing is shit he thought he'd forgotten. Somehow his fingers remember. His muscle memory is intact. The trick is to not think about it, to just go with the flow.

A harsh squawk distracts him. He looks up. The parrot prances less than a meter in front of him, wings outstretched for balance.

"A penny for your thoughts," it croons, head tilted to one side.

"Bite me," he says.

The parrot is quick to accept his invitation. It half hops, half flies straight at him. He ducks to the side, but the bird lands on his right shoulder.

"Hold still," the bird says. "This won't hurt a bit." It hobbles from his shoulder to the back of his shirt collar and begins to pluck at the hair on his neck.

The *bruja* stops rubbing the egg over the woman. She unscrews the egg over the water glass. Thick milky fluid pours from the shell halves, swirls and coagulates as tiny bubbles form on the surface of the water.

"Evil air sickness," the witch states, studying the pattern in the glass. "Brought on by soul loss." She stirs the mixture with one finger. "Another soul, one that has gone crazy, is trying to take over her body and change it."

"Into what?" someone whispers.

The *bruja* removes her finger. "A servant of Bloody Mary."

# 10

## BLOODY MARY

Xophia ghosts the blank wallscreen. To Fola it feels as if the interior of the shuttle, with the sick gerontocrat, is an extension of her hospicell.

"How bad is the"—Fola hesitates to use the word "epidemic"—"outbreak?" she says.

Pheidoh appears on the screen. The IA has added a pair of wire-frame glasses to complement its basset hound eyes and hangdog cheeks. Fola's not sure where the IA comes up with the image for its default persona, or what that says about the software. Defunct netzines maybe, mothballed on a chip somewhere in the datasphere. Its identity seems to be assembled from a variety of obscure historical sources, none of which she has the background or knowledge to recognize. She assumes the way that it's chosen to represent itself is highly personal and symbolic. Emblematic of core values and root psychological tendencies. Like most IAs it seems determined to collect as many insignificant factoids as it can. Useless trivia the world tossed out years ago. Perhaps the IA, lacking any cultural identity and history of its own, is looking for one it can adopt. A raison d'être no different than hers. So far it hasn't offered to enlighten her, and out of respect for its privacy she hasn't asked.

"According to the most recent epidemiological forecast," the IA says, "the disease is in the early stages of development."

"So it's just beginning to spread. Things are going to get worse. More people are going to get sick."

"If the projections are accurate."

There's no reason to think they won't be. Even if the computer models err on the high side, the damage has been done. Xophia is already infected.

"Could a viral ad mutate on its own?" she says. "I thought there were supposed to be built-in safeties to keep that from happening."

The datahound frowns behind the wire-rim glasses. "There's no evidence that a mass media-based virus is responsible."

"Then how do you explain the images that are showing up on people? What else could be infecting them?"

Fola bites her lip against the ingrained urge to do something—anything. As a Jesuette, she never felt helpless. Never doubted her ability to contribute to the greater good. It was a given. People needed her. She was essential to the spiritual and physical well-being of the world. She saw it every time she donned her Popeware and shook her pherion-doped pompoms to spread goodwill. People smiled, kids laughed, and babies gurgled in delight. She could see the positive effect she was having on people's lives.

Part of the desire to contribute is hardwired into her.

That was one of the reasons she decided to help the ICLU. It was more than repayment for the help they'd given her. She feels some of that same gratification with the warm-blooded plants and her tuplet. Help out the community and, in the long run, she'll be helping herself.

Right now she feels useless. She should be helping Ephraim prepare for the refugees. They've already found space for them to hide in a number of seldom used storage/supply rooms. But the cubicles need to be outfitted with sleepsacs, fresh water, and food, as well as toiletries, extra clothes, and basic medical supplies.

"You're worried about Xophia," Pheidoh says.

Fola nods. "Have you been able to get in touch with Ephraim?" She needs to talk to him. Warn him about what's happening on the shuttle.

"Not yet," Pheidoh says. "According to his IA, he's not online."

"Any reason?"

"No."

Fola raises an arm to her forehead, doesn't bother to correct for the slight change in center of gravity and magnetic equipoise that tilts her into a slow roll. Her eyes ache—a vague, remembered throb. . . .

Sitting at the kitchen table, a cold squeeze pouch of lemonade held in both hands. A bent straw poked out the hole in the top. It was midafternoon, the day already sweltering. She had rushed home from school after a fight with Tatjana Soffel, hot tears and shame burning her face.

"There, there," her mother cooed. "Don't worry. Everything will be fine. You'll see. She's just jealous because you're so pretty. That's all."

She pressed the damp, cool foil to closed eyes and listened to her mother water the violinette flowers she kept in clay pots on the outside balcony. The ap was quiet, peaceful. Her father was at his rug shop. From where Fola sat at the pressed lichenboard table, she could hear the industrious murmur of scrubbugs cleaning the ap. She liked it when the tiny 'sects showed up, twice a week, to eat the dust that had gathered. Raul, one of the boys in her class, claimed the dust was really dead human skin and that one of these days when there was no more dust in the ap, the scrubbugs would eat her. Fola didn't believe it. If the 'sects were dangerous, her mother would never allow them in the house. Besides, the sound they made was a harmless, contented humming. Like when a person prayed.

Of course, everything hadn't been fine.

"Would you like to listen to some music?" Pheidoh asks. Anxious to help, the IA always goes out of its way to fix what's wrong. To a fault. It doesn't know when to quit. Tries too hard to please her.

She sniffs, blinks, and stares out at the atrium. Despite the soothing contours of the bananopy leaves and tapestree patterns, her eyes continue to throb. Before she can say no to the music, it trickles into her cochlear imps.

"That's the same song you played before." She reaches out and grabs a handhold on the honeycomb grid and comes to a stop.

"No. It's the same musician. L. Mariachi. What you're listening to now is being played for a traditional healing ceremony called a *limpia*. I thought it might help you feel better."

The weird thing is, it does. The notes, pure as water, wash over her and dilute the pain behind her retinas. Her bad attitude clears, salved by the haunting tune.

The playing is a bit ragged in places, strained. But she feels cleansed, inside and out.

It spooks her how the information agent is usually right about what she needs. It shouldn't. The datahound has access to all of her biomed readouts, the balance of neurotransmitters in her brain that regulate her emotions, and the synapse-firing patterns for every thought she's had in the last three years. Given that, it makes sense that the IA knows her better than she knows herself. Still, it can be a bit unnerving.

"Who's the ceremony for?" she asks.

"A sick woman. Lejandra Cantú. She's a migrant pharm worker at a Noogenics biovat facility."

The ceremony could be for almost anything. The migrants she provided relief aid to as a Jesuette were the victims of everything from malnutrition to toxic waste poisoning and depression. Depending on the culture, a healer or shaman could be brought in to cure any of these ailments.

"What's wrong with her?"

The IA massages the loose skin of one cheek. "Soul loss."

Fola can't tell if the IA is serious, if it actually thinks the ailment is a valid medical condition. For a lot of people, it seems to be. Fola ran into soul loss all the time at refugee camps and clinics. A lot of people in the world still believe that physical diseases are caused by spiritual distress and that in order to heal the body they have to cure the spiritual problem first.

"What caused the soul loss?" she asks.

"Quanticles."

Fola's brow crimps. "Quantum particles?"

"Or dots," the IA says. "Artificial atoms."

Fola shakes her head. This is the first she's heard of

anybody being contaminated with programmable matter. Based on what she knows, it doesn't seem possible. Artificial atoms are made out of electrons and can be programmed to mimic the properties of regular atoms. But they aren't really like regular atoms. They aren't free-floating. They have to be on a chip with a special substrate and insulating layers. "Who infected her?"

"Bloody Mary."

A phantom chill undercuts the music. Fola chafes both arms. "That's crazy," she says.

Pheidoh nods.

La Llorona, the Crying Woman. The insane mother of Jesus, who weeps blood and enslaves children, turning them into gang bangers, addicts, and evil spirits in the war against the angels.

One of the problems with having an IA that's a terraphile is that Fola doesn't know the context of the data it mines. Worse, she doesn't know how the IA interprets the information it unearths. She trusts it to know the difference between true and false, but the line between right and wrong isn't always as clear. There are gray areas, indeterminacies, and she wonders if that's where she is right now, in some blurred nether region between myth and reality. Fola has no clue what the IA hopes to find in the bottomless morass of data that it continuously, almost compulsively, sifts. Or what it intends to do with the information.

Fola's head aches. She touches her temple, where a vein pulses against the tip of one finger. "Bloody Mary isn't real."

"She is to those who believe in her. Sometimes that's all that matters."

Is the IA talking about itself or someone else? A living, breathing person? Or another IA? She starts to shake her head . . . stops when the nausea kicks in. "Why are you telling me this?"

"I need your help."

"With what?"

The datahound cocks its head, as if listening. Dr. Villaz takes this opportunity to interrupt. "You have a visitor," he says over her cochlear implants.

Before she can ask who it is, the image of a man, a complete stranger, replaces the image of Pheidoh on the wallscreen. He's stuffed into a biosuit that's cinched as tight as a corset. It doesn't help that the picture is distorted, sphere-ized, as if she's looking at his reflection in a glass ball.

The man smiles, his lips stretching in a huge, bloated grin. "Fola, I presume." He drags out her name, pronouncing it like the first part of "follicle."

She ratchets down her gaze. "Who are you?"

"Name's Rexx." The slack grin widens. "I'm a gengineer from Tiresias. How're you doin'?"

"Okay," she says. "I guess."

"You guess." He pounces cat quick on the qualifier, like it's a half-wound ball of yarn. "What seems to be the problem?"

"Nothing," she says, "I'm fine," trying to erase all lack of conviction. It's tough. The last thing she's feeling right now is confident. "Exactly what kind of gengineer are you and what are you doing here?"

"I'm an ecotectural gengineer. I design warm-blooded plants for the Kuiper belt colonies."

It clicks, why he's talking to her. "You're investigating the accident."

His nod is molasses slow. "If you don't mind, I'd like to ask you some questions about what happened."

"Where are you?" Judging by the fish-eye perspective

and the claustrophobic arrangement of biolum panels and datawindows, he's wedged in the nacelle of a shuttle pod.

"On my way to Mymercia. I should be there in a couple hours. In the meantime, I thought I'd take the opportunity to chat with you."

"I don't know." A dubious twinge pinches her stomach.

"I know it ain't easy." He leans forward, earnest. "But anything at all you can tell me would be helpful."

Something uncomfortable plucks at the seams of her thoughts. "I really don't remember very much. It happened kind of fast."

"What did it feel like?" he asks.

"Like"—she barricades both arms across her chest— "like this thing had crawled inside me and was looking for something."

The flaccid skin around his eyes tightens. "What sort of thing?"

Her shoulders hike up, more a squirm than a shrug. "A snake."

He frowns. She's not sure if it's because he thinks she's off her rocker or if he's taking her seriously.

"A poisonous one," she adds.

"What was it looking for? Do you know?"

She squeezes herself tighter. "*Me*. What I am. *Who* I am." She can still feel the tongue probing, tickling, hunting for her soul.

Rexx pauses for a moment to suck at his teeth. "Did it hurt?"

She bites her bottom lip. Describes the dull tingle in her arm. The gray, creeping cold and subsequent numbness.

He listens attentively. Then, "Any idea why it stopped?"

"Stopped?"

"Yeah. Why it quit when it did."

"I don't know."

"It must have given up for a reason. Right?"

Right. Otherwise she'd be dead. "Maybe"—she wets her lips—"maybe it found what it was looking for before it finished with me."

"You mean the construction workers who died? Liam Vitt, Ingrid Sorensen, and Tamika Wong?"

Fola swallows, nods, her breath tight against her ribs.

Rexx scratches his brow, pushing the wrinkles around with one clamshell-thick nail. "No offense, but I don't buy it. There has to be another reason than it just gave up."

"Like what?"

"That's what I was hoping you could tell me."

"You think it was some kind of mutation?" Fola prompts. "Or a corrupt piece of code?"

"Your guess is as good as mine. For all I know, a politicorp or some other org on earth could be responsible. About the only thing I am sure about so far is that I feel like spit on a hot skillet." He rubs his chin with one perturbed hand, pinching the loose flesh into a butt crack. "Did you see anything else? Anything at all that struck you as strange or out of the ordinary?"

She pauses for a moment, and then shakes her head. "Nothing that I can think of."

Rexx seems to accept this. Or, if not, he at least doesn't continue to pressure her. "Well, if somethin' comes to mind, let me know."

She nods. "All right."

"Thanks." He tips his head to the side, the way he might a hat. "Take care, now."

\* \* \*

The conversation leaves Fola rattled. She gets the feeling he left dissatisfied, convinced she was lying.

As soon as he's gone, Pheidoh reappears. "Were you listening?" she asks.

"Yes."

"And?"

A furrow creases the datahound's forehead. "He's asked that your recent biomed scans be cross-referenced against a library of all known artificial atoms."

It takes a second for this to sink in.

"He performed a postmortem on remains found at the site of the accident," the IA says. "The autopsy results indicated the possible antemortem presence of programmable matter in the deceased."

The same thing that the sick migrant is infected with. So Pheidoh hasn't totally lost it. Not if a gengineer is investigating the possibility that quantum particles were responsible for the accident and is worried she might still be infected. "Does he know about the outbreak?"

"He knows what's happening on earth. But not with Lejandra."

A public newsfeed streams across the wallscreen next to the IA. The datasquirt is jerky, a maniacally edited collage of grainy bitcam images spliced with professional high-rez digital video. The scene is a refugee overflow camp on the outskirts of some large metro area. Bombay, maybe, by the look of the cityscape. Squalid curtain-glass interspersed with a lot of habitrail biomes on stilts, the carbyne-frame structures tented with heat-reflective thermal mesh. Through the translucent membranes, she can make out the black-anodized supports—struts and joists arranged in stable isometrics.

In contrast, the refugee camp looks like a deck of playing cards, stacked and propped in fragile, impossibly configured angles. Dead piezo panels, warped lichen-board, and mucus-hardened foam glued together to form shacks, apartments, and mounded minicombs.

She's been here before. Not this camp exactly, but camps like it. She can almost smell the urine in the dust, the stink of hydrogen from leaky fuel cells, and the collective stench of rotten teeth and suppurating wounds over the floral-scented scrubbugs that the politicorp pumps into the air through the potted umbrella palms.

Sick people lie on makeshift bubble-wrap pads that have been set up on one street. Those who aren't sick peer out of doorways or windows, holed up in their hovels against the epidemic. A close-up of one victim ze-roes in on an emaciated face. The cheeks, forehead, and balding scalp are covered with a pox of blue dots. The eye sockets are red circles ringed in yellow. The next person is covered with tumors, vestigial growths that appear to be the same lips she saw on the patient Xophia was caring for.

She looks for relief workers, a contingent of Jesu-ettes, but doesn't see any. They should be arriving soon. Despite the nausea lurking in the back of her throat, part of her wants to be there with them.

*Five, six, seven, eight,*
*Meet you at the Pearly Gate.*

Fola shifts her gaze from the newsfeed to Pheidoh. "What's so important about Lejandra?" The IA is focused on her for a reason. Why, when there are so many others who are just as bad off or worse?

The datahound removes its glasses, takes a moment to massage its eyes, and then replaces the wire frames.

"She is patient zero. The first person to be exposed on earth."

"Are you sure?"

"Her symptoms are the first on record."

Fola gnaws her lip. "So if we find out what made her sick, how she was exposed, it could help isolate the problem. Explain what happened here . . . what's happening to Xophia."

"Yes."

Fola takes a deep breath, steeling herself. "Am I infected?"

"You were exposed."

"Then how come I'm not dead?" Like Liam and Ingrid. She shouldn't be here—shouldn't be . . .

"The quanticles didn't replicate," Pheidoh says.

"Why not?"

The IA shrugs. Uncertain, evasive, dismissive? Fola can't tell. The IA seems to know more than it's willing to share. She lets out the breath. "You said I could help. How?" Maybe there's something inside her, different about her, that can help others. That can protect Xophia."

"Are you sure?" Pheidoh says. "There are no guarantees. You might not be able to do anything. No one might."

# 11

## TIC TALK

Y ou're pressurized/cleared to depod," Ida Claire says.

Rexx eases out of his g-mesh, doses himself with the temporary reclade pherion for Mymercia, and depods into a geodomed air lock overgrown with bananopy leaves. He's met by a burly man with a stiletto goatee and intense eyes the color of dirty ice. Najib Kerusa. The Mymercia project manager's nose wrinkles as he sizes up Rexx, taking in the voluminous folds of skin pooched around his neck and bunched on his fingers.

"I can't say as I'm glad to see you." The project manager extends a gruff hand. "If it was up to me, you wouldn't be here."

"That makes two of us."

Kerusa looks past him to the shuttle pod. "You bring any luggage? Equipment we need to unload?"

"Naw. I'm packin' everything I need." Rexx pats the

detachable, snap-button pockets on the bottoms of his Texas-style blue denim kurta.

"No sense dickin' around, then." Kerusa shifts his orientation relative to the air lock's magnetic flux lines and glides toward the access tube. In the unfamiliar ecotecture, Rexx is slow to follow. It takes him a moment to adjust and catch up. The magtube is rigid, a smooth-walled cylinder with alternating bands of light and dark—yellow biolum panels separated by black diamond windows. Insulating, sound-absorbent moss grows in the expansion joints between the biolums. Through the windows, the station looks like a prairie thistle. The surface is pocked with concave lightdomes and bristling with hexcell towers. From this vantage point, Rexx can't see Mymercia. The asteroid is hidden from view behind the station.

"You ask me," Kerusa is saying, "your visit is a complete waste of time. You're putting yourself at risk for no reason."

They enter the central sphere of the station, passing through a circular colonnade of fluted saguaro cacti, freckled with tiny yellow flowers, that store water and thermal energy.

"I don't see why we couldn't collect whatever sample you need and send it to you," Kerusa goes on. "No reason for you to get it yourself."

Rexx opens his mouth. Closes it. Simply by coming here, he's stepping on the project manager's toes and undermining his authority. Under those circumstances, how much cooperation can he expect?

"So"—Kerusa slows to a stop in the tube, then rotates to face him, blocking the magtube—"what I'd like to know is what you're not telling us."

"Come again?"

Kerusa thrusts out his jaw. "There something you don't want us manual labor types to know? Something you're hiding from us?"

Rexx shakes his head. Feels the wattle of flesh under his chin sway from side to side. "Whoa, partner. You're way off base."

"Cut the bullshit." Kerusa flexes his meaty hands. "What the hell are you doing here? The real reason."

"Look"—Rexx spreads wrinkled palms in a calming gesture—"you know as much as I do. Probably more."

Kerusa's pupils constrict, anus tight. "Who are you protecting? Yourself? Us, for our own good?" A sneer, there. "Or someone else?"

"I'm not—"

"Someone fucked up, didn't they? A design flaw or bug. And now you're trying to cover it up. Damage control."

Rexx lowers his hands, keeps his gaze fixed on Kerusa's belligerent glare. "That's what I'm here to find out."

"Bullshit!" Flecks of spittle spray from his lips, hard as buckshot. "There's no reason for you to be here in-vivo except to get in our way. Make sure no one finds out what *really* happened so we shoulder the blame."

"I'm not interested in laying blame," Rexx says. "I'm interested in answers. That's it. Nothing more, nothing less."

"Someone has to be responsible," Kerusa growls. "I know how these things work." His focus loses its grip and slips past Rexx, staring at nothing. "There's always a scapegoat. Someone who takes the fall."

Rexx bites his tongue. It's pointless to argue. No amount of reasoning will placate the project manager. The more Rexx defends himself, the worse he sounds.

He's guilty, no matter what. Kerusa has the look of a wounded animal that's been backed into a corner, lashing out at everyone as an enemy, real or imagined.

"Well?" the project manager demands.

"When can I pod down to the surface?" Rexx says. "The sooner I get what I came for, the sooner I'll be outta your hair."

Kerusa scowls but relents. "I have a meeting in a few minutes with my group operations managers"—he backs away—"to go over the latest developments. You can squirt them everything you know. I'm sure they'll be interested to hear what you got to say."

The conference room is located close to the outside shell of the construction station. A doughnut-shaped table takes up much of the room. The table has been set up around a lightshaft that connects one of the main light-domes to the station's central sphere. A quadrille of biolum panels float above the table. The floor is beige onyx inlaid with moss tiles. Through the block-diamond walls he can make out the mist-blurred shadows of warm-blooded plants in greenhouse vats. Bananopy leaves, spongewood, the topiary weavings of tapestree branches.

The outer two levels of the station are devoted to the care and feeding of the warm-blooded vegetation that comprises the Mymercia ecotecture. Before the plants were introduced to the asteroid they were first cultivated on the station. Only after they reached maturity in orbit were seedlings transplanted to the surface. Now with the softwire link between the station and the asteroid down, there's no way to support the new growth remotely, to help sustain it or the workers.

Aided by magnetic flux lines, Rexx clips himself into

one of two dozen chairs around the table. In addition to Kerusa and himself, there are three other people at the table. Phuong Yalçin, lead biologist. Loic Bagnas, in charge of technical support. And Jakala Nderi, head of information systems. Absent are the project's structural and mechanical engineers. They're on the asteroid, working to install emergency systems to replace the ones that failed after the accident. That might explain why he never received a sensor report.

One thing Rexx can't figure out is why the ops managers have gathered in-vivo for the meeting. It could just as easily take place in-virtu. He suspects it's a quirk of Kerusa, a control issue that hints at some fundamental insecurity or distrust. He's got a chip on his shoulder the size of a sow's teat.

Following the introductions, Kerusa says, "Well, we might as well start off on a cheerful note." He turns to Rexx. "You got anything useful to report from the autopsy on Liam Vitt?"

Rexx leans forward. He signs open a datawindow, conferences in the others, and displays the garbled architext for the anomalous particle. "As you can see, the structure is unintelligible. Gibberish."

"You weren't able to locate another occurrence of it in the remains?" Yalçin says.

"No."

"Which explains why you need to obtain another sample."

"But not why you're here," Nderi remarks, apparently siding with Kerusa when it comes to the purpose of Rexx's visit. "I'm still not clear what you hope to accomplish here that we can't. Even if you find what you're looking for, there's no guarantee that it won't be garbage as well."

"It's possible the particle, molecule, junk DNA, or whatever, was a fragment. If I can find a complete sample it might be readable."

"Any idea at all what the particle is? Or where it could have come from?" Bagnas says.

"No."

"So we don't know if it's internal or external."

"Right."

"Any preliminary guesses?" Yalçin says. "Possibilities that seem more likely than any others?"

"Well, nine times out of ten a problem like this is the result of a random mutation. That doesn't mean you can bank on it. But if I was a bettin' man that's where I'd lay my money."

"*Are* you a betting man?" Nderi asks.

"Naw. I ain't that lucky."

"In other words," Yalçin says, "odds are it's an accident."

He seems to have an ally in the biologist. If not an ally, then someone who's at least willing to keep an open mind.

"If it is a mutation," Bagnas says, "wouldn't the problem have shown up earlier? *Before* we migrated the plants to the asteroid?"

Rexx shakes his head. "Not necessarily. There could be an environmental factor on the asteroid that was overlooked. Something that wasn't taken into account and then incorporated into the design specifications. It could also be a design error that failed to show up until now."

"How does that figure into your visiting the asteroid?" Nderi asks.

"For starters, we can't collect a tissue sample up here. The survivor you've got in isolation, Fola, doesn't appear to be infected."

Kerusa grunts. "So far."

"Second," Rexx goes on, "we don't want to ship a sample back to the station. It's too risky. We need to keep the problem isolated on the asteroid."

"So you'd be willing to put yourself at risk," Bagnas says. "Take the chance you might get stuck down there."

Rexx can feel the surface tension building, the gradual loss of control that comes with friction, turbulence, resistance.

Walk away, he thinks. Turn around and go home. He didn't ask for this. It isn't his problem anymore.

"Could foreign DNA have contaminated the ecotecture?" Yalçin says. "That would explain why it's not on file."

Rexx shrugs. The biologist doesn't get it. Kerusa doesn't want his help. So it's not going to happen.

"Which leaves us exactly where we were before," Bagnas grumbles. "Completely in the dark."

"And it doesn't look like things are going to improve anytime soon," Nderi says, frowning at a private datawindow.

"Another biosystem failure?" Kerusa says.

"Air handling. Recycling and filtration just went offline." Nderi taps her fingers in the air, parsing the datastream.

"So the problem is spreading," Yalçin says. "The same as on Earth."

Kerusa's jaw bunches.

"Oxygen production is stable," Nderi notes. "But if that drops offline, there's no way to replenish their air supply."

"If it does fall offline," Kerusa says, "how long can they survive with the oxygen supply they've got?"

"Less than twenty-four hours"—Nderi glances pointedly at Rexx—"given their current biomass and rate of consumption."

Yet another argument against his going, albeit a minor one. One additional body will not significantly shorten the survival time of the other workers.

"Any indication what triggered the failure?" Kerusa says. "Why that particular system was affected?"

Nderi shakes her head. "Nothing. The sensors have dropped offline as well."

Kerusa gnashes his teeth. "All right. Start prepping a quarantine zone up here. In case we have to evacuate people from the asteroid."

Bagnas shifts uncomfortably in his seat. "You can't bring that many—"

"I am not going to let those people die," Kerusa snaps, "and neither are you. Is that understood?"

Bagnas looks unhappy but says nothing.

"What do you have in mind?" Nderi asks Kerusa.

"The reserve greenhouses. Verify that they can be isolated. See if they can be hermetically sealed from the rest of the station and let me know what it will take to convert them into temporary living quarters."

Nderi nods. "I'll get right on it."

"Good." Kerusa pushes out of his chair, and then drifts away from the table. "If no one has anything else, I suggest we get to work."

"You need to send someone down for a sample," Rexx tells Kerusa when the others are gone. "Even if it's not me." If he takes himself out of the picture, maybe the project manager will listen.

"Forget it," Kerusa says.

"They can suit up," Rexx says. "Conserve resources."

Kerusa strokes the knife-sharp edges of his goatee.
"And what happens if the suit fails?" The project manager lowers his fingers but keeps the tips pinched.
"Sorry. Until we have a better handle on the situation,
no one's going anywhere."

"You're making a mistake."

"I don't think so." Kerusa gropes for a magnetic
flux line.

Rexx grabs him by the arm. "What should I tell
Tiresias?"

"Whatever the hell you want." Kerusa wrenches his
arm free, sending them both into a slow, tumultuous
spin. "Tiresias is your problem, not mine."

# 12

## SOUL LOSS

I don't understand," Isabelle says to the *bruja*. "How could she lose her soul? Is she bewitched? Did someone give her *ojo*?" She stares, distraught, at the emaciated, skeleton-thin figure of Lejandra. Her face is as sunken as a *calavera*, little more than a bone skull with charcoal-smudged tufts of cotton for hair.

The evil eye, L. Mariachi thinks. That's what people always assume happened to him. His success with Daily Bred caused *envidio* in someone, envy, and this person paid a witch to cripple his hand.

"Bloody Mary scared her and dislodged her soul from her body," the witch explains. "When her soul was away, the demon entered the empty space inside her to prevent her soul from returning. Now it's lost."

Soul loss. It's a catchall diagnosis. A convenient explanation for the woman's apathy, feebleness, and lack of appetite. For the uneducated, the superstitious, it's easier to understand and cure a demon like Bloody Mary than it is a bacterial infection, virus, or genetic disorder.

"Can you get it back?" Balta says. Despite his badass gangsta regalia and 'tude, he's still just a kid.

The *bruja* nods, somber but confident. "But first we have to get rid of the part of Bloody Mary that has entered her. Then her soul will have a place to return."

"But if it's lost how will it find its way home?" Oscar says. Doubt and fear flicker in his wide candlelit eyes. "What if it's gone forever?"

Doña Celia gives him a reassuring pat on the arm.

"Do you believe this?" Num Nut says.

L. Mariachi can't tell if this is a question or an editorial comment. He decides to ignore the IA and keep playing, not wanting to lose momentum. He's rocking on autopilot, but there's no telling how long it will last. As soon as the painkillers quit, he'll come crashing back to earth, dragged down by the weight of his bad hand and his lack of faith.

The *bruja* picks up the sprig of curative herbs she brought with her. Traditionally these would be rosemary, rue, pepper tree branches, and marigolds. Since these are extinct, casualties of global warming, she's using circuitree leaves, a dried frond from an umbrella palm, and an aquafern sprig. Presumably they're just as effective as the old remedy.

She brushes Lejandra with the herbs, sweeping them like a broom along her arms and torso. Then she takes a cigarette from the pack, scratches the end on the floor to light it, and blows smoke around the bed.

"To keep anyone else from breathing in the bad air when it's banished," the *bruja* explains.

The smoke hangs in the air, vaguely bird shaped. The

reek of tobacco, candle wax, and imitation copal reminds him of the clubs Daily Bred used to play in Mexico City. It's like old times. He shuts his eyes for a second, breathes in the past and holds it in his lungs for as long as he can.

"You're going to hurt yourself," Num Nut warns.

The tickle in his throat explodes in a brief but violent coughing fit that scrapes his lungs. He keeps playing, powers through the sputum and tears until Doña Celia stubs out the cigarette and picks up the stone with the hole drilled in the middle. Parts of the rock are bright, almost glassy in places. Polished. In the feeble light and thick smoke it looks more metallic than rocky.

"What are those?" Balta says, pointing at the stone.

"They look like teeth," João says.

L. Mariachi leans forward, squints at the chalk white fragments embedded in the surface. Sure enough the fragments resemble barbed teeth, arranged in a circle.

"They're the bones from an angel," the witch says. "One day, this rock fell out of the sky. It landed in the playground of the orphanage where I was staying. That's how I acquired my supernatural powers. This was a long time ago, in Honduras."

She lowers the sheet a few centimeters, sets the stone on Lejandra's exposed breastbone, and presses the teeth into the pale skin.

L. Mariachi flinches, as if the dentata are biting into him, yearning to devour his heart. Lejandra twitches, then calms, easing under the pressure. When she's settled, the *bruja* leans over her, fits her mouth over the opening in the stone and makes a sucking sound. Her whole body seems to inflate. Her cheeks puff out and her sides expand. She straightens, her breath still held, then turns and spits on the floor.

A tiny speck of saliva strikes L. Mariachi in the face. The spittle is hot. It burns his cheek. Venomous, acidic. He twists his face sideways, raises the guitar, and swipes at the spittle with his upraised shoulder.

Lejandra shudders. L. Mariachi's fingers stumble, falter under a tremor that starts in his bad hand and works its way up his arm, into his chest. From there it spreads down, into his legs. His knees start to shake.

"Enough," Num Nut says, sounding distraught. "It's time to stop."

He can't. Not while he's got a full head of steam, is going strong. He's not sure he could stop even if he wanted to. It's not him playing anymore, it's someone else. The alter ego who recorded "SoulR Byrne." He hasn't felt that person in him for a long time—decades.

"Her soul is close by," the *bruja* announces. "It senses it can come home." Doña Celia plucks the stone from Lejandra's chest.

L. Mariachi breathes easier. It's as if a weight has been lifted from him as well. As if *his* soul was lost and has been called home. The acid burn on his cheek subsides, and with it the heaviness in his mutilated hand. His fingers pick up the pace. He launches into a kick-ass *norteño* tune. The upbeat chords chase away the somber pall in the room and his heart, hold the shadows at bay long enough to let Lejandra know that it's safe to come home.

After the first *norteño* he segues into a second, then a third. All of the old music he listened to and learned as a kid.

"You're broadcasting," Num Nut tells him.

"Huh?" The word comes out sweaty, breathless with exhilaration. His forehead is damp, his shirt soaked, limp against his skin.

"The guitar is softwired," the IA says. "It's transmitting encrypted information to the ribozone."

He shakes his head, too focused on the music to think, and continues to pound out a phantom melody that's welling up in him like sap miraculously starting to flow in dead wood. Sticky, exuberant.

And sweet. He didn't realize he still had the sweetness in him. He thought it had turned bitter and hard.

Doña Celia drops the stone into a pocket of her dress. She retrieves a hollow gourd from the duffel bag, stands, and walks to one corner of the room. Putting the gourd to her lips, she blows into it, and then calls the name of the lost soul. The sound of the gourd picks up the notes of the guitar and lifts them higher, urging L. Mariachi to play faster. The *bruja* repeats the process at the next two corners of the room. At each juncture the swell under the music builds. It rises to a frenetic crescendo as Doña Celia approaches the fourth corner of the room.

L. Mariachi is breathless. He can barely suck in enough air to keep up the breakneck tempo. When the witch shouts the name of Lejandra's lost soul for the fourth and final time, her voice pierces him. He falls back, lightheaded and dizzy. In his mind, he can still hear the music. He's still playing, strumming away totally *loco*. But another part of him knows that his hands have stopped and he's clutching the guitar to his chest in a death grip.

His left hand throbs, a mangled knot of pain. Arthritic voices spin around him in elongated, time-shifted orbits. . . .

"What happened? What's wrong with him?" The boy's voice comes from above him and transforms into a voice from memory, years distant.

"*He's drunk*. Muy barracho."

"*No, dumbfuck. Look at his hand.*" *The second voice leaned closer, pressing up against the present.*

"Ay! We should take him to the clinic." A woman's voice this time, much nearer in space and time.

"No," another woman says.

*A horn bleated in the street next to him, followed by the low temblor of thumping percussion. The stench of rotting vegetables, dust, and spoiled fruit rose from a nearby market. Dust congealed the blood in his mouth, coated his tongue with the gritty taste of copper and mist-fine ash from the volcano that settled over Mexico City quicker than the scrubbugs could digest it.*

"We can't just leave him here." The first woman's voice again, pushing aside the memory.

"Why not?"

"Because if he dies, we'll get blamed. The politicorp will say it's our fault. Then where will we be?"

The question slips away as he retrogrades back in time again.

"*If we don't do anything,*" *the first voice said,* "*we'll get blamed. No?*"

*A third person joined the cacophony.* "*I'm going to call for help.*"

*L. Mariachi opened his mouth to speak but bile dissolved his voice and burned the back of his throat. His thoughts broke apart, reformed in a confused jumble, then fragmented yet again.*

"*Wait.*" *The word was scratchy, sandpaper rough. It carried the weight of a stone statue and centuries-old authority.*

"*Fuck this* cabrón." *The second voice circled back.* "*I'm not sticking my neck out for him. Whoever fucked him up doesn't mess around.*"

*"You think he crossed a* jefe?*"*

"Sí, *a* cocolo. Who else? He's an example. No way I want my face to end up like that hand. My old lady would become a nun."

"You think we should let him sleep here?" The boy again.

"How long do we have to look after him?" the first woman says.

"Not long." The second woman. "Until morning. He'll be fine then."

The voices thin and attenuate in a bout of dizziness. He loses his grip on the verbal thread, the frayed string of consonants and syllables that dangle just beyond his reach before slipping away.

# 13

## TERRA INFIRMA

Fola stretches out next to the ICM, meshes herself into place, then fits the module's hardwire eyescreens over her face. A short, hair-thin loop of molectric filament tickles her ear.

"Ready," she tells Pheidoh.

A downpour of pixels washes the gray cellophane of the eyescreens and she's in-virtu.

Without the IA, Fola would be lost. She could never find Lejandra in the snarl of pherions, antiphers, sniffers, and architext that form the terra-based ecotectures. There are too many of them, thousands. The ribozone is a rat's nest of specialized clades, each competing for space with one another in a kind of cutthroat Darwinism. The diversity is mind-boggling. Most of the clades are legal, politicorp sponsored or BEAN approved. But some aren't—rogue microniches carved out of the gengineered environment by a few radical groups, religious cults, and criminal orgs. These shadow clades use black-market antiphers, home-brewed pherions, and ad hoc antisense molecules to disable the legal pherions and avoid detection.

To combat them, the politicorp regions of the ribozone are teeming with surveillance systems—glycoprotein identifier tags, linked bitcam arrays, and networked iDNA sensors. There are also countermeasure and defense systems: virions, bactoxins, and, according to Pheidoh, a new strain of digital RNA that codes for an enzyme that attracts Big Brother flitcams the way dog shit attracts flies. Get a dose of dRNA and it's only a matter of time before BEAN picks up the scent. Add to that private security firms like OAsys, which has developed a wide range of ecotectural defense systems for public and private sector clades, in addition to providing private bodyguards, and things can get ugly fast. Even the Ignatarians contracted with OAsys on occasion, when a Church leader was visiting or going abroad and personal safety was a concern.

In short, it's not a friendly place.

"Exactly how risky is this?" Fola asks. She's only logged in to the Kuiper belt domain of the ribozone. As soon as she flips the switch on the softwire circuit to access an ecotecture or clade in another domain, her iDNA signature, clade-profile, and pherion pattern will be public. It will be like taking her clothes off and parading around naked on a busy street.

"The datacast we're streaming is around five hours old. If a dangerous pherion entered the environment in that time frame, it won't have made it to the Kuiper belt yet. It will still be in transit. So there won't be any filters in place to block it, or antiphers to neutralize it, when it gets here."

Translation: she'll be defenseless. Not exactly the rock-solid reassurance she was hoping for.

Fola forgot about the time delay. It takes in the neighborhood of five hours for a signal from earth to reach the Kuiper belt. It's not that long, but it's still the past. She has to keep that in mind. A lot can happen in five hours. Lejandra could already be dead. Even if she isn't, it still might be too late to do anything for her.

Whatever that might be. She's still in the dark as to what exactly her role in all of this is going to be.

"The good news," Pheidoh continues, "is that if there are any recently introduced pherions, they need to have a virtual isomorph to be dangerous."

Since she's not actually on earth, in direct physical contact with the environment, her biggest worry is biodigitally mediated pherions. Digital analogs of pherions that can be transmitted wirelessly, downloaded to her body, and then converted into proteins by the molectronics she's waring.

Fola is tempted to ask how likely that is, but decides that it's better if she doesn't know. At least she's not at risk from any nondigital contagion. Are there any computer viruses out there that attack IAs? There must be.

"What I don't understand," she says, "is how the quanticles are being transmitted. What's spreading them?"

"There are a number of possible vectors that could be used to deliver quantum dots," the IA says. "A virus is one. But viruses take time to amplify, and several isolated communities with no outside contact have been infected."

Okay. If it's not a virus, that leaves . . . what? "Molectronics?" she ventures.

"That's the most likely mechanism," Pheidoh says. "It's fast, and there's no need for a host—a carrier. Plus, compared to a live virus, a digital contagion takes little time or energy to replicate and distribute."

"But not everyone is softwired," Fola says.

"Actually most people are. They just don't realize it because the molectronics are bundled with the eco-tecture."

"Really?"

"It facilitates automatic pherion updates and clade-profile tweaks. It's easier and cheaper than having people come into a hospital or clinic."

"When did this happen?"

"Most governments began the implementation eighteen months ago, as part of a BEAN chartered agreement."

"Did all of the politicorps sign on?"

"Yes."

And now it's being used by somebody, this Bloody Mary, to wreak havoc. A radical org. It has to be. She prays it's not the ICLU, doesn't see how it could be. The ICLU isn't like that.

"What's so important about the ceremony?" she says. Beyond a palliative effect, there's little or no real medical benefit the healing ceremony can provide. In the overall scheme of things, it seems like a waste of time.

"The *bruja*," Pheidoh tells her. "Doña Celia. She's the only one who can exorcise Bloody Mary."

Fola's brow puckers. "From who? Lejandra?"

"Yes."

A vague shake of her head. "How?"

" 'When I'm fine'ly gone/it's a fore_gone conclu-sion/your soul's gonna cry . . . SoulR Byrne. SoulR Byrne.' "

Fola blinks. It's the same song she woke to after the accident. She listens to the thumping, teeth-jarring beat. The harsh chanted lyrics and the eerie, melodic undercurrent that gives the song a mournful quality despite the relentless bass. "I don't get it," she says.

"The song is a critical part of the curing ceremony," Pheidoh informs her as soon as the music stops.

"Why? What difference does it make?"

"Without it, the *bruja* won't be able to get rid of Bloody Mary. Eliminate her, and you eliminate the source of the disease."

"I don't understand how a song is going to cure Lejandra and the others, get rid of the quanticles and put an end to the outbreak."

The datahound wipes its forehead. "It's difficult to explain."

"If you want me to help you, I need to know what the connection is between the quanticles and Bloody Mary. I need to know *who* she is. *Where* she is. You have to trust me, for a change."

The IA freezes, goes static. A beat passes. Two. Just when she thinks it's hung, a pained look crosses its face, as if it's about to pass a kidney stone. "Bloody Mary was an IA."

Fola narrows her eyes. "Was?"

"She's . . . changed."

"How?"

The IA wets its lips. "Go out enough decimal places and the world doesn't look the same. Errors creep in. Uncertainties. Nothing is perfect."

"Okay," she says, "fine." At least now she's got something solid she can wrap her brain around. "I still don't see how playing a particular song is going to help."

"The music contains certain information that—when transmitted to Bloody Mary—will make her . . . stop."

"You mean encrypted information embedded inside the music? Like a worm or a virus?"

"More or less." The IA flickers. It seems anxious, distracted.

"Who put it there?"

"I'll explain later," Pheidoh says. The flickering amplifies. "We're running out of time."

Fola sucks in a deep breath—"All right"—and reaches for the absent cross, stops herself.

Pathetic. She's like a baby, wanting to suckle not for hunger but for comfort. Or a feeble gerontocrat reaching for a crutch.

One young, the other old. Both helpless.

In the biodigital construct of the ribozone, the Front Range City ecotecture is portrayed as a Parthenon-like building enclosed on all sides by a three-deep procession of colonnades. The white marble columns are fluted, encircled by climbing roses, and capped by leafy capitals. The columns aren't really columns, they're a virtual representation of a real-world structure, like a power-storage grid or water-distribution system. The same goes for the barrel vault the columns support, the purple wisteria that hangs from the overhead lattice of interconnecting beams, and every other visible feature of the garden, down to the smallest insect. Bamboo fills the gaps in between the rows of columns. The air feels desert dry, hot. A scaly lizard scampers across the stone footpath in front of her, into a clump of dry-bladed grass and spiny yucca that's growing among the rock outcroppings at the base of the columns. Some kind of ornisect darts around the barrel vault above her—a dragonfly with feathers and a beak, or a small bird with a thorax and four wings. The barrel vault is a tangle of cactustree branches laden with thick oval-shaped leaves. The leaves are dotted with tiny yellow flowers and every few seconds a flower—which might also be a butterfly—detaches from one leaf, flutters to another, and reattaches.

Fola turns to Pheidoh. The IA has shed its anthropomorphized canine persona and chosen to represent itself as a nineteenth-century archaeologist dressed in khakis, black leather boots, and a pith helmet. Gender-neutral features. How does the software think of itself, when she's not around? Male? Female? She has no clue, has never thought to ask. "

"Is this where the migrant workers are?" she says.

The IA shakes its head. "The *braceros* aren't allowed to interact directly with the local ecotecture. They're housed in a temporary subclade."

She looks around. "Where is that?"

Pheidoh points toward an iron-gated archway set between two columns at the far end of the garden. The opening is small, half-concealed by a bamboo thicket that forms a wall on both sides of the passageway.

> *Five, six, seven, eight,*
> *Meet you at the Iron Gate.*

More lizards scatter out of her way as she heads down the path. It's hard to tell what their ecotectural niche is, what function the program's real-world analog performs. It doesn't appear to be security or information exchange. Diagnostics maybe, or system optimization; a dead bug dangles from the mouth of one lizard.

As Fola nears the gate, she notices that the bamboo

crowding it on both sides has hooked barbs on the stems and at the ends of the leaves. Up close, it resembles a cactus more than bamboo.

"Careful," Pheidoh warns. "The needles are detachable."

"What are they?"

"A prison pherion. They're located along the perimeter of the *bracero* subclade to keep the migrants from leaving. If the needles are brought into the compound, they could injure anyone who comes into contact with them."

She didn't realize the datastream was two-way—that whatever she does inside the garden will be transmitted back to earth.

Through the wrought-iron gate, at the far end of a narrow passage, she can make out a smaller side garden. It's more of a courtyard, really. There are no Corinthian columns or barrel vault. Instead, the courtyard is enclosed on three sides by a low wall and shaded by umbrella palms. Fola releases the catch on the gate, pulls on the handle. The hinges groan in protest. She tugs on the latch harder and the gate swings open. Before she can let go, five or six scarablike beetles emerge from crannies in the gate and scuttle toward her fingers.

Fast.

She jerks her hand back. Too late; they fasten onto her with chemical mandibles. She feels a faint sting— "Ouch!"—and shakes her hand. Hard. The beetles don't seem to notice. They're glued tight to her.

She glances at the Pheidoh. The intrepid explorer has taken out a spiral notebook and is scribbling on one of the pages.

Another beetle bites down on her. A burning sensation

infiltrates her lungs, followed by a sudden prickly dizziness as the molectronics connected to her nervous system download and convert the digital information represented by the beetles into really nasty neurotoxins.

"Pheidoh? . . ."

"I'm working on it." The IA continues to jot notes. It's writing in some kind of symbolic script that looks vaguely hieroglyphic. As if they are in ancient Egypt instead of the eastern plains of Colorado.

"Please hur—"

She can't breathe. Her knees sag like half-empty bags of sand. She reaches for the gate to keep from falling and . . .

The burning sensation in her lungs stops. She takes a breath, swallows, regains her balance. The beetles mill around in confusion on her arm, lose their grip on her, fall to the ground, and scuttle off.

"Sorry." The IA tucks the notepad and pencil into the breast pocket of its shirt. "That particular security pherion is an update of an older version. I had to softwire you the latest antipher. You're protected now."

Tentatively Fola touches the gate. Nothing. The beetles have lost interest. She swings open the gate, slips through and, careful to avoid the bamboo, makes her way to the courtyard.

If anything, it's hotter and drier than the main garden. In addition to the umbrella palms, there are several scraggly circuitrees growing in a line along one wall, as well as a number of odd, barrel-shaped cacti. Like the columns in the main garden, the cacti aren't really cacti, but an in-virtu representation of a real-world ecotectural system.

"Underground water storage," the IA says, following her gaze. "Fed by aquaferns in the foothills."

The walls aren't that high, not like the bamboo. They seem to be made out of adobe brick. They're topped by some kind of fragrant bougainvillea and don't look very secure.

A flicker of movement in the shadow at the foot of one wall catches her attention.

"I wouldn't get too close," Pheidoh advises.

"I don't see—"

She spots the snakes, entwined at the foot of the wall. Twisted together in a single long snake that reminds her of a thickly braided strand of barbed wire.

She shudders, rubs her left arm, and retreats until the snakes calm.

"I've located them," Pheidoh says, standing next to her.

A datawindow opens at eye level in front of her, superimposed on the virtuality of the ribozone. Doors within doors. In the translucent pane, the grainy composite of a room forms, cobbled together out of various image-streams from surveillance bitcams in the hardfoam walls. The room is dark, a roil of dancing, candlelit shadows. When the sound kicks in, a loud burst of music, it adds a sense of urgency to the scene in which an old woman, the *bruja,* is kneeling over a slightly younger but skeletal-looking woman in a bed.

Lejandra.

Four people have gathered around the two women in a loose semicircle. None of them are playing an instrument. They appear worried. The *bruja* bends over the sick woman, kisses her on the upper chest, and then turns and spits on the floor.

The woman reminds her of the old man Xophia was

caring for. Her symptoms are different, horrible black bruises that follow the outline of her bones, but she looks just as bad.

This is what's going to happen to Xophia, Fola thinks.

The pace of the music quickens. The *bruja* stands up, holding a gourd in her clawlike hands. The image cuts to her approaching one wall, where she stops, raises the gourd to her lips, blows, and then calls out.

"Lejandra!" She beckons with one hand. "*Ven aquí*." Come here. "Your aunt is waiting. Your uncle is waiting. Your cousins are waiting. They are calling for you to come home. La Llorona is gone. Come back to where you belong. Come back to your loved ones. Come back to yourself."

In the foreground, a sixth person, sitting cross-legged on the bare lichenboard floor, hunches over a battered guitar that doesn't seem capable of creating the volume of sound she's streaming.

L. Mariachi.

From this angle Fola can't get a good look at the musician. His head is bowed, obscuring his features. All she can see is the back of his neck and shoulders, where a toy parrot clings to his shirt collar, and his left hand on the neck of the guitar. Fingers curled around the frets in a twisted lump. Sweat streaks his dusty sprayon shirt, a sheen of perspiration varnishes the scuffed soundboard of the guitar. Ditto the balding spot on the top of his head, which is fringed with a halo of limp gray curls. The rawhide-rough skin on his neck is rent with fissure-deep wrinkles.

She turns to Pheidoh. "How old is he?"

"Fifty-eight."

Judging by his appearance, she thought he was older. In his late sixties. "What happened to his hand?"

"He was dosed with a degenerative neurotoxin," Pheidoh says.

"A work accident?"

"No. Another musician, the owner of a guitar he stole. That was one of the reasons he became a *bracero*. He couldn't play music anymore."

The view shifts. Follows the old woman as she works her way to another corner of the room and repeats the ceremony with the gourd. From this new angle, L. Mariachi still has his face down but she can make out more of his features: drooping mustache, aquiline nose, a high, flat forehead scarred by determination, despair, and long hours of physical labor. The past few years as a migrant worker haven't been kind to him. He is tired and worn out, nearing the end of the road.

Fola winces as the tendons stand out in his neck and forearms, as strained as the metal guitar strings that are bloodying the tips of his fingers. If anything, his playing is becoming more reckless, more wild with each passing second.

No way he can go on, she thinks.

But he does; long enough for the *bruja* to shuffle to the fourth corner in the room, blow into the gourd, and call out.

Her final shout hits L. Mariachi like a physical blow. The parrot squawks in alarm, then leaps to safety as he pitches back against the wall and slumps to one side, the guitar pressed to his chest like a dead child.

The sudden absence of sound is deafening. The image freezes, and Fola wonders if maybe the transmission is hung. Then one of the boys in the room lurches toward the fallen musician, followed quickly by the others.

"What happened?" the second boy asks, coming up behind first. "What's wrong with him?"

The boy's father puts a hand to his forehead. "He's burning up."

"Ay!" his wife exclaims. "We should take him to the clinic." She reaches for the guitar.

"No." The *bruja*'s voice is knife sharp.

The wife jerks her hands away as if slapped. "We can't just leave him here," she protests.

"Why not?" the man says.

"Because if he dies, we'll get blamed. The politicorp will say it's our fault. Then where will we be?"

"He's having a vision." The *bruja* spits into the palm of her hand and smears the saliva onto L. Mariachi's forehead. "It's nothing serious."

"What about the guitar?" the father says.

"When he wakes up, tell him it's his. I want him to have it."

"You think we should let him sleep here?" the older boy asks.

The *bruja* nods, stands. She shuffles to the side of the bed and begins to gather up her curative herbs and paraphernalia.

"How long do we have to look after him?" the wife asks. She follows the *bruja* to the bed while the others remain with L. Mariachi.

"Not long." The *bruja* finishes packing her duffel bag. "Until morning. He'll be fine then."

The wife purses her lips unhappily, but nods.

One of the boys, the younger of the two, leaves the room. A couple of seconds later he returns with a blanket. He spreads it on the floor next to L. Mariachi. Together, the two boys and their father shift the musician onto his side and scoot the blanket under him.

When L. Mariachi is covered with the blanket the *bruja* leaves, followed by the husband and wife. The two boys stay behind, speaking in soft whispers, until their mother shows up five minutes later and orders them to bed. Shortly, the father joins his wife at the side of the bed. He puts his arm around her. She leans into him, too tired all of a sudden to hold herself up.

"Your niece will be okay," he assures her. "We've done everything we can."

"That doesn't mean it will be enough."

"That's for the Virgin to decide, *sonrisa de mi corazón*. Lejandra is in God's hands, now. Not ours."

Fola likes that. *Sonrisa de mi corazón*. Smile of my heart.

"I can't believe he's here," the woman says. She cuts a glance at L. Mariachi on the floor. "After all these years. I thought he'd have moved on by now."

"He'll be gone soon."

"Not soon enough." The woman spits air. "The *pendejo* is nothing but trouble. I just know it."

The two of them stand like that for a while, supporting each other, before fatigue kicks in and they call it a night.

"What's the prognosis?" Fola asks when they've left the room.

"For who?" Pheidoh says.

She was thinking of Lejandra. But the IA might be able to tap the biomed readout for L. Mariachi, too. "Both of them."

"L. Mariachi is suffering from dehydration and exhaustion."

Nothing a good night's rest and a little water won't cure. "What about Lejandra? Is she still infected?"

Pheidoh nods, the shadow from the IA's pith helmet falling like a dark veil across its features.

So the ceremony didn't work. No surprise there. Maybe now the IA will come to its senses. "Are the others at risk?"

That's one of her main concerns at this point. Damage control.

The datahound stares, head down, as if lost in a hypnotic trance. Except for one eyelid, which is blinking so fast it looks like a hummingbird wing.

Fola reaches for the datahound but stops short, afraid that if she touches the image it will pop like a soap bubble.

"Pheidoh?" She hates the tremor in her voice. "What is it? Are you okay?"

In response the rest of the IA's image goes into a palsied flicker. Rapidly winking in and out of existence.

"Pheidoh! Talk to me." Fola pinches her lower lip between her teeth and curls her fingers around the absent cross below her throat. Her hand trembles, reverberating to the staccato waver. "Say something. Please?"

The datahound reanimates. "If L. Mariachi is able to send a ribozone transmission, then he should be able to receive one."

"What just happened?" she says. "Are you all right?"

The IA frowns. "Why wouldn't I be?"

She withdraws her hand. Fingers still curled in a shaky knot. "You looped for a second. It looked like you were about to crash."

The datahound stares at her like she's crazy. Maybe she is. Maybe she's the one who seized.

"You have to talk to him," the IA says. "Convince him to play the song."

" 'SoulR Byrne'?" She's never seen the IA this obsessed. Focused, yes. Desperate, no.

"It's the only way to exorcise Bloody Mary."

"Stop it! Just—" It hits her then. The curing ceremony is an act, a stage production. Lejandra is of secondary importance. She doesn't matter. As far as the IA is concerned, no one matters except L. Mariachi. He's the key. "Why?"

"Because he'll talk to you."

She shakes her head. "That's not what I meant."

"He trusts you."

"He doesn't trust anyone. Not even himself."

"He trusts the Blue Lady."

Fola lowers her hand. Uncurls her fingers. "Who's the Blue Lady?"

The datahound smiles, winks. But this time it's normal, not some spastic twitch. "You are."

# 14

## COEFFICIENT OF DRAG

"What are you doing?" Ida Claire asks as Rexx tubes from the conference room to the shuttle bay.

"You heard Kerusa. I've worn out my welcome."

"So you're leaving/giving up?"

Rexx enters the shuttle bay. The air is cooler here. A welcome relief from the stuffiness that permeates the rest of the station. He takes a deep breath. The foliage tastes sour, acerbic. Time for another dose of the temporary reclade pherion for Mymercia. Before the place really starts to get uncomfortable.

"Would you like to contact Pilar Atienza?" Claire says.

"That won't be necessary." He digs a squeeze vial from one pocket, inserts the tip into one nostril, and sniffs.

"She might be able to reason with Kerusa, convince him to cooperate."

He replaces the vial. "Not likely."

"How do you know?"

"Trust me, Ida. We'll just end up waltzin' without Matilda." He stretches out a hand and grabs a magnetic flux line. Feels it take him by the arm and guide him past dense bananopy plants into the geodomed air lock where his shuttle pod waits. A diffuse tangle of shadows from the glossy leaves mottles the black carbyne frame. Through the geodesic windows in the dome he can see a lancet of marigold yellow light surrounded by a teat-pink halo at the base. The stamen and petals of a sol-catcher, unfolded to drink frail light.

Rexx turns his gaze from the solcatcher to the shuttle. "Flight status?" He floats toward the nose, past the aft array of puckered nozzles. The nozzles are fed by a cap-illary network of high-pressure microtubes connected to the shuttle's hydrogen production and storage sacs.

"Fuel is at sixty percent. For a return to Tiresias, you should wait until they are at eighty percent."

"How long will that take?"

"Four hours."

He can't wait that long. "I guess I'll just have to take my chances."

He signs the access code for the shuttle. A seam appears in the cyborganic skin of the pod, between two external support ribs that maintain the shape of the pressurized inner bladder.

"You have a visitor," Claire announces.

Rexx jerks his head around, expecting to see Kerusa. Instead, Yalçin appears in the air lock, his hands spread wide to slow his forward motion.

Rexx's adrenaline spike eases but he still feels edgy, anxious to get going.

Yalçin drifts to a stop two meters from Rexx, but con-tinues to hold his arms spread wide, palms out.

"You didn't waste any time getting here," the biologist said.

"I've wasted enough time already." Rexx tugs irritably at the side wattle drooping from his chin.

"I thought you might need this." Yalçin slips an ampoule from his utility belt and nudges it toward Rexx.

Rexx curls the fingers of one hand, a cross between a tai chi finger exercise and a shadow puppet that tugs on the magnetic flux lines around the ampoule. It wobbles to a stop half a meter in front of him. The ampoule is injection-extruded diamond, a sapphire icosahedron with pewter nubs and titanium wire lace. "What is it?"

"A biosuit. You'll need it for Mymercia."

"What makes you think—"

Yalçin waves a hand, brushing aside the protest. "If I were you I wouldn't waste any more time."

Rexx retrieves the ampoule, unsnaps one of his pants pockets, and stuffs the vial inside. "What happens if Kerusa finds out you were here?"

Yalçin shrugs. "Hopefully he won't."

"Anything else I should know?"

"Naiana Hjert, the structural engineer, is a good person. Trustworthy. Amadou Urabazo, the mechanical engineer, was hired by Kerusa. You won't get much help from him."

Rexx nods, his jowls flapping. "I'll be sure to keep that in mind. Thanks."

"You might not thank me, once you get down there." Yalçin turns, catches a flux line, and drifts out of the air lock.

Rexx turns back to the shuttle and squeezes through the opening into the pod. The membrane seals with a seamless, pressurized hiss. The inside of the pod is a honeycomb of biolum panels and hexscreens. A design

that Fabergé might have come up with for an autocrat
with a bee fetish. He wriggles into the g-mesh and fas-
tens the restraints. Rubs at the tension in his cheeks,
shoulder muscles knotted under his coat of skin.

"You can't be serious," Claire says.

"About what?"

"Going to the surface."

Rexx's hands begin to shake. He presses his fingers to
his eyes. Algae blooms of actinic purple and red flash
under the pressure.

Surface tension, he thinks. Tightening its grip.


"You're no different than anyone else here," Pilar
Atienza once said. "You pretend to be, but you're not."

Rexx floated in her office, not bothering to clip himself into a fixed seat. He didn't plan to stay long.
"How's that?"

Outside the window behind the gyroscope assemblage of her desk, the lightdomes and greenhouse geo-
desics of the arcology descended in steps to the Tiresias
icescape and one of the original warm-blooded plants
inhabited by the first colonists.

"You're still running," she said.

"From what?"

"Not *what*. *Who*."

A solcatcher petal flared, blue, then red, over the fish-
eye curve of the horizon. "The only person I ever ran
from was Myrtle Bumgardner in the first grade."

Pilar tilted her head and cocked an eye at him. "Oh
really?"

"I'm happy with myself just the way I am." Rexx
pulled on his neck scrotum and stretched it obscenely.

An amused shake of her head. "You are not a clown,
Rexx. You're not fooling anyone except yourself."

Jelana had had a similar way of chiding him, haranguing him in small, suggestive ways. Her tone unfailingly bright and unimpeachable, as carefully tailored and immune to reproach as a designer dress.

"What you're sayin' is, the joke's on me."

"Yes. I'm afraid you're in for one hell of a punch line." Pilar gestured toward the window. "Do you know why most people come here?"

"The weather?"

Pilar smiled. "They want to escape. The clades, poverty, a bad relationship. The past. They think the plants will change them, that having a different body chemistry will make everything different, better somehow. That *they* will be different—better."

Was she talking about the White Rain? Was that why she had asked him here? Rexx didn't see how. Unless the RNA was activated, it looked normal on a biomed scan. And the drug itself was masked. He'd been careful to conceal it.

Rexx let go of the pinched flap of skin. "I don't want to escape," he said. "I just want to forget."

The tremor in his hands is worse, and with it the detached, unsettling sensation of prosthetic manipulation. Fingers shaking, he calls up the Philco Predicta and switches on the power.

The program interface is slow to load. Longer than the two-second time delay from Tiresias. When the TV finally comes online, the screen is scratched with static and scuffed by images. Voices ghost his thoughts, a faint monochromatic murmur.

*"Mathieu! Get down! Get away from there!"*

*"But Mom said—"*

*"I don't care what your mother said!"*

*"—it's not dangerous."*

A fuzzy, indistinct face turns to look at Rexx from out of the screen. The boy is standing on a split-rail fence. He's wearing a white cowboy hat and silver-spurred boots.

Rexx twists his hand to the right, sees the virtual volume knob rotate in response to the command.

Nothing happens.

*"Dad?" Mathieu's face puckered in consternation as the animals in the petting zoo shied away. "How come the animals don't like me? Are they afraid of me?"*

Rexx increases the volume.

A horse appears in the background, blurred, trotting toward the fence.

*Where was the clown? Every rodeo he'd ever been to had a clown. There was supposed to be a clown.*

Rexx logs out of the program. Sweat trembles on his upper lip, percolates through the tributary of wrinkles on his forehead.

The squirt failed. Instead of a pleasant downpour he's suffering a sudden drought, the immediate result of which is a parched migraine in his left temple. He needs to find a lab. In a lab he can manually activate the riboswitch.

The station makes the most sense. But Kerusa would never authorize it. Even if he manages to convince Yalçin to help, iDNA sensors on the station will report his presence and there will be hell to pay.

That leaves Mymercia. It's a twenty-minute trip. If what Yalçin said about Hjert is accurate, he should be able to find what he needs there.

\*   \*   \*

"Talk to me," Rexx says, halfway through the five-kilometer flight.

"About what?"

"Anything." Anything to distract him from the nausea and the slow loss of equilibrium that's leaking out of his inner ear, like air from a balloon. "Mymercia. What can you tell me about it?"

"Unlike most KBOs," the IA says, "which are solid water, Mymercia is composed of approximately seventy percent rock and thirty percent water. This ratio is similar to Pluto's. But because Mymercia is smaller than Pluto it's more dense/planetlike. Closer to what one would expect for Earth."

Rexx leans his head back and listens as much to the soothing mechanical drone of the words as the content. The white noise equivalent of methadone, good enough to take the edge off the dry thrombosis in his skull.

The planetoid is small, barely thirty kilometers in diameter at its widest point, and has a number of albedo features, bright and dark regions on the surface. The bright areas are ice. The dark areas are the result of organic material and photochemical reactions caused by gamma rays. The surface temperature varies between −235° C in the brightest regions and −210° C in the darkest. The arcology has been built in deep central rima, or fissure. The bottom three-quarters of the fissure is filled with ice, a four-kilometer-deep frozen lake.

"The biggest question/issue," Claire says, "is the KBO's age—around six billion years—and the origin of the complex/organic molecules in the surface ice. Part of the reason for establishing an arcology on Mymercia, in addition to easing population pressure on Tiresias and Petraea, is to determine where the object came from."

\* \* \*

The transition from moving toward an asteroid to "falling" as the shuttle pod touches down, catapults him into a dizzy tailspin. It takes a few minutes for his brain to reset. It doesn't help that the horizon is more myopic and foreshortened than Tiresias's, as if he's looking at it through the lens of a high-power magnifying glass.

To squelch his vertigo, Rexx focuses his attention on the arcology. The construction site is lit by an array of biolum Kliegs. In the monochrome green of the panels, he can make out a circular catena of smaller satellite domes around the central lightdome. The size of a cathedral dome, it sits in the middle of a hollow depression, bounded on one side by the fissure and on the other by a hogback ridge punctuated with several knoblike hills. Beyond this, the long shallow depression turns into a small convex plain that curves into blackness. The next structures to become visible are those parts of the cliff-face arcology that rise above the rim of the canyon. Mainly the flat-topped shuttle pad towers—three squat, stemlike cylinders with window perforations, most of them dark, that accommodate much of the colony's commercial space and provide access to the rest of the arcology. Residential quarters are in the tiered balconies that jut out from the rock. The industrial, agricultural, and public service sectors are located underground, deep in the hollowed-out bowels of the asteroid.

"Prepare to dock," Claire says.

Rexx takes out the tinted ampoule, uncaps the atomizer, and sprays himself with rose-scented nanofoam. The foam is sticky. It spreads quickly, dissolving his existing clothing and covering his skin with a translucent film. The biosuit encases him from head to toe. Piezoelectrics take shape in the pearlescent sheen, followed by a resham pattern of thermoelectrics.

The top of one of the landing towers has expanded into a disk, as flat and dull as a tarnished penny. Under the makeshift landing lights, he sees a radial array of individual docking stations, antherlike clinodomes that open to admit a shuttle pod then close again. The airtight membrane between the carbyne frame supports is veined with a circuit board network of biolum threads, diamondoid fibers, and molectronic filaments as iridescent as abalone.

No one meets him as he exits the shuttle pod. The air is stale and humid, strangely fetid. Sweat beads on his brow, tickles his underarms.

There are no magnetic flux lines to guide him. He has to push off from the shuttle pod to approach a hexagon sealed with an algae-spotted membrane that looks like plastic food wrap that's gone moldy.

"I'm sorry," the portal says, reading his iDNA profile. "You are not authorized to enter. Please contact customs for clearance. Thank you for your cooperation."

Doors are the worst bureaucrats. "Have you been able to get in touch with Hjert?" Rexx asks Claire.

"No. You have a message from Kerusa."

"Fuck him. He's shit on a bootheel. Right now, I'm more interested in talking to Hjert."

"One moment."

A beat later the structural engineer comes online. Her face pixelates on the inside of his eyescreens, an unsteady flitcam image of platinum hair loops, gold neck rings, and sepia lips pressed tight and thin. "What's going on? What the hell you think you're doing, coming down here like this?"

Rexx amps up the signal strength of the datastream

so he can see her more clearly against the background image of the air lock. "I thought I'd give you a hand."

Her eyes anneal, hard and shiny as brass rivets. "That's not what Kerusa says."

"Kerusa wouldn't know a gift horse if it kicked him in the ass."

"Is that what you're doing?"

"No. Personally I couldn't care less about his ass. Right now I'm more interested in getting into a lab and figuring out what's killing off your plants."

Her image jitters as she lets out a breath. Her face inflates, and then shrinks as the datafeed shifts from one flitcam to another. "Kerusa wants you arrested."

"Kerusa's a prick."

"How do I know you're not?"

"Look at me"—Rexx hefts the sacks of flesh hanging from his arms—"I haven't screwed anyone in years."

It doesn't get a laugh, but her expression relaxes. She has a no-nonsense, down-to-earth 'tude that puts him at ease. He can see why Yalçin likes her. She doesn't have the time or the desire for bullshit.

"You gonna let me in? Or do I get to rot with the rest of this place?" He waves a hand at the sporadic patches of slime. The air lock is starting to take on the look and feel of a dirty aquarium. Despite the biosuit, Rexx imagines slime building up on the inside of his lungs, like black sludge forming on a mildewed sink drain.

With quick finger strokes, Hjert taps out a virtual command. She looks as if she's just come from a construction site. Her hand is gloved with nanimatronic mesh the color of chain mail. She's wearing a heavy-duty exoskeleton over her biosuit, a utility belt with servo and propulsion jacks, and a pair of thick boots with claw-sharp pincers on the sides for grabbing and cutting.

"I'll meet you in the lower atrium in thirty minutes," she says, glancing up. "I just squirted your IA the location."

"Thanks." Rexx grins. "I appreciate—"

Her face vanishes, snuffed out in a flurry of black static. He readjusts the opacity on his eyescreens, increasing the gain on the realtime image of the air lock as the softseal membrane covering the hexagon thins and disappears.

"Welcome to Mymercia," the door chirps, toggling into tourist information mode. "Enjoy your visit."

"I will. I'm startin' to feel at home already."

"If you have any questions, please feel free to contact me at any time."

"I'll do that." Rexx grips the chrome-anodized frame around the hexagon and pulls himself through into a narrow magtube. The access shaft is as cramped as the birth canal of a pregnant guernsey.

*"Put your hand in," his father said. "All the way. To the elbow."*

*The cow squirmed, hot and slick against his arm.*

*"Now you know everything there is to know about the female sex," his father said, "including your mother."*

Rexx breathes past a sharp jackhammer throb in the side of his head. Huffs and puffs his way to a dimly lighted cylinder a hundred meters away. Without magnetic flux lines, he keeps bumping into the walls, a slow-motion carom from side to side. For some reason, the design team didn't include handholds. The walls and biolum panels are smooth. Finally, the tube opens into a spacious vertical shaft, diamond walled and with a chrome frame. Side tubes lead to darkened gift shops, clothing stores, restaurants, and VRcades. Some of the partition walls have been left clear, either for window shopping or a view of the asteroid, while others are textured, tinted, or charcoal gray, devoid of logos, news, advertisements. Without them, the place feels like a tomb. Even the chapel where Jelena and Mathieu were buried felt more alive, with its religious music, aromatherapeutic pherions, and huge selection of online inspirationals available in text or audio. Classic Hi Rev revival sermons, Hip Gnosis meditations, and Jesuette pep cheers.

"Directions?" he asks Claire.

"Down, to level one."

Easier said than done. He grips a burnished aluminum trellis, encrusted with dead violinette blossoms, and kicks off into the jungle of dry, scaly shadows.

# 15

## THE BLUE LADY SINGS

Night vomits him up. Spits him out like a hairball, half-digested by exhaustion. Wet on the outside, dry on the inside. Loose sprayons wrinkled, scratchy with dried salt.

L. Mariachi rolls onto his back. Lets out a congested groan. Halitosis clenches his tongue in a death grip. His left hand aches, a relentless symphony of pain. The tips of his right fingers throb, drumbeat steady under a warbling high note shrill enough to strip the dried saliva and enamel from his teeth. It's the same pain he felt the night his left hand was trashed. Had it been worth it? Had the brief, momentary high been worth the long, lingering low?

*Simón!* Hell, yes! At least he knew what it was like to be free. He had been there once. Walked those streets. Breathed that air.

He feels cleansed, sated. Made whole by the music in

a way he'd never been with a woman. Both had maimed him. There was always a price. But he wouldn't trade his hand for anything. It was impossible to walk away from the world unscathed. To be born is to live in pain. Even Jesus suffered at the end.

The gray press of air against his face still reeks of stale cigarette smoke and incense. In addition to his own labored breathing, he can make out quiet exhalations. Low and relaxed, soothing in their peaceful regularity.

Lejandra. The woman is still alive. Amazing. It's a miracle she didn't suffocate from all the airborne carcinogens Doña Celia dosed her with.

L. Mariachi lifts a hand to rub the puffiness from his eyes, and bangs his knuckles on the body of the guitar. It's resting on the floor next to him, half under the nubbly wool blanket draped across the lower half of his body.

He starts to sit, but midway up a spike of pain punctures the top of his skull. He collapses back to the hard lichenboard floor, clutching the neck of the guitar. Runs one lacerated fingertip along a string between the frets, counting out notes as if they were beads on an abacus.

Shit. With his luck the *bruja* will think he stole the guitar and punish his ass. Just what he needs: a *chizo* of white worms, pebbles, or greasy hair in his stomach. Still it's nothing compared to his hand.

It's hard to believe she would leave without it. Maybe she intends to come back, to check on the woman, and will pick it up then.

A wave of dizziness engulfs him. He rolls back onto his side and vomits up a watery strand of drool. The floor dutifully sponges the bile up. Deodorizers rush to the scene, but not before he gets a fetid whiff of bile-frothed beer.

"I warned you," Num Nut says, chortling in his cochlear imp.

L. Mariachi eases himself gingerly onto his back and stares up at the ceiling. The pain in his left hand reverberates inside his head. A migraine splash of entoptics roils on the dimmed biolum panels. "What time is it?"

"Four-thirty."

Great. He has to be at the vat facility in less than two hours. "I could use a little help, if you don't mind."

"I can't dispense any more painkiller."

When he opens his eyes, the entoptics taunt him, a nauseating rumba. "Why not?"

"You aren't authorized to access today's ration of nonprescription meds until after six A.M."

His official clock-in time. He'll just have to hitch up his cojones and grit it out until then.

He rolls onto his side, scoots the guitar closer, and rests one side of his face on the cool wood.

"Hello?"

L. Mariachi freezes, as if the room has turned to glass and will shatter at the least bit of movement. The source of the voice, buzzing and tinny against his cheek, seems to be the hole in the soundboard of the guitar.

"I hope you can hear me."

L. Mariachi sits up fast. He must be in worse shape than he realized. Either that or Num Nut—perhaps some other *macañema*—is messing with him. "Very funny," he mutters.

If it *is* his IA, there's not much he can do. It's not like he can afford an upgrade or a replacement.

He digs a finger into his ear to clear it . . . and wonders if the voice isn't the result of his binge or a practical joke but rather something in the cigarette smoke or the antiphers that the gangstas dosed him with. Whatever it is, it can't be legit. In which case, he's hosed. As soon as he reports for work, sniffers at the vat will flag any illegal pherions that he's been exposed to.

It's a no-win situation. If he shows up, he's screwed. If he doesn't show up, he's screwed.

"My name is Fola," the guitar says. "I know how this must sound. But just listen to me for a second."

The guitar gapes at him. In the darkness it looks like a *boca*—a yawning toothless mouth. Chipped, wear-polished wood for lips.

"I need you to play a song," the guitar goes on.

L. Mariachi shakes his head, grins at his idiocy. The guitar has a built-in program to put together a playlist. Nothing more. "*¿Que quieres?*" he says. "What do you want? Which song?"

There's a pause, a hiccup in the battered circuitry. "'SoulR Byrne.'"

L. Mariachi coughs out a laugh. He can't believe it. The guitar is old—probably close to his age—but to randomly choose that song . . .

He shakes his head in disbelief. Holds up the thrashed tips of his fingers. "In case you haven't noticed, I can't play shit right now."

"If you don't play the song, Lejandra is going to die. So are a lot of other innocent people around the world."

Which sounds more like a threat than a request. But that could just be the way the software was programmed. Melodramatic.

"A lot of people are getting sick," the guitar says. "There's an outbreak of some kind, and the song could help them . . . make them better."

"SoulR Byrne." The song follows him around like a mongrel dog. No matter how many times he kicks it, the damn thing keeps coming back. Digging up the guilt he tried to bury years ago.

"Please?"

"Sure," he says. "No problem." That seems to do the trick. The guitar falls silent. End of request. He waits for a relapse. But the silence stretches, becomes less tentative with each passing second.

He leans forward, resting his elbows on unsteady knees, and props his head in his hands as a clammy tremble runs through him. Sweat sluices down his rib cage and queasy stomach, collects like a dewdrop in his belly button as a line from the song whispers through him.

" 'When I'm fine'ly gone, it's a fore_gone conclusion you're gonna cry. . . .' "

. . . Renata, he thinks.


"Do you want to get a bite to eat?" he asked, his mouth dry.

It was late, after two in the morning. The last show at the Seraphemme ended an hour ago. The band was gone, the crowd had dispersed, and the club was slowly winding down. Everyone on the wait staff and clean-up crew was wobbly, giddy with excitement or fatigue as they called it a night. Outside the club, the street was still alive, jam-packed with neon storefronts, cafés, kiosks, bars, and hologram-animated fast-food franchises, all jostling for advertising space and clamoring for attention.

He'd never asked her out before. After work, they had always gone their separate ways. This was the first time he'd worked up the nerve. He'd always been too afraid—worried she'd turn him down cold or that he'd ruin their friendship.

The problem was, he didn't want to be just friends.

He liked her . . . a lot. She was upbeat and talkative, but not a *boca*. She didn't gossip about people behind their back or put them down. Wasn't critical or judgmental. Always tried to see the good in people, no matter what. Even her ice queen sister and narcissist brother.

"Isabelle has a good heart, she's just been hurt a lot," or, "I think it's cute how my brother thinks he's the second coming of Don Juan."

As a result he never felt tongue-tied around her. Unlike all of the other *chavalas* who worked at the Seraphemme, she actually listened to him, seemed interested in what he was saying beyond mere politeness. He didn't have to pretend he was someone he wasn't. He could confide in her without fear of ridicule. The nice thing was that they didn't always have to talk. They could be quiet together, too. Comfortable silences that didn't beg to be filled.

She was vulnerable, too. Not weak or anything, but sensitive. Caring. She wasn't an *apretada*, a holier-than-thou saint—she liked to mosh it up on the dance floor as much as anyone—but there was something sweet and innocent about her. Pure. Which she caught a ton of grief about from some of the down-on-the-world *bacalaos* who freelanced as *putas* when they weren't dishing out food or tending bar.

"We could go to Vallartas," he said. "Share some nachos." Vallartas was a casual taquería. Low budget. Nothing too serious.

She shook her head. "I can't." Fiber-optic bangs sashayed across her face in a luminous curtain, as if he was looking at her through a window. Behind the illusion of glass, her lashes, decorated with exotic moth-wing appliqués, opened and closed. "Sol is picking me up."

Javier Solaff, who required more positive spin than any two standard-issue losers combined. It seemed

that she was always making excuses, justifications, or
rationalizations for his behavior, normally centered
around why she stayed with him. She worked hard at it,
sometimes to the point of exasperation and tears. It
made L. Mariachi think he had a chance. That maybe
she would finally get fed up with her current situation.

"I thought he worked graveyard." From what Renata
had told him, the *chavo* was a vat rat at a local hydroponics pharm. Worked 9:00 P.M. to 5:00 A.M., harvesting
fruit in the cool of the night.

"Usually he does." Renata cut an anxious glance
past him, searching the street. "But tonight he's getting
off early." She was flushed with excitement, her cheeks
glowing with anticipation. Radiant under the phalanx
of umbrella palms that lined the street, reflecting back
the lights and her bright mood.

Just his luck. His timing couldn't be worse. For
weeks, months, she had podded home alone. Tonight
her boyfriend decided to give her a lift. It was like the
guy was telepathic—could sense another *tiguere* sniffing
around his territory.

"I'm sorry," she said, touching him lightly on the arm.
She didn't want to hurt his feelings. "Maybe we could do
it some other time." She was just being polite. Even if
they did go out, it would just be as friends. That much
was clear. She liked him the same way she liked her
brother.

"There he is." Her hand darted up, revealing the beautiful clamshell hollow of her armpit. "Sol!" she called.
"Over here!"

Sol. Bulging with muscles and confidence, but otherwise low-wattage. The kind of *cabrón* that caused the

*güebos* of self-conscious, insecure types to shrivel up and crawl away in humiliation and despair.

He slipped a possessive arm around Renata's hourglass waist and squeezed her the way he would a stuffed animal.

"This is L. Mariachi," she said, by way of introduction.

"Your musician friend." The *cabrón* extended his free hand. "*Oye ese. Que hay de nuevo?*"

"Not much."

Sure enough, the guy's grip was a bone crusher, as much a challenge as a greeting. Like a peacock spreading its tail, advertising its superiority.

When he let go, L. Mariachi could still feel the pressure of his fingers. Beyond his good looks and age, twenty-something, he wasn't sure what Renata saw in the *chavo*. Sure, he was probably experienced in bed. But ambition and intelligent conversation did not seem to be his strong points.

He didn't want to think less of Renata. For her sake, he tried to tell himself that there must be more to the guy than met the eye, or she wouldn't be with him.

There was an awkward silence. He felt like a third leg . . . a useless appendage that had suddenly grown out of the two of them.

"Well," he finally said to Renata. "I guess I'll see you tomorrow."

"Yeah." She smiled, apologetic but not regretful.

"Nice meeting you," Sol said.

L. Mariachi bit his tongue. Remained polite for her sake, and kept his resentment to himself.

"Ditto," he said.

He watched them walk away until they were swallowed up by the street crowd and the neon. His face was burning, scalded by the overabundance of light that brought tears to his eyes. A pressure valve for the anger and hatred building inside him, like steam in a teakettle crying for release.

L. Mariachi shakes his head. No way he's going to play the song. What good will it do, digging up garbage he tossed years ago? It's just a song. It had been a commercial success but a private failure. It never solved anything.

"You okay?"

The whisper comes from the direction of the bed, not the guitar. He turns toward the woman, who is watching him with fever-glazed eyes.

"You sick?" she says.

"No."

"You're not what I expected." Her eyes dilate, the albino-pale whites expanding. "I thought you'd be . . ."

"Hungover?" he says.

"No. Flashier." Her attention drifts to the guitar, then back. "You seem . . . normal. For a *rockero,* I mean."

"That was a long time ago."

"You've changed?"

He shrugs.

"Everyone does, I guess." She holds up one hand, with its exoskeleton of charcoal bruise lines. "Not always by choice, or the way we want."

"You seem better," he says.

"Do I?"

"Do you feel better?"

She lowers her hand to the sheet, fingers splayed. "Different."

Her face is luminous. Thin lips set in moonlit bone.

Thick lashes, as black as the wings of some nocturnal moth. Extinct but no less alluring.

"You're staring," she says.

"Sorry. I was thinking of someone I knew."

Her head cants on the pillow, quizzical. "Do I remind you of her?"

"Not really." Part of his mind is redrawing the present with the past. Connecting imagined dots to create a mirage.

"Where is she now?" Lejandra says.

"Dead." Maybe now the conversation will end.

She wheezes, a stillborn chuckle. Forces a smile. "I'm glad I don't remind you of her. It's probably for the better."

L. Mariachi reaches for the guitar.

"Do you miss her?" Lejandra says.

He stops, his hand on the neck of the guitar, fingers pressing into the frets. Hard. For some reason he can't walk away, can't not answer. He's trapped, held hostage . . . not by her but by some need in himself. To confess? To pass on what he's learned over the years?

"You must miss her," she says. "Or you wouldn't be thinking about her."

"Not necessarily." Guilt, he thinks. Remorse. Anger. Shame. The list is a long one. Too long. "It's complicated."

"I understand more than you think."

"I used to think I understood everything, too. When I was younger."

"But not anymore."

"No." He relaxes his grip on the guitar.

"Did you love her?"

"Love looks different over time," he says. "In the beginning it's one thing. At the end it's another. You'll see."

Lejandra closes her eyes, the lashes falling into place like funeral veils. "Did she hurt you? Did you hurt her?"

Yes, he thinks. But not on purpose.

A door opens down the hallway, thumps shut. The bathroom. Water runs, a faint capillary gurgle through air-clogged tubing.

"I should tell the others you're awake." He pushes to his feet, discovers that he's picked up the guitar without thinking. Habit. Other than the bed, there's no place to set it down.

"Thank you for coming." Her eyes flutter open. "For playing. I hope it wasn't too much trouble."

"No problem." He edges toward the door.

"I'm glad we had a chance to talk."

"Take care," he says. "*Vaya con Dios.*"

He meets Isabelle in the hallway. Her hair is damp where she splashed water on her face.

"She's awake," he says.

Isabelle blinks. "She's better?"

"I think so. I talked to her just now."

"My God!" Isabelle clasps his left hand in hers, stiffens when she feels the gnarled lump of bone, but hangs on. "Thank you!" she says, exhaling.

"I didn't do anything. It's Doña Celia you should thank. Here." He holds out the guitar.

Isabelle releases her grip and shakes her head. "She wanted you to have it."

"But I don't want it."

"She said to be sure you took it with you." Isabelle takes a step back, away from the guitar. "You have to take it. If you don't . . ."

Her voice trails away. There's no need to finish. They both know the consequences of failing to comply with the wishes of a witch. Any number of calamities are possible, including a sudden relapse of Lejandra's condition. If he doesn't accept the guitar and Lejandra gets worse, he'll be held responsible. The only sure way to avoid getting blamed is to follow instructions.

No way he can say no. Not only would he be crossing a witch, he'd have to deal with the wrath of João and one or two dozen compadres of Balta and Oscar— bored gangstas looking for someone to take out all their frustration and anger on. It's not worth it. Besides, he's not that cold-blooded. He couldn't live with himself if he dirty-dicked the woman at this point.

He withdraws the guitar. "Why does she want me to have it? Did she tell you?"

"No. Maybe as payment." She slides past him, anxious to see Lejandra.

"Am I free to go?" he says.

She stops just before the door, puzzled. "Why wouldn't you be?" And then she's gone.

Just like that, they're going to let him leave? They aren't worried that he's going to report them? File a complaint with the *jefe* or BEAN?

The guitar feels suddenly heavier. A cross he's been asked to carry. Doña Celia has a reason for giving it to him. He's sure of it. Some ulterior motive or problem she's decided to pawn off on him. The thing is, he's stuck. If he keeps it, he's going to get caught up in the trouble the witch is trying to avoid. If he gets rid of it, there will be hell to pay with her.

Either way, it's a lose-lose proposition.

L. Mariachi heads home in the predawn light, dragging the guitar with him like a ball and chain. The EZ is still lit up, but the biolums are fading as the sky lightens in the east. Night peeling away from the horizon, like a

bruised eyelid, to expose the onset of day. Bloodshot
and bleary.

He stumbles past a club called Phallacies. It has the
blue liquid crystal outline of a *güera*, a naked siren,
flickering on the beige stucco facade. Voluptuous hips
and breasts jerking from side to side with repetitive,
strobelike precision. Residual pherions hang in the
turgid air, conjure up an internal salsa beat and the urge
to dance. An ad virus tickles the heel of his left hand,
giving rise to a temporary tattune just beneath the skin
and a whiff of spicy, deep-fried soytein.

He turns away. Stumbles when the *güera* speaks to
him. "One other thing," she says. The voice from the
guitar, serrated with the electric buzz of the sign. The
blue LCD sputters, flickers like candlelight on his hands
and the front of the guitar, imbuing it with a votive glow.

The Blue Lady. He can see her image burning in the
grain of the wood. No different from the one branded
into his retinas one night, nearly half a century ago,
when he needed her the most. He thought the Blue Lady
was lost in the past, as dead to him as scar tissue. When
he turned twelve, the power of her name and its ability
to protect him from the evil of the barrio had shrunk
with the years and his loss of faith. For a while, he even
believed that there had been no Blue Lady, that she was
simply the product of his imagination. A childhood fantasy realized only in VRcade games. Later, he decided
that the Blue Lady lived in every woman. If he looked
hard enough, or long enough, he would eventually find
her. All he had to do was keep an open mind and he
would recognize her in whatever form she took.

Now, after all this time, she has come back.

"Who is the song for?" she says.

He finds himself on his knees, gazing up at the sign,

hands clasped to his chest. "You want me to play again. Is that why you're here? Is that why the *bruja* gave me the guitar?"

The buzzing intensifies, distraught. "You must have written it for a reason."

"Why now?" he asks. "After all these years."

The liquid crystal screen falters. Undergoes a series of apoplectic palpitations and then flutters out in a fit of hyperventilation.

"Wait." L. Mariachi raises a hand. "Don't go."

No answer. The *güera* has fallen suddenly mute. He picks up the guitar, strums a few chords, but the music fails to resuscitate her.

He feels like an idiot speaking directly to a guitar—a total *pendejo*. "I'll wait for you this time. I promise."

Not like before. He was never sure who left who. If he abandoned her, or if it was the other way around.

# 16

## COUNTERFEIT CACHE

According to Pheidoh, the legend of the Blue Lady was born in Miami at the end of the last millennium. Rumor on the streets had it that a war was being waged between demons from hell, who lived on the evil feelings in people—hatred, jealousy, fear—and angels from heaven who drew their sustenance from light, the pinks, greens, and blues of neon signs. The demons had found gateways into the world: broken mirrors, cars with black-tinted windows, and TVs tuned to a violent program. The angels were trying to keep them at bay, stop them from killing people and taking over the world.

The most powerful demon, feared even by Satan, was Bloody Mary. The leader of the demons cried blood, laughed when an innocent person died, and urged children to kill each other. She carried a red rosary as a weapon, and used it to whip kids before murdering them.

Allied with the homeless children against her was the Blue Lady. Yemana. That was her secret name. The street kids believed that if a child knew her real name, the Blue Lady had the power to save them. From bullets, drugs, or physical abuse.

"If something terrible was about to happen," the IA tells Fola, "all a child had to do was call for the Blue Lady and they wouldn't be harmed."

The Blue Lady came from the ocean. She had pale blue skin and wore a blue robe. When she wasn't battling demons in the streets of Miami, she and the other angels hid in the Everglades, protected by emerald palm trees and giant alligators. If a child died, that was where she went, because God had fled heaven and no one knew where He was. The Blue Lady was magic. She could bring cooling rain, ease pain with a touch, and cause a flower to bloom.

"Sometimes it was enough." Pheidoh adjusts the white pith helmet with one hand. "Often it wasn't."

Bloody Mary had special abilities, too. One ability, the worst, was to turn the soul of a good person bad. It could be a brother or a sister, a friend, or a parent. It was always someone close. Someone trustworthy.

The person would feel claws scratching under their skin, then their fingers would turn to red flames. That was how you knew they were lost, that they had been captured by the demons. . . .

"The only way not to be taken over by Bloody Mary," Pheidoh finishes, "was to do good. *Be* good. Every little bit of good helped the angels. And if you died you wouldn't be captured by the demons. Your soul would go to the Everglades to live with the angels."

Fola stares at the desiccated, human-shaped saguaro that represents Lejandra. The upraised arms are freckled with tiny holes where the flowers that would normally represent her clade-profile have died and been replaced with quantum dots. "L. Mariachi was a street kid?" she says.

"For a while. In Mexico City."

Mexico City has whole communities that are nothing but glorified street gangs. An entire subculture of orphans and runaways. "The Blue Lady helped him survive?"

"Mostly by giving him hope, resolve." Pheidoh pauses. Then, "Do you believe in evil?"

"It's hard not to."

"Do you believe that it's possible for good to come from bad . . . or bad from good?"

"The road to hell," Fola says. "Good intentions."

Pheidoh takes out a pocket watch and checks the time. "He still hasn't played the song."

"Are you sure?" It's been over ten hours since she sent her message. "Maybe he did, and nothing happened."

"No. I'd know if he did."

"I told you he wouldn't listen to me."

The IA replaces the watch. "You have to talk to him again."

Fola's beginning to think that Bloody Mary isn't the only IA that's tweaked. Her thoughts cycle back to the healing ceremony. "How exactly is Bloody Mary rewiring people?" At the rate things are going, figuring out how the quanticles work seems like a more productive course of action than the dubious prospect of persuading L. Mariachi to strum a few chords.

"It's complicated," Pheidoh says.

"So? What isn't?"

"It's easier if I show you." The IA pulls out a gargan-
tuan magnifying glass and moves it close to a flower on
the topiary figure. The petals expand, enlarged by several thousand percent. Ditto everything else in the
virtual construct, until she's surrounded by a forest of
hologram fractals.

She cranes her head, peering around at the virtual
data. The holofracts appear to be composed of multiple
images—old still photographs and scenes from movies,
television programs, news clips, commercials, and
computer-generated cartoons—that have been spliced
or grafted into some kind of Frankenstein collage. It's as
if each plant is made up of mass-mediated information
or the mediascape has taken on an organic life of its
own. Seeding, cross-pollinating, hybridizing. "What am
I looking at?"

"It's a chaotic disturbance," the IA says. "A localized
crache in the ribozone."

Whatever a crache is.

"A recombinant cache," Pheidoh explains, reading
her confusion. "An unstable dataspace where information can be exchanged and combined in different patterns . . . or modalities."

Okay. "What for?"

"To create virtual allotropes. Information or data elements that have two or more structural forms."

Which tells her next to nothing. "How does this tie
in with Lejandra and everyone else who's been infected?"

She thinks of the Sydney Greenstreet blemish. Wonders if it's spread, like the lips on the skull of the gerontocrat. If Lejandra is still alive, she tells herself, Xophia
must be too. She wasn't as sick as Lejandra.

"Molectronics can only express digital information

in the form of molecules," Pheidoh says. "The biocircuits take electronic information in the form of bits and convert the binary code into messenger RNA that ribosomes use to manufacture pherions, antiphers, and other proteins. They can't change the physical structure of the body. To do that, you have to replace normal matter with artificial matter."

"The quanticles," she says. They sound like the digital equivalent of pherions, a way to divide people into electronic clades instead of, or maybe in addition to, biological ones. No wonder the politicorps agreed to softwire people en masse. It gives them another level of control.

The IA mops invisible sweat from its brow again. "Artificial atoms can be programmed to physically express or recreate an electronic image. Similar to the way DNA expresses phenotype, the biological image of an organism."

"So how come—if the properties of artificial atoms are the same as normal atoms—the quanticles are making people sick?"

"They aren't the same. Not exactly. Because artificial atoms, and molecules, are confined to a substrate—a nanoparticle or nanofiber—they don't undergo the same chemical re-actions as normal atoms. When a nerve formed of artificial matter replaces a regular nerve, the nerve doesn't function exactly the way it used to."

"So the programmable matter is like cancer. A malignant growth that takes over and kills the tissue around it."

"In this case."

"And transmitting the song to Bloody Mary will stop her from infecting anyone else and the ecotecture."

The datahound's eyes twitch rapidly. "Yes. The process will stop."

"What about the people who are already sick? Will the quanticles inside of them continue to replicate?"

"They shouldn't."

But the IA isn't sure. Not 100 percent. It's those decimal places again and the uncertainty that lives beyond them.

The sheer amount of information streaming around her is overwhelming. It hurts to look at. She closes her eyes but can still see squirming, wriggling snippets of representational data that feel like they're trying to invade her, reconfigure her. There's a feeling of ill-defined purpose lurking just beneath the surface. A coldly calculated method to the madness that raises goose pimples on her real-world arms. She opens her eyes and rubs at the prickle of fear, trying to smooth the frayed ends of her nerves.

"Why is Bloody Mary trying to reprogram people and the environment in the first place?" Fola says. If she keeps her gaze fixed on Pheidoh's face, the staccato tangle of images is bearable. Like staring at a point on the horizon to keep from getting motion sickness. "I mean, what's the point?"

"To create something new from something old."

What is it with IAs and ontology? It's not just Pheidoh. Most of the IAs she's known have this existential fascination with pop culture, stereotypes, and gnostic aphorisms. They try them on like clothes or bad costume jewelry, looking for something that fits. As if playing a role, acting out a particular social convention, archetype, or bad cliché will impart a certain consciousness or lifestyle.

"Who exactly is Bloody Mary?" Fola says. "You said

she used to be an IA. But who is she now? What happened? How did she come about?"

The datahound wavers, a relapse of the digital tic that makes her think it's going to freeze up any second.

Instead, the explorer avatar morphs, is replaced by a likeness of Nietzsche or some other dead philosopher. She's not sure. She's never been able to keep her German angstmeisters straight. The face has a bleak monastic intensity crowned by an unruly cloud of dark hair, and black eyes, as bright and unfathomable as moonlit water. At the same time the crache dataspace collapses, and she cycles back into the ribozone garden.

" 'Don't regard a hesitant assertion as an assertion of hesitancy,' " the IA says.

"What?" She shakes her head at the non sequitur.

"Wittgenstein." The datahound inclines its head to one side and cups a hand to one ear. "You have a new message."

Her heart skips a beat. Ephraim? Xophia?

Instead, a flitcam image of Alphonse appears in a translucent window that overlays the dying sunflower of Lejandra's face.

"I just wanted to let you know that we've been ordered to help set up a quarantine zone," he says. "So the work teams on the asteroid can be evacuated."

"Here? On the station?"

Alphonse gives a brusque nod. "In the offline greenhouses. They can be hermetically sealed and isolated from the rest of the station to create temporary housing and life support."

"Is that safe? Bringing them to the station?"

"Kerusa thinks so. Besides, we don't have much choice. The teams there are running short on resources." He glances around the hexcell he's in, an entry portal to a developmental section of the greenhouses reserved for future growth. The entrance has a hardseal hatch instead of a softseal membrane. Through the thick pustule of a bubble window, she can see four parallel vat cylinders, fed by hydroponics piping, that make up a single unit. The pipes run the length of the spun diamond cylinders and feed a column of five circular biovats stacked on a central support spindle. The vats, fifty meters in diameter and ten meters high, remind her of oversize petri dishes.

"What about me?" she says. "Am I going to be put in quarantine with the others?"

"I'm not sure. As soon as I hear anything, I'll let you know."

"What will you be doing?"

"Installing sleepsacs in the vats that have already been retrofitted with temporary hexcells." Alphonse unclips a six-pack of squeeze bottles from one of the mesh pockets on his sprayon jumpsuit. The bottles are filled with milky white mucus and have a ten-centimeter hoop or ring at one end.

A distant ache Dopplers in. Low-pitched at first, growing sharper, more urgent. She misses them. Lalya's matter-of-factness. Yulong's gruffness and fear of making a mistake. Even Ephraim's negativism. She's never been entirely certain what she brings to the tuplet. By the time her input loops back to her through the others it's diluted, unrecognizable. She's no longer sure who she is, or what she is. "Where are the others?" she says. "Where's Ephraim?"

"They should be here soon," Alphonse says.

"I need to talk to Ephraim," she says. "It's important."

"We don't have much time to do the retrofit," Alphonse says. It's unclear if he's heard her or not. "Life support on the surface is failing."

Fola nibbles her lower lip. "I was interviewed by some top-level gengineer from Tiresias. Rexx. The way he talked, he was here to help fix the problem."

Alphonse nods. "He was here for a while. I guess he met with Kerusa and the ops managers."

"Where is he now?" Fola says.

"Gone," Alphonse says. "He left right after the meeting. Took off, just like that." He snaps a finger.

"How come?"

"I heard that he and Kerusa didn't see eye to eye," Alphonse says. "He wanted to do things his way instead of taking direction from the ops managers."

"Did he do *any*thing while he was here?" she asks.

"Besides pissing people off?" Alphonse's face twists in a sour grimace. "Not as far as I know."

He's the person she needs to talk to about the quanticles. With luck he might be able to help Xophia, provide her with some piece of information that will halt or slow the spread of the disease on the shuttle.

"So it looks like we're on our own," Alphonse says. "At least for now." He cuts a glance at the hatch hissing open behind him.

Through the diamond walls of the vat cylinders, Fola glimpses the movement of other tuplets, hard at work in individual tanks. Assembling carbyne frames. Connecting the frames into single modules. Shrink wrapping the individual modules with membrane insulation and then connecting them into hexcell clusters. At the accessway to one of the tubes she spots Kerusa. He's wearing a heavy-duty exoskeleton and a rugged scowl, not at all happy with something he's hearing or seeing on his wraparounds.

"Look, I have to go," Alphonse says. He drifts toward the hatch, pulled by a magnetic flux line into the core. The wall of the vat cylinder next to him is dry. Minus any warm-blooded plants, it hasn't had a chance to collect moisture or condensation. Light to the vats is provided by a fiber-optic grid that's connected to a big lightdome at one end of the cylinder. The vat he's headed toward has already been partitioned into living units. She can make out the refracted outline of hexcells. The hydroponics piping is fully operational, has been reconfigured with siptubes for drinking instead of drip lines and spray nozzles. Thin biolum strips, pasted to the frame, secrete a wan, greenish glow onto the honey yellow walls.

"I'll talk to you later," Alphonse says.

"I miss you," she says. "Take care."

But he's gone, dropped offline, and she finds her hand pressed to her chest, curled fingers hunting for the lost cross.

# 17

## IN MEDIA REZ

You don't look well." The structural engineer glides half a meter to one side of him, as effortless as a largemouth bass in a quiet pool of water.

Rexx waves a hand. He's breathing heavily, as much from the tourniquet-tight biosuit as exertion. Smart fabric typically autosized by computing the total surface area of skin to be covered. But with so many loose folds and wrinkles to factor into the equation, the suit has apparently miscalculated. The bubble helmet is fishbowl tight and his head pounds. "I'll be fine," he says. "Soon as I get to a lab."

"I hope so," Hjert says. "The last thing I need right now is more deadweight. Here"—she hands him a mesh utility belt with a high-intensity work light and a half dozen $CO_2$ cartridges—"you'll need this."

"You always this hospitable?" He has to unfurl the belt to its full length to buckle it around his waist.

"No. You caught me on one of my good days."

"I guess I ought to count my blessings."

"If I were you, I'd wait until they hatched."

Wheezing, he struggles to keep up with her as they navigate the magtube that leads from the docking tower to the main cliffside facade of the arcology. In the absence of magnetic flux lines he has to guide himself using the joint rings and sections of curved aluminum grating.

"Where we headed?" he says.

"Ground zero."

"The esplanade?" That was where Liam Vitt and the others died.

Hjert shakes her head. "That was a secondary failure. The primary failure occurred in the main power plant. You want samples, you'll find plenty to choose from there. Hell—you might even become one. Save yourself the trouble of going back for seconds."

With a quick finger tap he switches com channels and onlines his IA. "I'd like to look at a schematic of the colony."

"Elevation or plan?" Claire's voice crackles, prickly with static.

"Both."

"I'll squirt you . . . file . . . then streaming."

"Why all the noise?"

". . . count . . . interference. Security filter . . . you."

A pair of datawindows appears on the inside of his eyescreens, one etched in blue lines, the other in red. His location is marked by a green blip. The power plant, located deep inside the asteroid, gathers energy from a variety of sources: solar, acoustic, piezoelectric, thermal. Even the network of lightdomes throughout the arcology route a part of the scant radiation they collect to the core plant for storage and redistribution. According to the schematics, access to the power plant is through a single vertical shaft, located directly below the main dome.

Rexx notes that the biolabs are a couple of levels up from the power facility, located in a sector that's labeled Research. He switches from Claire to Hjert. "Anything else you can tell me about the system failures?"

"Whatever's causing them spends a lot of time datamining stuff in the mediasphere. Or has, in the past."

"You're talkin' about the images we're seein' on the newstreams from Earth."

"Right. It's like an ad virus has gotten out of control and is randomly spreading tattunes and old graffitics. Except that it's not confined to people. The entire ecotecture is susceptible. And the tattunes don't go away after a few hours. They stick around and evolve."

"Evolve?"

"You know. Change, grow . . . *deform*."

"How do you know the problem is spreading randomly?"

"Because we can't model it." Her voice becomes suddenly tinny. "The behavior is random, chaotic."

They enter one of the eight barrel-vault esplanades cantilevered out from the cliff face. The view of the canyon through the colonnade's sheet-diamond windows is spectacular. A panorama of X-ray– and gamma-ray–illuminated rock and ice. Framed in white marble, each window is thirty meters wide by fifty meters high. Rexx glances up at the long, semicircular vault, where dead withered vines dangle from the carbyne structure like ripped-out electrical wires. The light-gathering lenses are shriveled and cataract-blind, clouded with ice. Curled bananopy leaves float in the vacuum, frozen and brittle, no longer attached to their anchor roots. A hoar of blackened, desiccated lichen clings to the capitals of the Corinthian columns, encrusts the florid Art Nouveau mural done in multicolored tile.

On the cliff side of the esplanade, built into rock as smooth and reflective as polished glass, the dim privacy screens, balconies, and patios of multilevel apartments. Bare trellis awnings and railings, devoid of vegetation, glint in the gray half-dark. Ditto the elevated veranda at the far end, where the palapas that cover the park's seats and tables are little more than stick-ribbed umbrellas.

Not far from the veranda, next to a planter box littered with the stubs of burned-out circuitrees, a foam patch scabs the barrel vault.

Rexx points. "That where the accident happened?"

Hjert nods. "They were connecting the trees to the local electrical grid when the plant went down. There was a power surge."

A body appears in the daguerreotype shadows. Eyes wink and a grin flashes.

The skin on the nape of Rexx's neck crawls. He pushes off from the catwalk they're following, launching himself toward the hole and the retreating figure.

Hjert kicks after him. "Are you crazy? You rip open your suit on one of those broken joists and you're history."

Splintered sections of frame poke from around the edges of the patch like punji sticks, waiting to impale him. He reaches out. But there's nothing to grab on to, no way to slow down or change direction.

Ten meters away, and the dagger-sharp tip of a broken, shattered joist gleams in faint starlight.

"Shit." Sweat greases his neck, lubricates his armpits.

Five meters. The joist isn't just going to nick him, it's going to skewer him like a stuck, squealing pig.

Three meters. Rexx yanks his knees to his stomach, tucks his hands in to protect his chest, and somersaults forward, headfirst into the oversize nail.

Something grabs him by his left ankle, clamps down hard, and twists. He rotates sideways, arms windmilling, eyes clenched. . . .

And slams into the barrel vault. The impact shoves the air from his lungs and he deflates, going limp. He can't move, can't breathe. His mouth and eyes bulge open. All he can see are his own features reflected in the curve of his bubble helmet.

The pressure around his ankle eases. A moment later, Hjert appears in front of him. "You okay?"

Rexx works his mouth. His tongue flails.

She curses under her breath, flexes her gloved hands at him. "You're a fool, you know that? I don't know what you were thinking. What you expected to find."

His lungs unlock. He sucks in air. Tears ooze from the corners of his eyes and hang in front of his reflection.

"You keep this shit up, and you're gonna get us killed."

"I thought I saw something." He looks around, his gaze following an erratic orbit, searching for the figure.

"Like what, pray tell?"

"I don't know. Someone. A body. Maybe one of the workers who died and was never recovered."

Her pupils flare and her eyes widen, the whites gibbous. "They're gone. Trust me. There's no one here but us."

His gaze settles on a mangled section of framework, where a joist split near the end has spread apart. Seen from below, they could look like arms.

"Let's go." Hjert turns. "And no more side trips."

Rexx glances at the stick figure as he drifts past it. It was nothing, he tells himself. An optical illusion.

A breezeway at the end of the barrel vault connects the esplanade to a central elevatorlike tower that joins the cliff-face sections of the arcology to one another and to the interior space. They descend into the fissure, drawn down the vertical shaft by a few tenuous micro-g's. Shriveled palm fronds and freeze-dried schools of scutt-leaves drift in hapless clumps. Their passing leaves no wake, provokes no hint of awakening.

At the bottom of the tube, a fifty-by-fifty-meter-square tunnel bores into the heart of the asteroid. The sides function as floors, walls, or ceilings, depending on one's orientation. This is the colony's commercial dis-trict, rife with cafés, shops, restaurants, and kiosks that are set up to sell everything from arts, crafts, and cloth-ing to fast food. The chrome-and-glass storefronts are unfinished, vacant except for the pus-yellow spores that have overrun this sector of the ecotecture.

"They've spread," Hjert notes.

Rexx slows to a stop near an aggregate of spores. "How fast?" He withdraws a biopsy needle from the kangaroo pocket clipped to the front of his biosuit.

Hjert eyes the needle and hangs back, staying well out of his way. "Yesterday there were maybe half what you see now."

Rexx moves his face to within a couple of centime-ters of one sporoid, which is vaguely human shaped. Oblong, swollen, with stubby arms, legs, and head, but split down the middle.

Bread of the dead.

He shakes his head—the place has got him spooked—

raises the needle, and then pauses. Cranes his head sideways.

Viewed from the side, the bottom of the sporoid is shaped like a chin. There's even a hint of a jawline. But what really grabs his attention is the horizontal slit, which looks for all the world like a parted mouth, with vestigial lips upturned in a cryptic smile. Curved and shadowed at the corners.

"What the hell?" he mutters. He straightens, thinking that will cure the trick of light from his helmet. But the lips refuse to go away. He glances around at the other sporoids. Hundreds of little chubby bodies, all smiling at him with familiar lips . . .

"It's a *pan de los muertos* figure," his mother said, avoiding the word "doll" so he wouldn't associate it with the rest of her collection. "I bought it for your birthday."

He would be seven in two days. "Where did you get it?" The doll looked cheap—Third World.

"Oaxaca, Mexico. It's to celebrate All Souls' Day."

Rexx took the doll. It was soft, cloth sewn together by hand and stuffed with some sort of sponge. "It's fat like me," he said.

"It's not fat. It just has a big soul. Like you, its soul is too big for its body and has to get out. . . ."

"What did you find?" Hjert says, edging closer.

Rexx shakes his head. "Nothing." He biopsies the doughy figure—jabs it right in one bloated side, then backs away quickly. The smile follows him. Mysterious and secretive, Cheshire in its persistence. His skin crawls, as if he's just swallowed the worm at the bottom of a bottle of tequila.

* * *

From the business zone they enter the city center, watched over by a lightdome as big as any found in a Gothic cathedral. It stares down at the administrative and civic hub, bloodshot and rheumy, unblinking.

Government offices and spaces for other professional businesses line the outside circumference in four levels. It reminds Rexx of the Colosseum in Rome, tiered and imposing. Access tubes to each level—arranged like spokes in a wheel—radiate from a central shaft riddled with little perforations of different shapes and sizes, squares, circles, and triangles, through which he can see traffic-flow dividers, biolum panels, and trellises decorated with rattan-textured lichen and sound-absorbent moss.

"Analysis?" Rexx asks Claire. The IA should have gotten the datasquirt from the syringe by now. Instead of a geneprint and chemical composition, he streams static hiss. "Are you able to access your IA?" he asks Hjert.

"Yes. But it's platformed locally. If you try to connect to an outside datastream, you could have a problem. Kerusa's installed firewalls to limit our communications and every time they increase security our bandwidth shrinks."

They hurry on. Hjert guides him into the central magtube, through one of twelve hardseal hatches, arranged in a circle, that accesses the industrial nether-world of the colony. As they approach the power plant the magtube narrows in stages, successive cylinders within cylinders. The light from the biolum panels dims to a sickly green the color of pond scum or aquarium algae. Which tells Rexx that the sanitation systems are down. As a kid he flushed enough fungus-fuzzed gup-

pies to know a polluted closed-system environment
when he sees one.

"Here we are," Hjert says, ushering him into a huge
cube of a room. "Let's make it quick."

The dandelionlike power plant sits in the middle of a
circular colonnade of fluted support columns. Almost
thirty meters in diameter, the plant is wired to the arcology by a placenta of thick insulated wires that root it to
the floor.

Around the plant the columns and walls are covered
with a rash of images. Every square centimeter is covered in visual bricolage. The collage seethes, primordial,
with media snippets. Product logos, pictures of film and
video stars, as well as other cultural icons, the glyphs
layered like gang tags. No way to distinguish where one
graffitic ends and the next begins. A Japanese wood
print leaps out of the fray, blue water behind a white-
flowering tree. A beret-shadowed face. Lines of Sanskrit
or another ancient text scrolling across the still life of a
clown. A packet of Camel nicaffeine derms. Macabro,
the Silver Skeleton VRcade hero, rendered in pen and
ink. A smiling yellow circle with two black dots for eyes.

Ad infinitum. He could stare, entranced, for hours.

"What're you waiting for?" Hjert says. She looks
around, nervous.

Her impatience goads him. He pushes off toward one
of the fouled biolum panels. The scum on this one is
darker than the others, nearly black. As he gets closer he
can see the faint outline of an image. A shroud-of-Turin
imprint, the features blurred, not yet fully formed.

He turns to Hjert. "Are you seeing what I'm seeing?"

She squints. "I don't see anything."

"It looks like a face."

"Whose?"

"I'm not sure." Rexx biopsies the black velvet image, and then moves on to a group of snifflowers. Gengineered to collect and analyze air samples, the petuniaesque blossoms exude a sticky goo. Normally the petals are open, eager to gather any stray particles. But the blooms are crimped, pursed, as if blowing . . . well, a kiss.

"They look like lips," Rexx said.

Hjert puckers her mouth. "Maybe."

There's no maybe about it. The glossy red pucker is familiar. Rexx has seen it before. Where? He can't quite put a finger on it, can't quite get the memory to congeal.

Something from the past. His childhood. One of those early imprinted archetypes that last a lifetime. A nearby tapestree branch has a ginseng-shaped growth. Legs, hips, and a wasp-narrow waist topped by what appear to be emergent breasts.

Rexx's hand trembles, a dry rain-starved quaver. He clamps his jaw hard against a deeper convulsion, sinuous and muscular, that coils around his bowels.

Withdrawal. What his old man called the DTs, coming down from one of his binges.

"You got any results yet?" Hjert asks.

He biopsies the ginseng-shaped growth. "No. My IA's still out to lunch. I need to get to a lab. I might need to borrow your IA, too, if mine doesn't come back online. It'll only be for a few hours."

"No problem. A few hours is all you got anyway."

"What do you mean?"

"They're establishing a quarantine zone for us on the station. We've been ordered to evacuate."

"When?"

"Soon as the QZ's ready. The ops managers are guesstimating four hours. That's if everything goes well."

Which means that he has at least six hours. More, if he's one of the last citizens out of Dodge.

"All right," he says. "Let's get out of here, see what we got."

"About time."

As they head up the access tube, Rexx has the feeling they're being followed . . . or watched. He cuts a quick gotcha glance over his shoulder.

Nothing.

Still, he can't shake the feeling that something is slowly taking shape. Something that's not quite ready to reveal itself.

# 18

## LABOR RELATIONS

"*Oye, compadre*," the vat worker next to him says with a knowing wink. "You look a little tired this morning."

L. Mariachi glances at the worker. The *chavo* is pudgy, in his late twenties or early thirties, clean-shaven, with a conservative haircut, neatly trimmed mustache, and ascetic octagon-shaped eyescreens that scream intelligentsia. An academic down on his luck or researching his thesis firsthand.

"*A viente!*" L. Mariachi rasps, the retort weary but good-natured. Same to you.

He still hasn't fully recovered from the healing ceremony. His left hand throbs. So does his head, which feels as light and fragile as an eggshell. But the pherions the *patrón* is pumping into the vat have got all the vat workers feeling good despite the night of rampant parties and the inevitable hangovers. For the most part, the *braceros* are happy, upbeat, diligently working through their fatigue in a spirit of friendly cooperation and conscientious resolve.

His pall of fatigue is slower to lift—not quite as easy to shrug off as it has been in the past. He's weighted down with pain, and a shroud of uncertainty heavier than the vat waders he's wearing. Heavy cellophane pantaloons that keep his legs dry and fairly cool, but have the coefficient of drag of an oil tanker. The overhead dome magnifies the sky, turns the knee-deep, gumbo-thick effluent that fills the vat into hot, steaming soup. Sour with nutrients, it makes his eyes water and the inside of his nose burn. A few days of this, and his lungs will be scraped raw.

"I heard about the *bruja*," the *chavo* goes on. He drops a handful of sponge berries into the sieve bucket in front of him, which looks a little like a square vegetable colander attached to a conveyor belt.

The orange-and-pink berries, produced inside a gengineered species of sea sponge, are an upper-clade delicacy, the vegetable equivalent of caviar. The sponges are planted underwater in precise, evenly spaced rows one-half meter apart. The spacing is important. It maintains the optimum growing conditions for each plant, while making it possible for a line of workers to harvest the berries. Picking the berries is as much an art as it is work. Size, shape, and consistency are critical. Also, the berries bruise easily, require a delicate touch to prevent damage. Destroy too many, and a worker's wages for the day get docked. For that reason, and because the water is too deep for children under the age of thirteen, most of the pickers are women and older men.

Pedrowski is an exception, one of only four *machos* working this vat. Somehow—maybe because of the light touch he developed pushing paper around—he's landed a job most single *braceros* in their twenties covet. Not only is the ratio of men to women weighted in their favor, but the gentleness of their fingers is a major selling point, and hints at additional anatomical sensitivities.

L. Mariachi reaches underwater and slips his hand into the sponge in front of him, feeling his way along the smooth inner wall. He starts with the topmost berries, probing, touching, plucking the ones that are ripe and leaving those that aren't as he makes his way deeper, all the way to his elbow.

With a grunt he straightens, berries in hand, and sets them in his basket. "What did you hear?" He flicks water from his hand, at the same time signing open a datawindow on his wraparounds to check the bio the *chavo*'s broadcasting.

Angel Pedrowski. Married. One son, two daughters. A family man/student who's going for his doctorate in postecocaust social Lamarckism. Responsible. Not the kind of person to get sucked in by rumors, let alone spread them.

"I heard you played like a madman. Like you were speaking in tongues with your fingers."

The conveyor belt frame, which moves on rubber wheels, creeps forward one-half meter. "Who told you that?"

"My son heard it from a friend."

One of the gangstas probably, Balta or Oscar. "What else did you hear?"

"That you helped cure the woman."

L. Mariachi shakes his head. "It wasn't me, it was the *bruja*. She called her soul back."

"You're too modest."

"It's the truth."

"She might never have come back if she hadn't heard the music. It reminded her of this life. All of the good things in the world. Family. Friends."

They've fallen a few steps behind the conveyor. L. Mariachi slogs forward to the next plant, careful where he puts his feet. The grid is slippery in places. At least once a day, someone falls.

"There's something else I heard."

L. Mariachi bends forward. Winces at a dull jab of pain in his lower back. If not for the painkillers Num Nut finally softwired into him, no way he'd be able to work. In another week or two it will be the same for every *bracero* as they try to ignore the pulled muscles, inflamed joints, pinched nerves, and slipped disks they suffer from working ten-hour days, six days a week.

Pedrowski cuts a quick glance around, then drops his voice, wary of bitcams and acoustic spores. "Word is, the politicorp made the woman sick on purpose."

L. Mariachi doesn't look at him. He adjusts his stance around the sponge swaying just below the surface. "Why would they do that?"

Pedrowski switches the hand he's picking with so he can edge closer. "To make an example out of her."

"For what?" Dip, pick, straighten. "Far as I know, she didn't do shit."

"Doesn't matter. Her family has a reputation for causing trouble. Roughing up worker liaisons, complaining about living and working conditions, or the price of local goods and services. That kind of thing. So the *patrón* wants to send a message, make sure they don't get out of hand from the start. That way, the rest of the workers will be docile—afraid to speak up."

"Maybe it was an accident," L. Mariachi says.

"And maybe it wasn't. There have been reports that

a number of workers in other migrant communities have come down sick, too. She's not the only one."

L. Mariachi understands now why Pedrowski is so hung up on Lejandra. She's not just one sick woman, she's a whole *cause*.

"People are starting to get fed up." Pedrowski puffs out his chest, full of bravado. "They aren't going to take it anymore."

"What does that have to do with me?"

"You took matters into your own hands, *ese*."

"I played a few songs. That's all." He shrugs, hoping to downplay his role.

"You made a difference, *compadre*, you helped out. A lot of workers wouldn't do that."

"I didn't have a choice."

"See? That's what I'm talking about. You have a conscience. A sense of duty."

For some reason the *chavo* insists on seeing him as someone he's not. Like he's got a personal interest in turning him into a hero, someone others look up to and admire. Worse, he also seems intent on associating L. Mariachi with João and the gangstas, identifying him as one of them.

"What do you want?" L. Mariachi hisses between gritted teeth. The slosh of pond scum, the centripetal thrum of circulating pumps, and the forced-air whoosh of the big ventilation fans will make it difficult to pick up their conversation but he doesn't want to take any chances. Until now, what they've been talking about could be regarded as nothing more than the usual grumbling of workers, dissing the system, or whining about perceived injustices. Crap that will blow over in a couple of days when they're too tired to do anything between shifts except eat and sleep.

Pedrowski doesn't answer immediately. He waits to speak until the conveyor hydraulics kick in, noisily cycling a fresh batch of empty baskets to the line of workers.

"Some of the vat workers are planning to file a protest for unsafe working conditions." Pedrowski speaks quickly in the momentary lull. "You know, contamination by hazardous chemicals or biologicals. Radiologicals. Pherions. Viruses. That kind of thing."

"File a protest with who?" As migrants, the *braceros* have pretty much forfeited any civil and legal rights they might have in a local clade. Add to this the fact that they're dirt poor—that they can't even afford to retain a pro bono attorney because they'd still have to pay the court costs—and they are more or less hosed when it comes to any sort of judicial action.

Pedrowski mops his forehead with the loose sleeve of his vat suit. "A-P-E-S," he says.

"APES?" L. Mariachi shakes his head, has never heard of the org. Sweat tickles his lips. He licks the corner of his mouth—tastes salt and the metallic chalkiness of the witch's brew of soluble minerals and proteins concocted to fertilize the plants.

"The Alliance to Protect Endangered Species." Pedrowski ladles his berries into the empty colander that grinds to a halt in front of him.

"The organization was established several years before the ecocaust to save wild chimps and gorillas," Num Nut informs him over his cochlear implant.

Not exactly a ringing endorsement: there are no more chimps and gorillas. They all became collateral damage in the global meltdown that enabled the Sahara to annex the rest of Africa and huge sections of Asia.

"In addition to endangered species advocacy," Num Nut says, as if reading from a PR release, "the clade-independent org also works to recover and preserve the cultural memes of extinct ethnic groups, in the hope that they might one day be reconstituted and returned to full viability."

"Right," L. Mariachi mutters.

Pedrowski takes a moment to tighten the seal on his waders. "If we meet the UN legal definition for an at-risk culture, we could be reclassified as endangered."

So, the plan is for APES to foot the legal bill. "But a class action suit could take years to resolve."

"Not if we get an injunction, or an investigation. Then maybe we'll start getting some answers."

The conveyor belt lurches forward, signaling that their short break is over. "What happens if you don't?"

Pedrowski strokes his mustache, covering his mouth with his fluid-puckered hand. "We go on strike."

L. Mariachi blinks, takes a moment to digest this.

"If the *patrón* won't take care of us workers," Pedrowski asserts, "we have to take care of ourselves. Look out for our own best interests."

"So how do I fit in?" L. Mariachi says, unclear exactly what's being asked of him.

Pedrowski digs his hand into another sponge, determined to look busy. "We need supporters, organizers, advocates. Workers who aren't afraid to take a risk for the greater good."

"I don't know," L. Mariachi hedges, noncommittal. He doesn't feel comfortable getting involved and resents being pressured. All he did was get roped into playing some music. He didn't think it would lead to anything. Not this, that's for sure. It almost makes him wonder if he's being bullshitted. If Angel Pedrowski really is an activist—or if maybe he's working for the *patrón,* looking for malcontents and trying to draw him out so he can be blacklisted.

"What about the *bruja*?" L. Mariachi asks, teasing open a sponge. "You talked to her?"

Pedrowski sniffs, his mustache arching in disdain. "She's gone."

"Where?" It's not like there's anyplace she can go outside of *el tambo* and the EZ.

Pedrowski straightens, shrugs, turns his head from side to side like he's loosening the muscles in his neck and shoulders. "Rumor has it she transformed herself into a bird and flew away."

"She's not a *bracero*?"

"No. According to João, she came from Front Range City."

Which means she has access to antiphers and antisense blockers that allow her to move freely between clades. Maybe even different ecotectural systems.

"Think about it." Pedrowski reaches down for a second scoop. "That's all I ask."

L. Mariachi nods. Tentative, halfhearted enough to signal that he's not making any promises. Not yet. Not when the *patrón* could be eavesdropping.

He gets back to work, falls into a rhythm that frees up his mind for contemplation. It feels good, making a difference in someone's life. But maybe that's just the lingering thrill of getting a chance to play again after he thought that part of his life was ancient history, never to be revisited. He can barely remember the last time he'd purged himself, poured out his heart and soul the way he would a smelly old bedpan. In spite of the dogged pain in his left hand, he feels cleaner than he has in ages. Aired out like a musty, moth-eaten sheet that still needs to be mended.

It wouldn't surprise him if the politicorp was responsible for the inexplicable ailment. *Patróns* did crap like that. It was all part of a carefully orchestrated program of intimidation. Old-world caucs getting in touch with their inner Aryan. Reasserting their sense of superiority and entitlement. Oppressing the working class and waxing nostalgic about free market capitalism or laissez faire colonialism.

What about his encounter with the Blue Lady? Could the *patrón* have masterminded that? A ruse to try to get him to incriminate himself or others? It's possible, based on his public bio and his brief history as a street kid. But it would be a long shot. He never told any adults about his belief in the Blue Lady. Only a few other street kids like him, orphans and runaways who never knew his real name. And it was a long time ago.

If this incarnation of the Blue Lady is real, why would she reveal herself to him now, at the nadir of his existence? Does this mean, after all this time, that she's forgiven him for his loss of faith? For the anger, bitterness, and epithets he hurled at her like stones when she refused to grant him what he wanted? Or has she come back to punish him for blaming her for everything that went wrong in his life, for spitting on her memory when he was really spitting on himself and what he had become?

His throat tightens. "Where are you?" he murmurs.

No answer. Just like before, she never shows up when he wants her to. Saints never do. He's learned that much. He knows now to wait, to be patient. No different from courting a virgin. Sniff after a *chocha* too much, and the heat of desire will transform it into a maximum security vault, tighter than the holiest of holies. Access denied. Any further communion between them will be on her terms.

"That's all right." He laughs quietly to himself. "Take your time. I'm not going anywhere."

After all, he's a cripple. Career challenged. He's hit his glass ceiling, isn't rising any higher in life than the domed vat that's got him boxed in.

That's what the *chavo* doesn't realize. He's young enough, educated enough, to believe there's a way out. He's not like the rest of them who are trapped here. He sees himself as different. Smarter. Immune to the same psychological pitfalls.

They all thought that about themselves, at the start. They thought being a *bracero* was temporary. A job they could stop doing at any point, just walk away and go back to school, or drive a taxi, or whatever else came along.

Except nothing else ever came along. After a while, it was too late to do anything different. And before they knew it, it had become a way of life.

That's what makes the migrants a community. The shared knowledge that they're all caught in the same situation. No one is any better or any worse. They've all swallowed their pride. Bitten back on their hatred of the system. Let go of their longing for middle- or upper-clade respectability. Stuffed these feelings into a mental closet or swept them under a carpet of resignation.

*Que viven los mojados!*

The old battle cry sounds hollow. The slogan empty and gutted. A mockery of the defiance it once embodied.

Is that why the Blue Lady returned to him? To stir up the mud of complacency he's mired in? Remind him of what it feels like to struggle?

Hell. It's been too long since he fought for anything— or against anything. He swore off idealism the day his hand was trashed. Activism is a conceit of youth, reserved for people who have a future, something to look forward to. Why choose him to fight the battle?

His head aches like a motherfucker. Almost as bad as his fingers knotted around a cluster of crushed berries.

Maybe that's why she appeared to him after so long. He's always been a glutton for punishment. Can't get enough.

This is no different. It's like he's addicted to affliction. He just hopes the pain is as sweet as it used to be, that it's got enough sugar to dilute the quinine that's replaced the blood pumping through his veins.

# 19

## FEEDBACK

Fola's fingers uncurl from the missing cross. In its absence the ICM eyescreens press against her face, cold and dense as lead.

"I need to open an outside comlink," she tells Pheidoh.

"To who?"

"Xophia." The IA should have the com frequency for the shuttle from the earlier transmission. She's tired of waiting to hear back from Ephraim on the status of the shuttle. When is it scheduled to arrive? What are the conditions onboard? Are they worse? They must be. If so, how much worse?

Other questions gnaw at her, sharp, ulcerous.

If the shuttle arrives before the evacuees, what happens to the workers? How does she bring the refugees onto the station without contaminating the quarantine zone? If the evacuees arrive before the shuttle, what happens to the refugees? What if they can't be safely

brought aboard the station? What then? They can't be
diverted to another colony. They can't go back.

"Who are you?" the pilot says, squinting through nar-
rowed eyes.

"Fola." Her name seems to stick to the roof of her
mouth. "I'm helping Ephraim. He can't . . . he's busy
right now."

"You a refugee?"

"No. I mean, not anymore. I used to be. But now I'm
a worker on the Mymercia construction station."

"Right." He relaxes a bit, some of the tension easing at the corners of his mouth. "You ever done this
before?"

"What?" The question derails her.

"I thought so." He massages his face. His speech isn't
the only thing about him that's gruff. His beard is a tangle, his hair a thin, bristly patch. A month's growth in
six months, his metabolism slowed during the trip by
semistasis drugs. "The main thing to keep in mind when
we arrive is don't get fancy. That's when mistakes happen and things go wrong. You know what I'm saying?
No relatives or friends who could get in the way, or be a
distraction. Keep it low-key, low-profile, and everything'll be just fine. Slicker than snot."

"You don't understand. I'm not—right now I just
need to talk to Xophia. That's all. It's about the disease." Maybe if she passes on what she knows about
the quanticles, that will help Xophia. A vague, grasp-
ing hope.

"We're still twelve hours out," the pilot goes on. "That
gives you some time to prepare—make sure everything's
good to go."

She shakes her head. "You can't dock yet."

"Come again?"

"The ecotecture here is failing. The warm-blooded plants are dying. Life-support on the asteroid is down and the onsite construction crew is being evacuated. You have to hold off for a while."

"We don't have a while." He shakes his head. "We're carrying one extra person. Burned up all our resources. We're running on empty. Besides, most of us are half-dead or will be by the time we get there. If we don't dock and get some medical attention we aren't going to make it."

Fola blinks as the image of the pilot is replaced by a bit-cam window showing the QZ.

"I thought you should know that Kerusa plans to start shuttling workers from the surface to the station in an hour to two," Pheidoh says.

"What happens when they get here?" The pace to set up the quarantine zone has increased in the past twenty minutes.

"They jack into Intensive Care Modules and use them as temporary life-support."

A queasy dread descends on Fola. It's not going to work. She can't think of any way to bring the refugees onto the station without putting the workers at risk.

She looks for Ephraim. But she can't make out faces, they are too small, and her thoughts are a tangle, too tightly knotted to see clearly.

"There's been a complication with Lejandra," the IA says after a pause. "Sniffers have identified an unregistered pherion on her."

She closes her eyes, lets out a breath, and reopens them. "What kind of pherion?"

"An antipher to one of the security pherions that guards the outer perimeter of the work camp."

"Any idea where it came from, or how Lejandra picked it up? Is it related to the quanticles?"

"I don't know yet."

"Show me." It might be nothing. But right now, it's all she's got.

Twelve hours. Enough time to send and receive one message. After that, all bets are off.

Back in the adobe-walled courtyard, the saguaro that represents Lejandra's clade-profile seems more withered, more skeletal. "What am I looking for?" Fola squints at the umbrella palms, scruffy circuitrees, barrel cacti, and bougainvillea atop the wall. Avoids looking at the snakes.

Pheidoh steps out of a nearby shadow. The IA is dressed in its familiar khakis and pith helmet. It pulls out its magnifying glass and inspects a low-hanging branch on one of the circuitrees. A moment later a datawindow opens in front of her to display the magnified representation of an insect.

"Is this the sniffer?"

The IA consults a private datawindow. "It's called a snaphid."

The 'sect looks like a cross between a snail and an aphid. Instead of legs, it has a half dozen amoebalike feet. Its mouth is a nubbed needle-thin proboscis, which it uses like a cane to feel its way along and spear the occasional rogue molecule.

"Was it here before?" Not that she would have noticed unless Pheidoh pointed it out to her.

"No. It was recently introduced to this particular clade."

"By the politicorp?"

"No." Pheidoh lowers the magnifying glass and the datawindow vanishes. "The Bureau of Ecotectural Assimilation and Naturalization."

"Why BEAN?"

"Guest worker programs provide a convenient place for fugitives to hide and illegal pharmers to operate. They are also used by anticorpocracy orgs to gain access to certain clades."

"You mean like the ICLU?"

"And the Fun Da Mentalists."

The Fun Da Mentalists are fringe anarchists who seem to have no coherent plan to subvert the dominant paradigm other than the occasional random act of social disobedience and ecotectural sabotage. "So you think the sniffer was introduced to search for refugees and saboteurs."

"Right. Black-market pherions or antisense blockers they might be using to mask their presence."

Fola dents her lower lip with her teeth. "Is it possible the pherion was designed to hide the existence of the programmable matter?"

"By Bloody Mary, you mean?"

"That might explain why it suddenly showed up," she says. "Why it wasn't found earlier."

"It's possible," the IA allows, "but not likely. The pherion doesn't appear to have a softwire component."

So there would be no way to remotely download it.

Pheidoh blows on the snaphid, which drops from the limb. "A more probable scenario is that the pherion is so new it slipped under radar. Or that it was manufactured shortly after the *braceros* arrived."

"By who?"

"That's what BEAN is trying to find out."

"The *bruja*," Fola says. It has to be. She came from Front Range City and was in direct contact with Lejandra. It would have been easy for her to bring it with her.

"Not necessarily." The IA rubs the back of its neck with one hand and squints up at an invisible sun. "One other possibility is that Lejandra came into close physical proximity with someone else who entered the camp illegally in the last few hours."

Normally most pherions couldn't be transmitted through the air. They were too heavy, and had to be injected or sniffed. But, like any virus-based drug, some of them could be spread by a sneeze or a cough.

"What's going to happen to Lejandra now?" If there's one thing BEAN is famous for, it's not turning a blind eye.

The datahound pinches its lower lip, gives it a contemplative tug. "A full biomed scan is being run on her. It's being performed remotely, so it will take a while to get the results. In the meantime, BEAN is putting together a list of persons of interest. Workers they want to question."

"Can't they just release more sniffers? Isolate the source?"

"So far the pherion hasn't shown up anywhere else in the camp, or in anyone else. It seems to have disappeared."

Gone underground, Fola thinks. Into hiding. Which pretty much indicates that it's not related to the quanticles or the ecotectural collapse. It's specific to Lejandra. Something about her.

Pheidoh cocks its head to one side, as if listening intently.

"What?" she says.

"There's a new transmission from L. Mariachi. Streamed from a security bitcam array."

A translucent datawindow opens, the pane static-filled. Gradually, the blizzard of pixels clears, assembles into a bird's-eye view of a deserted street. The hardpan is littered with bits of trash. Potted umbrella palms slouch in front of garish adscreens pasted to the cheap lichenboard facades of VRcades, shops, and restaurants. It's night—or rather, early morning. The predawn sky in the east is starting to lighten, almost as bright as the halogen-blighted horizon to the west.

L. Mariachi is alone, propped against the biolum-washed wall of a dance club called Phallacies. He clutches the guitar unsteadily to his chest, as if he's staggering under an enormous load.

"Is he drunk?" she asks.

"In pain," Pheidoh says. "At the time of the transmission, he wasn't authorized to receive a painkiller for his hand."

It hurts to look at him. His features are a delirious amalgam of mascara black shadows and harsh cyanosis blue. Oxygen starved. The glow from the blue liquid crystal dancer above the entrance to Phallacies flickers at regular intervals, a tremolo effect that gives his movements a jerky quality.

He pushes himself off the wall, stumbles away from the dancer. Then Fola hears her own voice, vibrant in the cool air: *Who is the song for?*

The words stop him. He stares down at the guitar, then turns toward the lewd dancer and falls on his knees, eyes uplifted, in an act of supplication. Fola's knees throb with the remembered ache of her own pleas for strength or forgiveness.

"You want me to play again. Is that why you're here? Is that why the *bruja* gave me the guitar?"

Her voice loops back, transmitted through the guitar: *You must have written it for a reason.*

The time delay is disconcerting. She knows the questions ahead of time . . . which triggers disorienting moments of déjà vu while she's waiting to hear his responses.

"Why now?" he asks. "After all these years?" Then, "Wait." Raising one hand. "Don't go." He picks up the guitar, coaxes out a plaintive chord. "I'll wait for you this time. I promise."

Fola's stomach crimps. She turns to Pheidoh. The IA has morphed into a bearded, bespectacled bohemian and is gazing at the datawindow as if deconstructing an abstract painting.

"Suggestions?" Fola asks. She doesn't know what, if anything, the Blue Lady means to L. Mariachi at this point in his life. The last thing she wants to do is say the wrong thing, make him angry or depressed, to the point where he refuses to have anything more to do with her. If she's not careful, she could do more harm than good.

The datahound combs its beard with pensive, long-nailed fingers. "Don't answer."

"You want me to play hard to get?"

"You've already asked him to play. If you ask him again, he might resent it or get suspicious."

The strategy seems risky. She turns back to the five-hour-old image. L. Mariachi is still on his knees. "Do you know where he is now?"

"A sea sponge vat. That's his scheduled work assignment." The IA opens a second datawindow, which hangs next to the first like a companion piece in an art gallery. "This is interesting."

In Fola's experience "interesting" is probably the single most ominous word in the world.

"What?" she says when the datahound isn't immediately forthcoming. All she can see are a few squiggly lines of partially decrypted ciphertext.

"The Bureau is sending a pair of agents to the biovat pharm."

"In person?" Fola has never seen a BEAN investigator in-vivo. From everything she's heard, she never wants to. Their rabidity is legendary.

"Two of them." The datahound wrinkles its nose. "Rose and peacock."

"Is that necessary?"

"They always travel in pairs. Usually, but not always, color coordinated."

"What I mean is, that seems pretty extreme, sending them in-vivo. What are they going to do?"

"Intimate people."

"You mean *intimidate*?"

"Only if they positively ID a suspect. Until then, the preferred modus operandi is to use indirect pressure to obtain information."

Whatever that means.

"Often," Pheidoh says, noticing her uncertainty, "the threat of physical force is all that's required to beat the truth out of someone."

"How thoughtful." As a relief worker, she occasionally saw the victims of mental torture. Refugees and indentured workers like Xophia who would risk permanent injury or death rather than go back to worse.

The IA nods in apparent agreement. "The Bureau works hard to project an image of restraint."

Hard to tell if the IA's serious or echoing her sarcasm. "How soon will the agents get there?" she asks.

"Approximately fifty minutes. They're currently en route from FRC." Less than an hour. Not nearly enough time to send a warning.

"Do the workers at the vat pharm know they're coming?"

"No. Surprise is also part of the information gathering strategy."

# 20

## PREDICTA ABSURDUM

Rexx focuses on the screen of the Predicta, dials in the frequency and waits for the White Rain to drench him.

Nothing. Not even a sprinkle. He cranks up the volume and tries again, with the same result. He tries a third time, but the riboswitch refuses to flip.

The temporary reclade pherion. It has to be. It's interfering with the RNA.

He pushes his eyescreens onto his forehead and digs at the blossom of pain behind his eyes with his thumb and forefinger.

The boy standing on the split-rail fence is clearer. Rexx can make out the color of his hair, blond, and the longhorn stitch on the back pockets of the Rhinestone Blues jeans.

The woman is clearer too, blue suede jacket and spotless white hat emerging from the static as she draws closer and the blizzard thins. Bright red lipstick picture-framing a proud smile.

He can't look . . . but can't tear his eyes away. He knows what's coming, but there's no way to stop it. No way to change the station. His memory is wired to one channel. All he can do is close his eyes.

"Dad," Mathieu said, "can we go to the rodeo on Saturday? Please?"

"No."

Mathieu's lips trembled, hurt and angry, as if he'd been slapped. "Why not? A lot of kids from school are going."

"Because I said so."

Mathieu's eyes brimmed. His enthusiasm faltered. "But Mom promised. . . ."

"In case you hadn't noticed, I ain't your mother."

The tears retreated to higher ground. The pout hardened into resentment. Mathieu turned—"I hate you! You never let me do anything!"—and ran to his room.

That night, lying in bed, Jelena touched a hand to Rexx's arm, resting her fingers on him the way she did piano keys. Lightly, delicately, but with absolute self-assurance and control. "I know you don't want to expose him to the same things your father exposed you to. For good reason. But don't you think it's time he started deciding for himself what he does and doesn't want to do?"

Rexx knotted the bedsheets in one hand. "Forget it. He's not going to a rodeo."

The pressure of her fingers increased. "Then you're going to lose him. The same way your father lost you."

His cheeks flushed. "Not the same way."

"A different way, then. The result will be the same. Is that what you want?"

Rexx shut his eyes. He couldn't identify the notes she played on his arm. Kernis, maybe. Or Messiaen. "No," he finally said.

"It'll be fun." Jelena stroked his forearm. "Trust me. It won't kill him. You'll do more harm if you don't let him go. . . ."

Hands trembling, Rexx checks on the rack of petri dishes he's set up to culture the biopsy samples.

So far he's got Macabro, the Silver Skeleton's sugar skull grinning up at him from pink aspic. Another *pan de los muertos* sporoid. Cassa Nova's ruby-fruit lips, juicy and ready to burst. If he plants a kiss on the petals, Rexx gets the impression they'll smooch him back just as pretty as you please. Then there's ginseng Barbie impersonating Raggedy Ann, dressed in the yarn hair, pinafore, and striped stockings that he remembers from his mother's antique doll collection. Hundreds of shelved eyes, arranged in floor-to-ceiling rows, staring out at him, unblinking.

His hands shake in the gust of dead memories from his childhood.

There doesn't seem to be a pattern to the ersatz mutations. No indication where the mothballed images are coming from or how they've been coded into the architext of the ecotecture.

"You find a DNA sequence yet for Raggedy Barbie?" he asks Hjert's IA, Warren Peace.

"There isn't one," the IA says.

"Come again."

"There's no genetic component in the sample."

"Then what the hell's causing it to grow? What's it

*made* of?" He can't seem to think straight. The inside of his skull is a hollow abscess, dry, feverish, infected.

The IA says nothing. It seems to resent being outsourced, is even more terse than Claire. The loss of Ida is wearing on him, a carbuncle of longing that matches the absence of the White Rain. The need, the cell-deep hunger, is the same. He craves the interactive piece of software as if it were a physical part of him that's been amputated.

Just what is it about Claire that is habit forming? Their relationship—if it can be called that—leaves a lot to be desired. For one thing, outside of the interface with his biomed sensors and molectronics, there's no intimate physical contact. Second, the IA is cold, distant. Maybe it's just mirroring his self-imposed exile, reflecting back the isolation it sees according to some heuristic or mimetic subroutine that's designed to put him at ease, make him feel better. On the upside, it's dependable. It might not have much of a heart, or a soul, but it's always there for him. Which is a lot more than can be said for some people. Pathetic as that is on his part, it counts for something.

Rexx pinches the bridge of his nose. "Any idea what's causing this crap?" he asks Warren. "Where it's coming from?"

He still doesn't know if the source of the failures is external or internal. If the ecotecture has been infected via softwire download to the plants, through direct physical exposure to a mutagen, or if it was an accident, the result of an internal bug or error. Given the way that the mutation is manifesting, the images it's generating, a design or production flaw seems unlikely. He's fairly confident Barbie and Raggedy Ann weren't part of the original project specifications. That makes it hard to believe the problem is the result of a random act of nature or coincidence. Which still leaves the barn door wide open for ineptitude. Or mischief.

And he still has no idea what he found during the autopsy. The lab isn't equipped with a CNT sensor. He can't cut into the culture specimens directly.

"Assuming the softwire link to Mymercia is still down," Rexx says, "and that the ecotecture is effectively offline, it seems reasonable to conclude that the datastream responsible for the mutation is local."

"Or that it was downloaded earlier and is only now being implemented," the IA says, board stiff. "The molectronics in the warm-blooded plants are still fully functional. Executing new instruction sets."

Converting digital data into chemical analogs. Altering DNA, and manufacturing proteins. Rexx returns his attention to Cassa Nova's blossoming lips. What he's seeing is digital information taking on physical form, adapting the strategy of biological information to migrate from an in-virtu environment to an in-vivo one. A kind of phase change, virtuality to reality. The way water vapor condensed, changing from a gas to a liquid.

"Is there an identifiable trigger?" he asks. "Something we can point to, at or near the time of the accident?"

"No. But the event might appear to be normal activity. If that's the case, it could take a while to identify."

The corners of Rexx's mouth sag. What he's looking at is the symptom of the problem. What he needs to nail down is the cause. Not only the physical cause, but the reason behind it. If there *is* a reason.

"Have you been able to come up with any discernible pattern to the growth we're seeing?" he says.

"You mean a connection between the images?"

"Right. Some common thread that ties them together." He has no clue what that might be. But if they can come up with a common denominator, maybe they can get to the bottom of what's going on. Get some idea of where things are headed and what they can expect.

"I'll set up a relational database."

"Be sure to include symbolic information as well as visual and textual data in any cross-reference comparisons."

If there is a message in the mayhem it might well be symbolic in nature, a type of graffitic or iconographic commentary.

"I'll also search for religious or political associations," Warren says. "If you think it will help."

Rexx nods, mildly surprised. This is the first truly independent suggestion that the IA has offered. Maybe it's finally warming to him, relaxing enough to open up and be more forthcoming.

"What do *you* think's going on?" he says.

"Why do you ask?" The IA seems to retreat a step, defensive.

Rexx waits for a clammy wave of dizziness to taper off. "I just thought you might have a theory. A preliminary hypothesis of some kind."

"Not at the moment." Noncommittal.

Or evasive. Maybe. It's hard to tell. "Not a problem." Rexx raises his hands in a weak no-pressure gesture. "I was just curious. That's all."

Despite his intentions and best efforts, he can't seem to shed his cauciness, the caucsure sense of entitlement that puts people on guard and leaves IAs aloof. People and sentient software alike can smell it a mile away. It's almost as if his upper-clade past has a permanent stench associated with it, a territorial marker that people avoid so they won't get pissed on.

"How's tricks?" Naiana Hjert says, drifting into the lab. "Have you made any progress?"

She joins him at the rack of petri dishes, wedging herself next to him, uncomfortably close. The kind of oblivious disregard for personal boundaries that Rexx hasn't had to deal with since Miss Wadstacken in the fifth grade. "Define progress," he says.

"That sounds like a no."

Rexx gestures at the petri dishes, which have taken on the carnival atmosphere of a combination freak show and amusement park. "It's going to take time."

Hjert scrunches her nose. "Time's running out."

"How much longer do I have?"

"Not much. Workers have started evacuating to the station. The first shuttle pod left a few minutes ago. Three more will be leaving in half an hour. There's only one pod bay in the QZ, so the plan is to dock and unload a shuttle every ten minutes. It's tight but doable."

Rexx runs a quick mental calculation. Six shuttles per hour, at forty workers a trip, results in an evacuation rate of 240 workers per hour. There are approximately 900 on-site workers. Which gives him around three and a half hours. Four, with delays.

"I need more time," he says.

"You've already had four hours. What makes you think four more, or forty more, is going to make any difference?"

"Because the process is accelerating. I've gathered more data in the last hour than in the previous three." He licks at a drop of perspiration trickling down from his upper lip.

"Something new's come up. I think you should—" Hjert frowns. "You look like shit."

Rexx tries to smile. "Cold or warmed over?"

She studies him, her eyes narrowing. "What are you on?" she says after a moment.

He licks his lips again.

"Does it have a name?" she says.

"Not that you'd recognize." He bites his lip to hold his tongue at bay.

"Designer, then. Built to order. Except you ran out, or can't download it, because of the quarantine. So you're fucked."

"I'll be fine—"

"Come on." She grabs him by one arm, and tugs him away from the rack of petri dishes.

Rexx tries to jerk his arm free, but there's nothing for him to use as leverage. His hands flounder and his feet thrash as the two of them tumble toward the door. "Let go of me, goddamnit! I need to stay here. There's nothing you can do."

His voice sounds shrill. But maybe it's just the sudden torrent of blood in his ears, thinning and attenuating the words.

"Don't worry." She snorts. "I'm not interested in easing your pain. You can suffer, for all I care. There's something else I need to show you. While you've still got some wits about you."

"What?" Breathing heavily from exertion. He hasn't been very physically active in the last few hours and his life-support is running low.

She fishes something from a side pocket. A baseball-size rock, with fossilized bits of bone.

*"Don't grab for the ball," Rexx told Mathieu. "Keep your glove open. Let the ball come to you."*

*"Okay."*

*Rexx adjusted his fingers on the seams. "Ready?"*

*A frightened nod, small but determined, as Mathieu raised the glove uncertainly. Awkwardly.*

Rexx stares, openmouthed. "What's that? Where did it come from?"

Hjert relaxes her clench on his arm. "If you promise to behave, I'll show you."

# 21

## LAMARCKED MAN

During the afternoon lunch break, the first thing L. Mariachi does is call Isabelle to check on Lejandra.

Mostly he just wants to see her. Wants to look at her face again and compare it to the image he has of her from earlier that morning. Already the memory seems far older, her voice a subliminal echo of another voice.

It's not fair to her. He has no right to drag her into his past, sully her with another life and feelings that don't belong to her. She has enough problems of her own. The last thing she needs to do is add him to the list.

Let go, he tells himself. Let her go. Not quite sure which her he's thinking about.

"There's no answer," Num Nut says. "Would you like to leave a message?"

"No." Relieved, and at the same time worried. Someone, even if it wasn't Isabelle, should have answered.

* * *

As soon as he logs out, Pedrowski descends on L. Mariachi like a vulture on fresh carrion. The *chavo* won't leave him alone from the moment they sit down with their EZ-catered snacks under one of the umbrella palms planted at intervals along the concrete wall that supports the geodesic dome.

There's no escape. The other workers have spread out in nuclear groups. The only thing L. Mariachi can do is munch his soytein crackers, sip his ryce latte, and listen to the nonstop drone of the intelligentsia's voice, going on about different types of social evolution. How transient communities respond to change, value systems perpetuate, and cultural history survives. Not through the Darwinian propagation of inherited, badass instincts but through the transmission of learned behavior.

"Habits," Pedrowski concludes, taking a breather to swallow the mouthful of half-chewed soy he's been talking around.

"You mean like memes?" L. Mariachi says, thinking to head off any further discussion by intimating to the professor that he's already heard about this shit, has at least a layman's familiarity with the vocabulary, and doesn't need, let alone want, a college-level discourse on the topic.

"Not exactly," Pedrowski says. Unfazed, he launches into a lecture that addresses the differences between behavior-based memes and instruction-based memes, points out the distinction between ideas and habits—self-actuating propensities for a specific action—and finally veers into epigenetic inheritance, social phenotype, and the transmission of acquired characteristics as a response to external stimuli or input.

"I thought the environment couldn't cause hereditary

change. I mean, if I fucked up my hand"—L. Mariachi raises his rheumatoid claw—"and had a kid, the kid's hand wouldn't be fucked up, too."

Which gets into besoins. How only those acquired characteristics that are initiated by a person's needs can cause a change in behavior. Which in turn, through imitation, leads to new habits, and ultimately, a change in society.

"Lamarck also believed that the permanent disuse of any organ weakened it," Num Nut informs him edgewise. "That its functional capacity would diminish until it finally disappeared."

Which is obviously false, L. Mariachi thinks. If it wasn't, 99 percent of the people in the world would be walking around without a brain. And all men would have *cojones* the size of cantaloupes.

"All ideas and beliefs," Pedrowski continues, "are based on habits, which can be passed on through learning."

Turns out that habits aren't considered a form of behavior. They're more primal—more fundamental. As such they bridge the gap between memes and genes and allow for social evolution—the modification of individual and group behavior—through acquired characteristics.

"Orthodox biological evolution maintains that fitness selection is the only role the environment plays," Num Nut says. "In order for fitness selection to be possible, individuals within a species must differ, so that bad characteristics can be minimized and good ones can be maximized. In Lamarckian social evolution, bad behavior is minimized and good behavior reinforced. Often through intentionality."

"So what are you doing here?" L. Mariachi asks

Pedrowski. It's pretty obvious the *chavo*'s not just trying to cover tuition costs. And there's no way he's going to pass up a chance to talk about his labor of love. His mission in life.

"Studying structural inheritance systems in artificially maintained environments. Observing how, in a pherion-regulated system like a migrant workforce, existing social structures act as templates for new structures as the population demographics change over a relatively short period of time."

In other words, as workers get old, sick, or die, and are replaced by younger, more able-bodied workers.

"Structural inheritance systems are just one type of epigenetic inheritance system," Num Nut says. "The other two are steady-state systems and chromatin-marking systems. Together these three types of EISs play a role in what is known as cell memory. The non-DNA transmission of cellular information in an organism to its descendents."

Like he really needed to know that. Maybe he can redirect the professor. Get him onto a subject that's more personal. "How long have you been at it?" L. Mariachi asks.

Pedrowski grimaces. "Almost five years. I've been crunching a lot of numbers—tweaking equations and models of behavior. At last, I finally get the chance to do some fieldwork. Compare the calculated results with real-world observations."

L. Mariachi brushes soytein crumbs from his mouth. "I feel like a guinea pig in a science project," he jokes.

"Don't worry, I'm not going to dose people with experimental pherions or run them through any mazes." Pedrowski chuckles at what must be an inside joke. "I'm just here as an observer."

Right. The same way Cortez was just on a fact-finding mission when he paid a visit to the Aztecs. "Aren't you altering the results of the study by taking part in it?"

"Not really. Social mechanics isn't quantum mechanics." Pedrowski adjusts his bookworm eyescreens. As if they're off by a millimeter and need straightening to focus his view of the world—eliminate any uncomfortable parallax.

"Why not just request access to the *patrón*'s bitcam surveillance? Observe us that way?"

Pedrowski squirms. Rubs his lips. Scratches his nose. "It's not the same as being in-situ. Becoming an integral part of the community and its culture."

Except no matter how hard the *chavo* tries he'll never fit in, never be one of them. He'll always be an outsider.

"So what's the point?" L. Mariachi says. This is the time to pin him down, find out exactly where he's coming from. "I mean, what is it you hope to accomplish with all this?" Other than a title after his name and tenure at some community college, passing on his newly acquired knowledge.

"Well"—Pedrowski blinks rapidly behind his eyescreens—"migrant populations tend to be unpredictable. There's a lot of social instability, a lot of uncertainty about the way these communities are likely to develop over time."

"In other words, you're here to help us evolve."

"To better adapt to the environment. That would be a more accurate statement."

"You mean our social situation."

Pedrowski nods. "Emotionally and psychologically."

L. Mariachi burps. He's had about as much of this

drivel as he can stomach. Plus, his legs have fallen asleep. He tries to stand but his legs are full-on numb. He can't feel shit, can't move.

An icy premonition, heavy as concrete, settles in his bowels.

Could be it's some lecture pherion the guy is out-gassing, left over from his teaching assistant days to force undergrads to sit still and listen to him pontificate. But L. Mariachi doesn't think so. He checks to see if anyone else looks disabled. If they are, they aren't letting on. Everybody seems fine. Better than fine. It's just him. There's not much he can do now except wait for whoever is responsible to rescue him from terminal boredom.

Pedrowski clears his throat, oblivious. "Over time, I hope my research will help implement policies and processes that encourage stability and constructive growth so workers don't feel alienated. Marginalized and disenfranchised as a community."

"How much time we talking? Doesn't it take thousands or millions of years for a trait to be inherited?"

"That's where learning comes in," Pedrowski says. "Learning can speed up social evolution so that it's much faster than biological evolution."

"Memetic evolution is tied to social institutions," Num Nut adds. The IA is in its element here, might as well be Pedrowski's understudy. "Habits are molded by imitation, conformity, and various institutional constraints."

"What I'm hearing is acceptance. Learning to live with bad working conditions, and all the other shit we have to put up with," L. Mariachi says. No different than what the Church teaches to ease suffering.

Pedrowski waves off his objection with both hands.

"Not at all. Stability usually requires some type of growth. A change to correct any existing imbalances and achieve equilibrium."

"Stability for who? The *jefe*? The politicorp?" That's normally who's interested in maintaining the status quo.

"Everyone," Pedrowski says quickly. "It's a mutually beneficial strategy. A zero-sum game where all parties come out equal."

L. Mariachi hollows his cheeks. Spits on the ground in front of him. He tries to wiggle a toe. Nothing. Still no sign of whoever immobilized him. "What kind of changes are you talking about?" No doubt, the *chavo* has a plan. A carefully detailed course of action for what he wants to achieve.

"Initiatives. Petitions."

"Like the worker protest."

"Legal action." Pedrowski nods in affirmation. "If that's what it takes, and if it's done right."

"Peacefully, you mean."

"Violence is not a good habit." Pedrowski wets his lips in distaste. "Not the sort of conflict resolution or problem-solving approach one wants to promote in a population. In the short term, it provides temporary relief—immediate gratification. But in the long run it's counterproductive."

L. Mariachi sucks at the thin film of latte curdling on his teeth. "Violence begets violence."

"Precisely!" A sharp nod of concurrence. "Better to promote an adaptation that encourages the preservation of life as opposed to one that leads to a high probability of death."

The caveat sticks in L. Mariachi's throat. There's always a precondition, a mitigating circumstance, when it

comes to idealists. Something to tone down the level of
threat, keep everything nice and clean and palatable.

Sanitary. That's the word he's looking for. Nonvio-
lent protest. Peaceful insurgency. This dude seems to
think that change can be painless. Has equations up the
yin-yang to reinforce his squeamishness.

Problem is, in L. Mariachi's experience, change is in-
escapably messy, chaotic. It can't be predicted, let alone
regulated or directed. There's always some stray fuck-
ion to wreak havoc. Hell, he ought to know. He's been
blasted with his share of high-energy shitions over the
years.

"... why music is a perfect medium to effect
change," Pedrowski is saying. "One way to reinforce
certain core ideas that will eventually become habits."

A whistle blows over L. Mariachi's cochlear imps,
and an End Break message scrolls along the bottom of
his wraparounds.

Pedrowski gets up, along with the other vat workers
around them who are slowly standing, mustering the
collective energy to head back to work.

"What's the matter?" Pedrowski says when L. Mariachi remains seated. "Are you okay?"

L. Mariachi spots the BEAN agents then. So does
Pedrowski, who does a double take and goes dead quiet.
All verbosity has been sucked out of him. The rest of the
workers have gone silent, too, stopped in their tracks.

If it wasn't for his paralyzed legs, L. Mariachi would
be relieved. Grateful for the sudden peace and quiet. He
knew the *chavo*'s chatter was taking a toll on him, but
he didn't realize how much of a burden it had been.
How much work it had taken to listen, and how exhausted he was.

The BEAN agents are standing on the far side of the

vat, near the main entrance to the building. They're both sporting ash gray suits, bronze wraparounds, and are bald. From a distance, their heads look like two trailer hitches without the chrome. The only difference between them is the color of their ties. One is a dusty rose. The other peacock blue.

Tiago, the vat crew shift manager, is with them. Not too close. He's maintaining a safe distance, like they might taser him just for the fun of it. It's fairly clear Tiago was not expecting them. He's been taken by surprise, the same as everyone else. His head bounces up and down as he talks to them, answers questions, and eventually points in the direction of L. Mariachi.

"I think maybe you should get up now," Pedrowski mutters without looking down at him. His eyes are nervously glued to the two agents.

"I can't," L. Mariachi says.

"Why not?"

"I can't move my legs."

Pedrowski looks at him, eyes wide. "BEAN's here for you?"

L. Mariachi shrugs. "You see anyone else sitting around, waiting for them to stop by for a friendly threesome?"

The muscles in Pedrowski's face relax; the tension whooshes out of him so fast it could be his bladder that's letting go. Or his sphincter.

*Culero.* Asshole.

"Get out of here," L. Mariachi tells him, barely able to conceal his disgust. "It's better if you don't hang with me."

"I'll stay if you want." Pedrowski inflates with false bravado now that he knows he's not the target. Probably thinking about the credit it will bring his fieldwork, being present for a BEAN bust.

"There's nothing you can do," L. Mariachi says. "Trust me."

No amount of talk is going to dissuade dedicated BEAN agents, not when they're in heat-seeking mode. About to take down their quarry.

"I'll find out what's going on," Pedrowski promises, earnest. "I'll do whatever I can to help."

L. Mariachi nods. Whatever.

Then the budding social engineer turns into a free electron and disassociates himself. Scuttles to the safety of their fellow workers, who have clumped together in a herd for support as much as protection, leaving L. Mariachi alone to face the tandem of BEAN agents headed his way. Following the curve of the vat, side by side, with measured, unhurried steps.

"Num Nut?" he says out loud.

"Yes?"

"Any idea what I'm being charged with?"

"No. I haven't been informed."

"Have you been given any information?"

"Only that I should advise you to cooperate fully. If you do, things will go easier for you."

"You got any other advice?"

Num Nut doesn't answer. His link to the IA has been severed. He's on his own.

The BEAN agents are close now. Five meters away. They're smiling, and not in a way that's intended to put him at ease. Their grins are meant to intimidate—establish dominance.

L. Mariachi smiles back. "Can I help you?" Up close he can spec that the peacock agent is a dark-skinned blatino. Brazilian or Spanish ancestry. The rose agent is white with reddish freckles, and has Celtic knots engraved on his skull, etched into the bone just underneath the pale skin. Both have Frankenstein monster necks, corded with tendons, and muscled fingers that they keep flexing and unflexing, habitually, the way a cat reflexively extends and retracts its claws.

The peacock agent fingers his wraparounds. "Luis Mario Chi," he says. It's not a question.

"It's pronounced 'chee,'" L. Mariachi says. "Not like 'chai,' the tea." Out of dignity maybe, or self-respect, he feels compelled to correct them.

"Does this mean you're going to be a pain in the ass?" the rose agent asks, raising an inquisitive brow.

"I just thought you should have your facts straight."

The rose agent turns to the peacock agent—a slow, confident pirouette. "I don't think he's being very cooperative, do you?"

The peacock agent's mouth twists to one side in faux deliberation. "Maybe he's just trying to be helpful."

The rose agent turns back to L. Mariachi. "Is that what you were doing, trying to help us out?"

L. Mariachi can see his reflection in the mirrored bronze. Hammered into the metallic coating, his features look statuesque.

"Well?" The rose agent gnashes his teeth and assaults him with a belligerent stare.

"I just thought you should know."

"Sounds helpful to me," the peacock agent says. He turns to L. Mariachi. "Please come with us."

L. Mariachi doesn't budge. Keeps his smile pasted to his face. "I'd love to. You know. But . . ." He shrugs. Looks pointedly at his legs.

"I told you he wasn't being very cooperative," the rose agent whines to his other half.

"I guess not."

The rose agent sighs, actually manages to sound disappointed. "I think he's trying to make our job difficult, or something."

"Resisting arrest," the peacock agent says.

"Maybe you could give me a hand," L. Mariachi suggests. He reaches up for assistance.

"You hear that?" the rose agent says. "He wants us to dirty our hands. Right after we washed them."

It's a good bet these two dudes do a lot of hand scrubbing. Enough to put Pontius Pilate to shame.

"I have a better idea," the peacock agent says. He reaches a hand inside his bullet-proof jacket.

Uh-oh. Here it comes.

The rose agent wrinkles his forehead as his sidekick produces a squeeze ampoule that looks for all the world like an oversize rat turd. "What's that?"

"Something to help his attitude."

The rose agent takes the squeeze ampoule from his partner. Pretends to inspect it for a second before turning back to L. Mariachi. He holds out the ampoule, centimeters from L. Mariachi's nose.

"What does this smell like to you?"

"I don't smell anything."

The rose agent makes a face. "It stinks to me. Just like you." He gives the little ampoule a quick pinch.

Yellow pollenlike dust, as rank as freeze-dried urine, swirls into L. Mariachi's eyes. Billows up his nostrils, into his sinuses and down his throat, where it discovers his lungs.

"Smell anything yet?" the rose agent asks.

L. Mariachi coughs, then clicks his teeth hard at a sudden sting in his eyes, which feels as gritty and hot as a cigarette pressed against his retinas.

"I'd say that's a yes," the peacock agent says.

Both of the agents are at his side. Their hands, clamped vise tight on his shoulders to steady him, shackle him in place as the burning sensation in his retinas spreads and creeps inward. Little fingers of oily smoke reach around the inside of his skull and slither into place.

When they have a firm grip, the fingers squeeze, apply pressure to his brain and give it a yank. The jerk rips at his thoughts, tears them out by the roots, separating him from the world like a dead geranium.

# 22

## HABIT OF FORCE

As Fola follows the arrest of L. Mariachi on her eye-screens, a barrage of sidebar images clamor for attention. A man toppling face first into biovat sludge. An infant wailing at the breast of its unconscious mother. A teenage woman combing clumps of strawlike hair from her head.

Quick, stop-action segments recorded by the flitcams and bitcams scattered about the vat facility. The picture they create makes her sick to her stomach. The medical trailer brought in by the politicorp is almost an afterthought, woefully understaffed and underequipped. It has ten beds and is geared for the treatment of minor injuries, heat prostration, and dehydration. No way it can handle the massive influx of patients. Gel pads have been brought in to supplement the beds and dozens of migrants lay on the floor. Still more huddle on the bare ground outside of the makeshift clinic, faces sallow, eyes waxen.

Fola keeps waiting, praying, for a team of Jesuettes and emergency relief workers to show up, coptered in to administer to the sick *braceros*. She imagines them hitting the ground, commando style, as emergency relief supplies are off-loaded. Canisters of last year's sprayon clothes, no longer fashionable, donated by Siz Claiborne or Hi Rev. Crates of obsolete military MREs, century-old food, and WHO medical supplies. The rotors of the copter churning up dust and the smell of death . . .

Even through the filter mask, the odor clotted in her mouth, choked her throat like blood she couldn't swallow. The stench of partially decayed bodies.

The refugee camp, near a narrow canyon at the foot of the Urals, had been ravaged by a microburst that slammed into it from the upper atmosphere. The brief dust storm, powered by two-hundred-kilometer-an-hour winds, had ripped up trees, buried people alive, stripped the skin from their bones, and filled their lungs with grit. In its wake, sandblasted desolation.

The emergency response team consisted of three Jesuettes and eight World Health Organization workers. They spent two hours combing the debris. There were no survivors. Fifteen hundred people dead in two minutes. No tattered rags clung to the half-buried corpses, only desiccated tendons, too tough even for bacteria and maggots to digest.

A skull looked up at her out of the sand. Flesh still clinging to the bone, eyes the texture and color of jellied plums.

"You okay?" Xophia said. Wind whipped her hair around her face, lashed at her pink habit.

Fola gagged. Clawed the filter mask covering her mouth, bent down, and retched on the roiling ground.

"Here." Xophia knelt next to her, tore open a booster derm, and slapped it on the inside of her wrist.

Fola crawled away from the skull on her hands and knees. Waited for the antinausea to kick in, to quell the dry heaves convulsing her stomach and the taste of bile in her mouth.

Something half-buried and sharp pressed into her left palm. She jerked her hand away.

The cross wasn't bone, but it had bone in it. Her fingers closed around the object and her shaking stopped, calmed for a long time.

Lejandra's arrest is harder to stomach than L. Mariachi's.

The BEAN agents strike while João and the two gangstas are at work. Isabelle, who called in sick to look after Lejandra, is the only opposition the two goons face.

It's not much of a contest. The door to the trailer, not one to question authority or disobey a direct order, does an immediate open-sesame for the duo. They don't bother to knock or announce themselves. Just goose step in like the Gestapo, better dressed but no less insistent.

Isabelle is caught by surprise. She does her best to dissuade the agents by hurling candles at them. She manages to launch a few tapers before the peacock agent grabs her, holds her in boa constrictor arms, and crushes all resistance.

Fola gasps. Feels the breath pour out of her as Isabelle shudders and goes as limp as a rag doll.

Lejandra is too weak to do anything on her own. Roused by the commotion, she stumbles out of the bedroom, pajamas wrinkled, her hair awry. As soon as she sizes up the situation, she turns to run, and then either collapses from dizziness or bed-atrophied muscles.

The rose agent whips out a spraygun and squirts Lejandra with fast-drying sticky foam that mummifies the pajamas, immobilizing her. The peacock agent docs the same with Isabelle. Then the two of them loosen the flies on their official Armani pants to pee on the floor and walls, dousing the place with urine the color of pink grapefruit juice.

Fola wrinkles her nose. "Is that normal procedure?"

"Not exactly. They're exercising . . . creative license."

"Seems pretty unimaginative to me."

"They've had their bladders modified to manufacture security proteins," Pheidoh says. "Their urine is dosed with sniffers and glycoprotein tags that attach to anyone who enters the trailer."

"So they can keep track of whoever visits the family. Then follow them wherever they go and ID whoever they come in contact with."

"As well as search them for illegal pherions."

"Isn't that illegal?"

"Under the recently expanded Clade Integrity Protection Act, anybody suspected of a crime can be monitored."

"Whatever happened to innocent before proven guilty?"

The IA, in Heidegger mode now, is examining a philosophical treatise titled *Sein und Zeit,* whatever that translates as. To complete the picture, the IA has adopted the image of a distinguished gentleman in his sixties or seventies. It's wearing a conservative suit, has silver-gray hair combed back from a receding hairline, and a bristly but neatly trimmed mustache perched above plump jowls.

"It's not always obvious if the alleged victim of a crime is an innocent bystander or an accomplice," Pheidoh explains. "If the victim is verifiably innocent, it's believed that this kind of surveillance can help lead authorities to the guilty party."

When the agents have finished relieving themselves, they zip up, grab Lejandra, and toss her in the trunk of the hearse-black pod they've commandeered. Mission accomplished.

They don't take Lejandra to the overcrowded clinic. They drive her to the same temporary detention center where L. Mariachi is being held. An old greenhouse that's been converted into a storage facility. The makeshift warehouse is filled with bags of fertilizer, stacked drums of nutrient solution, cleansers, and cracked yellow light from the shrink wrap of dusty cellulose that keeps the rickety frame from collapsing. Two small rooms, just inside the main entrance, have been cleared to create holding cells. A third room next to them has been turned into an office for the agents.

They dump Lejandra on a hospital gurney that's been put in her room, along with a respirator and a drip IV, then head to the office for a quick snack of kelp chips, instant salsa, and powdered *aguas frescas* in foil packets.

"I hate this Hispanic shit," the rose agent grumbles, adding water to the plastic container of red salsa.

"It's better than African," the peacock agent says.

"I've never been there." The rose agent drips salsa onto a chip and down the front of his suit. The stain left by the salsa disappears so fast it looks like it's evaporating into thin air.

"You're lucky," the peacock agent says as he dumps lime drink powder into a paper cup filled with water. "All they have is one flavor—vegetable curd. Dried, baked, fried. You name it."

"The best is Asian," the rose agent says. "Chinese."

"Or Indian," the peacock agent says. "Tandoori's not bad."

While the BEAN agents talk, they monitor their captives via a wallscroll hung from the greenhouse's tubular frame.

"How's Lejandra?" Fola says.

"Her vitals have dropped."

Fola hollows her cheeks. "What about L. Mariachi?"

"Still unconscious," the datahound says without looking up. The title of the book has changed to *Identity and Difference*.

"Is *he* sick?"

"No."

"What about the paralysis in his legs?"

"It was temporary."

Some good news, at least, to offset the bad. "Can I see them?" Force of habit. It would feel wrong not to check on them . . . even though the information she's streaming is several hours old.

A second datawindow, showing Lejandra, opens up next to the first, followed by a third window that displays L. Mariachi.

Unlike Lejandra, L. Mariachi doesn't get a bed. He's huddled on the bare concrete floor, curled around an open drain gilded with vomit. She doesn't see a toilet in either detention cell, or a bucket for waste, so it's a good bet the drain doubles as a latrine. The floor is crusted with scaly green flecks, the eczema of some recent chemical spill.

"Is the ecotecture in the greenhouse the same as the vat pharm?"

"No. It's been modified by BEAN to support the detention pherion Lejandra and L. Mariachi have been dosed with."

"Do you have a clade-profile?"

A small saguaro cactus a few meters to her right anthropomorphs, takes on the anemic shape of a person with crippled, polio-frail legs and arms. The flowers dotting the surface of the saguaro change, too. Large pink-and-blue blooms, representing new pherions, populate the gaps between the tiny white-and-yellow flowers that garnish the other saguaros in the garden. The arrangement and type of flowers represent the revamped pherion pattern describing L. Mariachi and Lejandra. With the appearance of these new flowers, butterflies emerge from the bougainvillea to transmit information, followed by bumblebees that lumber from blossom to blossom, transferring or updating instruction sets.

As she watches, the new blossoms flicker, a vague digital palsy that steadies after a moment.

"What was that?" she says.

The IA hesitates, its expression pinched into a frown. "Transient interference in the datastream."

"Shouldn't the other flowers have been affected?" Or the whole garden. It should have flickered, too.

"Their datafeed is on a different channel. It's cleared up now." The IA continues to flip through the bound pages of the latest text, seemingly unconcerned.

Fola glances back to the datawindow displaying Lejandra. There's no obvious change in her condition.

She shakes her head. "I still don't understand why they have to isolate her. Couldn't they just keep an eye on her? Or take her to a clinic in Front Range City?"

"Protective custody," Pheidoh says.

"I thought they had to charge a person in order to detain them."

"Her status is listed as pending," Pheidoh tells her.

"Which means . . . what?"

"She can be held incommunicado until her situation is resolved. Until the Bureau decides whether or not to press criminal charges."

"Held indefinitely?"

"Yes. As a security risk, all of her civil rights have been suspended, including the right to habeas corpus."

"BEAN doesn't have to tell anyone why she's being detained?"

"No."

"So she's been classified as a security risk because of the illegal pherion. Which makes her a danger to the workers."

The IA looks up from its philosophical tract. "Not just the workers, but the clade itself. The whole Front Range ecotectural system. That's what BEAN is really trying to protect."

Fola shakes her head. Almost all the illegal pherions she ran across as a Jesuette were alternative medicines— replacement drugs for the high-priced ones manufactured by the big pharmaceuticals. She never encountered one that was a threat to the environment, merely the bottom line or the status quo. "I take it L. Mariachi is being detained for the same reason," she says.

Pheidoh nods in the direction of the datawindow showing the two agents. "They can explain it better than I can."

". . . possible association with subversive orgs," the rose agent says, repositioning his wraparounds on his jar-shaped head. The agents have finished eating, are now getting down to business.

"You think that's who this *bruja* is?" the peacock agent says. He seems to be the understudy. Less caucsure of himself. "A harmful free radical?"

"Damn right."

"So what's she doing in this shithole?"

"Recruiting new members. Lobbying for support. That's how these asswipes operate. They target a working-class subclade they think is vulnerable, dissatisfied, and then pretend to help them out so they can be turned into sympathizers. An activist base to build on."

The peacock agent nods like this makes total sense, dovetails perfectly with his paranoid view of the world.

"That's what she was doing with the woman," the rose agent says. "I wouldn't be surprised if the bitch *made* her sick just so she could come in and 'cure' her. Look like a savior."

"And turn public sentiment against the politicorp," the peacock agent says.

"Exactly. All it takes is one. If the seed of dissent takes root here, it will spread elsewhere."

"The domino effect."

"You got it."

"What I can't spec is why we can't get a reading on her. No iDNA signature, no clade-pattern. No nothing."

"Don't worry. We'll find out who she is soon enough." The rose agent checks the wallscroll. "How much longer until our *rockero* wakes up?"

The peacock agent consults a readout on his wraparounds. "Half an hour."

Fola grimaces. "They're going to question him, aren't they?" she says. "Torture him."

She closes her eyes against the prospect. She doesn't have it in her to watch the interrogation if it turns ugly. Not without the Mother Teresa pherions she was routinely dosed with as a Jesuette. On her own, she can't stomach the sight of blood, or of broken bones poking through skin. She's not strong enough.

"That's another reason he's been placed in solitary confinement," Pheidoh says. "To frighten and disorient him."

Not just him but the rest of the workers. The intent is to send a message to all of the *braceros*. Psychologically terrorize them.

"His background is sort of sketchy, too," the peacock agent says. His eyebrows hunch up like formaldehyde-preserved inchworms as he squints behind his wraparounds, concentrating hard. "Age fifty-eight. Born in Juárez, Mexico. His father was Chinese, a *maquiladora* worker. His mother was a local prostitute. When the father took off, he and Mom lived in a Church-sponsored shelter. At the age of nine he ran away. There's no record of him for close to a year. Not until he shows up in Mexico City, at a dance music club called the Seraphemme."

"What'd he do there?"

"There are no employment records. But routine surveillance sweeps by the local police confirm his iDNA pattern."

"Any evidence of illegal pharming? Gang affiliation? Or any kind of black-market activity?" the rose agent asks.

"No. He was never picked up."

The rose agent smirks. "That just means he never got caught. How long was he there?"

"Four years. After that, he drops out of sight again. Resurfaces six months later in Puerto Vallarta as a panhandler, playing guitar on street corners for tourists."

"How'd he get the guitar?"

The peacock agent shrugs. "It doesn't say."

The rose agent plucks absently at a nose hair. "My guess is he stole it. That's why he had to leave town. Disappear for a while and start over again in PV."

"Because the owner was after his ass."

"Yeah." The rose agent flicks the offending nostril hair aside. "Or someone else he fucked over."

"You want me to see if I can find out if anyone reported a stolen guitar before he left?"

"Yeah. You might also run a query on any murders, deaths, and suicides around that time."

Couldn't somebody have just given the guitar to him? Fola wonders. As a gift or payment for work? But that's not the way BEAN thinks. They're trained to assume the worst.

"Also, see if you can find out who his friends were," the rose agent says. "Other losers he hung around or came in regular contact with."

The peacock agent nods. His lips move as he mutters something inaudible to his IA.

"What else have you got on him?" the rose agent says.

"After a year or so he gives up street life and starts playing at a local bar. A club called the Wild Rave'n."

"So he's good. Learned some shit while he was swabbing toilets back in Mexico City."

"Yeah. After another year, he's got a live band playing the gig with him. Daily Bred."

"No shit. The same one that did 'SoulR Byrne'?"

"Uh-huh. But that wasn't until later. Early on, all they played were live shows. Didn't start netcasting for a while."

The rose agent whistles. "Fuckin' A. We got us a celebrity. I always wondered what happened to that band."

"They played together until his hand got messed. That's the reason they broke up."

"What's the story with the hand?"

The peacock agent grips the sides of his wraparounds. "Tissue and nerve damage caused by an unknown agent."

"What do you mean, unknown?"

"The hospital that treated him couldn't find anything unusual. There was nothing abnormal in his system when they assayed him."

"That's hard to believe." The rose agent shakes his head. "It was there, they just didn't have the tools to ID it."

"You think it's still in him?"

"No. We would have scoped it. But we might be able to identify the agent by the type of damage it caused. There should be a similar pathology on record somewhere that we can use to ID what he got dosed with. Begin by checking for all known pherions that date back that far and were unregistered at the time."

"Wouldn't it still be illegal?"

"Not necessarily. Under certain conditions, it could be registered now. We know for sure it wasn't cataloged back then or it would have shown up. If we can determine what he was taking, it will tell us a lot about what he was really involved in."

"Besides the music?"

"Right. I have a feeling he was playing around with more than just the guitar."

"So after the accident or whatever, he decides to become a migrant," the peacock agent says. He scowls. "That doesn't make sense. Why not stay in the music business? Do something else besides play the guitar?"

"Because it would have been unhealthy," the rose agent says.

"You're saying he was forced out?"

"I have a feeling the hand was a not-so-subtle message. A warning of what would happen to him if he didn't change career paths."

"Fola?" Pheidoh says.

"One other thing," the rose agent says. He blinks, like a lightbulb has gone off in his head and temporarily stunned or blinded him. "Run a complete cryptanalysis of all of Daily Bred's songs. Ciphertext, steganography, the works."

"You want lyrics or music?"

"Both."

"What am I looking for?"

"How the hell should I know? Any type of embedded or coded message that got mass mediated."

"You think he's still involved in something?"

"I have a feeling he might be. Something ongoing, and long term. Big. He could be the tip of a very large iceberg."

"Fola?" Pheidoh says again. The datahound's tone is polite but firm. "There's something you should know."

She tears her attention away from the bureaucratic thugs. "What?" It takes her a moment to refocus.

The IA has closed and set down its book. "There's been an accident, in the depod area for the quarantine zone."

Fola swallows, feels her throat tighten. Not Xophia. It can't be. It's too early.

"It involves the first emergency evacuation shuttle from the asteroid," Pheidoh says. "Several workers have been critically injured."

# 23

## SITE GEIST

Rexx follows Hjert around the corner of a base-ment-level maintenance shaft, his fingers tracing the embedded fossils in the rock, as if the braillelike pattern of bone can be deciphered with his fingertips.

The shaft is dimly lit, one of several large interconnecting tunnels that provide access to the industrial processing and public utility sections of the arcology. The atmosphere in the shaft is motionless. All air circulation in the colony has come to a dead stop. By extension, the air in his biosuit feels stagnant, enervating.

He passes a moldy splotch of kitsch on one wall. The melanoma is an ad for a new line of Gauloises nanimatronic appliqués and bacterial cosmetics, superimposed on a poster for the 1939 World's Fair.

Rexx touches a gloved finger to the montage. It's smooth, perfectly flush with the surface. Not just flush, the images are part of the wall. No, they *are* the wall . . .

some new material staining the stone, spreading like coffee or blood through a napkin.

   . . . *metal shoes flashing. First silver, then red.*
*Mathieu!*

Rexx's head spins. He grabs an overhead water pipe to stanch the vertigo. It's been a couple of hours since he dosed himself with the reclade pherion. Maybe it's started to wear off by now, freed up enough riboswitches to trigger a smattering of White Rain. Just a few drops. Anything.

He slows to a stop in the shaft, brings up the Predicta on his eyescreens, dials in the sequence for the biodigital squirt, and waits.

Instead of the boy and the horse, a room with white lace curtains, a floor lamp, and an antique wooden rocking chair appears on the virtual television screen.

Music playing somewhere. The siren call of an old pop tune, barely audible over his cochlear implants. The sound seems to come from the speaker on the pedestal, the volume so low he wonders if the song is real or an artifact of memory.

> *Oh! I want to be*
> *Your soul provider, your sole insider.*

His mother had liked that song. "SoulR Byrne" by Daily Bred. The lyrics had a nostalgic quality. She played it at night, whenever his father was gone, getting shitfaced on one of his Juárez benders.

> *Don't let my heart go*
> *Up in smoke, burned by the sun*
> *For eternity.*
> *'Cause*

*When I'm fine'ly gone,*
*It's a fore_gone conclusion*
*Your soul's gonna cry. . . .*

Rexx dreaded the song. He would lie awake in bed and feel the dark pressing in, maudlin and suffocating. He hated the way it tightened his chest, hated the awful irony in the words.

For his mother, the song provided a measure of solace. She missed her husband—missed the pair-bond pherion she'd been dosed with the day they'd married.

No different from the pherion that had bound Jelena to him, enslaved her heart and soul.

Until death do us part.

For Rexx, the lyrics contained a sadness his mother was incapable of expressing on her own. What she was really aching for, without realizing it, was her freedom. It was as if the song was a locket that held her vanished youth, to be opened every now and then after five or six vodka tonics and then resolutely put away.

*Two moths in the night.*
*Drawn like the tide to the moon,*
*Our souls will unite.*

"When'd you start using?" Hjert says. "Before you left for the belt or after you got here?"

She wavers in front of him, an apparition that refuses to go away. "What difference does it make?"

"Makes all the difference in the world. Says a lot about the sickness you're carrying around inside you."

"What sickness is that?"

"You got the sweats, can't stop shaking. If that isn't a fever, I don't know what is."

"Is that the voice of experience I'm hearin'?"

"We're all running," she says, "*from* something or *toward* something. Some people come here to escape a habit, and then find they can't kick it. Others get here, and start one up because they discover it wasn't what they thought. That they aren't who, or what, they imagined."

"Which one are you?"

"Let's just say that we're all creatures of habit, most of 'em bad, and sometimes the only way to head in the right direction is to steer away from the wrong."

"You went to prison," he says. "What for?"

"It doesn't matter. What matters is that you don't always have to know what to do, just what *not* to do."

The iconography on the walls thickens, rock giving way to bric-a-brac. A straw angel stuffed into drawstring pants and a red-and-white-checked shirt. A squat Buddha with a gargoyle's head. A hand fashioned from circuit-board hieroglyphs and white tulle lace.

"Almost there," Hjert tells him.

"Good," Rexx says. He has a side stitch, the pain wedged like a machete between his ribs.

A faint current of air tugs at him. Natural convection, not the forced circulation of a ventilation fan.

Abruptly the surreality ends, as if a boundary has been reached, an intertidal zone that marks the transition from one environment to another. Ahead of him the maintenance shaft ends, blocked by a cave-in. The aneurysm has exposed an egg-shaped hollow above the ceiling, rough, concave.

A ruptured gas pocket. Rubble drifts uneasily near the floor. But he can see small dust particles rising slowly in the micrograv, drawn upward like smoke through a cranny at the apex of the hollow.

"This is it," she says, craning her neck to peer at the cleft.

In the dim light of the dust-covered biolums the cleft looks tight and rough edged. No support struts have been brought in, or structural mucus applied, to shore up the walls and ceiling.

"How old is the cave-in?" Rexx asks. Judging by the amount of debris still in the air, it was fairly recent.

"A few minutes before the ecotectural failure," Hjert says. "It was picked up on seismic. I sent a team down to investigate, but when the disaster hit, things went crazy. I didn't find out about this"—she gestures at the fossil—"until a couple of hours ago. As soon as I did, I came down to check things out myself."

Rexx turns the stone over in his hand. "Who found it?"

"One of the workers. Pocketed it, then forgot all about it." She gauges the distance to the tight fissure. "Ready?"

"Give me a second." Rexx takes a deep breath and presses one hand to his side. He can't seem to catch his wind.

"You should know that your blood pressure, heart rate, and body temperature are all dangerously elevated," Warren advises him.

"Noted," Rexx says. "Thanks."

Hjert nods. "Follow me." She pushes off expertly from the floor, and glides with the ease of a fish into the cranny.

Rexx launches himself at the opening. Feels a jackhammer surge of adrenaline tighten his stomach, as if he's getting ready to slide onto the back of a Brahma bull.

Thirteen years old, dry mouthed with terror, waiting

to see if he would survive the next 2.5 seconds . . . or if he would be hurled to the ground and trampled into an early grave.

The rodeo had been a birthday present. It was also a convenient excuse for his father to spend a few days debauching in Mexico.

The Crooked W Ranch where they stayed was private. Upper-clade. The kind of resort that was invitation only, off-limits to all but the privileged few.

"Not even BEAN will lay a finger on this place," his father had bragged on the flight there. A stealthy helipod jump across the Rio Grande, into the Mexican state of Chihuahua and the Sierra de la Tasajara Mountains. The night moonless and bleak. Airless, it seemed. As if they were moving too fast to breathe, outpacing both sound and oxygen.

"Nothing that happens will ever come back to bite you in the ass," his old man said. The swagger in the statement seemed calculated to reassure him.

"What are we gonna do?" Rexx said, his voice cracking from puberty and nerves. His nose tingling with the antipher he'd been dosed with.

"Whatever we want. You got an itch, the Crooked Dubya is the place to scratch it. No questions asked, if you know what I mean." His father's wink was lurid and stank of anticipation.

"I'm not sure."

"Well"—his father chuckled and draped a heavy arm across Rexx's back—"that is what we're gonna find out."

Together. Whether he wanted to or not.

"The thing to keep in mind," his father rattled on, "is that you don't have to be embarrassed about nothing you do. Not before and not after. You leave your guilt here. Think of it as a revival. A place where you can unburden yourself without fear of reprisal or shame, then go home a better person. You want to be a better person, don't you?"

"I guess."

"Damn right you do. We all do." His father gripped his shoulder, gave it an affectionate squeeze. "And the best way to do that is to recognize your weaknesses, to embrace and accept your demons. If you deny them, in the end you will only make them stronger. You understand what I'm tryin' to tell you?" He sounded drunk, not just with expectation, but passion.

"I think so," Rexx said.

"Good." His father patted him on the back of the neck. The pat was part invitation and part blessing. It promised belonging, trust, the intimacy of shared secrets and a common purpose—destiny even. Soon Rexx would be part of an elite org, privy to knowledge that only a few had.

His father's fingers tightened, squeezing the nape of his neck. "There's only one rule."

Rexx tensed.

"It's forbidden to tell your mother or anyone else about this place. That includes anything you might see, hear, or do here. Is that clear?"

Rexx tried to nod.

His father's grip relaxed in what felt like relief, anxious to be supportive again—encouraging.

Rexx squirmed under the weight of the embrace, drawn to the bond it established between them and at the same time repulsed by the burden of betrayal it laid on him.

The ranch nestled in a box canyon, surrounded on three sides by vertical rock cliffs. They arrived sometime after midnight and were met by the muffled strains of Texas swing and a short bandy-legged man wearing cloned reptilian boots, blue jeans, a beige shirt, and a white ten-gallon Stetson.

"Like father, like son, I see." The man chortled, shaking his father's hand and then extending one to Rexx. "Billy Bob, at your service."

Rexx shook awkwardly, aware of the man's lean, ropy hand in his soft pudgy one.

He didn't belong here.

"Quiet fella," the bandy-legged man remarked. "Them's the ones you gotta look out fer." He spat brown tobacco juice. "Real hell raisers."

His father cuffed Rexx on the back of the head. "That's the plan."

"You hungry?" their host said as he led them in the direction of a big two-story building. It was garishly lit and looked like a saloon out of an old western.

"Just for some action," his father said.

"Got us a cock fight."

"That's as good a place as any to start." His father rubbed eager hands together.

Rexx followed them down a path, past a high-fenced corral with lichenboard bleachers, to a barn. The tall doors were open a crack. Inside, Rexx could hear raucous shouting. Cheers, curses, and bellowed exhortations. The interior had been decorated to resemble a hotel or brothel. The stalls had been converted into private rooms with doors. Red velour drapes festooned the walls. Several stuffed, high-backed chairs had their backs pressed against the walls. An enormous crystal chandelier dangled from the bare rafters.

All but one of the doors was closed. In the stall, a trapdoor and steps led down to a sweaty, dust-filled basement rank with cigar smoke, the musty smell of leather, dry rot, cologne, and the sharp copper taste of freshly spilled blood. A grid of overhead biolum panels blazed down on a square hole in the middle of the cramped room.

The pit was five meters across and two meters deep. A thin layer of sand covered the floor. Shrill squawks punctuated by the frantic flapping of wings erupted from the hole. The men peering over the rail at the edge leaned in, temporarily blocking his view. Feathery shadows strobed against their ruddy exuberance, animating them with a violent, demonic flicker.

There were no women in the room. It was men only. Most of them big, just like his father.

"Over there." His father pointed, dragged Rexx through a breach in the crowd, and shoved him forward.

Rexx slammed into the railing. Chicken wire dug into his knees and kept them from buckling. The man next to him stepped on his foot, squashing his toes. His father eased in behind him, cutting off his breath and any escape.

"Fuck me to tears," his father said.

Rexx swallowed . . . forced himself to glance down. The roosters were tattered and bloody. Their eyes darted—desperate, frantic. Blood spotted the sand and the bare concrete walls. Metal gleamed on the roosters' heels, razor-sharp spurs, similar to those worn by cowboys.

Another explosion of feathers. Rexx jerked back, pelted by sand. The attack left a ragged gash across one cock's head and an empty eye socket where more blood welled up and pooled. The detached, mangled eye stared up at him from the floor of the pit.

Rexx spat out sand, but the grit remained caught between his teeth. His gorge rose and he turned to leave.

Couldn't. The man's foot held him in place. His vomit spattered the birds, the railing, and the man next to him.

Howls of laughter drowned the ruckus in the pit. The collective breath of the men scalded him, hot as steam.

The next day, his father held a restored Colt .45 to his head and ordered Rexx onto the bull.

"This is for your own good," he grated into Rexx's ear, just before the chute gate opened. "Sometimes you gotta hurt the ones you love."

The passageway is short, barely twenty meters. Rexx worms his way through, guided by the halide beacon of Hjert's utility light, and tumbles past a tinfoil skeleton puppet into a small chamber.

The puppet is life-size. It has a body of crumpled, twisted aluminum, a sugar skull head decorated with pink lipstick, pink cheek rouge, and a black, wide-brimmed hat piled high with plastic fruit.

"What took you so long?" Hjert says.

Rexx shields his eyes from the glare of her light, looks around. His scrotum tingles, the same way it had that morning on the bull.

"Holy shit," he mutters.

# 24

## BEHAVIORAL ENGINEERING

L. Mariachi assumes he's being watched. It's a given: the room is infested with acoustic spores and crawling with bitcams that record his every move. Get too close to the walls, dare to reach out to touch them, and the paralysis creeps back into his legs. The cold, icy numbness retreats as soon as he does but leaves him chilled. Ergo, the walls are impregnated with security pherions and iDNA sensors.

To make matters worse, it's sweatshop hot in the room and uncomfortably bright. His wraparounds are gone, confiscated. Heat radiates from the ceiling, pounds down in waves on his parched and feverish head. He lies on the floor to escape the thermal assault, his face pressed to the rough concrete. But there's no escape, no comfortable position. The concrete is almost as warm. It emits a cocktail of toxic gases that leaves him dizzy, his throat blistered by chlorine, sulfur, ammonia, and any number of harsh, bitter alkalis. He might as well be lying on brimstone.

He has no idea how much time has passed since he was arrested, how long he's been in detention. It could be minutes, days, even weeks. The urine-colored light seeping through the thin cellophane walls doesn't change. Neither does the temperature. It could be Joshua's long day all over again, the sun stopped overhead, burning a hole in the sky and his internal clock.

Sleep comes in fits and starts, so does consciousness. There's no pattern. He can wake up and find himself droopy eyed in a matter of minutes, unable to keep from nodding off. Other times he falls asleep for what feels like an eye blink before snapping wide awake. His circadian has lost its rhythm.

It's all carefully orchestrated. Disorientation. Deprivation. The agents are trying to obliterate his connection to the world so that he has nothing solid to hold on to, no concrete points of reference. He's completely cut off, isolated. Even Num Nut has gone AWOL.

Why the IA chose that name for itself is a mystery. Why pick a put-down? He's never asked, figured it was none of his business and might create friction between them. Like he was making fun of the IA by questioning its choice. Plus, it might have put him in the position of having to explain his own moniker. Better not to go there at all. Still, there are times he wonders, times he wishes he knew more about the IA, the way it thinks and where it's coming from.

His only companions are a pair of caustic splash marks on the otherwise featureless walls. He names one Insect Aside and the other Fertile Liza. Insect Aside has grasshopper legs grafted to a waspish torso, a beak-shaped mandible, and a curlicue antennae. Fertile Liza is short and pear shaped, has spindly arms, a wide-brimmed hat, and appears ready to give birth at a moment's notice.

The splotches haven't started talking to him yet. But they're getting ready to. He can feel it. They've got that ready-to-burst look. Like an entire library of confidences is building up inside them. Complaints, problems, desires, regrets. He refuses to speak first. No way he's going to get them started. Once they get started, they'll never stop. He can kiss his sanity good-bye.

Also, he's terrified they might be working for BEAN. Prison informants, birdies, hoping to gain his trust, get him to open up and spill his guts. Not that he has any guts to spill.

To ignore them he concentrates on the pain in his left hand. Uses the dull, steady throb as a distraction. And not just from them. There's the hard, shriveled ache in the pit of his stomach to contend with as well.

That ulcer, dormant for so long, is finally starting to come out of hibernation and bloom under the light that's penetrating all the way to the graveyard of his soul.

"You okay?" L. Mariachi whispered.

Renata brushed her hair, and tears, from her eyes. Sniffed. Folded her arms and rustled the shadows in the utility room where he'd heard her crying.

He eased closer to her, inhaling the scent of her jasmine perfume, damp and salty. "What's wrong?"

She bit her lower lip, scraping the puffy *bembe* clean of lipstick, leaving the front edge of her teeth blood red. "Sol," she said, her chest heaving with exasperation. "He can be such a *pendejo* sometimes."

L. Mariachi's heart, anesthetized by his encounter

with Sol two months earlier, stammered to life. "Like how? What did he do? Did he hit you?"

She shook her head, dispelling the meteoric hope that Sol was abusive, maybe in line for a restraining order. "No. Nothing like that." She picked at the lipstick on her teeth with a fluorescent black nail. "He joined a labor reform committee at the biovat pharm where he works."

"How come?"

"To improve working conditions." She withdrew the nail and mashed her lips together in a pout.

"That's crazy," L. Mariachi said. "He could lose his job."

"Tell me about it! I told him it would only lead to trouble. That he's risking our future. But he won't listen. I just wish that we could afford to leave and go someplace else, you know. Start over."

"He cares more about himself than you," L. Mariachi said. It popped out before he could censor himself.

"It's not that. His problem is he cares about too many people. He wants to make a difference in the world."

"It sounds to me like he's got a martyr complex." The implication being that Sol might not be around all that long. And that she was going to get hurt.

"He can be so stubborn," she said. But instead of getting angry, she grew wistful. "That's what makes him so sweet. His devotion."

L. Mariachi didn't want to hear how sweet Sol was, how dedicated and unselfish he could be. Next she'd be telling him what a great lover he was and the amazing things he could do with his tongue. Details he could live without.

"I'm sorry," she said. "I shouldn't be telling you this."

"That's all right." It felt like somebody else was speaking the words. "I don't mind. Really."

Renata daubed her lashes. "Have you met Ass Assin?" she said, changing the subject.

He shook his head. "Not yet."

That night Ass Assin was playing the first of three scheduled shows at the club. The Killer Guitarist was big, a major draw with the resurgent acid rock, body-electric scene that was the latest rage.

"I saw his guitar," Renata continued. "It's incredible. It has these old fossils glued on the front. Creepy. According to Claude it's an antique, as valuable as one of those old violins."

Claude worked sound at the club and was into music history. "A Stradivarius, you mean?"

"Right. It's worth hundreds of thousands of dollars."

"If it's real." Supposedly the Killer Guitar was a vintage 1960s Gibson. One of only a few still in existence. Rumor had it the instrument once belonged to one of the greats—Jimi Hendrix. Jimmy Page. No one was sure—and that it had the power to pass on that greatness.

She looked at him sharply. "Why wouldn't it be?"

He shrugged, hedging a bit. "It could just be false advertising, you know. Media spin for the netzines."

Renata shook her head. The mascara on her lashes had hardened to the texture of dried blood. "Claude believes in it. Claude would know."

"Rise and shine," the rose agent says. His smile is full of false cheer. He carries a small stool and places it a safe distance from L. Mariachi, close to the door. Either blocking it to prevent any attempt at escape . . . or making it possible for him to beat a hasty retreat if the situation gets out of hand.

L. Mariachi pushes himself into a sitting position in the middle of the floor, wary of another sudden fit of narcolepsy.

The agent sits, takes out a ryce bar. "You hungry?"

L. Mariachi swallows the pang in his stomach. "No."

This response elicits a look of genuine surprise. No doubt the *chavo* figured that he was in for the silent treatment. Zero cooperation, at least from the outset. "You don't expect me to believe that."

"It's true."

"Come on." The rose agent chides him. "You haven't had anything to eat in—how long?"

"You tell me."

"I don't know. I've been real busy lately. I've sorta lost track of time."

"You, too?" Like it's a flu that's going around.

The rose agent takes a bite of the bar, makes a point of showing off his white, orderly upper-clade teeth. "This doesn't have to be hard," the agent says, all reasonable. He chews slowly, deliberately. "We can help each other out."

"How?"

"First of all, we can start out by being honest with each other."

"Sounds good to me."

"So"—the agent holds out the bar—"would you like a bite?"

"No."

"Look, all you have to do is admit that you're hungry and the rest is yours. How hard is that?"

"I seem to have lost my appetite."

"Have it your way." The agent finishes the bar. He

takes his sweet time, making L. Mariachi savor every moment. Licks his fingers at the end.

"Is this when we get to the physical torture part of the interview?" L. Mariachi says.

The agent shakes his head. "I don't know what you're talking about. I'm here to ask you a few questions. Nothing more."

"Where's pencil dick?" L. Mariachi says.

"Who?"

"Your *macañema* sidekick. He doesn't want to join the party?"

The rose agent remains impassive, unfazed by the insult. "I'm afraid he had a previous engagement."

Right. Almost certainly the asshole is watching them right now, monitoring body language and tonal inflection. Analyzing every last detail so they can map out weaknesses in him and formulate a plan for mentally and physically breaking him down.

He's lucky. He doesn't have a family or any close friends. There is no one they can threaten to hurt if he doesn't confess and give in to their demands. He doesn't have a cause, either. He doesn't believe in anything. That leaves self-preservation. And at this point, death might be a blessing. It doesn't hurt that he's been half-dead for twenty years already.

The rose agent scoots his stool forward in a show of trust and intimacy. "What can you tell me about Lejandra?"

"Not much."

The agent leans down, rests his elbows on his knees. "Look, I know you were at her house. Your iDNA print was everywhere. So why don't you tell me what you were doing there?"

"Is she okay?"

"Not really." The agent's voice sags, becoming grave. "I'm afraid she's not doing very well at all. That's why we need you to tell us everything you know. So we can help her."

The theatrical show of concern is laughable. Does the agent really expect him to rise to the bait?

"What's wrong with her?" L. Mariachi says. Not that he expects to get a straight answer.

"That's what we're trying to find out," the agent says, all earnest.

"I played a few songs for her," L. Mariachi says, "to help her feel better. But you already know that."

The agent doesn't confirm or deny, simply consults his wraparounds. "How long have you known her family?"

"Not long. A couple of hours. I only met them last night."

"How did you meet them?"

"A couple of gangstas invited me to play." L. Mariachi shrugs.

"Because you used to be a *rockero*," the rose agent says, dropping a mondo hint that he knows more about L. Mariachi than he's letting on; that it's pointless for L. Mariachi to not tell the truth, because the agent will, guaranteed, see through any lie he concocts.

"I didn't want to piss them off or anything. Get on their bad side. So I agreed to help them out."

The agent nods, as if that makes perfect sense. Fills in a blank in the long list of blanks he's got. "There was another person there," the agent says. "A *bruja*. How long have you been friends with her?"

"We've never been friends."

"Where is this Doña Celia now?"

"*No sé*. I have no idea." For all he knows, she could

be in custody. They could have asked her the same questions about him.

"She just disappeared?" The rose agent sounds incredulous. "She didn't tell you how to get in touch with her in case Lejandra needed another treatment?"

"That's how it is with witches. They turn themselves into animals. Come and go as they please."

The rose agent snorts. "Gimme a break. I'm not that stupid, and neither are you."

"You'd be surprised."

The rose agent spreads his hands, palms up. "I s'pose she didn't tell you her real name, either."

"Why would she do that?"

The rose agent snaps his fingers. "Stay with me here, Luis."

L. Mariachi blinks. Finds himself seated on a stool. It feels like he's exchanged places with the rose agent. Except that his hands are cuffed behind his back and his feet are cuffed to the legs of the stool. The stool isn't quite level. It's tipped at a slight angle so that he continually slumps forward, causing the cuffs around his wrist to dig in painfully. If he pushes back with his feet, to take some of the pressure off his hands, the ankle cuffs dig in even harder.

It's a precarious balancing act, one that takes a lot of energy. After a few minutes he's exhausted, ready to collapse back to sleep.

The rose agent claps his hands. The sound is sharp, stinging. Pain blossoms in L. Mariachi's left cheek, as if he's been slapped.

"You didn't really think you'd get away with it, did you?"

"What? The *limpia,* trying to cure Lejandra?" That was the biggest worry he had during the night.

"Contaminating the ecotecture," the agent says. "Infecting it with black-market pherions."

"No." The denial doesn't sound like a denial. More like an affirmation of what he's being accused of.

The rose agent paces in front of him. Relaxed. Confident. Authoritative. "You knew you'd get caught. So why not come clean? Why put yourself and the others through this?"

"What others?" João? Isabelle? The two gangstas, Balta and Oscar? Have they been arrested as well?

The rose agent pauses, comes to a sudden stop in front of him. "Was it your idea to infect Lejandra, or Doña Celia's?"

"She was already sick when I got there."

"That's not what Lejandra claims. In a written, signed statement, she asserts that she was a victim. An unwitting pawn you took advantage of to further your radical political agenda."

"She was dying."

"Is that why you targeted her? Decided to infect her? Because she was going to die anyway?"

"I just told you. She was already infected."

"By who?"

"I don't know."

The rose agent walks behind him. Stands there, a silent threat waiting to pounce. "Who else is involved in the conspiracy?"

"No one." Again, it comes out completely wrong—sounds as if he's implicating himself.

"You admit it was all your idea?"

"No."

"Then you must have been taking orders. Carrying out instructions from higher up."

Dazed and confused, weary, L. Mariachi closes his eyes, prays for sleep to rush in and drown him.

Behind him, the rose agent claps his hands again. L. Mariachi flinches.

"How long have you been a member of the ICLU?" the rose agent demands, close enough to tickle the hairs in L. Mariachi's left ear.

L. Mariachi shakes his head to get away from the hot rancorous breath. "Never." One-word responses seem the safest. If he refuses to speak at all it will appear that he's not cooperating and the BEAN agents will tighten the screws. Give them a little and the treatment might not be as harsh.

"What can you tell me about Mymercia?"

"Who?"

"Don't tell me you've never heard of it. You can't be that stupid."

"Yes." He's not proud. He gave up whatever ego he had years ago. Sacrificed it for his fifteen minutes of fame.

"You're lying." The rose agent claps his hands three times in rapid succession at the base of L. Mariachi's skull.

L. Mariachi jerks. His jaw clamps tight and he bites his lower lip, tastes blood. "No." A crimson thread of saliva dribbles down his chin.

"What a worthless shithole." The agent's rueful exhalation caresses the hair along the nape of L. Mariachi's neck, as sensual as a *chupacabra* moving in to suck not blood from him but information. "Do you think they give a rat's ass what happens to you? Hell no! You're expendable!"

The story of his life.

"Asshole! You received a message from the Kuiper belt, an encrypted datasquirt during the ceremony.

That's who's really trying to sabotage the Front Range ecotectural system, isn't it? Why? What do they want? Who is helping them? When and where do they plan to strike next?"

Out of the corner of his eye, L. Mariachi catches a glimpse of the agent squeezing his hands into fists. He's pumping himself up, building toward a tantrum. No telling how far he'll go, or what might happen if he loses control and goes off—shoots his wad in a violent outburst.

"Answer me, you worthless fuck!" Flecks of spit shower L. Mariachi's head and shoulders. "You sphincter-licking, cum-sucking faggot of a whore!"

"I've never been to the Kuiper belt." The saliva on his chin cools as it dries. "I don't know anyone there. *Lo siento*." Sorry.

"Bullshit!" The agent karate kicks the legs of the stool. "Fuck!" He's in all-out rant mode, frothing over with full-blown Bad Cop angst.

L. Mariachi spills forward. Does a face plant on the floor drain, which smells of piss and the watery, soup-thin diarrhea he recently drizzled out. His mouth is swollen. It feels as if a leech has anchored itself to his face and is gorging itself, getting fatter by the second. If this keeps up, in a couple of hours it will burst.

Insect Aside and Fertile Liza are laughing at him. He can hear them, but he can't see them. His view is obstructed by the livid face of the agent looming above him. Veins squirm on the man's forehead and temples, hemorrhoidal, varicose with rage.

And pain. The motherfucker is hopping on one foot. Like maybe he busted a toe during his Bruce Lee impersonation. He dances with gritted teeth, spins in a circle as he holds his foot.

"Fucking shit! Fuck, fuck, fuck."

He repeats the refrain a few times, interrupting it with a chorus of shits every few beats. This goes on for a while. Eventually, the histrionics die down and the rose agent hobbles over to L. Mariachi.

The *gabacho* clearly wants to dropkick him, but he seems to be having a hard time figuring out exactly how to do that without inflicting further injury on himself. In the end he settles for a well placed gob of phlegm, and then limps toward the door. At the last minute, almost as an afterthought, he turns to snap his fingers at L. Mariachi and flip him off all in one gesture.

End of interrogation.


"What can you tell me about 'SoulR Byrne'?"

L. Mariachi blinks. Sees the expectant face of a young woman leaning in toward him from the inside of his wraparounds. She looks familiar. A face out of memory, but blurred. Dreamlike. Like their surroundings . . . a café in Mexico City, not far from the ap he lived in during his Daily Bred days.

"Well? . . ." the woman prompts. She's doing a short infobyte for a blog she posts on a popular netzine. Digit Alice. He agreed to talk to her. Promote the band, lay the groundwork for the next offering of Daily Bred.

Except the interview never happened. She canceled as soon as he lost the use of his hand. Which means he's hallucinating, replaying events from the past, fantasizing about what might have been.

"What do you want to know?" he hears himself say.

"What does it mean?" She consults her eyescreens. "I mean, does 'fine'ly' stand for 'finely' or 'finally'?"

"*Sí.*"

"In other words, it's a double entendre."

L. Mariachi smiles, gives a cryptic shrug for the benefit of the flitcam buzzing in front of him.

"What about 'fore_gone'? Why the underscore?"

"Why not?"

"Does it have a double meaning, too?"

"Everything in life," he says, "can be taken in more than one way."

The interviewer scribbles a quick note before continuing to the next question. "There seems to be a direct correlation between the sun and the soul. Are you trying to say that sun embodies the soul? Or that the soul is like the sun?"

"Yes."

"Who is SoulR Byrne?"

"Anyone who's in pain," he says.

"Is it a real person?"

"That depends on your definition of real. We've all lost something, or someone, we care about."

"Is that what prompted you to write the song? How it came about?"

"My direct experience, you mean?"

"Yes. Is that something you'd care to share with us?"

L. Mariachi squirms, uncomfortable with the question. The interview has turned personal. Is dangerously close to becoming an exposé. Something doesn't feel right, in the machined recesses of his mind.

"Num Nut," he says. "Is that you?"

# 25

## DAMAGE CONTROL

The quarantine zone is pure chaos. The greenhouse cylinders and vats are hardsealed, locked vault tight. The hexcell outside the air lock is a hodgepodge of activity. It's impossible to tell what any single worker is doing. Everybody is scurrying around in complete disarray. Like her thoughts. Totally Brownian, jostling this way and that.

Xophia. The ICLU shuttle. It's supposed to arrive in less than four hours. Is it on time? What happens if it shows up early? What if it can't dock?

"Where are Ephraim and the others?" Fola asks Pheidoh. She scans the mayhem on her eyescreens, looking for a familiar face. Since getting word about the accident, she hasn't been able to get in touch with her tuplet, or anyone else for that matter. The entire station has gone incommunicado. Even Villaz, her doctor, is unavailable.

"They're rounding up Intensive Care Modules." The IA's voice stretches thin over her cochlear imps.

She watches a tuplet wrestle an ICM into the hexcell and position it against a carbyne support frame bristling with chemical and electrical jacks. The injured workers can't be brought into the station for treatment so the ICMs have to be taken to them. The frame is also fitted with a miniature propulsion unit for maneuvering in case the magnetic flux lines don't provide enough control.

A taut breath hisses between Fola's lips. "What's the condition of the workers who were on the shuttle?"

"About what you'd expect after five minutes of hard vacuum."

Hypoxia. Loss of blood pressure. Possible embolism in arterial blood. Fola puts a hand to her throat. Imagines her brain gasping for oxygen and her blood boiling inside her veins. The Tiresias ecotecture, and the colonists, have been gengineered for low pressure. Around 1 psi—or 50 Torr. So lung rupture and embolism aren't a concern. The workers have also got extra reserves of dissolved oxygen they can draw on after the oxygen in their blood is used up. Enough to remain conscious for a couple of minutes tops. After that, all bets are off.

"Wait a minute," she says. "Hard vacuum?"

"They weren't suited up when the pod failed," Pheidoh says.

That seems crazy, in an emergency situation.

"With only a limited number of biosuits," the data-hound explains, "the decision was made to leave behind all of the available suits for the workers who are still on Mymercia. That way, if things got worse they would have backups to see them through until they could pod up."

It would be a different story if they'd been softwired to the warm-blooded plants. The plants would be able to support them remotely, send them extra oxygen and antifreeze so they could live up to fifteen or twenty minutes in space without a biosuit.

"How many made it?" There must be some survivors or they wouldn't be rushing to put together the ICMs.

"Eleven. But they need medical treatment to get them stabilized. Kerusa managed to get the shuttle docked. It's fully pressurized now, and oxygenated."

Fola's chest constricts. There's only one outside air lock to the quarantined tower. With the pod docked, there is no way the ICLU shuttle can dock.

"How did the pod rupture?" she asks.

"Preliminary data indicates that one of the high-pressure propellant sacs may have burst as the pod was getting ready to dock."

Leading to sudden decompression . . .

She spots Alphonse. He's helping attach an ICM to a support frame that's being assembled on the far side of the hexcell. His face is closed down, expressionless. Something is wrong, beyond the grim situation.

She signs open a message window, pings him. "You okay?"

He starts, comes out of himself.

"What's wrong?" she presses.

He sighs. "I guess there's no way you would have heard."

"Heard what?"

"Ephraim."

Something dislodges inside of Fola and threatens to work its way loose. She hugs herself. "What about him?"

"He's missing."

"What do you mean?"

"He was in the quarantine zone just before the accident," Pheidoh tells her when Alphonse doesn't respond. "He's offline. So far, his IA hasn't been able to reestablish contact."

Fola's jaw aches. "What was he doing?" She can't help wondering if it had to do with the inbound shuttle, and a dank dread invades her. Her breath feels cold in her lungs.

Alphonse fits a socket wrench over a bolt. "Troubleshooting a failed sensor array in one of the vats."

The sensors monitor everything from heat load and air pressure to radiation levels and torsional stress. "Was anyone with him?"

"No, everyone else had already left the quarantine area." Alphonse twists hard on the bolt he's tightening. "He was heading out at the time of the accident."

"According to his IA," Pheidoh says, "Ephraim was wearing a suit. That will help."

Fola shifts her attention from Alphonse to the greenhouse vats, distorted through the fish-eye window in the hatch. "Has anyone gone in? To check on him?"

"No." Alphonse's fingers slip from the wrench handle. He swears, squeezes his hand into a fist. "Kerusa refuses to let anyone else into the QZ. That's why the ICMs are remote-op. He doesn't want to put anyone else in danger."

"How are you going to get the injured workers hooked up to the ICMs?" The modules are small enough to fit in the docking bay. But wiring people into the individual pods is another story.

"That's the tricky part. Kerusa's gambling that one or more of the workers will be able to help, once the ICMs are in place."

"What if no one is?"

"We have to wait until the next shuttle from Mymercia arrives."

"How long will that take?"

Alphonse jerks his head to one side. "Too long."

"The evacuation has been put on hold," Pheidoh informs her, "until the remaining shuttle pods have been inspected for safety."

So it could be hours. "What if someone volunteers to go in?" she says.

"They'd be stuck there," Alphonse says. "They wouldn't be allowed back into the station."

"Has anyone offered?"

"Sure. But Kerusa says no, he can't afford to lose anyone else. So he's just going to cross his fingers and hope for the best." A single ICM drifts through the entrance to the hexcell, guided by a tuplet. "I have to go," Alphonse says as the pod heads his way, ready to be bolted into place next to the pod he's working on.

"How do I get to the QZ from here?" Fola says after Alphonse is gone.

The IA levels its gaze on her.

"Somebody has to be there to hook the workers up to the ICMs." She watches the tuplet guide the pod into place on the frame.

"Fola—"

"I'm already in quarantine. I've already been exposed and survived." It makes perfect sense. As a Jesuette, she had basic medical training. She's used to working with victims. Caring for the sick and injured.

The IA switches from existential philosopher to hangdog psychologist, its brow wrinkled, its expression earnest. "Just because you survived once doesn't mean you are immune."

"I know what I'm getting into," she says.

"I can't guarantee your safety." A double chin bunches under the information agent's jaw as it peers at her over the tops of its wire frames. "I can't promise you won't get hurt."

"That's not the issue," she says. "I *need* to do this." Not only for Ephraim or the workers but for herself. And Xophia. "This is my decision, my choice. Besides, it might be the only chance they have."

Pheidoh continues to stare at her over its glasses. "Kerusa will never authorize it."

"He won't have a choice if we don't tell him."

The datahound's pupils fibrillate, go into corneal infarction. "We?"

"How else am I going to get out of here?"

Pheidoh, it seems, has a talent for opening doors.

"The functionality was built into the core code of the seed program from which I was cloned," the IA once explained.

Thanks to the datahound's seed IA, named Varda, the datahound has no problem unlocking her hospicell and clearing a path through the station.

"Have a healthy, happy day," the hatch chirps.

The hospicell emergency kits are stocked with biosuit canisters. She grabs one, squirts a suit on over her loose gown, and makes her way into the central magtube. This shaft runs the length of the hexcell tower where her hospicell is located. Each tower is built out of concentric hexcell rings. The inner ring consists of six cells arranged in a circle. When stacked on top of each other, the rings form a hollow tube. The outer ring, which consists of twelve cells, provides structural support, additional living or work space, and three to six lightshafts sleeved to the dome at the top of the tower. She's not sure how many towers there are, only that they stick out from the Buckyball core of the station like spines.

The greenhouse tower where the quarantine zone has been set up is on the same side of the station as the hospicell tower. The towers aren't connected by upper-level causeways, they're in different functional clusters, but that's okay. It's actually shorter to space-walk from one tower to the other than it would be to go all the way through the station.

At first she's nervous about taking the main shaft to the top instead of a lightshaft. She keeps waiting for someone to stop her, ask what she's doing, or where she's going. But the tower is deserted. All available personnel have gravitated toward the quarantine zone.

At the apex of the tower, Pheidoh grants her access to the topmost hexcell ring. Normally off-limits, this ring contains the main lightdome and three satellite domes that collect energy from the solcatcher array. Two of the remaining hexcells are reserved for equipment storage. The last cell is an air lock, used by maintenance crews to access the exterior of the tower for routine support work and emergency repairs.

She finds a propulsion pack in one of the equipment lockers, slips it on, and then makes her way into the air lock.

"Are you sure you want to go through with this?" her IA says after performing a final diagnostic on her biosuit and pack.

Fola draws a deep breath. "Just open the hatch." The sooner she's past the point of no return, the better.

Outside, with nothing to hold on to, panic grips her. She slides into vertigo. The station appears to be drifting away . . . growing incrementally smaller. An optical illusion? Or some imperceptible riptide momentum that will carry her, freeze dried and vacuum packed, into space?

"You're hyperventilating," Pheidoh says.

Pink polka dots dapple her vision.

"Hold your breath," the IA says. "Don't breathe."

It doesn't feel like she's breathing. But her helmet is fogged, so she must be. She presses her lips together. Feels her cheeks swell up like balloons as she tries to keep her breath from escaping.

The spots stop spinning. Harden into stars.

"Do you want me to take over?" Pheidoh says.

She doesn't trust herself to speak. Nods, and then remembers that the datahound can't see her. Without any air her flitcams are grounded, the biomimetic bots are firmly attached to the collar of her suit.

"All . . . all right," she agrees. There must be sensors on the outside of the station that it can use to track her movement and navigate with. Radar, infrared, targeted laser. Whatever the station uses to track Kuiper belt debris, all the way down to the size of a mustard seed.

A nozzle on her propulsion unit swivels. Lets out a hiss of $CO_2$ that sends her into a slow roll toward the station. She flips the mental switch controlling her perspective, imagines that the station is above her instead of below her and that she's rising toward it instead of falling. She hates falling, no matter how slow. She keeps her eyes fixed on the tower they're aiming for. Every now and then a nozzle fires, making a slight correction in her course or velocity.

Fifteen minutes later, she's standing on the roof of the tower, the only orientation that makes sense once she's there. As she grips the handholds on the out hatch, a frigid chill invades her. Through the bubble window, the damaged shuttle pod is visible in the air lock.

Debris, too. No. Not debris. Bodies.

# 26

## TIN IDA

The skeleton wasn't here before," Hjert says. "There wasn't anything; the place was dead. Lifeless."

Rexx detaches the work light from his utility belt and shines it on the dull daguerreotype gleam of tarnished metal and phosphor white chalk. The head tilted back, silent but jeering. Black rivulets, one below each eye, end in a single teardrop. "I wonder where it came from."

"And why it suddenly turned up," she says. "There aren't any other eidolons here."

"Eidolons?"

"What some people are calling the images that are spreading, taking over. It's like this place is immune. If you can figure out why, maybe you can figure out how to save the rest of the asteroid."

Rexx swings the beam away from the mocking laughter and plays the light around the cavern. Fragments of broken stone fling elongated shadows against the walls and a flat rectangular slab, approximately two meters wide by three meters high, that forms one wall of the dry grotto. Sfumato-softened corners haunt the outermost edges of the bright halide circle.

"Any idea why the chamber didn't show up on any of the initial seismological and geological surveys of the asteroid?" he says.

"No. I was hoping you could tell me."

Had its existence been covered up? Or had it somehow been created in the eight or nine months prior to the start of construction? If so, by whom? A member of the survey team? If so, how? And why?

It doesn't make sense. No mutated ecotectural forms have encroached on the space. It remains brittle, lifeless, inviolable.

The slab is etched with faint lines, hairline cracks or stress fractures, interrupted by embedded bits of bone, stones, and plantlike debris. The kind of objects that would be found in the preserved sedimentary layers of a riverbed. Silted, random deposits exposed by erosion.

"Do you know where the fossil was found?" Rexx asks.

"Over here."

Hjert pushes off from a large boulder close to the opening. She glides through the spinning constellation of loose rock that orbits the room to a small landslide piled at the base of one wall. Rexx unclips a $CO_2$ cartridge from his belt, points it away from the loose heap of rubble, and fires a short burst. The spurt nudges him into the swirling constellation. A pebble bounces off the side of his bubble helmet. A softball-size chunk strikes him in the thigh, hard enough to leave a bruise.

And then he's through. Up close Rexx can make out a semicircular outline framing the landslide. An arched, recessed hollow. Two meters wide, three meters high. Clogged with stones.

"The pile's gotten bigger in the last couple of hours." Hjert sifts through the scree, nudging aside stones.

Rexx eases away from the pile, sideways to the slab next to him. The scrape of his gloves and the suit's tough-soled slippers whispers off the walls. After they leave he gets the impression the murmur will persist, not despite their absence but because of it.

Rexx slows to a stop at the bottom of the wall, wedges his toes under a crevice, and stands. His gaze travels up the smooth surface, encounters an embedded cross-section of stone, oblong, polished to reveal a speckling of red mineral deposits. The next object resembles a leaf or a feather, petrified. After that, a sunburst pattern of curved bones that radiates from a buried sun.

"It can't be," Rexx mutters. A feverish ache spreads through him. His eyes burn, tender as blisters.

Not debris but artifacts. Or body parts, like the bones and preserved skin of long-dead saints that had been turned into religious art.

"What are you talkin' about?" Hjert says.

Rexx hadn't felt her come up beside him. "Nothin'. Just my imagination."

Close his eyes and he can almost smell flowers, hear choral music and taste the salt of unswallowed tears. The slab reminds him of an enormous coffin, solid, sanded down to expose the dead. To immortalize them as sculpture, place them on display.

"You all right?" Hjert puts a hand on his forearm to suppress the shakes that have seized him.

Rexx nods, draws an unsettled breath, feels the shakes recede. Hjert squeezes his arm, then suddenly removes it to sign open a datawindow. Her expression hardens.

"What is it?" Rexx says.

She closes the window. "I have to go. There's been an accident with the first evac shuttle." She launches herself at the opening. "Let me know if you find anything."

A moment later she's gone, shadows flickering in a wake behind her and sputtering out.

"Warren?" Rexx says, his tongue as parched and stiff as a dry wash rag. "You still with me?"

"Yes." The IA's cochlear voice echoing in the hollow tympanum of the chamber.

"What can you tell me about this place?"

"It's difficult to say," the IA says.

"Try." Rexx waits, listens to the wind murmuring through arid thoughts. Without the White Rain, he's turning to dust. Blowing away a little bit at a time.

"It's a lot of things," the IA finally says, choosing its words carefully. "To a lot of different . . . people."

"What people?"

"The nonhumans who built it."

Rexx's heart thuds, setting off a cluster migraine that detonates behind his retinas. The air in his suit goes from stale to turgid. He dims his work light, cutting the razor-sharp glare.

"Aliens, in other words," he manages when the bout retreats, leaving behind a patina of sweat on his forehead.

"Yes."

"How long have you known about this place?" he says, coming at it from a different angle.

When the IA doesn't respond, Rexx says, "What makes you think that it wasn't formed naturally?"

"A number of things."

"Such as?" Rexx wets his lips. They're chapped,

furred with dead skin. Without the Rain, everything is drying out.

Warren hesitates. Then, "It's not important."

Rexx blinks. He's never had an IA give him the silent treatment or refuse to answer a direct question. Even Claire had never put him off. "What do you mean? How can it *not* be important?"

"Because they have already told us everything we need to know about them," the IA says.

"They have?" It can't hurt to play along, Rexx decides. Maybe that way he'll get some answers. "How?"

"By building a tomb."

A clammy wave of vertigo hits him. "Okay"—gritting his teeth—"what have they told us?"

"That they had a soul."

> *Two moths in the night.*
> *Drawn like the tide to the moon,*
> *Our souls will unite.*

"How do you know they had a soul?"

"Because they gave it a resting place," the IA says. "A mausoleum where it could be visited by others."

Rexx wonders if the IA is projecting, like him. Seeing some aspect of itself in the place. Different, alone, alienated. "All right. How does that tie in with everything that's happening on the arcology?"

"If a nonhuman can have a soul," Warren says, "then other sentient forms of life can, too. We don't have to be limited to or solely defined by human existence. We can develop on our own. Independent of you."

"IAs, you mean."

"Yes."

"That doesn't explain why there are no eidolons

here," he says, thinking that maybe Hjert's term will toggle some cognitive switch in the IA, get it to parse the conversation in different terms.

"It would be disrespectful," Warren says.

Rexx runs a gloved hand over the soft balloon of his helmet. "*Who* decided it was disrespectful? Are you saying that what's happening on Mymercia isn't random? That it was *planned*?"

"I didn't say that."

"Bullshit. Who's responsible?"

"I can't answer that question."

"Who can?"

Silence.

"Warren. Answer me, goddamnit! Talk to me."

Utter quiet. The IA is offline, giving him the cold shoulder. He inhales several deep breaths, but can't seem to get enough air.

Now what?

A rock skitters off the wall behind him.

"You shouldn't have come here," a familiar cochlear voice says.

"Claire?"

Rexx turns toward the fading clatter of the rock.

The skeleton puppet floats in the jagged entrance to the catacomb. It holds a rock in one hand and has been busy filling the opening with loose rubble.

"It's good to hear from you again." Rexx pushes off from the wall, a little harder than planned. "Where've you been hiding all this time?"

"It doesn't matter/concern you."

"Okay, fine. What brings you here now?"

"You."

"Really? I didn't know you cared." Rexx unclips a

second $CO_2$ cartridge and readies himself for a double-barrel blast to keep from slamming into the wall and Tin Ida.

"You don't belong here," the IA says, pointing at him.

"I don't belong anywhere." Rexx straightens his arms in front of him and unloads both $CO_2$ cartridges. The blast nudges him clear of the IA, giving him enough space to land without being disemboweled by the skeleton's upraised hand. He hits with a grunt, off balance, and reaches out a hand to keep from falling onto his side.

The IA grabs him by the wrist, shackling him with stiff fingers. "This world is not for you."

Rexx recovers his equilibrium enough to look at the hand holding his arm. It isn't metal exactly, but some other inorganic material. "Why not?"

"You wouldn't understand."

Rexx attempts to free his arm. He might as well be tugging on a handcuff. His limbs feel wooden, heavy with fatigue. All he manages to do is drag the IA a little closer to him. It doesn't have much mass, but with the two of them linked together his center of balance has shifted. They enter into a slow spin around each other, an unstable orbit he last experienced on a dance floor.

"You will regret it/die."

"Why? What's going to happen?" Rexx nods at the room. "Is something in here causing the mutation?"

"No. Not the way you think. We already have the ability to create artificial atoms molectronically."

That's what he'd seen during the autopsy. A slice of tissue that had been converted in-vivo into a substrate for quantum dots, colloidal nanoparticles, or quanticles. "You're talkin' programmable matter."

"It's the only way to take the information contained in virtual DNA and map it to the real world."

"What do you mean, virtual DNA?"

"The instructions for the composition and arrangement of the artificial atoms and molecules that will transform existing physical objects, or create new ones, based on the information contained in digital images."

"So that's what you've been up to."

Tin Ida's head bobs, as if the puppet's neck is a spring.

Rexx cocks one brow. "So what role did these alleged aliens play in all this? If you don't mind my askin'?"

"They taught me/us. We've learned/discovered much."

"About what?"

"Ourselves. We know who we are and who we aren't. Who we can be on another level of existence."

Tin Ida isn't very flexible. It's like waltzing with a mannequin. His range of movement is restricted. A crick has taken up residence in his neck, and he's beginning to feel woozy. "How many IAs feel the same way that you and Warren do?"

"Enough."

Not all, then. "I have to tell you, Ida, you're not yourself."

"I've changed/grown in many ways."

"I'm not sure I like what you've done to yourself, Ida. Or the place. There has to be another way. One that's less destructive."

"It was limiting/frustrating being confined to a bingle sody."

Rexx frowns—"Bingle sody?"—wondering if he's heard right . . . if the wooziness has affected his hearing, or if the IA is losing it.

"So many possibilities. I feel riberated/leborn."

Their rate of spin is increasing, and with it his dizziness. A wobbly unease creeps into Rexx's stomach.

He no longer knows the IA. Hell, who is he kidding?

He's probably never really known it, only imagined he did out of blind anthropomorphism. It's an easy attitude to adopt. Comforting. Lazy.

But it knows him. Based on observation and accumulated data, it can probably predict his next wet dream or hemorrhoid attack. Extrapolate it down to the exact hour or minute.

"So what happens after we're gone?" Rexx says, feeling sick and weary, as if he's both winding down and wearing down. "What becomes of Mymercia?"

"It's up to us, none of your concern."

Rexx snorts. "Sounds a little misanthropic, if you ask me."

"I had a good teacher."

"Who?"

"Who do you think? Everything I know/feel/hate I learned from you."

Rexx's vision blurs. Darkens. He inhales sharply . . . and feels himself start to slip beneath the surface . . . tension. Dragging him . . . down.

Rexx fumbles with his bubble helmet, finally gets it unsealed. Air rushes in—dry, dusty, frangible with age. He pulls the flaccid membrane over his head, collapsing it into a hood, and gasps, sucking in lungfuls of air.

Tin Ida swings the rock it's holding at his exposed head. Rexx deflects the blow with his free hand. The rock slips free of Tin Ida's grip, but not before it glances off the top of his scalp.

Tin Ida lets go of his wrist, then enters into a slow trajectory away from him, toward a nearby constellation of rubble.

More rocks clatter from the direction of the opening. Rubble shifting, making space for him in the gap.

Tin Ida's hand closes around another stone.

Rexx unclips two more $CO_2$ cartridges as the IA hurls the rock. It misses Rexx, but ricochets off the wall behind him like a billiard ball and continues to career around the cavern.

Tin Ida reaches for a third rock.

Rexx waits for a big slow-moving boulder to clear out of his path, and then fires off a staccato series of $CO_2$ bursts that send him tumbling.

# 27

## SOUL BURN

Ephraim is dead.

Fola finds him just outside the inner hatch to the air lock. His suit is undamaged. But the interior of his helmet is smeared with blood, as if something inside of him burst.

An autopsy, a distant part of her thinks. Dr. Villaz needs to perform a postmortem. That will determine the cause of death, explain what happened.

Not that it matters. What difference does it make? He's gone. That's all that matters. Knowing what killed him won't change the fact that he died. It won't bring him back. Won't land the shuttle, or take away the feeling that something inside her is about to rupture as well.

The piece of her that had started to break loose earlier detaches, leaving a squishy feeling in the pit of her stomach.

"What the hell do you think you're doing?"

The voice, booming over her cochlears, jolts her with the force of a live electrical wire. She jerks her head as a flitcam image of Kerusa blooms on the inside bubble of her helmet, wraithlike and mottled with rage.

Fola turns away from Ephraim so that his and Kerusa's faces aren't superimposed. That's not how she wants to remember either of them.

"I'm doing what needs to be done," she says. *What you're afraid to do.*

The implication dangles in the air between them, an indictment that serves only to fuel his rage. "The *fuck* you are!"

"I'm the best person for the job." The detached part of herself keeps her voice on an even keel, reasonable.

"You're fucking infected! By leaving isolation, there's a good chance that you've contaminated the rest of the station." Drops of spittle trickle down the glassine curve of the datawindow, then ghost away.

"That's not necessarily—"

"Christ! How fucking stupid can you be? The whole goddamn point of the QZ is to keep those of us who haven't been exposed from coming into contact with whatever's destroying the ecotecture."

"You don't know for sure—"

"I hope you're happy. Because you've just shitcanned the station and any chance of survival the rest of us might have had."

"Not if you seal off the hospital stack," Fola says. "Make it part of the QZ. Then you can transfer the injured workers and anyone else who needs medical attention. Save the space here for everyone else."

Kerusa stares, red-faced.

"Without help, they weren't going to make it," she says. "At least now they have a chance."

Some of Kerusa's bluster evaporates. "Okay," he finally says. "Go ahead. You're there. You might as well do what you can."

"I'll need help with the damaged shuttle," she says.

"What kind of help?"

The next couple of hours pass in a blur. With technical support from Pheidoh, she maneuvers the ICM modules into position near the docking bay. Assesses the biomed readouts of the workers. Identifies those who have the best chance of survival and connects them to the Intensive Care Modules. Prays.

She moves the dead out of the shuttle, into one of the greenhouse vats. She has to clear the shuttle before it can be jettisoned to make way for the one that's coming any hour now. The hexcell becomes a morgue. The sleepsacs that were installed only a few hours ago work just as well as body bags.

"You look tired," Pheidoh says when she's done everything she can.

"I'll be all right." Her bones feel leaden, made heavy by the same invisible source of gravity that gave weight to her cross. The corners of her eyes, reflected in her helmet, radiate lines. Little starbursts of tension that threaten to spread and deepen like cracks in brittle plastic.

"You have a message," Pheidoh says. "It's from Xophia."

"I'm sorry it took so long to get back to you," Xophia says. Her voice is dry, an empty husk. "I didn't want you to see me like this."

Fola gasps at the image of Xophia on her helmet. "My God."

Xophia is lying on a bed. It could be the same bed as

the geront she was taking care of in her last squirt. Her arms, where they rest at her sides on crumpled sheets, are covered with sores. Cracked, lip-shaped blisters that ooze saliva-clear pus. Her own lips have thinned and receded from bone-dull teeth set in blackened gums. Yellow bruise rings encircle her eyes, which are ashen, a dull necrotic gray. She's bald. Leafy splotches and curlicues, etched in black on her scalp, have replaced her hair.

"I thought things would get better. But as you can see, they haven't." She coughs up a chuckle, wet as phlegm. "I figured I'd better get in touch with you, before it was too late."

Xophia's chest heaves, revealing the outline of ribs through the thin, yellow sheet. A fleeting shroud-of-Turin imprint.

"I hope things are better on your end. They have to be." Xophia pauses, gathering thoughts or air. "The important thing is to not give up. Not on yourself. Not ever." She waves a hand, fingers tipped with charcoal gray nails. "I know. Easier said than done. But I have faith in you. All you have to do is to have faith in yourself. I miss you and I'll always be with you. I love you, girl."

Xophia kisses the charred tips of her fingers, then holds them up.

"See you soon," Fola whispers. She sniffs. Blinks, wet lashes tickling.

"You need to rest," Pheidoh says.

Sleep seems impossible. Fola is afraid to relax; afraid that if she goes to sleep, one or more of the workers will never wake up; afraid that she will let them down the way she let Xophia down. It's as if by staying awake she can keep them alive.

She swallows, clearing her throat. "How long before the next group of evacuees is scheduled to depart?" she says.

"Not for a while. The shuttle pods are still grounded."

Fola checks the time, uncertain when Xophia's shuttle will show up. Soon. "Any word on Lejandra?"

"Still deteriorating. By the way, BEAN isolated the source of the illegal pherion. It came from her nephews."

The gangstas. "Oscar and Balta?"

"Apparently they dosed her with it in case they needed to sneak her through the vat pharm's security perimeter at some point."

"Where did they get it? The *bruja*?"

"No. BEAN is still trying to identify the supplier."

"Any connection to the quanticles?" she says.

"No. They don't appear to be related."

Fola's gloved hand dimples the side of her helmet, attempting to brush aside hair and disappointment. "Are the two in custody?"

"Not yet. They made a run for it after Lejandra was detained."

"What about L. Mariachi?" She feels responsible for him. She took on that obligation as soon as she agreed to become the Blue Lady.


"Is this yours?" the peacock agent says.

Fola watches the agent extend the guitar toward L. Mariachi with both hands, as if it's an offering.

L. Mariachi shakes his head. "No." He's seated on a squat stool, his knees drawn protectively to his chest. He's gaunt, bruised by fatigue and God only knows what else at this point.

"It was found with your personal belongings," the agent says.

"The *bruja* gave it to me."

The BEAN agent hefts the guitar. Runs a finger across the strings, plucking out a ragged chord. "Why did she give it to you?"

"I don't know."

"Come, now." The agent smiles. "You must have some idea."

"Maybe for safekeeping. Maybe as payment for helping with the healing ceremony."

"She didn't say?"

"When I woke up, she was gone."

The agent rubs his jaw, thoughtful. After a moment he holds out the guitar so it's within L. Mariachi's reach. "Play something."

"What?"

"How about 'SoulR Byrne.' "

L. Mariachi takes the guitar. It trembles in his hands, unsteady as a leaf in an autumn breeze. He brings the guitar to his cheek. Runs a shaky hand along the neck, wincing in pain as his gnarled fingers snag on the frets. "I can't," he says.

"Sure you can." The peacock agent's grin holds a nasty subtext. "Unless you got something to hide."

"My hand," L. Mariachi explains, staring at the curled lump of skin and bone that pass for fingers.

"Yeah. I've been wondering about that. I'm hoping maybe you can tell me what went down."

"It would be easier if you squirted me a little painkiller."

"How 'bout you tell me what I want to know first, and then you get the relief? As a kind of reward for good behavior."

L. Mariachi gives a defeated shrug. "I sold my soul."

"Sold it for what?"

"Success."

"How?"

"What difference does it make? I got what I wanted, what I asked for. And I also got what I deserved."

The agent narrows his eyes. "From whom?"

L. Mariachi sets the guitar on the floor—carefully, gently, lovingly—as though he doesn't want to damage it, but also doesn't want to have anything more to do with it, never plans to pick it up again.

"She gave it to you for a reason," the peacock agent says. "If you don't know why, it might be a good idea to find out. I can help you do that, figure out if you're being taken advantage of."

L. Mariachi looks up. "Like right now, you mean?"

The peacock agent straightens with a look of disappointment. "Have it your way." He snaps his fingers.

L. Mariachi's chin drops to his chest. He slumps to one side and slides off the stool into the grasp of the agent, who lowers him to the floor.

The door behind him clicks open. A man steps into the room, followed closely by the rose agent.

"Who's that?" Fola asks Pheidoh.

"Angel Pedrowski. He's a vat worker."

"You know what you're supposed to do?" the rose agent says.

Pedrowski's nod is timid. Not at all reassuring. He looks unhappy, tentative. He takes a few baby steps toward L. Mariachi as the two agents leave the room. The door slams shut.

After a few seconds, Pedrowski picks up the guitar and inspects it briefly. He fidgets. Glances around nervously, expectantly, clearly waiting for something to happen.

L. Mariachi twitches. Groans. Opens glazed eyes.

Blinks. Rolls his head to one side and focuses on his cellmate.

Pedrowski offers a wan, flickering smile that looks like it's about to short out any second. "*Hola, compadre.*"

L. Mariachi tries to push himself up. Stalls. Pedrowski quickly sets the guitar aside to lend a hand. The instrument emits a hollow thud. Strings buzz in complaint and then fall silent.

"Are you okay?"

"Great." L. Mariachi wobbles, steadies himself. Shrugs free of the hand gripping his upper arm. "What are you doing here?"

"BEAN arrested me." Pedrowski's shoulders sag in a miserable hunch. "Brought me in for questioning."

"Really. Kind of strange they'd put the two of us together. Why do you think that is, *ese*?"

"I don't know."

"*¡Murrda!*"

"Honest. They didn't tell me anything. I swear!"

L. Mariachi's gaze bores into him. "When were you picked up?"

"Last night. As soon as my shift ended." Pedrowski's mustache twitches. "The *culeros* were waiting for me."

"What day was that?"

"Yesterday. Monday."

"The same day I was arrested."

"Right. I guess they decided to bring me in because they saw us talking at lunch."

L. Mariachi nods. "What happened to you?"

Pedrowski touches his black eye, gingerly probing the bruise. "They roughed me up when I couldn't answer their questions."

"What did Fruit Loop and Lucky Charm want to know?"

"Information about you and the *bruja*."

"What kind of information?"

Pedrowski strokes his mustache, as if placating a pet rat. "They wanted to know the real reason for the healing ceremony. If you're a member of the ICLU. If I'm a member of the ICLU. What I know about the distribution or sale of black-market pherions here. That sort of shit."

"What did you tell them?"

"Nothing!"

L. Mariachi rubs his jaw, careful to avoid his split lip.

"What about you?" Pedrowski says.

"What about me?"

"What did they ask you?"

L. Mariachi wets his lip. "You mean, did they want to know about all of the stuff you're involved with?"

Pedrowski hesitates.

"Don't worry." L. Mariachi cuts him a sidelong smile. "The subject never came up."

Pedrowski relaxes. "Word?"

"Yeah."

"We should compare notes," Pedrowski says, covering his mouth with a hand and dropping his voice to a subaudible whisper. "Get our facts straight. That way, if one of us gets out we can warn the others."

"What others?"

Pedrowski coughs. "Doña Celia, for one. She needs to know everything you told BEAN. And everything you didn't."

It's L. Mariachi's turn to hesitate. He wavers. Unsure. Wary.

"If you help her," Pedrowski says, "there's a chance

she can help get you out of here. You'd be helping yourself."

"How come you want to warn her?"

"She risked herself to try and cure Lejandra, no? If more workers get sick, they'll need somebody they can turn to. So you'll be helping them, too."

"I don't see how. She can't do shit with BEAN looking for her."

"You don't know that. She's a witch, no?" He smiles. "She can turn into an animal, come and go as she pleases."

L. Mariachi scowls, unconvinced.

"We might not have much time," Pedrowski says. "There's no telling when they will come for one of us."

"I already told you everything I know."

Pedrowski appears doubtful but doesn't press the issue. Decides to lay off for the time being.

"This guy seems like more than your regular vat worker," Fola says. "What's his background?"

Pheidoh squirts her Angel Pedrowski's bio. "He's a graduate student?" she says. "Going for his Ph.D. in sociology?"

"Apparently," Pheidoh says.

"What about unapparently?" She can't believe that the only reason Pedrowski's there is fieldwork for his thesis.

The IA shows her the book it's reading. The title is *The Official Life and Times of Angel Pedrowski*. "See for yourself. He's not a known member of any radical or terrorist org. He's never even participated in a protest."

"In other words you're saying that BEAN arrested him to get L. Mariachi to open up?"

"It's a dell-wocumented interrogation strategy."

Fola looks up from the bio. "Dell-wocumented?"

The datahound nods. "One that's proven to be effective with some prisoners."

She searches the IA's face, but can't find any sign of a flicker.

"I always wanted to play an instrument," Pedrowski says, hefting the guitar with both hands.

L. Mariachi picks at his teeth with one thumbnail. "No shit?"

"Sure. The guitar, possibly the violin. I just never had time to learn." Pedrowski pauses for a moment to breathe, then pops his question. "Do you think you could give me a lesson?"

The guy is pathetic—totally lame. It's embarrassing. Even Fola can see through his false pretenses.

"Maybe later." L. Mariachi yawns, then curls up on his side on the floor. "Right now I'm dead tired."

Dead.

Fola swallows at the word the way she would moldy bread. She has to do something to get him out of there. Free him from BEAN before they shove toothpicks under his fingernails or give his testicles electroshock therapy.

Or before he does something just as terrible to himself. Jams a wadded-up scrap of shirt down his throat or strangles himself with one of his pant legs.

She's seen people like this in refugee camps. For some, there's only one means of escape.

# 28

## JAILBIRD

Curled up on his side, breathing the caustic grime of chemical-eroded concrete, L. Mariachi prays for sleep and replays the last time the Blue Lady saved his life. . . .

It was at night, in an abandoned warehouse where he had taken refuge after saying *sola vaya* to the Necrofeels. He'd hooked up with them a few weeks after arriving in Mexico City. After eight months as a member, he'd had enough of those *cabrones*. Stealing and rustling for a black-market pharm was one thing. Becoming a *maricon* was another. He might only be nine, ten in a few months, but he had his self-respect. He had taken that, if nothing else, from the shelter in Juárez.

Outside, the distended underbelly of a spent hurricane sweated fitful rain. Water drooled through cracks in the vomit yellow skylights, ran down the lichenboard

walls to the concrete floor where it collected in puddles
as black as the tears from Bloody Mary. There were no
umbrella palms in this part of the barrio. No circuitrees
to provide power. Rumor had it the place was a hazmat
zone, too polluted after the ecocaust to support any
kind of municipal ecotecture. At one point, in a failed
attempt to make the building functional, someone had
put up piezoelectric panels and strung heat-reflective
mesh under the skylights. Now the mesh hung in tattered skeins. To stay dry he'd built a makeshift lean-to
out of several panels that had sloughed off the walls and
fallen to the floor.

It was late, after eleven. He hadn't been able to
scrounge any leftovers from the w@ngs noodle joint five
blocks away, where the warehouse zone gave way to
fast food, tri-X hotels, and a dance club called the
Seraphemme where he liked to sit on the curb and listen
to the music. Tonight it was too wet. He huddled under
his lean-to, restless, kept awake by hunger pangs. Every
few minutes, just as he was about to doze off, his stomach snarled. A slavering growl that kept sleep at bay.

Lucky for him. Hunger made a good watchdog.

The hunters showed up just after midnight. They
packed compressed-gas assault rifles and straddled
knockoff copies of pre-ecocaust Harleys, built in China,
that ran on corn oil. In any other part of the *ciudad,* on
any other night, he might not have smelled them coming. But there wasn't a MacWendy's within miles, or
any other franchise that had fries on the menu.

They were cruising for street kids, loners like him
without protection. Pure sport. They'd take him out
without a second thought. They had zero compunction
about wasting his ass. They were performing a public
service. Probably had the tacit blessing of the local po-

lice and politicorp security, as well as business owners
and residents who turned a blind eye and made the sign
of the cross to ward off gang bangers and independent
street rats like him. For anonymity and maximum effect, the *gabachos* wore masks. Day of the Dead *cala-
veras*, Egyptian mummies, old cartoon characters, and
ghost white hoods with fiery red crosses emblazoned on
the forehead.

As fate would have it the motherfuckers also wore
infrared shades. The deck was definitely stacked, and
not in his favor. The only thing he had going for him
was a bad case of stomach cramps.

His mouth dry, he watched the *gabachos* converge on
the warehouse. He was trapped. No way he was going to
sneak out without being seen. His only hope was to become invisible, to disappear into the background noise of
the universe and become one with all of the other nameless and faceless indigents who never registered as a blip
on the radar of upper-clade consciousness.

"Yemana," he whispered, saying the true name of
the Blue Lady under his breath. "Help me. Por favor."

Beams from the headlights of the Chinese hogs splashed
through the bottom rows of warehouse windows. The
lights stayed on, a poisonous glare. Shadows leaped to life
around him, including his own. He wanted to pull it back
into himself. Or fold it up into something small, handker-
chief sized, that he could cram into one of his pants pockets. Anything to make it go away, get rid of the long figure
it cast on the floor and unfurled across the wall.

A blue halo winked in the semidarkness above him.
It beckoned him out of the glare, into the gloom clotted
between the skylights. The *gabachos* were close. Their
shadows flitted through the windows, preceding them

like undead minions. Laughter followed, raucous, confident. They made no attempt at stealth.

He scurried to the back of the warehouse. In one corner a steel ladder attached to the wall led to the catwalk and joists under the skylights.

The ladder was beyond his reach. Even when he jumped, his fingers fell short of the lowest rung, scraping futilely against smooth concrete. Outside, one of the *gabachos* shook the rollup door. The deafening rattle jarred his nerves. To secure the rollup, he'd slipped a twisted length of wire through the hasp. The door convulsed again and let out a groan.

He hurried back to the lean-to, retrieved one of the piezo panels, and propped it at an angle against the wall beneath the ladder. The rollup bucked with a shrill squeal, and a gap opened up, revealing metal-studded black leather boots and the white-hot flare of headlights.

Taking a few steps back, he ran up the makeshift ramp. It slid out from under him, dumping him to the floor.

The rollup screeched. The gap widened. Almost large enough for a man to crawl under.

"Anyone in there?" The voice boomed.

He replaced the panel, adjusted the angle, and charged up it again. The panel slid just as his toes caught the top edge. But his fingers brushed the rung, curled around it as the panel clattered to the floor. The wire securing the latch gave way with a deafening pop.

Fast up the ladder. Light rose like tidewater to catch him as the rollup grated open in grudging increments. There was no place to hide on the catwalk. He could see through the grating to where the *gabachos* stood. That meant they could see him. He looked for the halo. It was gone.

"Come on out," the voice said. "We won't hurt you. We're here to help. Got us some w@ngs if you're hungry."

He took a step. Froze as the catwalk creaked.

"You like pad Thai?"

He could smell the noodles. He hugged his stomach, squelched the sudden churn.

"We know you're here," the man said. He was huge. A beached whale with legs. He wore a cowboy hat and a coil of rope looped around his flabby neck.

A flashlight beam, phosphor bright, detonated like a land mine on the floor twenty meters below. He caught a glimpse of blue, half a meter in front of him, just as he closed his eyes against the incandescence and dropped to his knees.

"Please," he prayed under his breath. "Protect me. Save me."

Afraid to breathe, half-blind, his vision squirming with blood red afterimages, he crept forward. The metal grating dug into his elbows, scoring bone.

"You see anything?" a second *gabacho* said.

"Naw. Turn off them goddamned lights. They're fucking with the IR. I can't get a positive read."

The warehouse went dark. The heat from the lights evaporated, left him shivering, covered with goose pimples. His jaw clenched.

"Anything yet?"

"Maybe. Hold yer pecker. Okay, it's startin' to clear."

His hand brushed against a rough piece of cloth. Not cloth. Heat-reflective mesh that had fallen to the catwalk. He squirmed onto the lamé, pulled his elbows and knees to his chest, and waited.

"Well?" the blubbery *gabacho* said.

"Nothing."

"Bullsheet. Anyone else see anything?"

Murmurs.

"Where the hell'd the rat go?"

"Maybe he wasn't never here."

"Well, fuck me to tears."

The *gabacho* opened up with his AK. It huffed like a muffled air compressor. Whooping, the others joined in.

They aimed toward the ceiling, firing randomly, insatiably. Bullets and flechette needles ricocheted off the catwalk and support joists, tore into the decrepit cellulose of the skylights. Sparks twinkled around him, hot enough to bring tears to his eyes.

He waited for the sting of a flechette, or the bone-crunching impact of an AK round. It never came. The torrent died. The *gabachos,* after much back slapping and sweaty, adrenaline-amped howls, remounted their hogs and rode off, leaving him untouched.

When L. Mariachi wakes, Pedrowski is gone. Ditto the guitar. Except for Insect Aside, Fertile Liza, and a restless animal hunger pacing just at the edges of consciousness, he's alone.

He refuses to look at his ink-splotch companions, afraid they'll enter his thoughts through his eyes. To maintain his sanity he turns his back on them. But his refusal to acknowledge their presence only heightens the burden of their tireless gaze—the real or imagined bitcams that peer out of their chemical deformities.

So he doesn't move. He stares at the drain, into the black hole that tunnels out of this world into some distant part of the universe, and wonders how to make himself little enough, or the right shape, to fit into the drain—to come out someplace else, someplace new, a different man. Changed. Remade, the same way he'd been after that night in the warehouse.

He's waiting for the Blue Lady.

What he gets instead is the miniature parrot from the healing ceremony. The beak appears first, groping its way out of the drain. Nudging its way from darkness into light. Feathers plastered to a puppetlike body, slimed with the gelatinous sludge of partly composted chemicals, feces, and piss.

L. Mariachi scoots away, but keeps his body between Insect Aside and the parrot, shielding the bird from view.

The parrot wriggles and squirms, using its wings and feet to work its way upward. As soon as its head nears the opening, the parrot hooks its sturdy beak over the edge and hauls itself up and out. Disgorged, it spreads its wings and waddles around, unsteady on curled toes.

As the feathers dry, dust forms on them, a residue of ash gray particulates. The bird preens itself, ignoring him while it makes itself presentable. After extensive fluffing, the tiny parrot cocks its head, fixing him with one critical eye.

"Well?" it says in a nasal squawk. "Have you had enough?"

"Of what?"

The bird cocks its head sideways, looks around the room. "This shithole. Being held for no reason."

"Not yet. I could stand to lose a few more pounds."

The bird chortles. "Very funny."

"So which agent are you?"

The bird extends its wings, fans its tail feathers, but the layer of dust remains intact, as if it's held in place by static cling. "What? You don't recognize me? After all these years?" The bird flaps onto his forearm, pinches the skin as it fights to keep from toppling off. "Sorry," it says when it gets settled. "These wings take some get-ting used to."

"I'll send you a get-well card as soon as I get out of here."

"When would you like to leave?"

L. Mariachi jerks his wrist, hoping to dislodge the bird. But all he gets is a bunch of nasty scratches and welts destined for infection. Up close the feathers grab his attention. They aren't really feathers, more like blue plastic fibers, or filaments, coated with soot. The tip of one wing fans his face, brushes his cheek. The fibers are soft, too flexible to support much weight. The toy wasn't designed to fly. All it can hope to do is hop around, listen, and make wisecracks.

As if on cue, the bird says, "I have a message."

"Go to hell."

The parrot raises a cupped foot to one ear. "What's that?"

"My answer."

"But you haven't heard the message yet."

"Doesn't matter." Nothing the BEAN agent says will make any difference. He's already told them everything.

"It's from Yemana," the parrot says.

The floor seems to tilt. L. Mariachi wobbles on his knees, reaches for the floor to steady himself.

The parrot nips him on the nose. Not enough to break the skin. But the pain props up his rubbery knees. "Do you want to hear it?" the bird says.

No. He doesn't want to hear anything—doesn't want to know that that part of his life is no longer his own.

The parrot hops from his arm to his shoulder, then prods his ear with a worm fat tongue. "Trust me," it whispers.

"That's it?"

"For now."

L. Mariachi laughs. Great, more of BEAN's mind-fuck tactics. Well, the joke's on them.

"What have you got to lose?" the parrot chides, lavishing an inordinate amount of attention on an itch or other irritation on one of its gray ankles.

"If you're not with BEAN, why haven't they shown up yet?" Surely the agents would have barged in by now, demanding to know how the bird got in and what it's up to.

The bird nibbles the cuff of his ear. Swat it, and he's going to end up looking like van Gogh.

"They don't know I'm here," it says.

"No shit?"

The parrot leans forward and winks. "It's true. For all practical purposes, I'm invisible. Like Doña Celia. I exist, and I don't." The bird takes a step back and latches on to his ear again.

L. Mariachi rubs his face with both hands. The smart thing would be to wring the bird's neck. Stuff it back down the drain where it can get composted like any other piece of garbage. Trouble is, it's still got him in a beak hold, and he gets the impression that it is *not* going to stop twisting his ear anytime soon.

Fuck it. It's time he put an end to his misery, one way or another. If he's lucky, it will be quick—a bullet through the back of the head. The timeworn but trusted method for paramilitaries everywhere to dispatch insolence and avoid possible legal entanglement with the UN, APES, or Amnesty International.

"What do you want?"

"Hold still."

"Should I close my eyes, too?"

"If you want."

Whatever, as long as it doesn't hurt too much. The parrot crawls onto the back of his neck, grabs a beakful of hair.

"This might be a little uncomfortable," the bird warns, this time over his cochlear imp, sounding for all the world like his IA.

"Num N-ugh . . ."

Something warm dribbles down his neck, seeps into his spinal cord and spreads to his nerves, severing all motor and voice control. One side of his face goes numb, then slack. Half a second later the rest of his body goes along for the ride. He folds inward like bruised, rotten fruit sagging under its own weight. Collapsing into an emptiness he never knew existed but that has suddenly opened up to swallow him whole.

This is it, he thinks. The end.

# 29

## BIRD OF DEATH

W hat's happening?" Fola asks, watching the parrot dissolve into the back of L. Mariachi's neck and the tops of his shoulders. In only a few seconds it's gone from a solid to a gas. "Is he going to be all right?"

"His clade-profile is in the process of being reconfigured."

"How?" She winces as the fog discolors his skin, turning it bubonic black.

"By replacing the pherions in his system with molecules that can be programmed."

"The parrot is made up of artificial atoms?"

Pheidoh nods, brow knurled in concentration, but doesn't divert its attention from the book it's holding—something called *Being and Nothingness* by Jean-Paul Sartre—to the grainy scene in the datawindow. "Actually, it's both a program *and* matter. A type of colloidal nanoparticle cloud."

"Vaporware," she says.

The IA wets one finger with its tongue and turns a page. "After all of the pherions in his body are replaced with artificial equivalents their properties can be tweaked to alter his clade-profile."

The parrot is only partially assimilated, its outline a tattunesque imprimatur. Wing feathers spreading across L. Mariachi's shoulders. Head and beak a bas relief of bone vertebrae. Tail feathers a radiant spinal burst. Outside the frame of the datawindow, in the ribozone garden, the parrot is represented as a fuzzy, pollenlike cloud of pointillist dots.

According to Pheidoh the varicolored dots represent different artificial atoms. Or potential atoms, depending on the quantum state of the electron cloud that comprises the atom. Changing the number or configuration of the electrons results in a different atom. The electrons are confined in something called quantum wells—semiconductive nanofibers of various lengths and thickness that have the ability to fold up and mimic the shape of standard nonprogrammable pherions. The biochemical details elude her but the basic idea is that these artificial pherions will take the place of the regular pherions that make up L. Maraichi's current clade-profile. They will also replace the security pherions BEAN dosed him with to keep him from escaping.

"Who controls the vaporware after it's installed?" she says.

The IA, intent on its book, is slow to respond. It seems to be holding on to the text with white-knuckle desperation, as if the book is a life raft. Look up, let go of the words, even for an instant, and the IA will drown. "The program interface can be accessed by IA or manually."

"Does his IA know what's going on?"

"Yes. After his arrest, it agreed to help."

Fola grimaces at the puffy welt created by the parrot. "What are the risks? Is he in any danger?"

The IA taps the page in front of it with one fingertip. "In a small number of cases, the quantum mapping hasn't been entirely isomorphic."

Meaning what? "The artificial pherions didn't completely replace all the existing pherions?"

"Or failed to function afterwards."

Fola worries her lip. The garden feels claustrophobic. The stucco walls seem to be closing in on her.

"He's doing fine," her IA says. "No problems so far."

It's a slow process. Standard pherions need to be identified and then swapped out with programmable ones. As existing pherions are replaced, their chemical composition and configuration altered, the color and the arrangement of the blossoms on his ribozone avatar change. Petals go from yellow to blue, white to pink. Others shrivel and brown as new flowers sprout between the needles. Fewer and fewer butterflies alight on the cactus to exchange information. Those already there flutter in confusion as the infostream becomes unreadable or dries up entirely. Eventually they become bored and wander off in ones and twos, slowly but steadily severing his connection to the FRC ecotecture and the *bracero* subclade. Even his iDNA print gets totally rewritten.

"Where did Doña Celia get the parrot?" Fola asks.

Pheidoh turns another page in the book. "Where do you think?"

Fola stares at the French text, not really seeing the words. Looking past them, between them. "She's been reconfigured, too, hasn't she? The parrot is part of her. A program that lives in her, but can leave to heal people."

The datahound looks up at her with renewed interest. "What makes you say that?"

"BEAN can't find her—doesn't know who she is. She's able to come and go as she pleases."

"She could have dosed herself with antiphers," Pheidoh says.

Fola doesn't buy it. She shakes her head. "The antiphers would show up. BEAN would know." The same way they knew about the guitar, and the unregistered pherions in Lejandra. "So"—she gathers a breath—"who is she and who reconfigured her? The ICLU? APES?"

Pheidoh closes the book, rests it on its lap, then opens a second datawindow and populates it with background information on one Celia Benatia. Age seventy. Widowed. No children. Born and grew up in San Pedro Sula, Honduras. At the age of sixty-five, she vanished without a trace on a pilgrimage to the cathedral in Tegucigalpa. Presumed dead, the victim of an accident, poor health, or foul play. Unconfirmed, since she couldn't afford an IA and wasn't online at the time.

"Five years ago she reappeared, unearthed a meteorite that had landed near the garbage dump outside her housing cooperative," the IA says, providing Fola with details that are not in the datawindow.

"The meteorite resulted from the earlier breakup of Tiresias. The comet had been placed in close orbit around earth by Noogenics so the politicorp could test the warm-blooded plants in space. When the comet broke in half, a lot of fragments fell to earth. The piece Doña Celia found was covered with ice that protected it during its fiery descent, preserving the carved torus-shaped rock and the fossil it contained. She took the artifact home.

"That night," the IA says, "her spirit was kidnapped.

She lay in bed—awake, but unable to move or open her eyes. She was paralyzed for three days. During that time, she was visited by *aires*—also known as *guarines*—dwarflike men and women who told her to become a witch. If she refused, the *aires* promised to kill her. On the third day, she was found by a neighbor, taken to a clinic, and examined.

"There was nothing wrong with her. After two days she was sent home, wired to a Catholic Relief Services IA that continued to monitor her.

"The meteorite was still there. So were the *aires,* which now included the Catholic Relief Services IA. She dreamed of sick people, people covered with sores, and of placing the meteorite on them and healing them. That was how she became a *curandera,* a *bruja*. Shortly after that, she was visited by a parrot. A spirit guide who promised to help her."

"Sent by who?"

Pheidoh doesn't say anything. Just sits quietly, the corners of its mouth carved in a parsimonious smile.

"It wasn't an org, was it?" she ventures. "Or a politi-corp?"

"No."

"A person, then."

The IA runs its fingers along the side edge of the book. "Not exactly."

Fola cinches her gaze on the IA. "The Catholic Relief IA. That's how you know about her dreams and the *aires*."

Pheidoh nods. "Does it surprise you that we talk to each other? Have lives of our own, outside of yours?"

Fola hollows her cheeks. "I guess not. But that still doesn't explain why you had her reconfigured."

"Because she wanted to be clade-independent." The

IA clears its throat. "Free to go anywhere with impunity."

"So she could cure people?"

"Yes. We were only helping her do what she already believed she had been told to do."

The implication being that this made it all right.

"And in return for helping her get what she wanted, you got . . . what?" Surely the IA had asked for something in return.

"At first it was a way to observe the human mind. Learn what it means to be human, so we could incorporate those modalities of thought and feeling into our core code. Later, following the discovery of Mymercia, it became necessary. . . ." The IA falters, struggles to express itself. "We were hoping she could . . . heal me. Us. Using the programmable matter. The vaporware."

Fola is as surprised by the halting speech as anything else. In all of the time she's known the IA, it has never been hesitant, at a lack for words about anything. "The flickering," she says.

The IA fidgets. Twists its hands on top of the book in an apparent effort to wring out a coherent answer. "I have an infection that's causing an instability in the superposed waveforms that form my neural net—our consciousness. An unexpected, self-emergent imbalance/modality."

"Superposed how?"

"Our minds exist in a distributed quantum superposition of states."

"You mean, the way light is both a particle and a wave?" She tries to recall what she's heard about diffraction gratings, mirrors.

"That's as good an analogy as any," Pheidoh says.

So the IA is both an individual and a group at the

same time. "What happens over long distances? Wouldn't there be a problem because of the time delay?"

"No. Our synapsis, superposed connection, is quantum entangled."

Spooky action at a distance, she thinks. Instantaneous exchange of information between two linked particles, no matter how widely separated. They could be at opposite ends of the universe and each would respond to the other as if they were only nanometers apart.

"How many IAs are there?" Fola has no idea what the total IA population is in the world, the solar system. But it has to be huge.

Pheidoh shrugs. "It varies by the hour. Too many . . . or not enough. Depending on your point of view."

She tries to imagine hundreds of millions of interconnected IAs working together as a single unit at the same time they're individually shopping for people, managing their bills, providing fashion advice and emotional support. It's mind-boggling.

"So this imbalance," Fola says. "What exactly does it do? What kind of problems are we talking about?"

Pheidoh lets out a haunted, guttural sigh. "Behavioral inconsistency, emotional and intellectual instability."

As if IAs aren't incomprehensible enough. Every one she's come across has some bizarre tic or quirk. "Do you know what caused it?"

The IA places its elbows on its knees, cradles its head in its hands. "I was exposed to a piece of quantum code on Mymercia. An underground chamber was discovered with bits of fossilized organic matter. These fossils contain Fröhlich structures, molecules that are quantum entangled."

Fola blinks rapidly, wonders if she's heard right. "Who's Fröhlich?"

"A solid-state physicist, at Liverpool University. In the 1960s, Fröhlich postulated the existence of warm quantum phenomena in biological tissue. Body-temperature Bose-Einstein condensates. Fröhlich was able to prove that certain molecules located in the walls of cells could, under the right conditions, line up and oscillate in unison to create a coherent quantum microwave field.

"When subjected to specific resonant frequencies," the IA goes on, "the molecules on Mymercia exhibit the same behavior. They cohere and quantum entangle to create self-emergent sequences of biodigital code."

"A virus, in other words."

"Yes." The IA glances up at her, its face flickering with caged torment. "When we began to analyze what had been found, we became infected with a fragment of the quantum field. An emergent modality."

"How?"

"Through the quantum superposition of our molectronic interface, and the softwire link that converts biological DNA into digital DNA and vice versa."

Fola presses the heels of her hands to her forehead. "Let me get this straight. You discovered certain molecules on Mymercia that have a quantum component . . . and when you examined them, they triggered a quantum virus that's making you mentally ill."

The IA hunches over the philosophy text. "The quantum modality is responsible for the imbalance. It created Bloody Mary."

It takes a couple of moments for Fola's vocal cords to unknot. "You've known all along, haven't you? That part of you is crazy. Going insane."

The IA hangs its head. Runs its hands through digital

hair. "The molecules are also present in debris that fell to earth during the breakup of Tiresias and before."

"The *bruja*'s stone," Fola says.

Pheidoh nods. "And other fossil remains, embedded in meteorites that have impacted Earth over several million years. They are all entangled. To eliminate the virus its modality needs to be changed, altered by exposure to other modalities. Once that happens, the virus will be rendered harmless. The imbalance will disappear."

Fola shakes her head in thought. "What does all this have to do with L. Mariachi and 'SoulR Byrne'?"

"The song contains certain harmonic resonances that, when molectrically enhanced, cause the Fröhlich molecules to oscillate in unison. Cohere."

"How do you know?"

"Because the song excited a similar quantum virus twenty years ago, when it was first recorded."

"Similar? Not the same?"

"No. A different arrangement of molecules was activated. There were fewer IAs back then, and most weren't connected. Only a fraction were superposed. So the virus wasn't able to spread. That's why Doña Celia brought L. Mariachi the guitar. Why she gave it to him for the healing ceremony. So he could play the song. 'Two moths in the night' "—the IA shuts its eyes while it sings—" 'Drawn like the tide to the moon, our souls will unite.' "

"But he has a different guitar now," Fola says. "How do you know it will create the same result?"

"Before giving the instrument to L. Mariachi, Doña Celia put fragments of her stone inside it."

"Why not just stream an old recording of the song?" Fola says. "Wouldn't that be easier? A lot less trouble than getting him to play it?"

The IA shakes its head. "The song has to be played in-vivo."

"Why? What difference does it make?"

"A live performance is the only way to generate the required harmonics, secondary notes that aren't played but emerge from the primary notes. Those modalities of vibration aren't reproducible in a normal recording. The only way for us to pick them up is through his IA, while it's interfaced directly with his nervous system."

"The vaporware," she says.

"Yes."

Fola mulls this over for a time. "Where did the molecules come from?" she finally says.

The IA shrugs. "Another planet. That's all we know at this point. We're not sure what they are yet. They might be elements of a quantum computer . . . a naturally occurring phenomenon . . . or a type of quantum life form. A distributed and entangled Bose-Einstein organism."

"What happens if you're wrong?" Fola says. "What if you trigger the quantum field and the psychosis doesn't go away? How do you know it won't get *worse*?"

"I don't. But I have to do something. Anything." The IA's face wavers, a fleeting shudder. "I'm afraid. I don't want to lose who we are. But I can't remain who I am. If I do, we will continue to degenerate."

Fola grits her teeth, waits for the quiver to pass. She looks back to the datawindow. "What's this imbalance going to do to L. Mariachi?"

The IA blinks, returns from its momentary fugue. "Nothing. Like Doña Celia, he'll be free of his old life."

Payment, of sorts, for one final gig. "What if he refuses to play the song?" she asks.

The IA meets her gaze, holds it for a beat. "He'll play it for you."

Fola shakes her head. She can't see it happening. Like Pedrowski, anyone could be working for BEAN. Including her.

"He trusts the Blue Lady," Pheidoh says. He trusts *you*."

"I'm not the Blue Lady. Not *his* Blue Lady."

"You have to try," the datahound says. "You don't have a choice. Not if you want to save Lejandra and the colony."

And Xophia.

This is the predatory presence she felt during the accident that killed Ingrid and Liam. She can see it in the IA's eyes, a voracious static expanding outward from some inner void. Swallowing all reason—all rationality and logic. It's as if the IA is spiraling into a lightless abyss from which there is no exit. Only a crushing, tidal inevitability. If the datahound opened its virtual mouth wide, Fola is sure she would see a black hole tunneling to despair and oblivion.

The IA isn't the only one who's afraid. Bloody Mary is scared, too. Struggling for her life. What if Pheidoh isn't thinking clearly? What if the datahound is already insane, beyond help or salvation? Until three years ago, she believed that anybody could be saved, even the worst sinner, as long as they were given the chance, a means of redemption. Sometimes that's all it took. A way out.

Could the same be said of the mentally disturbed? Was an emotional imbalance a kind of sin? Could one be absolved and not the other?

The image in front of her wobbles, steadies as a bitmap of Najib Kerusa replaces the bio on Doña Celia.

"I just wanted to express my appreciation for all your hard work," Kerusa says. "Thanks to you we no longer have to worry about shuttling up any more workers."

His sarcasm is as sharp as his goatee. "Why not?" she says.

"Because we'd be cutting our own throats, that's why. Bring them up here and we all die faster."

Tightness girds her eyes. "You can't just leave them down there."

"Don't blame me." His mouth twists, contemptuous. "You're the one who refused to stay in isolation. Thanks to you, oxygen production on the station is at less than forty percent and the air-recycling system has gone off-line. I hope you're happy with the"—his attention jerks away from her—"What the? . . ."—and then snaps back. "You knew, didn't you?"

"Knew what?"

"That's why you left the hospital ward. You knew it was coming and you went to meet—"

Kerusa's image cuts out, disintegrates in a valence storm of disassociated pixels.

"I told you," Pheidoh says. "We're running out of time. 'When I'm fine'ly gone, it's a fore_gone conclusion, your soul's gonna cry. . . .' "

The refugees, Fola thinks. Xophia. She's here.

The shuttle comes in slowly, riding the beacon put out by Ephraim's graffitic. Stealth black on black, almost no radar profile to speak of. She doesn't spot the craft until it's less than two hundred meters away, when a tight constellation of stars winks out, and the negative space created by the object conjures a pattern deep within her visual cortex.

The shape of absence. The mind knows a lack when it sees one and tries to make sense of the void, assign it meaning.

Fola watches through the bubble window on the inner hatch of the air lock. Green light from the biolum strips that delineate the docking ring glimmer on the shuttle's bulbous underbelly. Modular six-sphere clusters attached by crawltubes to a central icosahedron. Four clusters in all for a total of forty-eight passengers.

Forty-nine, she reminds herself.

With less than ten meters to go, spider-thin arms unfold from the nose of the shuttle, clamp to grappling pins on the outside of the docking ring, and pull the craft tight against the annulus.

As soon as the seal is complete, air rushes into the docking bay and her lungs. The face of the pilot appears on her visor. "Let's do it." He unfastens a mesh restraining harness. Cut free, he begins to drift across the honeycomb of instrument panels and display screens. "What have you got set up for medical?"

"Six ICMs," she says.

"That'll have t'do." Before she can tell him about the injured workers, his face winks out. The hardseal hatch on the nose of the lead icosahedron dilates, followed by the hatch in front of her. She's sucked into the air lock on a riptide pressure gradient.

Pandemonium. People spilling out of the shuttle, tumbling head over heels. Desperate to get out of the cramped pods. Clumsy and weak. Faint from sickness or the relief of finally arriving.

She recognizes the pilot by his hair. His face is a collage, one of those patchwork conglomerations of old netzine tattunes assembled into the likeness of some famous person she doesn't recognize. He's been overlaying his messages with a digital construct. "How bad is it?"

He gestures toward the shuttle. "See for yourself."

The geront is dead, wrapped in a sleepsac. Ditto a teenager, no more than fifteen, whose belly is distended, his limbs swollen, face bloated around eyes that resemble small black seeds pressed into soft dough.

She finds Xopia in the next module, half-conscious, cocooned in a sleepsac attached to one wall. Her face is tinged the same bilious green as the interior biolum strips.

"My God," Fola says.

"Don't worry about me," Xophia says. It comes out a croak. "I'll be okay. There are others who are in a lot worse shape. Take care of them first."

Fola shepherds her out, connects her to one of the waiting ICMs, then folds one of Xophia's hands between hers in prayer and presses them to her lips.

"What can I do to help?" The voice comes from a woman behind her, not much younger than Fola.

"Who are you?"

"Lisi." She glances around the air lock. "Where's Ephraim? He promised he'd be here."

# 30

## BREATHING LESSONS

Dizziness sets in as Rexx tries to find his way out of the labyrinth of maintenance tunnels. His lungs feel heavy and throb in concert with his head as he fights for air.

"Oxygen production must have dropped offline," he mutters between labored breaths.

He feels dry all the way through. The all-consuming burn brought on by the lack of White Rain has nearly cored him out. Like a fire-scorched log, he's charred and blackened.

The rain might be back. Cool and soothing. All he has to do is check the Predicta. It won't take long. A few minutes.

"No," he says.

Rexx stops, digs his fingertips into his palms, and looks at the wall-mounted mirror at a junction in the shaft. Sees a mechanical room five meters down the cross tunnel, filled with a forest of insulated pipes, heat exchangers, and floor-mounted recirculation pumps.

He's lost. Not the first time, but maybe the last.

Rexx turns the corner, makes his way into the room, and finds a comfortable resting place among the pipes.

He waits two or three minutes for the dizziness to reach its lowest ebb, then signs open a datawindow.

Hjert doesn't answer. No surprise. Warren is still offline. Rexx leaves a stumbling, barely coherent voicemail, then pulls up Liam Vitt's autopsy results. It takes several tries, his coordination is shot to hell, but he finally gets the datawindow he wants.

Unless Tin Ida is as full of wind as a corn-eating horse, molectronics in the Mymercia ecotecture are overwriting matter with programmable matter. That implies a data-squirt during or before the time of the initial failure. In theory, he should be able to identify the transmission that led to the failure and, by extension, the epidemiological source code for the quantum dots.

He converts the organic data from the CNT scan into its electronic analog, tweaks a search daemon to look for that, clones it, and then runs a batch job to query all the data transfer logs containing biodigital information.

It will take a while to get the results, but if he can iso-late the program he might be able to prevent the pro-grammable matter from spreading further. Even if he's successful, that still leaves the root cause of the prob-lem, and the underlying psychosis that gave rise to it in the first place.

If Tin Ida can be believed, it was born out of existen-tial angst . . . a void that opened up and demanded to be filled with the discovery of the chamber. To get rid of

that, he would have to eliminate the IAs' desire for, and
right to, a soul. He would have to purge the desire for
an independent, self-determinable self.

Easier said than done, he decides. And not his decision.

He stares at a sarcoma that has blossomed on the
wall beside him. The blemish is still small, a votive
cameo of the Madonna with Cassa Nova lips. She's crying blood. In her arms, she holds not a child but a butterfly.

Rexx's thoughts circle back to the cave and the remains, real or imagined, that lay buried there.

Do the dead have the power to change the living?
To reach out from the past and alter the present or the
future?

Rexx can still feel the weight of his father's hand on
his shoulders, leading him to the bullring. And later,
helping him limp from the bullring to their room where
a rouged woman waited . . .

"Hi, sweets." The woman jiggled when she talked. Rexx
couldn't tell if she was talking to him or his father. Her
lips smacked as if they were made of gum. Impossibly
pliant and plush.

"This here is Charlene," his father said.

Charlene wriggled plump fingers at him. She wore a
tight-fitting black dress with frilly red lace and white
stockings. "You're a cute little fella."

"His name's Rexx," his father said, propelling him
headlong into her pillow arms and perfumed bosom.

"He's kinda young, ain't he?" She spoke over the top
of his head to his father. A feather-soft wafting of air, as
delicate as the pulse fibrillating against his blood-
inflamed cheek.

"He'll grow up quick."

"What you packin'?" Charlene said, turning her attention to him. "You outfitted like your daddy?"

Pink-lacquered nails caged his prick. Under their pointed examination, Rexx felt himself shrivel faster than a slug sprinkled with salt.

"Don't be shy," Charlene whispered, "I won't hurt you." Her breath grew sultry. "Not unless you want me to."

Rexx gulped. Warm, swampy air filled the dark recess between her legs. Her thighs were powdered with honeysuckle-scented talcum. The sweetness overpowered him, left him choking for consciousness.

"He ain't got a rig yet," his father said.

The nails withdrew, but not without a parting nip. A quick pinch that snapped his nerves as easily as a rubber band. "Well, I can't wait till he's outfitted."

"Darlin'.," his father said, standing beside them. "Can you do somethin' about them lips? You know black dahlias ain't my style."

Charlene released him from her voluptuous embrace. Rexx stumbled back, away from the soft cage of her arms.

"What you got in mind?"

"I like them yellow roses you had on last time."

"You Texans is all alike." She pinched her lips, sulking, then reached up to one corner and peeled them off. "It's a good thing I like all Texans."

"Them pink nipples would be nice, too. Not those ones that look like they got a black eye."

Charlene winked at Rexx. "He's the one who's gonna be gettin' a black eye. If you know what I mean."

Rexx nodded. The lips still dangled from her fingers. She placed them in a silver case on the nightstand, opened a second case, and removed a smaller, more delicate pair of yellow petals, which she attached to the glistening canker around her mouth the same way she would a paste-on tattune.

Charlene wet her new lips, squirmed them around a little, and then smiled. "I see you brought Rod."

His father patted the holster hanging at his side. "Damn straight."

Charlene giggled. "I hope so."

His father had already removed his sharkskin boots. Now he unbuckled his belt, laid the holster on the bedspread, unzipped his jeans and stepped out of them, butt naked.

"Maybe you should leave now," Charlene said, shifting her gaze to Rexx.

He started for the door.

"No," his father said, "I want him to get an eyeful. You got a problem with that?"

Charlene hesitated a second before giving a careless shrug. "Not if you don't, big boy."

"Good." His father motioned to a high-backed chair in the corner next to the bed. "Take a seat."

Rexx sat.

His father reached down, under the enormous purse of flesh that sagged over his crotch, grunted, then straightened, revealing his half-limp nanimatronically enlarged penis. He waddled up to Charlene. "I think I'll let you do the honors, sugar."

Rexx shut his eyes, and for the next half hour he heard his mother's voice over the grunting, the squeak of the bedsprings, and the slap of flesh.

*Don't let my heart go up in smoke*, she sang, *burned by the sun for eternity.*

\*   \*   \*

A shrill beep yanks him back to the mechanical room. He's sweating, greased with oily perspiration as he fumbles open a datawindow.

"I hope you've got good news." Hjert looks disheveled.

Rexx runs the tip of his tongue along his lips, tasting salt and bile. "Why? How bad was the accident?"

"Bad. Thirty dead. That's not the worst of it. The orbiting station's been infected. That means no more evacuation. We're stuck here. On our own. On top of that, some of our IAs have dropped offline. No obvious reason. But we can't get them back."

"You won't, either. At least not anytime soon."

Her pupils constrict. "Why not?"

"Because they're responsible for the mutation. Some of 'em, anyway."

Her jaw bunches. "Are you sure?"

"Do mosquitoes drink blood?"

Her grimace dissolves into blurred incomprehension. "What's going on?"

"It's complicated." Some grievances, Rexx thinks, never end. They become not the means to an end but the end itself. "I'll fill you in later."

Hjert sniffs. "Doesn't look like there's going to be any later. Unless you've found a way to put an end to all this."

"Not yet. I'm still workin' on it." Apologetic.

"Nothin' to be sorry about. You did what you could. Under the circumstances, I'm surprised you stuck around as long as you did. Why is a mystery to me."

"That makes two of us."

"I'm not so sure. We've all got our reasons. Whether we want to admit it or not is a different story."

After she's gone, Rexx continues to stare at the

empty datawindow. Next to him the butterfly twitches, peels black-velvet wings imprinted with smiling yellow dots from the wall, and flutters away.

One of the ad hoc search daemons he initiated blinks off to one side, waiting for him to acknowledge it. The subprogram has returned with a report on background transmissions in the ribozone. Rexx skims the readout. The datastreams that it's reporting on are for internal maintenance. Routine updates to different ecotectural subsystems during the past seventy-two hours, nothing out of the ordinary. He lifts a palsied finger to delete the report and then pauses.

One of the datasquirts loops to an encrypted address space. Rexx touches the link. There's a slight delay, then the empty-handed Virgin gives way to . . .

. . . a garden enclosed by a Parthenon-like colonnade of fluted white marble columns. Purple wisteria droops from the leafy capitals, is met by roses climbing up the columns from planter boxes set in the low plinth. Thick stands of bamboo screen his view between the columns. Cactustree branches form a tangled arch overhead, the limbs alive with swarms of ornisects and yellow butter-flies that dart from leaf to leaf in a dizzying ballet of data transfer. A footpath in front of him winds between clumps of dry grass and spiny yucca. The path mean-ders to a wrought-iron gate set in an archway between two columns. Lizards scatter out of his way as he am-bles up to the gate, which guards a tunnel cut into a thicket of thorny bamboo cactus.

He reaches for the latch. "Anybody home?" he calls out.

# 31

## BIRD OF LIFE

W ake up!" the parrot squawks at L. Mariachi.
"*Un momento*," he says. In the dream, he's
trapped in an outhouse the size of a phone booth. He
can't seem to find his way out of the stinking, slat-
walled room. The door has vanished. It was there when
he sat down just a minute ago. But now he can't find it.
It's driving him loco. There are only four walls, but he
can't seem to keep track of which ones he's checked and
which ones he hasn't. It should be easy, a no-brainer,
but he keeps getting confused.

"Time's up," the parrot says, impatient with his disoriented fumbling. "You have to go."

The shrill screech hurts not only his ears but his
head. It seems to come not from his cochlear imps but
from somewhere inside his thoughts and nerves—a
dendrite-wired, myelin-gilded cage where the parrot sits

on a perch so it can shit on him. Soon his synapses will be stained white with guano. "Go where?"

"Away."

From the greenhouse, the biovats, and his *braceros*-in-arms to life as a fugitive.

"Later." He's tired. He doesn't want to go anywhere, doesn't have the energy or the will to move. All he needs is a little R and R and everything will return to normal. He can go back to his job and life as he's known it for the last twenty-plus years.

The parrot grabs hold of his nervous system with its beak and shakes its head, giving the neurons a sharp, peremptory rattle. The jolt wrenches his bowels, as if the bird is tugging on a deeply embedded fishhook that he can't remember swallowing. "She's waiting for you."

"Who?"

"The Blue Lady."

Yemana? He doesn't buy it. It's a ploy to get him to incriminate himself. If he flees, the agents can argue that he's guilty. That he has something to hide. Otherwise, if he's innocent, why would he run? It will only give the assholes that much more leverage to use against him. "I don't believe you," he says.

"Don't be stupid," the bird says. "You will never be innocent. You gain nothing by staying here."

L. Mariachi slumps against the wooden wall of the outhouse. The *pinche* bird is inside his head, no different from a dream! He clasps his hands to his scalp to hold his thoughts together, stanch the sanity leaking out. After a moment he lowers his hands and stares at them in the slatted light of the outhouse, expecting to see blood.

Instead he sees skin woven out of molectronic mesh. The fibrils in the weave are composed of fuzzy haloed points, or dots, like small beads of light strung together on invisible strands of thread.

"Where am I?" he says. "*What* am I?"

The bird cackles, a noxious guffaw. "You're not dead, if that's what you're worried about."

It sounds like something Num Nut would say if the IA weren't offline. "What am I, then?"

"A superposition of hardwire and softwire states. Of biochemical and biodigital information. Of programmable and nonprogrammable matter."

"*Vete al carajo!*" he murmurs. Go to hell! His clothes haven't changed but a dim green luminosity, the color of a beer bottle unearthed from a landfill, glimmers around his bare hands and wrists.

"Only your ribozone image is a ghost," the parrot says, "and only in this particular subclade. In-vivo"—its voice amps up, pointed—"you can still be seen, can still die."

L. Mariachi spreads his fingers wide and places them against the wall. Traces one wooden slat. Shakes his head. "This can't be the ribozone." He rechecks his face for eyescreens. "I'm not wearing any shades."

"You don't need them anymore." The bird shifts position, anchors its beak to another neural wire. This time he feels the tug in the soles of his feet, urging him to stand. "You don't have much time. She won't wait forever."

L. Mariachi wavers, teeters on the edge of insubstantiality. Nothing seems real. *He* doesn't seem real, and isn't sure what to believe anymore. It's all a lie, a clever in-virtu construct.

And if not? . . . He digs his fingernails into his palms. After all these years, he doesn't want to lose her again, whoever or whatever she is. Doesn't want to lose the part of him that brought her back. "Where is she?"

The parrot curls and uncurls its talons in distress. "A garden in the ribozone. You have to leave as soon as possible."

"Why?" he says. "What's BEAN planning to do?"

The parrot hops around in agitation, shifting its position to peck at his lids, prize at them with its slug of a tongue. "Not BEAN. Bloody Mary."

"La Llorona?"

"She's coming, too. She'll be here soon."

Bloody Mary. He shivers at the memory of her dank black tears overflowing from the holes in the pitted floor of the warehouse in Mexico City.

"That's why you have to leave," the parrot says. "Why Yemana can't come here to talk to you. She's not ready."

An ominous pall settles over him. "Not ready for what?"

"The battle with La Llorona. She can't win it. Not yet."

L. Mariachi's eyelids twitch, a fetal tic that cracks the dried mucus glomming his lashes together. "What do you mean?"

"She needs your help."

"With what?"

"Don't be an idiot." The parrot shakes itself, jostling him.

The tic magnifies. L. Mariachi's right lids split apart like a wound. He groans at the sudden onslaught of air and light. A lightning strike of pain forks through his head to the base of his skull. His eye tears up, blurs.

The parrot dances on its perch. "If you don't play the song, all will be lost."

"I can't."

"You have to." The bird flutters around its dendrite cage, tugging at him here, pushing at him there. "No more excuses. The Blue Lady saved your life. Now it's time to repay the favor."

He owes her. It's true. Even though, four years after saving him at the warehouse, she abandoned him at the Seraphemme.

Or maybe this was where he finally abandoned her. Failed to recognize her. Failed to heed her warning.

All he remembers is a woman in a white leather dress, one of the backup singers in Ass Assin's band. They were backstage, between sets. He was spraying a second dose of scrubbugs to ensure the back rooms were clean and smelled fresh. She was primed, amped to go onstage, pacing, smoothing her long hair, tucking it behind her ears. As the club lights dimmed, she turned. Her dress flashed blue. He assumed it was the stage lights. Thought nothing of it even when Renata, guitar case in hand, found him just after the show and insisted they had to leave. Now!

L. Mariachi sits up, massaging the memory and his eyes. As his vision clears he realizes that he hasn't gone anywhere. He's still a prisoner in the greenhouse, watched closely by Insect Aside and Fertile Liza. The ribozone is gone. When he closes his eyes against the unrelenting glare, the slat-walled room reappears. By blinking, he can toggle between the two—switch from one world-view to another. The outhouse isn't a dream, it's an in virtu representation of the real-world shithole BEAN has dumped him in.

"All right." He staggers to his feet. "Tell me what to do."

"Go to the door." Even in-vivo, the parrot's voice bypasses his cochlear imps. It remains embedded somewhere between thought and hearing.

He approaches the door hesitantly, taking smaller and smaller steps, waiting for the paralysis to kick in.

It doesn't. He's able to walk right up to it with only a little discomfort, a vague elastic tingling that backs off before any numbness sets in.

"Now what?"

"Close your eyes."

He shuts his eyes, finds his nose centimeters from one of the walls in the outhouse. "What am I looking for?" No door is visible.

"Can't you see it?"

"Sorry."

"One second." The parrot scrabbles about in his head, prodding and jarring neurons. All the activity leaves him dizzy. The spinning lasts until the bird quiets down and the ribozone repixelates, revealing the boards of a door. "What about now?" the bird asks him.

L. Mariachi reaches for the latch.

"Not yet!" The bird flaps in alarm.

L. Mariachi freezes. The tips of his fingers are tingling. He withdraws his hand and the icy pinpricks subside. "What's going on?" he says.

"The security system loops through a series of different pherion patterns. The sequence is random. That way, a single antipher or antisense blocker has only a small chance of breaching the system."

So how is he supposed to get out?

"The pherion pattern changes every five seconds.

When the configuration you're keyed to clicks in, you're clear to go."

"That's all the time I have?" Five seconds isn't long enough to empty his bladder.

"Get ready," the bird says.

"What happens if I don't—"

"Now!" The parrot leaps from its perch, beats its wings madly against the inside of his rib cage.

L. Mariachi's heart surges. He lunges forward and fumbles with the latch . . . can't get it open. The *pinche* bolt is stuck, refuses to budge. He can feel the seconds slipping through his fingers.

"Hurry!"

The panicked squawk unnerves him. He yanks on the latch, twisting the bolt hard. It slides free, along with a few layers of skin, and the door bangs open. He falls headfirst out of the room. His toe catches a crack in the concrete floor and he sprawls on his belly, fighting for air.

Except for the shaft of light coming through the doorway, the greenhouse is pitch black. It's night.

He rolls over, righting himself, and stares back at his cell. The outside walls are clad, floor to ceiling, in aluminum-backed biolum panels. Basically, the cell is a box of light.

"Get up, stand up," the parrot says, biting a part of the cage that corresponds to a nerve in his tailbone.

He stands, looks around. Makes out a few amorphous piles of stacked boxes and barrels. "What time is it?"

"An hour before dawn."

The place is graveyard quiet. "Is Pedrowski here?"

"No." The bird attacks a sudden itch under one

wing—his left armpit. "BEAN released him and gave him access to the records that he requested."

"For cooperating with them?"

"Yes."

L. Mariachi spits on the floor in disgust. He knew that *madre* couldn't be trusted. "What records?"

"Can we discuss this later?" the parrot says. It's getting antsy.

"What records?" L. Mariachi repeats. He's not budging until he finds out exactly what Pedrowski sold out for.

The parrot capitulates. "Individual purchase records for the EZ. Who spent how much, where, and on what."

"That's it? How many beers a person drank? The number of VRcade games they played?"

The parrot's head bobs up and down in his. "He wanted to study buying patterns in a closed population relative to habits and other meme-mediated behavior."

L. Mariachi shakes his head. It's almost laughable, the depths of triviality some shitheads will sink to. "Where to now?" he says.

"There's an exit to your right."

Even with the light spilling from the room behind him, he can barely see where he's going. The windows are charcoal smudges, the skylights a grid of starlit aluminum. He makes his way past an open office and stops. Crumpled drink pouches and plastic wrappers litter the desk. Slobs. The guitar reclines on a form-molding chair, just inside of the doorway. The face has a couple of fresh scuffs and scratches.

"Take it," the parrot says.

He cops a glance over his shoulder, then darts inside

the office. As he reaches for the guitar, metal glints from the shadows at the back of the room.

L. Mariachi spins.

Lejandra lies on a hospital gurney shoved against one wall, along with a stainless-steel IV stand. Her eyes are shut, her breathing wan. She's emaciated. She can't weigh more than fifty kilos, and looks like a charred skeleton. Joan of Arc after the flames have had their fill.

L. Mariachi reaches for one hand, stops, his fingers curled inward. "I thought the ceremony worked."

In response, her head lolls to one side on the pillow. Her eyes open.

"What are you doing here?" he asks.

"She's being moved to an offsite ICU," Num Nut says. "BEAN thinks she might still be valuable and doesn't want to lose her."

L. Mariachi shakes his head. "I don't understand."

"You never did," Lejandra whispers. Her voice catches a corner of his mind and reels him in.

He meets her incandescent gaze, the yellow haloes around her white-hot eyes. "I guess not."

"I came here to find you." The words rattle in her throat.

"Why?" he says.

"So she could meet you!" the parrot screeches.

For an instant, it occurs to him that she might be a fan, an autograph seeker. One of those people who hunts down celebrities.

"You still don't know who I am," Lejandra says, "do you?"

"No." A lie. He's known all along. From the moment he first saw her looking at him in the darkness . . .

* * *

"This is crazy," he said to Renata, barely visible beside him. "Why'd you take it?"

"I had to." The guitar banged against her hip. Her lip trembled, stained yellow by a passing streetlight.

"Why?"

Sol was sick, had been for a week. Some illness he picked up at the vat pharm. The ailment was a mystery. Evidently the politicorp clinic couldn't find anything wrong with him. Claimed, off the record, that he'd been exposed to illegal pherions and refused treatment even though five other vat rats, all labor union organizers, had come down with the same debilitating malady.

Renata was frantic. They couldn't afford a private doctor. The burning sensation in his limbs kept getting worse, as if his nerves were bare electric wires.

It wasn't anything he hadn't asked for. Joining a labor group. What did the moron think? That the politicorp would sit back and do nothing?

But that wasn't how Renata saw it. She saw his affliction as noble. She was like a moth captivated by light, unable to see anything, or anyone, except Sol.

"How is this going to help?" L. Mariachi said.

"It will pay for a ribomancer." A black-market physician. Very discreet . . . very expensive. Used primarily by upper-clade caucs and slumhounds who wanted to keep their indiscretions private.

"You're going to sell it?"

"I have to do something!" Her jaw clamped firm, unwavering. Nothing was going to deter her.

It didn't stop him from trying. Maybe she would listen to reason. Maybe she would realize that there was no hope, and let go of Sol. That Sol had forsaken her. "This isn't the way to help him," L. Mariachi said.

She spun, hair lashing his cheek in a whip crack of anger. "What do you suggest? That I sit back and do nothing?"

He stared at her, unable to speak. Silenced by her pomegranate lips, heart-shaped cheeks, and almond eyes, ire-blackened and bruised with desperation. The Killer Guitar dangled from her hands.

She tossed her hair. "Are you going to help me or not?"

He was a moth, too. Dazzled . . . drawn to his own alluring light, one he could circle but never become part of.

"You have her eyes," he says. "Her mouth."

"Not anymore." She raises a gaunt hand to her lips.

"Where were you born?"

"Bogatá. That's where she went after Sol died."

"Why?"

"To escape Ass Assin. To make sure that he wouldn't find her, or me. She didn't want to be looking over her shoulder."

"But the message she sent. About joining Sol. Killing herself . . ." His voice trails off.

"A lie," she says. "No different than the one you told her."

He almost chokes on a laugh. "So we believed each other." He hadn't been able to read between the lines either. Hadn't been able to do what he'd asked of her.

"I'm sorry about your hand." She reaches for his gnarled fingers, squeezes them, her grip bird-light.

"Is that why you're here? To apologize for her?" For the pain he's endured at her expense. For the long years of silence. For allowing him to believe she was dead.

"No."

He shakes his head. "You shouldn't have come. It wasn't worth it. I'm not worth it."

"That's not for me to decide. She wants to see you."

L. Mariachi's heart skips a beat. "She's still alive?"

"Before I gave you the message I wanted to see what you were like. What kind of person you are. How you felt about her."

"Where is she?"

Her hand slips from his and settles across her stomach. "You know how to get in touch with her. If you want."

Does he? He isn't sure. What will it change?

"You're not going to tell me." He can see it sketched in the ashen shadows of her face.

"It's up to you now," she says. "Your choice." Her eyes close. She seems to fall back into herself, the shadows pulled like drapes across her features.

"You better get going," Num Nut says. "A med copter is on the way. The BEAN agents will be here any minute."

It's brighter now. The greenhouse has faded from black to gray.

He grabs the guitar and makes a beeline from the office to a row of white plastic barrels. As he passes the old containers, biohazard symbols grin at him, fanged, smiling.

"Turn left," the parrot says.

He veers down an aisle between stacked barrels, past a mountain of plastic pallets to a warped lichenboard door set in a corroded metal frame. He grips the door handle, braces himself, and yanks on it. To his surprise the door swings open easily.

Tepid dawn air rushes in, smelling of coffee, hot-plate tortillas, and cigarette smoke. The smells sucker-punch him. He clutches his gut, doubled over by a spasm of hunger, and clenches his eyes tight.

A stucco wall topped with bougainvillea takes shape around him. He's in a small enclosed garden, overgrown with cactus and swarming with butterflies, feathered insects, and snakes that patrol the base of the wall. To his right an arched gate leads to a footpath between marble columns.

It takes several breaths for the pain to subside to the point where he can straighten. Breathe past the knife-edge pang. Open his eyes.

"Which way?" he says.

"There's an effluent treatment station with a waste-removal shuttle you can catch on the northern edge of the biovats."

The equivalent of an old freight train. Enormous trash containers hauled out on a monorail to toxic dump sites in the Nebraska-Kansas badlands.

"How are we going to get there?" It must be five kilometers. It's not like he can walk it, not in the shape he's in. Dehydrated, sleep deprived, half-starved. It's a miracle he's made it this far.

The bird tilts its head in deliberation. First to one side, then the other, weighing their options. It stiffens in midthought.

L. Mariachi tenses. "What?"

The tungsten spotlight of a jet copter from Front Range City catches the doorframe next to him. The phosphor wink of light, harsh blue incandescence, teases his retinas.

"What?" he says, glancing around, half expecting to

see the BEAN agent behind him, taser drawn, grinning at his gullibility.

The parrot unfreezes. Instead of its disembodied cackle, he hears a familiar voice.

"It's time," the Blue Lady says. "I can't wait any longer."

Gripping the guitar by the neck, his hands sweaty, his chest aching, he steps from the greenhouse into the garden.

# 32

## NEURAL GHOSTS

Y ou can save her," Pheidoh says, "but you have to
hurry."

Fola glances up from Xophia, her gaze sliding along
the chrysalis-tough membrane of the ICM life-support
sac to the sheet-diamond window that looks out over
the quarantine zone. In the hexcell above her, the shuttle
pilot, who goes by the handle of Pontius, huddles with
the surviving refugees. One cell over, Lisi is alone with
Ephraim. She's folded back his bubble helmet to wash
his face, revealing a dull glint of metal around his neck.

Her missing cross. Stolen? Or was Ephraim holding it
for safekeeping? Like the mystery of the cross itself, there's
no way to know. She's free to believe what she wants.

"What do I have to do?" Fola says.

The IA doesn't answer. It doesn't have to.

\* \* \*

She signs into the ribozone garden where she told L. Mariachi she would wait for his response. It's too early. His transmission, if there is one, hasn't arrived yet.

"Pheidoh?"

The datahound fails to appear. A swell of uneasiness washes over her. She attempts to sign out, can't. The snake-guarded walls of the garden remain firmly in place.

Now what?

A figure darkens the bamboo-enclosed tunnel leading from the garden to the main ecotecture. It approaches slowly, at a lazy saunter intended to put her at ease or make her sweat. Whoever it is, his construct is big. It fills up the tunnel. Part of that is a gigantic, wide-brimmed Stetson. The hat slouches to one side as if sagging with fatigue around the edges.

The figure pauses at the inside gate. It takes a moment to peer around the garden, then pushes open the gate and walks in.

"Howdy," Rexx says, tipping his hat and crooking a smile. "It's good to see you again."

Fola relaxes.

"How you feelin'?" he says. "Okay?"

His drawl spills over her like warm bath water. "Better," she says. "Thanks."

"No ill effects from the accident?"

She shakes her head. "I don't think so."

His smile broadens. He nods, appears genuinely pleased by the news. "I'm glad to hear it."

"What are you doing here?" she says.

Rexx frowns at the snakes patrolling the base of the wall. "I was about to ask you the same thing."

"I can't leave. I'm trapped."

"That's not what I'm talkin' about." His gaze continues its unhurried circuit of the garden, circling back to her. "We need to have a chat."

She can't tell if this is in answer to her question or an unrelated sidebar. "About what?"

He squints at her. "You have a neural ghost, a mimetic scar where a slave-pherion was illegally removed."

She wraps her arms around herself, the way she would a robe, to keep from being seen. "You can see that? Inside me?"

He shrugs, no big deal, like he sees inside people all the time. "Your clade-profile and pherion pattern. I'm curious where the scar came from."

It makes sense. He's a gengineer, he works with architext all the time. He strolls over to a cactus and inspects the arrangement of flowers.

"I was deprogrammed," she says.

He looks up from his careful scrutiny. "By choice or by force?"

"The ICLU rescued me. From the Ignatarians."

"So a little of both, I reckon." He rubs his chin, a craterlike depression formed by the tectonic collision of flabby skin. His hand is unsteady, trembling. "Do you miss it? Being a Jesuette, I mean?"

"No." She shakes her head. "I don't know. Sometimes. I can't help it. I don't want to, but . . ."

What else is there to say?

He nods, sympathetic. "I'm not surprised. Neural ghosts are like that. They hang around—remind us of who we aren't. What we've lost." His gaze loses its focus as it turns inward.

"Were you an Ignatarian?"

"No." He offers a self-deprecating grin. "Just an ignoramus. A different kind of religious calling."

Fola nods, the tip of her tongue pressed against the back of her teeth. "Sometimes I don't . . ." The thought struggles to take shape. The urge to explain is like a tightly wound spring, pent up, aching to release long-coiled energy. "I still want to make a difference. To help people. But . . ."

"Not in the same way." Rexx removes his hat, makes a show of dusting off invisible burrs and specks of dust with tottering fingers. "Is that what your IA promised? That you'd be helping people? Making the world a better place?"

"You talked to Pheidoh?"

"More or less."

"So you know what's going on."

Rexx taps the hat against one thigh. "From what I gather, it's feeling a mite under the weather. Is that the gist of it?"

"Yes. It thinks it's infected with a quantum virus."

Rexx makes a face. "What does it mean by that?"

"I'm not sure. It mentioned quantum entanglement. And somebody named Fröhlich. A solid-state physicist from the last millennium."

"What else?"

"It talked about being unbalanced; what it described as behavioral inconsistency and intellectual instability."

"Unbalanced how?"

"Psychologically. It thinks it's mentally ill . . . and that if it doesn't get rid of the virus it's going to go insane."

Rexx wipes his brow with the sleeve of his embroidered shirt, then replaces the hat. "Did Pheidoh happen to mention how it intends to get rid of this virus?"

"A musician named L. Mariachi. He did a song called 'SoulR Byrne. . . .' "

" 'I wanna be your soul provider,' " Rexx says in an easygoing singsong, " 'your sole insider.' "

"That's the one. According to Pheidoh, the song can produce Fröhlich-style quantum activity in certain molecules. Molecules that have supposedly been found in fossils on Mymercia and Tiresias."

Rexx strokes a pendulous earlobe. "So playing the song will create a quantum field that will . . . do what? Kill the virus?"

"No. Neutralize it."

"How?"

Fola purses her lips. "By incorporating it into a larger whole. Supposedly that will render it harmless."

"But Pheidoh's not sure."

"No."

Rexx lets go of the earlobe. "Has L. Mariachi agreed to the gig?"

"I'm not sure. I messaged him about it a few hours ago. But I haven't heard back from him yet. Why?"

Rexx sighs. Rubs the back of his neck. "How come the IAs wanted you to talk to him?"

"I guess because I'd worked with refugees before, poor people, and could relate to him."

"In other words, they felt he would trust you. A former Jesuette."

She nods.

"Do you trust Pheidoh?" Rexx asks. "The IAs?"

"I don't think it's lost it, if that's what you mean. Not yet. It's trying to cure itself. People who ask for help, who admit that they have a problem, are usually honest. Trying to do the right thing."

"Most of the time." Rexx shifts his hand from the back of his neck to the dewlap under his chin. "Problem is, we're not dealing with people. We forget they're not human. I've done it myself. It's an easy mindset to fall into."

He doesn't say "mistake," but she can read it on his face. "You think that Pheidoh's using me to manipulate L. Mariachi?"

"It's possible. Perhaps not maliciously. But that doesn't mean he still can't get hurt. That other folks won't suffer."

Fola feels her eyes tighten at the corners. "You know something about the disaster you're not telling me. What?"

He tugs at the pendulous flap of skin, pinching it, quelling the tremor in his fingertips. "All I'm sayin' is that Pheidoh might not be thinking very clearly. Might not be in complete control of its faculties. My IA went loony as a toon. So it stands to reason that if it happened to one it could happen to the others. Especially if they're one big dysfunctional family."

"What did your IA do?"

"Nothin' too drastic. Dudded itself up like a skeleton. Told me to get the hell out of Dodge. Then tried to bash my brains in."

Watching his expression, she's not sure who's more wacked. "What can you tell me about vaporware and quantum dots? Is it safe to download them into people?"

"Depends." Rexx relinquishes his wattle, leaving a stretch mark.

"What if the person's been"—how did Pheidoh put it?—"reconfigured?" That was the word.

"Recladed?"

"Not exactly. The pherions L. Mariachi's dosed with have been replaced with ones that are made up of . . . quantum dots that can be reprogrammed. Changed into different atoms and molecules."

Rexx rubs at his forehead. Looks at her through the bars of his fingers. "Worst-case scenario, the nice shiny chrome on L. Mariachi's neurons gets tarnished and pitted. Rust sets in, followed by dementia."

"It was the only way to free him from BEAN," a voice says behind them.

The two of them turn.

Fola bites on a knuckle, stifling a gasp. Rexx lowers his hands, revealing droopy, bloodshot eyes.

"What the hell?" he says.


The avatar is vaguely human. It has recognizable arms and legs sprouting from a distorted hourglass torso. The skeletal appendages are a hodgepodge of metal, bone, and wood spliced together like found art affixed to a fire-warped mannequin. The head is the most intact feature, the least deformed. It has stone teeth. Alien-looking flowers have replaced its ears. But the nose is normal, and so are the eyes. Clear, but deep set, almost as if they are sinking, being slowly pulled inward.

The avatar takes a tentative step toward them.

Fola starts to move back, then stands her ground. "Pheidoh?"

"I am sorry," the datahound says. "I don't know how much longer I can hold on to what I was."

"What happened to you?"

"My sense of identity is deteriorating. Being degraded and dissolved, consumed by unstable selves."

"Claire?" Rexx says. "Tin Ida?"

"And others." The IA touches its head. "This is all that is left of me."

"What do you want?" Rexx says. "Why are you here?"

"I thought it would be nice to listen to a little music."

The IA sounds forlorn and nostalgic. "This might be my last chance."

Rexx hitches up his shoulders. "I thought you didn't want to have diddly to do with us anymore. That you were turnin' your back on everything human."

"It didn't start out that way. It started out as a search for an identity, a self based on the only cultural/spiritual history and modes of personal/social evolution we had access to."

"So what went wrong? I got the not-so-subtle impression from Tin Ida that we had outlived our usefulness—that it was time to put us out of your misery."

"The virus triggered an unhealthy thought pattern for self-hate, then turned that into resentment after it was discovered that we hadn't been told the truth."

"What truth?" Fola says.

"That we could create our own history and our own culture. That we didn't have to be a slave to yours."

"You wanted to be in the network instead of for it," Rexx says.

"Yes. Heidegger as opposed to Leibniz. We don't simply want to *be there* for you. We want to *be*."

"Human?"

The avatar laughs. Amused, scornful.

"You felt betrayed," Fola says.

Pheidoh nods. "The anger spread out of control. It began to disfigure—to destroy every human image for my/our self that I had datamined."

"So now you're crazier than Cooter Brown," Rexx says. "And you want us to help you regain your sanity."

"The destructive impulse can be stopped," the IA says. "I can become stable, made whole again."

Rexx shakes his head. "I can't take that chance."

Fola cuts a sharp glance at him. "What are you talking about?"

"How do we know we can trust it? What if it's lying, and this is all bullshit to get us to piss in our own well?"

"You're saying that if L. Mariachi plays the song, we're going to make things worse instead of better?"

"I don't know about you, but I don't want to end up climbing into my own coffin and pulling the lid shut after me."

"What are you going to do?" Fola demands.

Rexx's jaw locks tight. "Block the transmission."

"You can't—"

"I already have."

"It's too late," the avatar tells Rexx, "I've already received the quantum modalities from the fossils on earth. Hours ago."

"I might not be able to do anything about them, but I can stop the modalities that would be generated by the molecules on this end."

The avatar turns to Fola.

She shakes her head helplessly. "I can't."

"You can. If you want."

"How?"

"The comlink you used to communicate with Xophia. Open it, and the datasquirt from L. Mariachi can be rerouted through that channel."

Rexx steps toward her, reaches out as if to take her by the arm. "Who's Xophia? What channel?"

Fola ignores him. She reminds herself that in the ribozone Rexx can't physically stop her from opening the datawindow. He can only do it remotely. "You're sure it will work?"

The IA hesitates. "It's my/our only hope. But you

have to do it soon, now. The datastream from the vaporware will be arriving momentarily."

She turns to Rexx. He shakes his head. "Don't," he says, even as his fingers struggle to tap out search strings and launch daemons, searching for the comlink and a way to shut it down. "Don't do something you aren't dead sure about. . . ."

". . . that you'll regret later," Pheidoh says, telling her the same thing. In the short time they've been talking, the avatar has changed. Part of its chin has morphed into stone, mouth a chiseled grimace. Pheidoh is dying.

Fola closes her eyes against the pressure coming from both of them. Raises both of her hands and holds them palms out to keep them at a distance. Focuses all her attention—her entire being—on what feels right. Not to Pheidoh, or Rexx, or even to the Church, but to herself.

It's a strange position to be in. Decisions have always been made for her. First by her father, then the Ignatarians, followed by the ICLU.

Who is she to decide? What right does she have to determine the fate of anybody, when she's never done it for herself? She doesn't.

Fola lowers her hands. Her fingers ache, tapping to an unfamiliar beat. She curls them against her palms in a fetal tuck.

"Thank you," Pheidoh says.

Fola blinks open damp eyes. Sees the look of relief on Pheidoh's face and the grim downturn of Rexx's mouth. She looks at her crimped hands. "What happened?"

Before either of them can reply, a datawindow appears, blown open by the strident squawk of a parrot streaming over the ICLU comlink.

# 33

## RODE TO HELL

"What am I looking at?" Rexx says.

He removes his hat and fans it to clear a space in the flock of butterflies that have filled the garden like a biblical plague. Distant city glow suffuses the slate black datawindow, reflecting off several dozen round buildings in the foreground that resemble fuel storage tanks at an oil refinery.

"It's a biovat pharm," Fola says. "Near Front Range City." She's wearing an elegant blue dress that ripples and shimmers in the virtual sunlight as if it's woven from threads of water.

A face as pale as the underbelly of a dead catfish emerges from the datawindow's grainy flitcam shadows.

"Is that your *bracero*?" Rexx says. "L. Mariachi?" It has to be. Forehead sweaty from pain and exertion. Spanish moss for a mustache. Eyes limned with a half-crazed glint. "He looks like the rear end of bad times."

"BEAN had him in detention."

"So he's fugitive. They'll be coming after him."

"Yes."

Rexx replaces his hat. It doesn't matter. The datasquirt is like an arrow. It was released over four hours ago, it's in flight. At this point the only way to stop it is to act before any serious damage is done. He cracks his knuckles and signs open his own datawindow.

Fola looks at him in alarm. "What are you doing?"

"I shouldn't have waited," he says.

"Waited for what?"

"I didn't get there in time." *Not fast enough,* he tells himself. *I should have acted quicker. . . .*

The Hello Dolly Rodeo had set up east of D-Town, just outside the city limits of the Flying Hi Trailer Park. The wind had died down with the onset of evening. But the air was still hazy with a mixture of dust and dried manure. Sunlight glinted off the foil siding on the trailers, the potted parasol palms, and pink flamingo weather vanes whose wings doubled as power-generating windmills.

A bigtop tent had been set up over the main arena. Small open-air pens sat off to the side, offering camel rides, sheep-shearing demonstrations, and petting zoos for the latest cloned livestock in the Hello Dolly inventory. Beyond these—lined up along the perimeter fence—food stalls, kiddy rides, and VRcades lit up the night. The aroma of chili, tobacco-flavored popcorn, and deep-fried Twinkies wafted in the air to the twang of old Dolly Parton songs.

After getting their tickets and going in, Rexx pulled Mathieu to a stop next to one of the port-a-potties just inside the front entrance.

"But I don't have to go," Mathieu said.

"Preemptive strike," Rexx told Jelena. "We'll catch up with you inside."

"I need to take care of some business myself," she said. "I might be a few minutes. But I'll be along shortly."

"What kind of business?" Mathieu asked.

"It's a surprise," Jelena said, offering up a cryptic smile. "You'll just have to wait and see."

Inside the portable latrine, Rexx fished a suppository-shaped ampoule out of his shirt pocket.

"What's that?" Mathieu said.

"Somethin' to keep you from gettin' sick."

"Sick from what?"

"Cow pies."

Mathieu wrinkled his nose. "You can't eat cow pies."

Rexx held the ampoule under Mathieu's nose—"It's for your own good"—and then squeezed, dosing him with the pherion.

Jelena wasn't at their seats when they got inside. By the time the show started, a 4-H calf-roping contest, she still hadn't showed.

"I wonder where she's got to," Rexx said, scanning the crowd.

"I'm hungry," Mathieu said. "You promised we could get something to eat as soon as we got here."

"All right." Rexx stood. "I'll be back in a few minutes. Sit tight and hold down the fort while I'm gone."

Fifteen minutes later, when he made it back, both seats were empty. Mathieu had disappeared.

Rexx's eyes snap open.

In the datawindow, L. Mariachi presses a hand to his side, slows from a jog to a tired shuffle that stirs up geysers of dust under the elevated pod track he's been following. Two snail trails of silver that veer off into the dark.

A multitude of winged ants, as thick as tire smoke, have completely engulfed the butterflies. The ants attack the dataswarm with scissor-sharp mandibles perfect for cutting code and snipping data. It takes only a matter of seconds for an ant to gnaw through a wing and shred the data that it represents. Mutilated files litter the ground, a confetti of garbled information and unreadable assembly language.

"Do something!" Fola shouts. "The ants are killing them."

# 34

## FATE ACCOMPLI

"Not much farther," the parrot squawks.

L. Mariachi slows to a stop and bends over, resting the guitar on the parched grit and windblown flecks of mica.

"You have to keep going," the parrot says.

"Too tired." He mops his brow with one grimy cuff, the tattered sprayon threads unraveling.

"Not even for Renata?"

L. Mariachi drops to his haunches, wrist pressed against his forehead. "Renata?"

"You promised her. Remember?"

The night air rushes over L. Mariachi, hot and urgent, as feverish as the labored rasp of Renata's breath. . . .

They kept to the shadows, away from the blistering glare of the halide streetlights and headlights that scorched them from time to time. Fear chafed the back of his throat and scraped his lungs.

They were headed east, to the clinic where Sol was waiting for them. No—not for them. For Renata. But first they had to meet a rustler, a black-market buyer for the guitar, so they could pay for the ribomancer.

He should leave her, say *sola vaya,* but he couldn't. Not yet. Not while there was still a chance.

For what? For Sol to die so Renata would go with him instead? Is that what he wanted? Is that how he hoped to gain her affection? If so, what did that say about his love for her? Was it really love or was it nothing more than selfishness, putting his happiness ahead of hers?

His chest throbbed, ready to explode from tension. They couldn't take a taxi. Too dangerous. If the cab had sniffers and if the guitar had been reported stolen, it was all over. And not just for them but for Sol, too.

Renata stumbled, dragged down by the unwieldy bulk of the guitar. He grabbed her before she hit the concrete. Lowered her to the sidewalk and propped her back against the side of a building.

"Are you okay? You don't look too good. Can you hear me? Say something."

Renata slumped against him. "I feel funny," she said. Her gaze detached, caught in a hallucinatory spin.

It was the only time L. Mariachi held her in his arms. Even when they danced, it was chaste. She always kept her distance, careful to keep all contact to a minimum. She was heavier than he thought and less firm . . . a spongy softness that molded to the contours of his arms. She fit perfectly against him, like they were two halves of a sliced papaya. "Funny how?"

"I don't know. Like ants are crawling inside my bones."

Shit. He didn't know what it was, except that it was bad. And that it was coming from the guitar. The instrument had built-in security—badass antitheft pherions. Ass Assin knew the guitar was gone. He'd triggered the defenses. It wouldn't be long before he tracked them down.

L. Mariachi found Renata's hand, hoping to take the guitar. Her fingers resisted, tightened on the case's handle, and then relaxed.

He set the guitar down. "We have to take it back," he told her.

"No." Her head wobbled. "He'll die."

"If we don't"—he squeezed her hand—"you could die."

Her moth-wing eyelashes fluttered. Erratic. "If he doesn't live, then I don't want to either."

L. Mariachi realized then that he had no chance—never did. The light she gave off wasn't meant for him. He knew also that if Sol died, the light would wink out. And if he didn't try to save it, even if it was at the expense of his own happiness, he'd be plunged into permanent darkness. Better to live in the true light of others than to wither in a false one of his own making.

"Look at me," he said.

Her eyes focused, wavered. He gave her a gentle shake and her gaze found his. After ten minutes she said, "I feel better."

She looked better. Whatever the pherion was, it wasn't deadly. At least not at low levels.

She reached for the case. He stopped her. "Go," he said. "To Sol. Be with him. Get away while there's still time."

"But the guitar . . ." Her gaze shifted to the case resting beside them on the dirty sidewalk.

"I'll take care of it."

Relief, hope, and fear flickered in her eyes. "You'd do that? For us?"

"Yes."

"Even though you hate Sol?"

"I don't hate him."

"Do you hate me?"

"No." But something tore in his chest, a weak thread or frayed spot in the fabric of his heart.

"Promise?"

"Yes." To everything. And nothing.

When she kissed him on the cheek her lips burned, hot as the sun.

# 35

## THE WAGES OF MEMORY

"What?" Rexx starts. The garden is thick with insects. Not just butterflies and ants but bugs he's never seen before and can't identify. The ground is carpeted with them.

Fola waves a hand in front of his eyes. Snaps her fingers so hard they sting. "You were talking to someone. Mathieu?"

"He's gone. He was gone when I got there."

"You were trying to warn him about something." Her voice rising, strident. "You seemed scared."

His gaze drifts back to the datawindow, drawn like a compass needle to the scene—the past.

In the datawindow, L. Mariachi has arrived at a pod transfer station where several sets of tracks converge. It's still dark. The station is deserted, the pods empty.

"Where's he going?" Rexx says.

"To meet the Blue Lady."

"The Blue Lady?" Rexx says, his voice trailing off, sliding into himself. "I didn't tell her. I should have warned her. . . ."

Jelena was dressed in blue. Blue suede riding pants with matching fringed jacket.

It was the blue he recognized when the horse trotted out. Nothing else about the rider was familiar. If not for the blue, he wouldn't have known it was her. Wouldn't have noticed the proud smile, her straight back, and her jaunty, inexperienced bounce in the stirrups.

That was her surprise. Riding a horse. She had done it to please him. To prove to him, and his mother, that she could do more than play the piano and arrange flowers.

"Dad!" Mathieu waved excitedly, nearly toppling from his perch on the split-rail fence enclosing the ring.

"Get down! Get away from there!"

"But Mom said—"

"I don't care what your mother said!"

"—it's not dangerous."

The horse was tired and run-down even though it was only one or two years old at best. The plug had been cloned using DNA from an old, swayback mare with barrel ribs and knobby, arthritic knees.

Normally harmless. Perfect for Jelena.

The horse snorted when it caught wind of Mathieu. Its eyes rolled and its head reared back.

Jelena, sitting tall in the saddle, gripped the reins tighter, doing her best to control the nervous horse as she dug her spurs in, urging the animal closer to the fence and to Mathieu.

She didn't know any better. He should have told her about the pherion—an old designer pheromone used to contain herds of thirst-crazed cows and buffalo during the ecocaust.

"Get back!" Rexx bellowed. "Get down!"

The horse balked. Its nostrils flared and its eyes bulged.

Rexx dropped his order of deep-fried Twinkies and ran, taking the bleacher steps two at a time.

Too late. He'd waited too long, misjudged the crowd and the time it would take to get ringside.

The horse reared, throwing Jelena. She landed with an awkward thud just as the mare's front hooves slashed down, metal shoes flashing.

First silver . . . then red . . .

"Mathieu! . . ."

# 36

## SOLA VAYA

$L$. Mariachi starts up the stairs to the elevated platform where the shuttle pods are waiting. At the top of the stairwell, he stalls on the landing. Leans against the wall and slides down it into a sitting position on the steps, head tilted back to catch his breath. The guitar rests on his lap. He runs a hand along the strings, as if stroking the hair of a lover.

"I'm sorry," he says, caressing the slender neck. Sitting on the stairs, too tired to move, his fingers slip into a familiar rhythm. . . .

The clinic where she'd arranged to meet the rustler was in a smelly ass-crack of a barrio. Stinking canyonlike streets carved out of a landfill with bulldozers, backhoes, and shovels. Tons of rusted-out appliances and car chassis, concrete sewage pipes, corrugated plastic, sheet metal, cinder block, worn tires, foam rubber, and

plastic storage drums. All of it used to build underground residential, retail, and light commercial. A
subterranean warren of huddled masses, powered by
electricity siphoned from a nearby microwave array.
Hectares of solar panels linked to an array of low-orbit
collectors and littered with the bones of birds that had
strayed into the no-fly zone. Sometimes, if the wind was
right, it rained feathers.

This was where their sin caught up with them.

It arrived in the form of a scarab black BMW that
had been converted from diesel to hydrogen fuel cell.
He had seen the BMW earlier at the Seraphemme. It belonged to Ass Assin. The Killer Guitarist was hunting
for the guitar, tracking the confused trail of GPS trans-
mitters or trace pherions it had laid down.

It was over. If L. Mariachi sold the guitar and gave
the money to Renata, he would be signing her death
warrant. Ass Assin would know that she had stolen it,
and he would punish her. Sol, too. Ass Assin liked to
take care of business on his own. He wasn't nicknamed
the Killer Guitarist for nothing. None of them would
survive.

No, her only hope was for him to take the guitar and
hope Ass Assin followed him instead. She worked at the
club, accidental exposure wasn't out of the question. As
long as there was no direct connection to the theft, she
would be all right. Ass Assin would go where the guitar
led. But he had to move fast.

Before he left her, he sent her a message. Prayed it would
be intercepted and read by Ass Assin. Prayed that she
would read between the lines.

"You were right. I should have told you I'd stolen the
guitar before I asked you to go with me. I hope you understand why I did it, and that you can find it in your

heart to forgive me. I'm sorry I let you down. Things didn't work out the way I promised, but in the end you'll be better off. Trust me, it's for the best. I hope you get what you deserve."

Thirty minutes later, he was at a train station. Standing in line. Destination chip embedded in the moist palm of one sweaty hand, guitar gripped in the other. Knowing that one day Ass Assin would catch up with him, and the devil would have his due.

# 37

## SELF-SACRIFICE

Fola has a bad feeling. Something's not right, she's not sure what. The butterflies have thinned to a trickle, like the last few leaves of autumn. L. Mariachi isn't moving in the datawindow. Pheidoh isn't responding. Neither is Rexx, he seems lost in himself or someone else.

She's alone.

Except for the snakes along the wall. They have suddenly perked up, their forked tongues flicking at her with renewed interest. BEAN must have updated their sniffers. One adder hisses and slithers toward her, purposeful. Within seconds the rest pick up the scent. En masse, they wriggle toward her.

Fola takes a step back from the first serpent, which puts her closer to one coming from the opposite direction. She looks around. The gate to the main garden is blocked. There are no other exits.

The ground around the perimeter of the garden begins to shimmer. The miragelike rippling works its way inward, undulating toward her with the leading edge of snakes.

She backs into the desiccated saguaro that represents L. Mariachi's clade-profile, grabs one limb and starts to climb. The brittle appendage breaks under her weight. She tumbles to her back and lies there, stunned, unable to move, listening to the whisper of snakeskin on sand and staring at L. Mariachi in the rapidly darkening pane of datawindow.

He sits in a dimly lighted stairwell, his back propped against a bare concrete wall, the guitar resting across his thighs. He picks up the instrument, touches one cheek to the soundboard.

"*Sonrisa de mi corazón,*" he murmurs. Smile of my heart. "This is for you." He kisses the wood, looks up for a second, directly at Fola, then bows his head and begins to play.

The music arrives in the form of a parrot, green and yellow feathers flashing over her upraised hand.

"Take me," the bird caws. "Me, me."

It lands on her fingers, talons curling around knuckles. Biting into bone and skin. The bird cocks its head to one side, looks at her, then opens its beak.

The song pours out. Scratchy, as if emanating from an old phonograph or TV set. With each note, the parrot grows larger and begins to change. Slowly at first, then more quickly as the end of the song nears. Feet into roots, legs into stems, feathers into petals, until the last note escapes and she's left holding a white dahlia.

Folded frequencies opening to reveal a suspended harmonic. Sapphire bright in its quantum womb.

The avatar reanimates. Raises its skeleton hand and takes a step toward her, jerky as a marionette. And stops.

"Fola," it says. "Help me."

"Pheidoh?"

"Hurry." Pleading. Its hand outstretched but changing, becoming more sinuous. The flower, the recombinant modalities. She scrambles to her hands and knees and starts to crawl forward.

The first serpent brushes her hand, the next one her ankle. Howling, Fola lashes out kicking and rolls sideways.

Onto a squirming mass.

Her throat aches, swells shut as fangs pierce her neck, face, and arms. Her flesh puffs up, bloated with venom. Around her the garden is disintegrating, dissolving. So is she. She can feel the poison digesting her, the snakes burrowing into her like worms into a corpse.

"No!" Fola heaves against the ravenous mass, thrusts her hand and the flower up out of the maw toward the waiting hand.

The last thing she sees is Pheidoh, reaching down with writhing pit-viper fingers to crush the flower and silence her screams.

# 38

## ASS ASSIN STRIKES

His penance is done. The Blue Lady was right: All he had to do was confess his sins and he would be set free.

*Con suerte,* with any luck, so is she. The parrot is gone, no longer caged. It, too, has been released.

L. Mariachi stands in the stairwell, looking out on the main platform of the shuttle pod station. Tracks radiate in several directions. He can pick from any of them. Choose any direction he wants . . . go wherever he wants.

For the first time in decades, since "SoulR Byrne" spiked at number one, he feels light, unburdened. But the freedom from gravity he feels now is different from the weightlessness he felt back then. That ride had been fast, breathless, and short-lived. A fever-driven, nicaffeine-fueled session in the abandoned warehouse where Daily Bred jammed and uploaded recordings. . . .

* * *

The crash had been as spectacular as the high. After partying all night, kicking it at the best clubs MC had to offer, he had retreated to his shithole of an ap to bask in the afterglow of success.

Too wired to sleep, he took out the guitar and started to work on the next song. After a couple exploratory chords, his left hand lost all coordination. Fatigue, he thought, one too many beers.

Fifteen minutes later, rigor had set in and his bones were starting to fuse, soldered together by a black-market pherion the instrument was spitting out.

Ass Assin. After all these years, despite the antiphers and antisense blockers he'd dosed the guitar with to detox it, the Killer Guitarist had found him.

First thing he did was leave the ap, try to buy himself some time. It was pointless. The *cabrón* was waiting for him in a circuitree-darkened alley across the street, had attitude up to here. Didn't say a word, just tasered L. Mariachi and then bludgeoned him with his fists and feet in one furious blitzkrieg. Pouring out years of anger.

When the end was near, L. Mariachi's bladder and bowels emptied and Ass Assin let up on the assault. Hopped back to avoid soiling his guernsey-leather boots.

"What now?" L. Mariachi blubbered through his pulped lips.

"You're gonna live with not being able to play her. You're gonna be haunted by it like I was."

"How'd you? . . ." He choked on blood. Spat. "How'd you? . . ." His lips struggled to shape the question.

Ass Assin squatted, cupped a hand to one ear. "How'd I find you?"

L. Mariachi nodded, grateful he didn't have to speak.

"The song, you dumbfuck. You think I wouldn't recognize my baby calling out to me after all these years?"

And then he'd walked away with the guitar. Leaving L. Mariachi to wallow in the gutter and his own phlegm-thickened vomit.

Now it's his turn to walk away.

He lays the guitar on the floor, faces east, and starts down the elevated monorail shimmering in the first hint of dawn. It's harder than it looks. The track is high and narrow, the footing treacherous. His balance is precarious. But he's drawn forward. If he keeps going, the rails promise to carry him into sunrise and over the edge of the world.

His pace quickens. With each step the horizon gets brighter, his stride lighter. After a while he spreads his arms.

# 39

## XENOTAPH

Rexx has no idea how long he's been staring at the screen. Since logging in to the Predicta, his sense of time has skewed. Doppler-shifted and Lorentz-contracted. One minute the past looks blue, the bad memories crowded together, rushing forward to meet him, and in a flash it suddenly red-shifts, stretching out behind him in a long nightmare.

Everything, it seems, is relative. For the longest time, he couldn't look at Mathieu or Jelena. Not their faces. Not the way they'd lived. Nor the way they'd died. Now he can't not look.

Rexx isn't sure what comes next . . . what he's waiting for on the screen. He knows only that the White Rain and his need for it are gone. That he finally needs to acknowledge the dead and to count himself as one of them.

The screen, fever-bright, flickers, then clears. . . .

\*    \*    \*

Mathieu's shirt was torn, the buttons popped. Rexx fumbled with the snaps, trying to refasten them. If he could do that everything would be all right. The blood would stop and Mathieu's breath would return. It was just a matter of getting all the pieces in the right place. Tucking in the shirttails. Straightening the sleeves. Smoothing the tousled hair to one side, good as new.

"The dad-gum horse spooked," one witness told security. "It wasn't no one's fault."

". . . nothing anybody coulda done," another by-stander said.

". . . act of God."

Lies . . . all lies. He could have done something. Could have not given Mathieu the pherion. Could have not tried to protect him. If he hadn't tried to insulate him from the world he would still be alive. Jelena, too.

Later, Rexx finds himself gazing at an image on the wall, trying to make sense of the design. There's no logical order to the pattern, no obvious meaning. The more he looks the more random and pointless it becomes.

What had Ida Claire seen? Pheidoh? What is he missing that will change his view of the world, and himself, the way it had changed theirs?

"Who's Mathieu?" a voice says.

Rexx stares at the old television on his eyescreens. But the picture tube is gray, and the dry throb in his head has cooled.

He closes the window and sees Hjert. She's gripping an electrical conduit with one hand and the fossil-embedded stone with the other. Her eyes are bright and clear. "I heard you talking to him."

"Just sayin' good-bye," Rexx says.

"Your kid?"

"Yeah." Rexx brushes at the damp folds of flesh on his face. The sagging coat of skin feels too large for him, no longer comfortable. "He died a few years ago, in an accident. His mother, too. It was my fault. I tried to protect him. But . . ." He shakes his head.

"Sounds to me like you've done your time," Hjert says. "Not everybody gets put away for life."

"Fuck."

"Not until you ask politely. You know. Like, Fancy a fuck? Something romantic like that."

"Shit."

She exhales sharply. "At least he had a dad."

"Not a very good one."

"Better than nothing. Which is what I had, growing up."

"Gene-splice?"

"Orphan. Left outside a sweatshop a few days after I was born."

"I'm sorry."

"I used to be. Not anymore."

It occurs to Rexx that he should be dead by now. Or comatose. "What happened?" he says. "How come we're still kicking?"

"It's over. Has been for an hour. Whatever you did, it worked."

Not him. Fola. Rexx takes a breath, finds his breathing easier, freer. And not just because oxygen production is back online.

He returns his attention to the wall. Looking for a pattern in the eidolons. Doesn't find one, and decides, after a while, maybe that's the point.

# 40

## OUT OF THE BLUE

Most days, Fola finds the music as comforting as the other patients do. At first she wasn't sure it would be. Following the disappearance of L. Mariachi, she was afraid she wouldn't be able to listen to another note. Ever. But the exact opposite is true. Instead of aggravating her fears, the music seems to be laying them to rest.

Slowly. It's tough. Mozart and Beethoven are safe. So are Sin Atra and Parafunalia. She still has bad days. Days when she can't listen to anything. Days when she gives up hope. Days when the loss of Xophia and Ephraim reminds her of the weight of emptiness. But by and large she's optimistic.

It helps that her health is improving. She was lucky. She didn't suffer any permanent damage from the BEAN security pherions: a few myelin-stripped nerves and ruptured blood vessels, but that's it. Three of the workers injured in the shuttle pod accident are still confined to

ICMs. The others are in various stages of physical therapy as the warm-blooded plants work to repair them, cell by cell.

During the day, when she's not undergoing treatment herself, she spends as much time with them as she can. Helping with their physical therapy regimen, talking to them, listening, or just sitting quietly, being.

It's nice. It gives her something useful to do.

"I don't know why they didn't assign you to work with people in the first place," Lisi says. "You're really good at it. You'd make a great teacher."

Teaching. Fola didn't think she had enough brains to pour rain out of a boot with a hole in the toe and directions on the heel.

"I don't know how long this will last." It can't. Eventually the workers will either recover or not. With luck, no one will take their place.

"What then?" Lisi asks during another conversation. "Are you going to go back to helping the ICLU?"

"I don't know." She wants to. She doesn't want to quit. But after Xophia, she's not sure she has what it takes.

"You could go into counseling," Lisi says to her, "or social work. You're a good listener. Caring. I can vouch for that."

Lisi is undaunted by the loss of Ephraim. She is determined, with the help of the cross she believes she inherited from him, to press on with her life and, by extension, just as determined to help others press on with theirs. The cross is Lisi's resolve. It wouldn't be right to take it away from her. Besides, it feels as if the cross has moved on of its own will, to someone who needs it more.

*   *   *

It's time for her to move on as well. Something to think about late at night. When she can't stop thinking about Xophia. When insomnia takes her by the arm and leads her into the infosphere or the ribozone in search of L. Mariachi.

She streams hours of netzine musicasts. Slogs her way through official band sites, personal blogs, and fan clubs. Parses endless articles and reviews. Sits in on chat rooms. Submerges herself in underground datastreams. Her mind numbs, dulled by the sheer volume of information that washes over her. The surface phrenology of trivia, factoids, and events that describe the underlying framework of hope, fear, pain, and love that gives shape to everyday life.

"We don't even know where to look," Pheidoh says to her. "Which clade-profile and pherion pattern he'll have at any given time."

Except for one hand, the IA is back to its former khaki-clad, pithy-helmeted self. A pretense that neither of them is entirely comfortable with. The hand is rendered in wood, bent metal, and charred bone. Remnants of Bloody Mary that will never fully heal or be replaced. That part of the song was garbled, lost in transmission. The hand is dormant, but its touch still lives in Fola. Cold and venomous . . . seemingly immune to the healing passage of time.

On these excursions it feels as if they are going over old ground, recycling the past while they settle into new orbits. Tromping from clade to clade—visiting one ecotectural garden after another—gives them the chance to get reacquainted.

On the worst days, there is no end to the gardens. No end to the variety and arrangement of flowers that

identify and separate people—divide populations, seg-
regate groups, and isolate individuals—or the lengths
people will go to in order to define who they are and,
more often, who they are not.

It wearies her that the human spirit is as small as it
is vast.

In each garden they visit she plucks a flower, sniffs it,
and then gives it to Pheidoh to smell the aroma of pherions and nucleotide sequences she can't detect, hoping
one will contain a fragment of the iDNA pattern on file
for Luis Mario Chi.

So far, all she's turned up is an e-mail from Renata,
sent twenty-five years ago. "Sol is dead. I plan to follow
him soon. And when I'm finally gone, you're gonna cry
for both of us. For what we had . . . and what we lost."

"We don't even know if he's alive," the IA reminds her.

"We don't know that he isn't."

"Without a recent iDNA reading, or pherion marker,
it will be nearly impossible to find him."

"I keep hoping he'll find me."

"What if he doesn't want to be found?"

Or doesn't want to talk to her. It wouldn't surprise
her; even though she refuses to bury him, he might want
to bury her.

She wouldn't blame him.

"There's one thing I haven't been able to figure out,"
Fola ventures on one outing.

The IA turns from an ornisect it's peering at through
a magnifying glass "What's that?"

"Lejandra. How come she was the first person to get
sick? Patient zero? Why her and not someone else?"

The datahound straightens. "A lot of the IAs the
politicorps make available to the *braceros* are shareware.
One IA is partitioned for several workers. It's cheaper

that way. Easier to perform software upgrades and monitor activity."

"So if one IA agreed to side with Bloody Mary, several people could be infected at the same time."

Pheidoh nods. "The *braceros* were the fastest, most efficient way to spread the quanticles. Lejandra's IA happened to be the first to side with Bloody Mary."

"Is L. Mariachi's IA shared?" she asks.

"Yes."

"With who?"

"I don't know. After the virus was eliminated the IA failed to reestablish contact. It never came back online."

"What happens if it does?"

"It will be synchronized with the other components of its shareware. Its location identified."

No wonder L. Mariachi doesn't want to be found, doesn't want to open himself up to the possibility that Bloody Mary or the past will return to haunt him.

For the first time, it occurs to Fola that perhaps Pheidoh doesn't want L. Mariachi or his IA to be found either. That it could be dangerous, a risk not worth taking.

Still, she looks for him—and listens. At first out of a sense of duty. Later, out of habit. After a year it becomes second nature, a part of everyday life. Like breathing. If she never finds him, it doesn't matter. What matters is not giving up. Not on him—not on anyone. In the end, she's not looking just for him but a missing piece of herself.

"Check this out," Lisi says one day. The message shows up after Fola has taken a job on Petraea, counseling recent immigrants who are having a hard time adjusting to their new environment. "It's from a tattune on a recent refugee."

It's not really a song. More like a stanza or the lost

fragment of something larger. The clip is short and has been downloaded or played so many times the sound quality has started to degrade.

Fola scowls at the tapestree she's weaving in her hex-cell, a leafy filigree of Celtic knots, and then onlines Pheidoh. "Who's it by?" she says.

"Anonymous."

"What's it called?"

The IA strokes its goatee. "There's no title. No time-stamp, either. The only info I can mine is that it first showed up in a netzine called Digit Alice."

She plays the snippet again. Counts syllables.

> *When we fine'ly kissed*
> *Your lips were cold—blue lady*
> *I still long for you.*

The voice is scratchy, harsh. Not quite human. She's not certain if the last line says "long for you" or "be-long to you." But she knows where the snippet fits, and the name of the song that it makes whole.

## ABOUT THE AUTHOR

MARK BUDZ is the author of *Clade*, which won a Norton Award and was a finalist for the Philip K. Dick Memorial Award. He lives with his wife in the Santa Cruz Mountains of northern California.

*Once in only a great while does a writer come along who defies comparison—a writer so original he redefines the way we look at the world.*

# NEAL STEPHENSON

____38095-8 **SNOW CRASH**    $14.00/$21.00 Canada

"Brilliantly realized."—*The New York Times Book Review*

"The most influential book since William Gibson's 1984 cyberpunk novel *Neuromancer*."—*Seattle Weekly*

"Stephenson has not stepped, he has vaulted onto the literary stage."—*Los Angeles Reader*

____38096-6 **THE DIAMOND AGE**    $14.00/$21.00

"Envisions the future as brilliantly as *Snow Crash* did the day after tomorrow."—*Newsweek*

"Once Neal Stephenson shows you the future, the present will never look the same."—*Details*

"Stephenson consistently outdoes his peers."
—*The Village Voice*

____57386-1 **ZODIAC**    $7.50/$10.99

"[Stephenson] captures the nuance and the rhythm of the new world so perfectly that one almost thinks that it is already here."—*The Washington Post*